## *"So you're engaged?"*

Daniel frowned. "Where's your ring?"

Shifting in her seat, Baily said, "Technically...I'm not...we really haven't quite...he hasn't actually..."

"He hasn't proposed yet." Ha! Daniel felt triumphant, although he had no idea why.

"He hasn't proposed, but he will. He's waiting for me to come home."

"How long's he been waiting?"

"Uh, seven years," she muttered under her breath.

Daniel started to laugh. "You're telling me your soon-to-be fiancé has been waiting for you for seven years. What on earth have you been doing, picking out bridesmaids' dresses?"

His question was met with stony silence. "I'm sorry for laughing. Hey, I'm not even married."

"Big shock there," Baily retorted.

"See, I won't even rise to your bait. Now, tell me about this guy."

"Harry? He's the supportive, sensitive type."

Daniel groaned. "Oh please, spare me the sensitive man stories."

Inwardly he fumed. The thought of Baily in a lifeless marriage didn't sit well with him. She was the throw-everything-off-the-table, toss-her-skirt-over-her-head-and-take-her-hard-and-long type. *Oh, hell!* Where had that thought come from?

*For more, turn to page 9*

# Czech Mate

## *I hope the old guy speaks some English.*

Mentally crossing her fingers, Wendy knocked on the door of Peter Havel's hotel room and waited.

Another knock, another wait.

She sighed as she recalled the last visiting professor they'd had. Lifzmeir. Frail, elderly—and so preoccupied with neutrinos he couldn't keep track of his sweater.

More knocking. More waiting.

Darn it, she didn't have time to baby-sit another absentminded genius! Just as her knuckles were about to contact the surface of the door again, it opened....

Wendy felt her throat go dry as she stared at the massive, muscular, golden expanse only inches away.

*It's a chest,* she realized finally, her fist still suspended in midair.

*A hard, naked, magnificent male chest.*

"S-sorry. Wrong room," she croaked—just as the Chest, incredibly, expanded even more and a deep, husky voice purred, "Good morning."

*For more, turn to page 197*

HARLEQUIN DUETS

ISBN 0-373-44154-1

Copyright in the collection:
Copyright © 2002 by Harlequin Books S.A.

The publisher acknowledges the copyright holders
of the individual works as follows:

BAILY'S IRISH DREAM
Copyright © 2002 by Stephanie Doyle

CZECH MATE
Copyright © 2002 by Catherine Hudgins

This edition published by arrangement with Harlequin Books S.A.

® and TM are trademarks of the publisher. Trademarks indicated with ® are registered in the United States Patent and Trademark Office, the Canadian Trade Marks Office and in other countries.

Visit us at www.eHarlequin.com

**Printed in U.S.A.**

# Baily's Irish Dream

## Stephanie Doyle

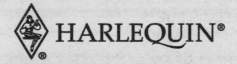

TORONTO • NEW YORK • LONDON
AMSTERDAM • PARIS • SYDNEY • HAMBURG
STOCKHOLM • ATHENS • TOKYO • MILAN • MADRID
PRAGUE • WARSAW • BUDAPEST • AUCKLAND

Dear Reader,

This book was inspired by so many things: my thirtieth (cough, cough) twenty-ninth birthday; my very Irish mother, who is determined to see me married; but most of all the best vacation I ever had—a five-day drive across this huge and magnificent country.

I'll never forget what it was like to see so much beauty, so much vastness and so much commonality between American towns all over the country. It was a trip that I will never forget, and then I realized it would be the perfect backdrop for Daniel and Baily's story.

It's amazing what these two seemingly different people discover they have in common when trapped inside a Volkswagen Bug for three days with a cat who thinks she's a former president!

So sit back and enjoy this story as you would a long, leisurely car trip. Just don't ask if you're there yet. You'll know you've reached the end of the trip when you get to the happy ending.

I love to hear from readers! You can e-mail me at stephd_romance@hotmail.com.

Have fun!

*Stephanie Doyle*

## Books by Stephanie Doyle

HARLEQUIN DUETS
65—DOWN-HOME DIVA

Charlie, we'll always have Chugwater.
Good luck to you and Glynn in your life together.

# 1

---

"Done. End. Finished. Gone. Goodbye. Get out of my way. No more. No way. Not me. *Adiós. Au revoir. Hasta la vista.* See you. So long. *Sayonara.*"

"So what you're saying is that you're leaving."

"Yep." Baily looked up from her task of trying to fit too many articles of clothing into a too small suitcase. Her friend Janice looked utterly confused.

"You could always tell your parents no. You are an adult, after all."

That was questionable. Regardless, Baily had given her word. And if her parents' persistence wasn't enough to make her return home then her own honor was.

"Don't you think I've tried to reason with them? Don't you think I've explained that I'm a real, live grown-up? It simply doesn't work. Besides, Harry is a really nice guy." Any anger that Baily had over the situation quickly melted away. No one could ever be angry with Harry. Baily dropped the lid on the overpacked suitcase and threw, as she would term it, her nicely rounded bottom on top to give it extra incentive to close.

Janice sat atop the second suitcase and sighed with frustration. "It's barbaric, I tell you. Forcing you to come home to marry the chosen suitor. Why did you ever agree to that kind of deal in the first place?"

"I wanted adventure, and it was the only way they would let me come to Seattle." Snap. Baily felt the locks catch under her weight. She didn't know whether to be glad that the suitcase shut or mournful that it shut so easily.

Janice debated that last point. "They couldn't have stopped you."

"Obviously you've never seen the size of my brothers. Trust me, they could have stopped me." Baily glanced around the empty apartment, checking to see that the movers had gotten everything. All that was left were her two suitcases and Miss Roosevelt.

"Barbaric," Janice muttered as she shifted her weight on the second suitcase, trying to close it.

"You said that already," Baily returned, smiling at her friend's irritation and knowing how illogical it must seem to a person who wasn't raised a Monohan.

"Medieval! Did I say that yet? What about your job? The school is really going to miss you."

"I'll get another teaching job when I get back to New Jersey. There is always a job for a teacher who doesn't mind middle school kids."

"It's still wrong."

With a sigh, Baily moved to sit on the suitcase with Janice, both of their nicely rounded rumps filling the tiny space and then some. Snap. Apparently, it was diet time again. "Listen, my parents only wanted to secure my future. They gave me seven years to explore the west. And I had a glorious time. But the more I think about it, the more I agree with them. I miss my family."

"You're going to marry a man just because you miss your family?" Janice was incredulous.

No, of course not! Okay, maybe a little. How did Baily explain all that to Janice? Janice would tell her to hold out for true love and other such ridiculous romantic notions. Baily, once a devoted romantic, had simply given up on the idea that true love existed for her in the cosmos. She had met too many men, had dated several of them, and not once had Cupid struck a blow.

"Harry will make an excellent husband. He'll be loyal, faithful, loving…"

"And he'll come on command, sit when you tell him, and he won't make puddles on the rug," Janice said sarcastically, moving off the suitcase to stand in the middle of the empty room.

"Hey. Don't knock it. Housebreaking a man is harder than it looks." Okay, so Harry had all the qualities of a fine dog. There were worse things in life. Harry would give Baily children. Something a dog certainly couldn't do. Just think of the children, Baily reminded herself. Unfortunately, that meant that she had to think about how she was going to get those children with Harry. Ugh-hh.

"You're not taking this seriously. This is your life, Baily Monohan. You're about to throw it all away," Janice fairly shrieked.

"Not throw it all away. More like start it all over… again."

"Are you sure?"

"I'm sure," Baily announced with a firmness that surprised her. She was making the right choice. In her mind she knew that. It was just her heart that was doing little anxious flip-flops every time she thought about spending the rest of her life with Harry.

With a determination she knew she was faking, Baily stood and lifted her two suitcases.

"Theodora! Let's go, Miss Roosevelt. We're leaving!"

"Miss Roosevelt" peeked out from her perch on one of the kitchen shelves. "Meow."

"Now, Theodora," Baily coaxed, "we talked about this. You agreed. So stop being so stubborn and move your tail."

Reluctantly the cat joined her. An indignant mew at Baily's feet let her know it wasn't without complaint. It was obvious Theodora wasn't at all happy about moving, but she apparently knew she wasn't going to have any say in the matter.

Janice shook her head in wonder. "You treat that animal like a human. It's not natural, you know."

"Shh. Do you want her to hear you? You know how she gets when someone reminds her that she wasn't the president of the United States. I know I'm encouraging her delusions, but it's less crying this way." Baily gazed down upon the black ball of fluff with loving adoration. "Are you ready, Madam President?"

"Meow." Theodora practically sighed, as if she realized she had no choice.

"Tell me again which of you is the delusional one?" Janice asked under her breath, not exactly sure she wanted an answer.

The two friends made their way out of the apartment with the President in tow. Baily popped the trunk of her antique yellow Volkswagen Bug and shoved the suitcases in place. There was a litter box already set up in the back seat and a six-pack of Diet Pepsi on ice in the passenger's seat. Baily was ready.

"Are you sure you are okay driving across the country by yourself? What about the maniacs that prey on helpless women?" Janice wondered out loud.

"Way to put me at ease." Baily had driven out to Seattle with her brother, Nick, the first time. At the time, Seattle had seemed as far away from New Jersey as she could get. Nick, a Philadelphia police officer, had insisted that she be accompanied. Currently he was rebounding from a nasty divorce and was unfit company for fish. No way Baily wanted to put up with his ex-wife bashing for three thousand miles. Which meant that this was a solo trip. She wasn't exactly thrilled about that, but she also had to be practical. Besides, how dangerous could it be?

Okay, so maybe she was a little nervous. But she was tough. One had to be to be a Monohan. Just in case, she'd packed a can of Mace.

"Be careful. And whatever you do, don't pick up hitch-hikers." Janice threw her arms around Baily and clung tight. "I'll miss you."

"I'll miss you, too."

Baily situated herself in her car and drove off. Through semi-watery eyes, she watched as Janice became smaller and smaller in the rearview mirror. The next time Baily looked up, Janice was gone.

"Well, Theodora, it's just you and me. Are you ready to go home?"

"Meow."

"Me, too."

DAMN! DAMN! DAMN! Damn! Daniel Blake simply refused to believe his ears. It wasn't possible. It couldn't be happening. Not to him. Not now. Not Sarah. With an impatience born of fury, he stabbed the rewind button on his answering machine then hit the play button once again. Maybe during the process of rewinding, the tape would somehow alter itself and a new message would play. One that did not cause his pulse to leap and his blood pressure to soar.

*Beeeep.* "Hi, Danny! It's me, Sarah. I've got wonderful news. You're never going to believe it. Well, I mean you'll believe it because I'm telling you it's the truth, and you know I don't lie...."

Daniel closed his eyes. It was his sister's habit to explain every exaggeration she ever made. He used to find the quality endearing. It declared her honesty. Now it was just time-consuming, and he was in a hurry to get to the punch line. Again.

"So what I really mean is that you'll probably be stunned. Oh, here it goes... I'm getting married! Can you believe it? Me, married. It's Pierce, of course. I know you have your reservations about him, but trust me he's really a doll, and sweet, and funny. I could go on forever. I mean not really forever because I would run out of words, but...well, you know what I mean. He says he can't wait. So we're doing it on August 3."

Seven days! Actually six, since the message was a day old.

"I know what you're thinking...I always wanted a big wedding with all the trimmings, but with Mom and Dad gone and Pierce not having any family, either, we decided to keep it small. Just you and a friend of Pierce's. Oh, and I know that's only seven days away, but it should only take you three or four to get here if you drive all day. That's probably faster than the train what with all the schedule juggling you'd have to do. So I'll expect to see you at the end of the week. Can't wait!" *Beeeeeep.*

His sister's voice seemed to echo throughout the house. She was going to marry that sleazy, two-bit fortune hunter, and he only had six days to stop the wedding. Six days. It simply wasn't enough time. For a moment he considered flying, but the idea was gone as soon as it had entered his head. He had given his word to Sarah that he would never fly, and his word was his bond. She was right about the train schedules being a hassle, too. There was no point in trying to reason with her on the phone, either. She may be flaky, but she could also be very stubborn. The only way to handle this was face to face. Which meant getting in his car and driving.

Without wasting any time, he opened the suitcase that was still filled with his clothes from the trip he had just returned from late last night. He had driven down to San Francisco to meet with a potential client interested in his unique software package. Daniel's product was one of a few that the large timber company had shown an interest in, and he had a hunch that his trip had all but sealed the deal. Still, nothing was concrete, and the last thing he needed was something to distract him from winning the bid.

Family, however annoying, came first. His only choice was to do what Sarah suggested: drive to Philadelphia. Not to attend her wedding, but to stop it. His vice president, Bruce, could handle the California bid while he was away.

Decision made, Daniel's next step was to find some clean clothes to replace the ones he'd just dumped in the hamper. Thankfully his maid had taken care of the laundry in his absence. Neatly laundered jeans and crisply ironed cotton polo shirts hung in his closest. Barely taking the time to fold them, he shoved them into the suitcase. A quick check to see that he had his wallet, and he was ready. He practically sprinted down the stairs of his Seattle, Washington, home and out the door, only to climb back into the car he had recently vacated.

After a tiresome drive back from California he'd had visions of unwinding for the day before getting back to work. Now he was going to have to make a marathon drive across the country to where his incredibly naive sister was about to make the biggest mistake of his life. Her life, he corrected himself.

At least she had given him six days. It could have been worse. Daniel figured he could make it to Philadelphia in three if he really pushed it. That would give him plenty of time to scare off the would-be husband and to lock Sarah in a convent. In that order.

Armed with a plan, he secured his seat belt and checked his rearview mirror. He spotted a beige Ford sedan parked too close to his driveway. The driver was still in the car. Daniel hit his horn to let the man know he was about to leave the driveway. As Daniel backed up, he shot the man a look to let him know he didn't appreciate him blocking his driveway. The man in the car averted his eyes.

"Damn tourist," Daniel muttered under his breath. Was there anyone on the planet who knew how to drive other than him? He doubted it.

Just stick to the plan, Daniel told himself, and this nightmare would soon be over.

# 2

"WILL THIS NIGHTMARE ever be over?" Daniel asked himself after being forced to put his foot on the brake yet again. It was only day two of his trip, but at this rate he would never reach his sister's wedding in time. Not when the vehicles in front of him insisted on driving as slow as his late great-grandmother. A Volkswagen Bug and a semi both conspired against him by only driving sixty miles per hour each in their own lane. For a brief moment Daniel considered passing the truck on the shoulder of the road, but it would be just his luck to get caught in a rut and end up with a flat tire. What he needed to do was to get the attention of the woman in the car in front of him.

He knew it was a woman because it was hard to miss the mass of red hair that spilled over the headrest of her seat. However, she clearly wasn't aware of his presence behind her. Daniel hunched forward over the steering wheel in the hope that by bringing his body inches closer to the lady in front of him she might sense his desire to pass. Since she remained at a constant speed, he had to assume she hadn't picked up on his mental vibe.

He tried another ploy and flipped on his headlights. A reflection of bright light bounced off her silver bumper. He could see his high beams clearly. No such luck from Red.

The woman was obviously too distracted to check her rearview mirror. The curls that he'd noticed before were bouncing around her head. She was bobbing and weaving and thrusting an occasional finger at the passenger in the seat next to her. If Daniel had to guess, she was either having a seizure or singing to a very short companion. It must have been his imagination that conjured up the image of pointy ears peeking around the front seat. She wasn't actually singing to a cat?

"HOW WAS I?" Baily asked, slightly out of breath from sining along with the radio. Baily was no Aretha Franklin, but Miss Roosevelt didn't seem to mind. Madam President had soul.

Baily waited anxiously for the next song. In the interim she took stock of where she was. A glance in her rearview mirror revealed an ominous black Mercedes practically sitting on her back bumper.

"Jeesh. Sorry, buddy," Baily muttered a little sheepishly. "I didn't realize you were back there." After all, Aretha demanded full concentration. She hit the gas and attempted to accelerate enough so that she could pull ahead of the semi next to her. Her Bug had other ideas.

The car sputtered a bit and sped up a mere five miles per hour on the decline. Since the truck was also picking up speed, there was no way Baily would be able to pass it let alone pull in front of it. Poor car, she thought. She'd pushed it too hard, and it let her know that it didn't appreciate it. Her only recourse was to slow down and pull in behind the semi.

SHE WAS SLOWING DOWN! There was only one option left. Daniel laid his hand on the horn and left it there out of sheer frustration. Frustration at the woman in front of him for driving too slow. Frustration at his sister for marrying the wrong man. Frustration at having to walk away from his business at a crucial time. It was undignified to shout at the top of his lungs, but there was nothing in the rule books about using a car horn to let off a little steam. The noise was an awful wonderful sound that made his ears ache joyously. The blare filled the car, zoomed out around him, and echoed against the vast Montana landscape.

MISS ROOSEVELT SHRIEKED and dove for cover under the seat. "Oh!" Baily shouted with indignation. The big bully. She'd been trying to move over to do him a favor and he had gone and scared her baby. The semi passed, and she immediately swung into the lane behind it. The truck picked up speed and was soon out of sight. Baily, meanwhile, couldn't help but stare at the man in the Mercedes as he pulled even with her.

WITH ONE LAST FINAL PUSH, Daniel released his horn. A dreamy sort of peace invaded him. Damn that had felt good. If he smoked he would have had a cigarette. Nothing like a good blow of the horn to relieve a little stress. Heck, now that the car in front of him had moved, Daniel no longer felt the sudden rush to get ahead. He pulled up slowly alongside the yellow Volkswagen Bug. Belatedly he turned to get a better look at the driver, wondering if she was as pretty as her hair.

"BIG...JERK!" Baily shouted, rolling down her window in an effort to make herself heard. Unfortunately it was doubtful that he heard her because his car window was still rolled up. Not that he would be overly offended by such a comment. Baily really needed to work on the whole swearing thing. She had lived too long with her mother's words ringing in her head. *A lady simply doesn't swear.* Obviously her mother never had to put up with jerks that drove Mercedes.

WHAT WAS HER PROBLEM? Daniel thought. He hadn't heard her, but it didn't take a genius to understand that she was furious. After all, she was the one who wouldn't pull ahead of the truck. When Daniel had tried to encourage her forward, she'd had the nerve to slow down. Of course now Daniel realized that she had only slowed down so that she could get behind the truck. More than likely the little car didn't have the acceleration required for a high-speed pass. It was Daniel's turn to feel a bit sheepish.

The only thing to do was to apologize. No chance she would hear him through two car widths. Daniel improvised with a shrug of his shoulders and a harmless smile that said, "Hey, I'm sorry. I didn't mean to honk so loud."

BAILY GASPED. "The nerve of that man! He's smirking and shrugging at me like he doesn't even care that he turned five of my hairs gray with that blasted horn of his."

The meanest action she could think to do popped into her head. Without a second's hesitation she did it.

SHE STUCK HER TONGUE OUT at him! Here he was trying to apologize, and she was showing him tongue. Obviously she was disturbed. Probably an escapee from some kind of mental facility. The best thing to do would be to hightail it out of there before she did something really crazy.

Like the pig face. Daniel hated the pig face. The one where the person pushed his nose up on his face and slanted his eyes back toward his ears. It chilled him just thinking about it. With one last glare to show her that he didn't appreciate her driving etiquette, Daniel hit the gas pedal with the full weight of his foot.

A mistake, considering he hadn't taken his eyes off the redheaded driver. Daniel never saw the cow that had slowly made its way through the opening in the fence along the side of the road until it was actually on the road itself. He knew it was too late the minute he saw the big bovine. Completely oblivious to the damage the dumb animal was about to cause, the cow mooed at the oncoming car.

Daniel slammed on his brakes so hard he feared he would push the pedal through the floor of the car. The vehicle swerved then spun out of control. He tried to steer into the skid, but the car didn't respond in time. Before he was aware of what was happening, he'd skidded off the road and crashed into a fence post. The air bag inflated, and Daniel was thrown back against the seat.

It all took exactly two seconds.

"Moooo."

Well at least the cow made it.

"Mister! Mister! Are you all right?"

The air bag now deflated, Daniel was able to move within the car. First he took stock of his body. Both his legs and arms were okay. His chest and the rest of his body had been protected by the air bag. He bumped his head and he felt a burning sensation on his cheek from where the air bag had scraped his face. Other than that he was fine. And lucky.

His car…not so lucky.

"Answer me!"

Daniel turned his head and met the worried green eyes of his redheaded nemesis. "Why?"

Baily sat back on her haunches. That was an odd answer. "Because I want to make sure you're okay."

"Obviously I am, or I wouldn't have been able to answer you, now would I?"

Good point. He was awfully calm for someone who had just gotten into a car wreck. And by the looks of it the car was totaled. The hood was practically wrapped around the thick fence post. The fence post, however, looked fine. "Didn't you see the cow?"

No words were necessary. Daniel's sour face said it all.

"Okay, you didn't see the cow," Baily concluded.

Daniel attempted to open the car door. Not an easy task since the entire frame had been pushed in. Baily saw his intent and aided him by pulling on the door while he pushed. Together they managed to create enough space for him to escape. Finding his legs a bit unsteady, he took a few calming breaths before he inspected the damage.

"You should sit down while we wait for the cops."

"What cops?"

"You know the cops that come after you've been in an accident," Baily told him naively.

Daniel raised his arms to indicate the vast space around him. The only thing for miles was Baily's Bug, Daniel's wreck and a cow. "And just where do expect these magical cops to sprout from?"

"Oh." She saw his point. The road they traveled wasn't a hotbed of activity. The semi was the only other vehicle Baily had noticed for hours and by now it was long gone. "I don't have a cell phone or anything."

"Who doesn't have a cell phone in today's world?" he asked incredulously. He didn't know why he cared, but it seemed wrong for a woman to be on the road alone without a cell phone.

"Me. I'm a schoolteacher on a budget. It was either a cell phone or my monthly manicure."

"Cell phones are very useful in cases of emergencies, accidents…"

"Yes, but well-painted nails are a joy every day," she said holding out her pretty pink nails for inspection. He didn't seem impressed. "I take it you have a cell phone."

"Of course I have a cell phone," he stated haughtily.

He reached for his right pants' pocket and found it empty. Then he reached for his left pocket and also found it empty. Looking down at his pants, he realized they weren't the same ones he'd been wearing on his trip back from California. The ones with his cell phone still in the pocket. They were on the floor of his bathroom where he'd last left them. Not here. With him. In the middle of Montana.

"No cell phone?"

He almost wanted to growl at her.

"So what should we do?"

Again, Daniel was beyond words. He moved around the car slowly and carefully. The hood, the engine, the frame—the whole damn car was trashed. He began to swear with the skill of a sailor.

Baily smiled uncomfortably. It wasn't that she hadn't heard the words before. Growing up with five brothers, she could give vocabulary lessons in swearing. She just envied the ease with which he did it. Boy, if her mother could hear him now, she'd shove enough soap in his mouth to keep his language clean for years.

Finally, after he'd surveyed the wreck and realized that he wasn't going anywhere, Daniel turned his attention on the woman. "You," he accused.

"Me?" Baily asked.

"This is all your fault!" It was a lie. He'd been driving too fast, but it felt good to blame someone else for his stupidity.

"My fault! You were the one who almost hit that poor cow and drove off the road."

"Poor cow?" Daniel searched and found the cow off to the side of the road munching on some grass. "The cow is fine! What about my car?"

Baily spared a glance at the car. "It's pretty much totaled."

"Ah-hh," Daniel yelled in frustration.

Perhaps this would have been a good time for Baily to get in her car and get the hell out of Dodge. Who knew what the man would do next? Honking and yelling, he was obviously the emotional sort. But she couldn't leave. Although she'd denied it, she did feel partly responsible for the accident. She wasn't about to admit it to him, but he had been staring at her tongue. The tongue she'd so childishly thrust at him. It was why he hadn't seen the cow until it was too late. For that reason, she had to at least offer her assistance.

"What am I going to do?" Daniel yelled. Now that he had regained some of his senses, he realized that he was in big trouble. Totaling his car wasn't part of the plan. Being stuck out in the middle of nowhere with a redhead wasn't part of the plan, either.

Baily refrained from making a comment, but she had asked a similar question only moments before. They were still all alone. Not counting the cow.

That's when the trepidation hit. She was alone in Montana with a strange man who liked to beep his horn and swear. The smart course of action, the one the self-defense books suggested, would be to get into her car, drive to the nearest phone, and call someone to help him. That idea, however, didn't sit well with Baily. Not while she was still feeling slightly, just slightly, guilty.

Besides that, the poor man appeared to be desperate. It was a safe bet he hadn't staged the accident as part of some diabolical plot to kidnap, rape and murder her. Had that been the case he wouldn't have been driving a Mercedes. No one totaled a sixty-thousand-dollar car just to commit murder. He could do that in a Ford.

"Listen, I could drive you to the nearest gas station. You could call a tow truck."

Daniel stood there for a moment and contemplated his choices. There were none. That had already been established. It was just that he had a sinking suspicion getting into the yellow Bug with its redheaded owner was going to be a life-altering decision. He couldn't see how, but his gut was never wrong. And it was telling him the woman was trouble.

Baily opened the driver's side door of her car and got in, then leaned her head out the open window. "Hey! Are you coming or what?"

Daniel removed his suitcase from his trunk. He opened the hood of the ancient Bug and shoved his suitcase inside. Then he closed it and stared at her through the windshield.

She stared back and shrugged her shoulders as if to ask what was taking him so long. Sighing, he moved around the car to the passenger side and got in. Or at least tried to. It was an effort, but he managed to squeeze himself into the compact automobile, feeling the car lurch as his weight was added.

"Meeeooow!"

"What the hell was that?" Daniel bellowed.

"Poor, poor, Miss Roosevelt. Did the big bad man take your seat?" Baily held Theodora in her arms, crooning to her as if she were an overly spoiled child. Which, in fact, she was.

"A cat." So it had been a cat she'd been singing to.

"I hope you're not allergic," Baily announced, "because let me tell you who is going to get the boot if you are."

Her smile was evil. Daniel returned it with full force. "Not the cat?"

Satisfied, Baily decided to play nice. "Her name is Theodora Roosevelt. You can call her Miss Roosevelt or Theodora or, if you prefer, Madam President. She likes that name best, but I try not to encourage her delusions of grandeur too often.''

He was in Oz. That must be it. His car had driven off the road, a tornado had picked him up, and now he was in Oz. Either that or he had just agreed to drive the next twenty or so miles with a lunatic.

Baily introduced her cat to her new passenger. ''Miss Roosevelt, this is...I don't know your name.''

''Blake. My name is Daniel Blake.'' Daniel thought about offering his hand, but he'd be damned before he shook a cat's paw.

''Oh,'' Baily commented. Starting up the car, she maneuvered herself back onto the highway. ''My name is Baily Monohan.''

''Bailey, huh? Is that like the movie, *It's a Wonderful Life*? George Bailey, wasn't it?'' It would be typical for her to be named after a fictional character. She, herself, was fictional-like. The red hair, the green eyes, the cat.

''No. It's Baily as in Irish Cream.''

''The drink? Baileys Irish Cream?''

''Yes,'' explained Baily, ''only it's not spelled the same. I was born around Christmastime you see, and my father...well Baileys is his favorite drink at Christmas. So he had a few when mother went into labor. I was born and he named me Bailey, but he spelled it wrong on the birth certificate. It's sort of the family joke.''

''Good thing your dad wasn't drinking tequila. Any brothers or sisters? Maybe a Jack Daniels or a Wild Turkey?'' Daniel chuckled at his own joke.

''Very funny. And original, too. No, my brothers are Nick, Michael, Billy, Sean, and James. All very Irish and very proper. But I was the first girl, you see, so my parents were stumped. Not to mention I was number six, and they were running low on options.''

''Six children!'' The thought of having more than six people in his house at the same time made Daniel nervous. Families in general made him nervous. ''Big family.''

Baily shook her head, laughing. ''You don't know the half of it. Three of my brothers are married with children. One still lives at home, and one is temporarily living at home because he just got a divorce. Other than Nick and James, the family has practically quadrupled in the last ten years. It's really a lot of fun.''

''I wouldn't know about families and fun,'' Daniel remarked grimly. His family, his sister, was the reason he was in his current predicament. It finally dawned on him the magnitude of his dilemma. ''I'm never going to reach my sister in time.''

''Is your sister in trouble?''

Daniel redirected his attention back to the woman. He hadn't realized he said his thoughts out loud. ''Yes, my sister is in trouble. Thanks to the accident, I'll never make it in time to save her.'' Daniel pushed his hands through his hair in frustration and grimaced when he found a goose egg that had suddenly sprouted on his head.

Baily witnessed the grimace out of the corner of her eye. ''Are you hurt?''

''Hurt?'' That was the understatement of the year. ''My car is totaled. My sister's life is about to be destroyed, and to top it all off I've got a bump the size of Mount Rainier on my head.''

Baily had to humph a bit at that last comment. Really, the size of Mount Rainier?

''You don't believe me?'' Daniel bellowed. Reaching out he took her right hand off the steering wheel and shoved it over the lump on his forehead that had only been partially covered by his brown bangs. Baily brushed her fingers through his thick chestnut hair, trying to ignore the silky feeling of it and how it made her fingers tingle. It wasn't too hard to find the lump. A startled gasp left her mouth before she could stop it.

"It's really big," she stated, as if he didn't already have that information. "Maybe I should take you to a hospital."

The concern in her eyes and the tremor in her voice made him realize how much his little speech had affected her. Good, he thought evilly.

"I don't need to go to the hospital," he assured her. Rubbing a hand over his face in an attempt to alleviate some of his frustration, he murmured, "What I need is to get to Philadelphia."

"Philadelphia? Did you say Philadelphia?" Baily asked, thinking she hadn't heard what she thought she'd heard. It was too much of a coincidence.

"Yeah. What about it? I don't know what the hell I'm going to do now. It's going to take days to fix my car, and I don't have that long to wait. I could rent a car, but where the hell am I going to find a car rental place around here." Daniel muttered to himself as he sorted through his options. "I'll never make it in time." What would happen to Sarah?

Before she could stop herself the words seemed to pop out of her mouth. "I'm going to New Jersey. South Jersey, actually, right over the Ben Franklin Bridge just a few miles from Philadelphia." It was a ridiculous thought. Surely she wasn't offering to drive this complete stranger across the country. It sounded like it though, didn't it? It might not be so bad. She would have someone to split the driving time, and she wouldn't be so defenseless. Unless of course he turned out to be a psychopathic killer. What had Janice said about not picking up hitchhikers?

The ashen color of his skin made the red bump stand out even more. He didn't look like the average menacing hitchhiker. Besides, the company wouldn't hurt. It would give her someone to talk to besides Miss Roosevelt. As for him being a stranger, he didn't feel like a stranger.

He'd seen her tongue.

She'd felt his bump.

In the short time they had shared the car ride, Baily was pretty confident that she could trust this man. Of course she was sure that was what every woman had said when she'd first met Ted Bundy.

"Or," she suggested, "I could just take you on to the next town like we originally planned."

"What am I going to do there?"

"What am I, your guidance counselor? I don't know. You could have a tow truck pick up your car for starters. Then see about a rental."

"A Hertz? In the two street blocks they call towns around here? I don't think so," he stated sarcastically.

Baily was now beginning to get angry. He was quick to shoot down her ideas, but what was he coming up with? "Well what do you want to do?" Baily shouted back.

The shouting was beginning to get to him. His head throbbed. The best thing to do was to make peace first. "Look, I'm sorry. I'm just frustrated. I've got to be in Philadelphia in five days at the latest. I know this isn't all your fault."

"*All* my fault? It isn't any of my fault!" That was her story and she was sticking to it, guilty conscience aside. "If you hadn't beeped at me…"

"If you hadn't put your brakes on…"

"If you hadn't been on my bumper…"

Daniel clenched his teeth. This was getting them nowhere. "The point is, my sister's life depends on me getting to Philadelphia."

"If it was that important, why didn't you fly?" It

seemed like the obvious solution. "You can probably get an airline ticket at Billings. That isn't so far. I could drive you there."

"I don't fly," Daniel replied without explanation.

This man could try the patience of Mother Teresa. "Your sister's life is on the line, and you can't get over your fear of flying?"

If he clenched his teeth any tighter, he knew they would break. "I didn't say I was afraid of flying. I said I don't fly. There is a very big difference. The end result is still the same though. I don't fly. I won't fly. Now let's move on to the next suggestion."

It should have dawned on him then the way he had so casually brought her into his decision-making process that this wasn't any ordinary woman who had entered his life.

"I offered to drive you to Philadelphia," she pointed out, feeling as if they had wasted a long time just to get back to the point from which they'd started.

It was a good offer, but the last thing he wanted to do. He couldn't drive across the country with this woman. Not this woman.

"I can't do it," he announced, giving voice to his thoughts.

"Why not?" Baily waited for his reasons. She had a hunch this was going to be good. "What's the matter, isn't my car luxurious enough for you?"

His knees hit the dashboard. The top of his head scraped the roof of the car. The only place to put his arms was in his lap or around a cat named Madam President. The Bug wasn't his big roomy Mercedes. But he'd be a fool to tell her that. The problem was less substantial than that. He stared at her hard and something inside him screamed at him to jump out of the car now while he still had the chance. "I simply can't drive with *you* all the way to Philadelphia."

"What's the matter with me?"

Nothing obvious. The trouble was hidden. It was there in the way her jean shorts rode up high on her thighs and the way her shirt clung to her breasts. It was the way her hair bounced around her shoulders as if it were alive and the way her green eyes sparkled with mischief.

"Well, look at you, for one thing."

Actually, the whole picture had only just registered in Daniel's mind. He'd seen her profile; he'd seen her standing in front of him. He'd seen her hair, of course. But it was only a second ago that all of those images filtered back through his mind and he put them all together into one extremely attractive, heart-pumping package that would disturb his equilibrium. Which was exactly the last complication he needed at this time.

Baily glanced down at herself. She was wearing a pair of cutoffs and a white T-shirt. She didn't see the problem. "What is wrong with the way I look?" she asked defensively. She was no beauty but no one had ever told her that she was too repulsive to drive with.

Daniel didn't know how to articulate it. "It's your red hair, and the eyes, and the freckles. All I have to do is look at you to know that you are going to irritate me like no one on this planet has ever irritated me before."

"Listen you overbearing, Mercedes-driving jerk! I didn't have to pull over to help you. I didn't have to offer to drive you to the next town. I could have left you there looking for the cell phone you don't seem to have. I certainly didn't have to offer to drive you to Philadelphia. But you're in a bind. And your sister, whom I've suddenly developed a great sympathy for, is in trouble. So why don't you just say yes, then shut the hell up. Because let me tell you, you have already irritated me more than anyone I've ever known. And I've been irritated by the best, pal.''

Daniel snorted. He refused to agree to anything until he had a chance to weigh his options. He wouldn't know what those options were until they reached civilization.

It was twenty silent miles to the next town. One that had a gas station, a quickie mart, five dwellings and nothing else. Certainly no rental car facilities. Even if Daniel had wanted to wait while the car was being repaired, there wasn't an available hotel room for at least another hundred miles. His options were becoming fewer and his hope of avoiding a three-thousand-mile car trip with a batty redhead was becoming dimmer.

The only bright spot was that the gas attendant, Doug, was the helpful sort. He took Daniel's credit card number and assured Daniel that he would bill him fairly for the damage to the car. Daniel told the man he'd be back in less than two weeks to pick up his car. No problem for Doug as there was plenty of room in his garage. Western courtesy. It wasn't a myth. Doug also mentioned that Jackson Hole, just over the border of Montana, would have the rental car facilities Daniel needed.

''See, your problems are solved. I'll take you to Jackson Hole. I was planning on stopping there anyway. And Doug said he would take good care of the car.'' Baily had trusted the attendant completely.

''He'll probably be joyriding in it once he gets it fixed,'' Daniel said cynically. Nobody was that nice. Then again he had just accepted a ride from a woman who had selflessly offered to drive him where he needed to go. Maybe he was the one with the problem.

''Well, we're off,'' Baily announced.

Daniel groaned as he struggled to fit his frame back into her car. She started the engine and the car sputtered to life.

It was going to be the longest trip of his life. That he knew, absolutely. If nothing else, the cramped confines of the car would more than likely cause him permanent injury. To keep his mind off his already sore knees he looked around for something to distract him. Unfortunately, that would be Red's too tight T-shirt. Even while she irritated his mind, she stirred his body. A lethal combination.

A thought occurred to Daniel, but he was almost hesitant to ask. "Are you married? What am I saying, of course you're not."

She had opened her mouth to tell him no, but then closed it when he answered his own question. "What is that supposed to mean? Don't I look like someone who might be married? Don't you think I could get a husband if I wanted one? Don't you think it's possible, even a little, that someone somewhere might find me vaguely attractive enough or interesting enough to marry? Huh?"

"Sensitive subject, I see," Daniel remarked while he watched her face turn several shades of purple.

"Meow," Miss Roosevelt concurred from the back seat.

Slightly embarrassed, Baily tried to compose herself. Okay, maybe she was a little too sensitive about the whole topic of marriage. Besides, there was nothing to worry about now. She was going to marry Harry.

"All I meant was that if you were married, your husband would most likely be with you and you would be wearing a ring. Since neither of those things are true, I assumed you weren't married."

Daniel's logical explanation only turned her cheeks rosier. "I'm not," she quietly replied.

"That's what I thought," Daniel said smugly.

A little too smugly, Baily decided. "But I'm going to be."

Not quite sure what she meant, he conceded, "Sure.

Most people think they'll get married and have a family someday.''

"No, I mean I'm getting married. When I get back to New Jersey," Baily clarified.

He was at an absolute loss to explain the sudden sense of regret that washed over him. It was as if he tried to capture something in his grasp but it was gone before he could close his fingers around it. Then he shook his head. He was being ridiculous.

"So you're engaged?" Daniel concluded. "Where's your ring if you're engaged?"

Shifting slightly in her seat, Baily thought of a few legitimate excuses, but none of them rang true. "Technically...I'm not...we really haven't quite...he hasn't actually..."

"He hasn't proposed yet." It was a statement. Ha! Daniel felt triumphant. Although he had no idea why.

"He hasn't proposed, but he will. He's waiting for me to come home." There, that was reasonable. It was also the truth.

Daniel was confused. And really, none of this was his business. He should let the subject drop, lean his head back and catch a few winks. That was sound thinking.

"So he's been waiting for you in New Jersey while you've been Seattle."

"Yes."

"For how long?"

She squirmed in her seat a little bit, then muttered something under her breath.

"I'm sorry I didn't catch that."

"Seven years," she said clearly.

There wasn't any reaction at first. For a second, Baily thought he might have fallen asleep. That was until she glanced quickly to her right and saw his face turning red and his eyes watering up. Shortly after that, the laughter started.

Five minutes later he was still laughing. Baily's anger grew proportionately. She didn't know what had made her say anything in the first place. That wasn't true. Maybe she'd wanted to share the story with someone. Get someone else's feedback to decide whether or not she was making a huge mistake. Stupid idea. Now on top of everything else she was completely humiliated.

Breathing in deep gulps of air, Daniel tried to get control of his body. He couldn't say why he found the story so amusing, but he had a feeling that the laughter had been building inside him from the first moment he'd seen her. Seven years. She certainly could deliver a punch line. Once he was calm he was able to ask his next series of questions.

"Okay, give. You're telling me your soon-to-be fiancé has been waiting for you for seven years. What the hell have you been doing, picking out bridesmaids' dresses?" Daniel amazed himself with his witty banter.

His question was met with stony silence. Taking in her profile, he could see her proud chin was raised slightly. While he waited for her reaction, he took the time to study her other features. He couldn't help but notice that her nose sloped up at the cutest angle. Her lips were firm, but were currently stiff with irritation. Long lashes dusted her cheeks when they closed. If he looked close, he could even count the number of freckles that covered the right side of her face. Seventeen.

"I'm sorry for laughing," Daniel apologized, unused to the sound of those words echoing off his own lips. "I really want to know the whole story."

"Why? So you can make fun of me some more?" Baily was no masochist.

The long highway stretched in front of them, and Daniel

felt penned in by the confines of the small car. The question and its answer was just a way to pass the time. At least that was what he told himself. "I won't make fun. Hey, I'm not even married."

"Big shock there," Baily retorted.

"See, I won't even rise to your bait. Now tell me about this guy… What's his name?"

Sniffing past her indignation, Baily muttered, "Harry."

"Henry?"

"Harry. His name is Harry, and I've known him since I was ten. We grew up together. Dated in high school. Dated in college. Everybody assumed that we were going to get married. I wanted to experience a little more of the world before I settled down. My family was adamantly against me leaving. Harry was bothered, too. I guess."

"You guess?"

Baily winced at the implication. "You have to know Harry. He's the supportive, sensitive type."

Groaning, Daniel stopped her. "Oh, please, spare me the sensitive man stories. Whoever put those two words together should be shot."

Baily ignored his sarcasm and continued with her story. "Well, he is. So when I told him I wanted to move to Seattle, he said that was fine. He said he would wait and that he loved me. My parents weren't nearly as supportive. They made me promise that if I wasn't married by the time I was thirty that I would come home where I belonged and marry Harry."

"You're kidding. And that worked?"

"My birthday is in three weeks. My thirtieth birthday."

Daniel issued ultimatums to Sarah all the time. They never worked. He needed Sarah and Red to meet. Maybe Red would rub off on her and— Scratch that thought.

"I don't think I need to point out to you that you are

an adult. You don't have to obey your parents. Although I do respect the fact that you are honoring your word.'' Daniel couldn't think of a woman he knew that he would have ever described as honorable, yet it was a characteristic he admired greatly.

Finally, she thought, here was someone who understood what it meant to keep one's word. However, Baily had to admit that it wasn't the only reason she was heading east. ''I wouldn't break my word, that's true. But I also think it's time for me to get married. I want a home and children. A family. Harry can provide that. The truth is, having almost reached the age of thirty, I'm beginning to believe that true romantic love doesn't exist.''

''Damn right!'' Daniel agreed readily.

''Somehow I knew you would agree with me.''

He wasn't exactly sure how he should take that statement. He decided it was a credit to his logical way of thinking. Therefore, it was obviously a compliment, and he thanked her.

Baily chuckled. A man like him would view her comment as a compliment. Maybe it was wrong to judge him so quickly without really knowing him. But his short brown hair, his clean-shaven jaw, his green polo shirt, and his crisp new blue jeans with a brown belt that matched his casual shoes said a lot about the man. He was the bottom line, the practical choice, and the reasonable solution type.

''What I meant,'' Baily clarified herself, ''is that love isn't like the storybooks. It doesn't hit suddenly. It isn't passionate and fiery and out of control. Sure some people say they experience that. But how long does it last? Instead I've decided that love is like a warm comforter. Snugly. Cuddly. Secure. Harry and I will love each other and our children. It won't be a story for the fairy tales, but then fairy tales are fiction. Harry and I are nonfiction." Baily nodded her head with conviction. She was definitely doing the right thing. How could being part of warm loving family, one that she would help to create, be wrong?

"Very practical," Daniel added. Not that he understood her need to be married and have children, but at least she wasn't one of those women who believed love would make everything all right. However, the thought of Red trapped in a loveless, lifeless marriage didn't sit well with him. He saw Red as the fiery, passionate type. She was the throw-everything-off-the-table, toss-her-skirt-over-her-head and take-her-hard-and-long type.

Oh, hell! Where did that thought come from? It was one thing to notice a woman's chest in a T-shirt; it was another to envision that chest naked. No, he told a certain part of his anatomy. Don't even think about it. Don't even twitch, you son of a bitch. Not her. She is absolutely out of the question.

That part of his body wasn't listening. In fact the mere image of her thighs spread in front of him open and waiting for him to claim her was enough to make his sex do more than just twitch.

"Are you all right?" Baily caught a glimpse of a really pained expression on his face. "Is it your head? Is it bothering you?"

"Yes," he replied gruffly. "It's my head." It was sort of the truth.

"Your problem is you're still cranky. Why don't you rest for a while? I'll let you know when we get there," Baily suggested.

Perhaps that wasn't a bad idea. He could close his eyes and catch up on the sleep he so desperately needed. Then he would wake up refreshed and in charge of his own body. He would expunge all thoughts of Red as a sexual being while he slept and life would once again make sense. It was a wonderful idea. Closing his eyes, he yawned once then sighed deeply. One last thought occurred to him before he drifted off.

"You said you would wake me up when we got to where we were going, but Jackson Hole is hours away. I won't sleep that long." And there really wasn't anything else that was noteworthy along the way.

"Oh, I meant when we get to Yellowstone, of course."

# 3

"YELLOWSTONE! Yellowstone National Park? But we don't have to go through the park to get to Jackson Hole. That's south. We want to go east." Daniel pinched the bridge of his nose in an effort to stem the pain of his headache.

"And eventually we will. I just want to take a little detour. You certainly don't want to miss Yellowstone, do you? Elk, bear, caribou, Old Faithful! It would be a travesty to be this close and not visit." It made perfect sense to Baily. She was a traveler by nature. She needed to accumulate new sights and experiences to keep her senses fed. And the first time she'd driven across country Nick had been in charge. He didn't allow for detours. This was a perfect opportunity.

"Did I mention that my sister's life was at stake? I don't have time for detours."

"Maybe it's about time that we talked about your sister. It would help if I knew exactly what kind of danger she was in. I can't imagine that her life is truly in jeopardy or else you would have found a way to overcome your fear of flying."

Daniel, with his severe features, intense hazel eyes, and broad shoulders, didn't look like a man who feared much. It was hard to reconcile the man who overwhelmed the space inside her small car as someone who had fears like other normal people.

Sighing, Daniel patiently explained. "I told you, I'm not afraid to fly."

"Yeah, yeah, I know. You *don't* fly." Baily attempted not to roll her eyes. She didn't succeed, which was fortunate because when she did succeed it always made her dizzy.

"That's right. Like you, I made a promise, and I don't intend to break it." His voice changed somehow, and immediately Baily knew that she had touched a vulnerable spot inside the man.

"Who made you promise not to fly?" An important person in his life, that much Baily surmised. It made her wonder how many other important people were in this man's life. She would bet her life savings there weren't many. Although considering that her life savings was the sum of eight hundred dollars, it wasn't much of a bet.

It was an area of his life he didn't think he wanted to share. He'd known this woman less than a day. She didn't have the right to know about his personal problems. He should probably tell her to go to hell. Then he remembered how vulnerable she'd looked when she told him about her purported fiancé. It had taken both trust and hope on her part that he would tread softly on her feelings. Would she do the same?

More than likely. She had a quality about her. "My sister made me promise not to fly. My parents were killed in a plane crash many years ago. And it was our misfortune to be there when it happened."

Tears burned Baily's eyes, appearing so quickly they stunned her. "I'm so sorry. How old were you?"

"I was seventeen, but Sarah was only ten. Obviously, she took it harder."

It wasn't so obvious to Baily. She bit her tongue, but

she couldn't stop herself from silently wondering why Daniel shouldn't be just as hurt by the loss of his parents.

"She's been fragile, even frightened, ever since," Daniel continued. "The next year I went to college. That first Christmas I planned to fly home, but Sarah made me promise that I wouldn't. Then she made me promise that I would never fly...ever. It was probably wrong of me to indulge her, but if you had heard her voice trembling on the other end of the phone. She was so scared I wanted to make that fear disappear."

"Surely she's overcome that fear or at least would understand if you flew occasionally. You live across the country for Pete's sake. How do you ever get home?" Baily thought about how difficult it was for her to be separated from her family for so long. Even the plane trip was long and arduous. If she didn't have the option of flight open to her, she never would have made it home for Christmas and other family occasions.

Not easily, and not often, Daniel wanted to answer. It was just as well, too. Home only brought with it uncomfortable memories of a time long gone. Those memories and the sense of loss they brought with them were what had goaded him into leaving in the first place. That first year he had taken a summer job in Alaska, cutting wood, and seen the need to standardize the cutting and replanting process. After college, a software company recruited him, and he'd honed his skills until he was ready to venture out on his own with software designed to track the lumber business. In the ten years since he'd lived in Seattle he'd made it home only once a year, every year. Both he and Sarah accepted the fact that neither one of them would step foot on a plane again.

"Sarah hasn't overcome her fear and I don't want her driving by herself. I get home about once a year. Sometimes I drive, other times I take the train. Either way I'm not home as often as I would like. But my business is in the northwest, so there's nothing I can do about that.''

It was odd that even after living in Seattle for more than ten years, he still considered Philadelphia his home despite his intentional neglect. Daniel thought about the implications of that statement. When would Seattle be home?

Since it was evident that this wasn't his yearly trip home, Baily was still left with questions concerning his sister. "You said Sarah's life was at stake. She's not sick, is she?" If that were the case Baily would be willing to drive twenty-four hours a day if necessary to reach her. A sister shouldn't be sick and without her family to comfort her.

Baily remembered breaking her ankle in a game of tag football with some of her larger students. She'd been laid up in her apartment all by herself. Friends had come to help and visit, but it wasn't the same. No one stayed with her. No one commiserated with her when her ankle itched so bad that she wanted to scream. No one brought her ice cream with extra chocolate syrup on top. That hurt more than the ankle.

"She's not sick." For that he should be grateful, he supposed.

Baily waited, but no other answer was forthcoming.

"Well, is she in danger?"

Daniel thought about that. He doubted that Pierce was the violent type. Sarah was most likely physically safe. It was Pierce who was about to suffer some serious pain in the near future, as soon as Daniel got his hands on the wretched fake. "No, Sarah's not in danger."

Again, Baily waited. "Is she about to be run down by a heard of buffalo, uprooted from a ranch in Montana and transplanted to a farm in Pennsylvania, that somehow got loose in the city of Philadelphia and is now on a tragic course headed directly for her?'' Baily smiled mischievously thinking he might laugh.

He didn't. ''No, that isn't the problem, either.''

Frankly, Baily was out of options.

''She's in love,'' Daniel muttered, as if that were far worse than any of the before-mentioned suggestions.

Confused, Baily prompted him to elaborate. ''In love? That is why her life's at stake? Because she's in love?''

Daniel was again reluctant to share personal information with this woman. He had a sneaking suspicion she wasn't going to approve of his tactics.

His reticence was clear. Baily watched as he struggled over whether or not to divulge the information. She decided that she would make it easier for him. ''Hey, if I don't have a good reason to head east immediately, I might take the opportunity to stop and see the Grand Canyon. And that's south. I mean, really south.''

Gritting his teeth, he spilled the story. ''She's in love with a man who's going to rob her blind and leave her shattered. That is what I'm referring to when I say that her life is at stake. Okay maybe not her life, but definitely her future. As her brother, it's my job to protect her. So I'm on my way to Philadelphia where I will proceed to stop the wedding and save her future.'' Both arms crossed over his chest, Daniel stared resolutely out the windshield at the road ahead. The discussion was over as far as he was concerned.

Baily, however, was not quite ready to let the matter drop. First things first. ''How do you know this guy is going to steal all her money?''

Daniel struggled to put his thoughts into words.

''He's…he's…''

''Yes?''

"Slick," Daniel finally said, as if that explained everything.

"And..."

"And?"

"Yes," Baily reiterated. "And. And. As in, what else, or in addition to, or as well as. And."

"What?" Daniel had lost her train of thought. Not to mention his.

Exasperated, Baily screamed, "Exactly! What? Surely you've got more to go on than the fact that he's slick!"

"You don't have to shout." Typical woman, Daniel thought, always flying off the handle at the least little thing.

Question: a woman drives a car at sixty-five miles per hour on a highway and shoves a man who weighs one hundred and eighty pounds out of the speeding car. How many years does the woman serve in prison for justifiable manslaughter? Answer: zero. She was justified. It was a trick question.

In a calm and rational voice Baily asked, "What's his name?"

"Pierce Larson. And doesn't that just smack of a con man. I mean really, Pierce? Pierce Larson." Daniel repeated in what Baily believed to be an English accent.

He sounded ridiculous. Giggling, Baily asked, "Is he English?"

"No," Daniel replied, unsure of how to react to her laughter. As a rule, people didn't laugh at Daniel Blake. Then again Daniel didn't often say much that would be considered humorous.

"So he's slick and you think his name is fake. And that is the reason, the only reason, you want to stop your sister's wedding?"

"Yes."

"We're going to the Grand Canyon."

"Come on. Seriously, Pierce? It sounds as if it comes from one of those silly romantic books about the English earl who falls in love with a chambermaid. Really, the name couldn't be any sillier unless it were…"

"Baily," Baily supplied with a mischievous grin. Somehow she knew that her name was on the tip of his tongue.

Not in least perturbed, Daniel replied, "Exactly. Baily is a silly name. So much so, I think I'm going to have to refuse to call you by such an appellation."

"It's going to be a while before we get to Jackson Hole. What do you plan to call me for all that time? 'Hey, you' might not work if we find ourselves in a crowd at the next pit stop."

"I'll make sure I poke your shoulder when I say, 'Hey, you.'"

"It's funny because you look like a rational man, but it's becoming clear to me that you rarely make sense."

"I don't make sense? Miss I'm-going-home-to-marry-a-man-I-haven't-seen-in-seven-years, and I'm bringing my cat who, by the way, thinks she's the president of the United States, is telling me *I* don't make sense."

With an affirmative nod, Baily confirmed, "Yes, you don't make any sense."

Maybe she did have a slight point, but Daniel certainly wasn't about to admit that to her. "It's more than that. He knows exactly what to say, yet he says nothing. I've asked him several times what he does for a living. He tells a fine story and goes into great detail, but after a fifteen-minute dissertation I still don't know what he does. He says nothing about his family or his background. As far as I can tell, he comes from nowhere. He's nothing more than a leech. In addition to all that, he doesn't look at her like…"

"Like what?" Baily asked genuinely curious.

"Never mind," Daniel said, shaking off that thought. He was going to say that he doesn't look at his sister like a man in love. But that would have been preposterous since Daniel himself didn't believe in love. Neither did Red, he reminded himself.

"No, tell me." Baily didn't know why it was important for her to know, but she couldn't seem to stem her curiosity about the drama in which she had embroiled herself.

"When Sarah looks at him, he's all smiles and kisses. When she turns her head, it's as if he takes off a mask and underneath is another person. I'm convinced he's conning her."

Baily believed him. Although she had no doubt that Daniel was too protective for his own good, he didn't seem the type to interfere unless he thought it was necessary. "Perhaps you don't want to let your little sister go," Baily suggested. She had been on the receiving end of her brothers' protectiveness and knew from firsthand experience that it stemmed from them not wanting to let her grow up.

It was Daniel's turn to laugh, but he wasn't amused. "Believe me, I would be more than willing to give Sarah away to the first decent man that would have her. She needs someone to watch over her and protect her, and I am simply not there enough. Pierce Larson, however, is not a decent man. I'm sure of it."

Daniel wanted nothing more than to relinquish his role as Sarah's guardian. Mostly because he knew he hadn't done the job to his own satisfaction. If she were married to a good man, a strong man, Daniel could absolve himself of the guilt that plagued him.

"Why didn't you try to run him off the last time you saw him?" Baily wondered. For the time being she decided to believe that Daniel was probably correct in his assumptions, which meant she might as well lend her hand to the cause of ousting Pierce from Sarah's life.

"I tried," Daniel explained, seeing that Red was with him in his efforts. Great, now he had a partner. A female partner. In the next few hours they were sure to come up with some idea of how to get rid of Pierce without sending Sarah straight into his arms. "I thought he had gotten the message. I was mistaken."

"Let's rule out the obvious. Number one, you can't bribe him. That would be the worst mistake."

Cautiously, Daniel asked, "Why do you say that?"

Baily sighed as she realized she was dealing with an amateur in these matters. "Don't you ever watch TV? When the rich father—or brother, as the case may be—" Baily used her hand as a pointer to indicate Daniel without actually looking at him "—offers the sleazy boyfriend money to stay away from his daughter, or sister, as the case may be, the sleazy boyfriend always tells his girlfriend. The girlfriend becomes so enraged with her father, or her brother—"

"As the case may be," Daniel supplied. "I get the picture."

Baily continued. "…for insulting her boyfriend and trying to interfere with her happiness, which she is convinced rests with the sleazy boyfriend that she immediately elopes with him. Simple."

"Ha!" Daniel shouted, his finger in the air with triumph.

"What do you mean, 'ha'?"

Wiggling his eyebrows, Daniel told her smugly, "I did offer him a bribe. That was months ago and they haven't eloped."

"No, they didn't elope. They just decided to get married and only gave you…how many days' notice was that?"

"Seven. Now I have only five days left to get there."

"Seven," she repeated. "Enough time for you to make it home and walk your sister down the aisle. The bribe obviously didn't work." If smug was a woman, she would look like Baily.

"Maybe I didn't offer him enough," Daniel muttered, not willing to concede total defeat.

"If this guy is as slick as you say he is, then we're going to have to do better than a bribe." The sound of her brain clicking into devious action seemed to emanate throughout the tiny car. Even Miss Roosevelt looked up from her pillow in the back seat.

"'We'?" Daniel asked. When she said the word, it made it sound as if they were going to be together longer than they were. For whatever reason, the idea of them together for longer than a day didn't sound as horrible to Daniel as it had that morning.

"Lord knows you're going to need the help. A bribe! How cliché." Baily ignored his mention of the word "we," but she couldn't help but be affected by the significance of it. We. Frightening thought.

Daniel chuckled and let his head fall back against the seat. He was content now to forget his worries and to let Red try to wrestle with the problem of how to separate Pierce from his sister. He was also long overdue for that nap he'd planned to take. "Wake me when you need a break."

"I'll wake you when we get to Yellowstone. You can't miss Yellowstone," Baily informed him, her voice as serious as stone.

"I wouldn't think of missing Yellowstone."

In minutes Daniel was asleep and the occasional snore filled the car. As much as she could, Baily took her eyes off the road to peek at her passenger. It was odd, but he reminded her of a new toy that was fun to play with. He challenged her, made her laugh, and also made her feel comfortable in his presence. They barely knew each other yet they had basically spilled their life stories to one another.

As a child Baily had received many toys. She would play with them nonstop, for hours on end. After a time, though, she would get bored and move on to her other toys. But every so often there came a special toy. Those toys became her best friends forever. Those toys she took to bed with her and snuggled with them under the covers to pass away the hours of the long, dark, lonely night. Those toys had become part of her life and she felt less than whole when she was without them.

In a slight whisper Baily asked, "What do you think, Miss Roosevelt? Should we keep him?"

"Meow."

"I agree," Baily replied.

Daniel, who woke at the sound of Baily's voice, spent the next few hours trying to decipher what the cat had said.

"WE'RE HERE!"

Daniel felt the car jolt to a stop. Surprised that he had actually dozed off, he took a few minutes to get his bearings. There were cars in front of him, in back of him, to his right, and to his left. Either they were stuck in a really bad traffic jam or they were in a parking lot.

"Come on, sleepyhead. I let you sleep through the elk sighting, but this is Old Faithful," Baily informed him. She pulled Miss Roosevelt from her spot with difficulty, as Theodora was also unwilling to relinquish her nap time. "I swear between the two of you you're like a bunch of babies. There will be time to sleep later. Right now we have a national treasure to see."

"Meow," Theodora complained.

"I agree with the cat. Wake us when you get back," Daniel groaned. He'd been in the middle of a wonderful sexy dream, and he wanted to return to it. A vision of Red flashed in front of his eyes, and he suddenly realized that she'd been the focal point of his dream. Since that kind of thinking had been outlawed this morning, Daniel forced himself to wake up, but his eyes wouldn't cooperate.

Baily decided to encourage him.

The loud blaring noise of a horn rang throughout the car, and Daniel wondered whether or not they were in a state that permitted spanking. Her point made, he opened his door and left the car.

Satisfied, Baily removed her hand from the horn and scooped up Theodora in her arms. She moved around the car and began to follow Daniel as he headed in the direction of all the other tourists.

"Sorry about the guerrilla tactics to wake you up, but I'm convinced you would have been devastated if you had missed this," Baily apologized.

"Devastated," he assured her insincerely.

In front of a large clearing where the hot springs were located, Daniel could see a huge clock on the side of the recreation center. It was eight minutes to countdown until the ever-faithful gusher blew.

The two moved up to the barrier that kept the tourists at a safe distance from the hot water. Daniel turned to see that Baily was practically jumping out of her skin with excitement over what was about to happen. He was about to tease her, after all it was just some bubbling water, but somehow her excitement became infectious. Even Miss Roosevelt's ears had perked up.

"The pressure from the heat of the spring builds up until finally it must be released," the tour guide lectured to the group standing around the barrier. She continued with a complete explanation of how the spring worked.

Baily hung on every word. Then water suddenly began to spout from the opening in the ground. It wasn't exploding yet, just a bubbling of water that indicated the time was at hand.

"Isn't this thrilling?" Baily turned and with her free hand she clasped Daniel's, squeezing it tightly as the water began to shoot up higher and higher.

Daniel looked down at their joined hands. He didn't feel any spark of electricity. He didn't see fireworks in the distance or hear the clamor of bells in his ears. Instead he felt the crush of people around him, smelled the stale steam that emanated from the water, and saw two hands joined. His and hers linked together. He sensed a swirling in his stomach and decided that he must be hungry.

"Wow!" The water was twenty feet high now, exploding from the ground like a rocket headed for space. Baily jumped up and down, subconsciously imitating the water. Theodora whined at the treatment, but Baily was heedless of her irritation. She didn't just witness Old Faithful—she experienced it as no one else around them was doing.

All too soon it ended. The water subsided, as did Baily's jumping. She turned to Daniel who seemed to be more enthralled with her than he was with the spectacle. "Wasn't it wonderful?"

"Yes it was," he answered truthfully.

Baily thought that he sounded a bit cryptic, but she didn't pursue it. "Well, let's make tracks. We want to make Jackson Hole by nightfall. There will be a place where you can rent a car. Then tomorrow you can head east." For what ever reason the words turned sour in her mouth.

And the words sounded sour to his ears. But it made

sense for him to get his own car. Didn't it? Of course it did. This woman was trouble. And he was too damned attracted to her. He couldn't deal with that attraction and save his sister at the same time. Besides, any attraction he might feel for Baily would be a lesson in futility. They might be driving in the same direction, but emotionally they were headed their separate ways: one toward a home and family, the other as far away from a home and family as he could possibly get. The only thing to do was to separate.

Without argument, Daniel followed Baily back to the car. Purposely, he moved to stand by the driver's side door. Now that he had decided to leave her, he wanted to get the leaving over with as soon as possible before he did something stupid such as reconsider his options.

Baily looked at him suspiciously.

"If you want to make Jackson Hole by nightfall, trust me—this is the only way," Daniel reasoned, and stuck out his hand for the keys. Baily acquiesced and handed him the keys. As soon as he had them in hand, Daniel completed his thought. "You drive like an old lady."

Affronted, but not really because it was more or less the truth, Baily made herself comfortable in the passenger's seat, snuggling Theodora into her lap. Her legs bumped into her cooler, and she remembered that she had put another six-pack of Diet Pepsi on ice this morning. A cold soda sounded delicious to her while she still felt the residual heat from all that steam at Old Faithful.

"Do you want a soda?" she asked, her hand remaining in the cooler in case he answered in the affirmative.

"Diet?" Daniel questioned. Baily's nod prompted his answer. "No, thank you."

With a shrug Baily pulled out a can for herself and cracked it open. She took long, audible gulps and sighed after she pulled the can away from her lips. She was like a commercial; she compelled Daniel to watch. Once again her actions were bolder than Daniel thought they should be, bolder than anybody else's actions would have been. She didn't just drink the soda, she consumed it. He couldn't help but be distracted by the sizzle of the soda, the sound of her sigh, the sight of her neck arched back and her throat as she swallowed. Then to really drive him nuts she placed the perspiring can against her neck, her cheeks and her forehead to cool herself.

Catching his gaze, Baily asked, "Are you sure you don't want one?"

"I don't like diet soda," he explained. "Besides, what do you need diet soda for anyway? You have a perfect figure."

Smiling at the compliment and blushing slightly, too, Baily replied, "I hardly have a perfect figure, but what I do have I owe to diet soda. It's not so bad once you get used to it."

Another gulp oozed down her throat and Daniel crumbled. "Okay, give me a sip."

"Why don't I just get you your own?"

"I don't know if I'll like it, and I don't want you to waste a whole can on me." *I want that one,* he thought. *I want to put my lips where yours have been and taste the sweetness of your mouth, which I'm sure, is far sweeter than any soda could ever be.* He kept that opinion to himself.

Baily seemed almost reluctant to give him the can. She, too, was thinking about where her mouth had been, and where his would be, and where hers would be after his had been there. It was practically kissing!

Reaching his hand around the can, Daniel actually had to tug it away from her. "I don't have cooties."

With a laugh that gave no hint of humor, Baily relinquished her soda. She watched him as he put his lips over the rim and craned his neck to take in the sweet, carbonated fluid. His bottom lip was fuller than his top lip and it flattened against the can, leaving a trace of moisture where his hot breath had formed dew against the cold can.

Gulp. Baily swallowed. And she wasn't the one drinking. Daniel handed the can back to her with a satisfied, "Ah."

Then he waited.

Baily looked down at the can. She saw where his lips had been and felt him stare at her between the glimpses he shot at the road. All she had to do was wipe his presence from the can with her fingers. It would have been a clear signal to him that she meant to keep her distance from this stranger who had so suddenly entered her life.

Instead she lifted the can to her lips and took a deep swig. What the hell, she thought. Maybe it was time to start living a little more dangerously. After all, she was headed home to Harry. Life couldn't get any less dangerous than Harry.

For some reason Daniel was inordinately pleased. "So are you one of those diet fanatics who always watches their fat content?" he asked, turning the conversation back to the mundane to ease the sensual tension they had just created.

"Yes," Baily sighed. "Sad to say I am. But I do have the occasional lapse. Actually it's more than occasional, as you might have noticed by the way my shorts snug my rump a bit to…snugly."

He had noticed. But he had liked the result.

"I have this awful craving for chocolate-chip cookies," she admitted. "It's like an addiction."

"You mean the soft gooey kind with big chunks of

chocolate,'' Daniel elaborated. He often suffered from similar cravings.

Baily closed her eyes with desire. ''Oh, yeah! You pull it apart and the chocolate drips from one end of the cookie to the other. Yum-mm.''

''And walnuts,'' Daniel added. ''I love it when they add the walnuts.''

Baily's mouth popped open and she sat up a bit straighter, her expression incredulous. ''You don't really like the walnuts.''

Taken back by her fervor, Daniel corrected her. ''I love the walnuts.''

''Nobody loves the walnuts.''

''I *love* the walnuts,'' Daniel insisted.

Baily simply couldn't believe it. ''But that's impossible. Everybody knows that the easiest way to ruin a perfectly good chocolate-chip cookie is to throw in walnuts. It's a myth. Everybody really hates the walnuts.''

''Not me!'' Daniel retorted, irritated at her suggestion that he was a freak just for liking walnuts in his damn cookies. ''I adore the walnuts. I worship the walnuts. A cookie isn't a cookie without the walnuts!''

''You know it's people like you who ruin it for the rest of us. I can't go to a bakery these days without having to specifically ask for cookies without walnuts. It should be the other way around. You freaks should simply do your walnut eating at home and let the majority enjoy their cookies the way they want them.'' Baily was incensed. Just the other day she had bought a cookie only to find that it had walnuts in it. Yuck.

Daniel wasn't about to let up so quickly. ''Ha!''

''Again with the 'ha.'''

Undaunted, he continued. ''Did you ever think that

maybe us walnut-eating people were the majority, and that's why all the bakeries make their cookies that way?''

"No."

It lasted for hours. The great walnut debate continued long into the afternoon and into early evening. Textures, taste, fullness, richness, all were debated with one being pro walnut, the other con walnut. It wasn't until they reached Jackson Hole and found a motel that they both realized that they had spent an entire afternoon arguing about a nut.

Getting out of the car and stretching, they looked at each other.

"We're nuts, no pun intended. You do realize that? We've spent hours talking about cookies."

"Well, if you hadn't been so insistent...."

"I was insistent? What the hell were you?" Daniel asked as he started toward the hotel lobby to check in.

"I wasn't insistent. I was right," Baily shouted over her shoulder. "And wait a minute, wait a minute! Let's first find a place where you can rent a car, then we'll check in."

"Fine," Daniel said huffily. "Once that's done I'll be out of your hair forever."

Forever, Baily thought.

Forever, Daniel thought.

# 4

"I can't believe this has happened."

"It's seems like par for the course for you on this trip. You haven't broken any mirrors lately, have you?" Baily asked, hitching Theodora up over her shoulder. The cat had been cooperative so far, but if they didn't settle her in their room soon for her nap she would be impossible to travel with the next day.

"No, I haven't broken any mirrors or walked under any ladders. I have spent too much time with a black cat and its wacky mother."

"Oh, is this going to be my fault, too?" Baily asked. They stood outside the car rental place, which was only a few blocks from the motel where they had parked. Baily had suggested they see about the rental car first as it was getting late and the place might close. Daniel had agreed. To stretch their legs, they'd decided to walk the few blocks through the crowd of tourists that filled the streets of the trendy new boomtown in Wyoming. Through the tourists and one pickpocket, that is.

"I didn't steal your wallet," Baily reminded him.

"It was your idea to walk!" It was a ridiculous accusation said out of aggravation. Still it felt good. No wallet. No credit cards. No license to rent a car even if he did have his credit cards. He could get his V.P. to wire him some cash first thing tomorrow morning, but what was he going to do about his license? More importantly, what was he going to do for a room tonight?

Unfortunately, the answer to his question had red hair and was an endless source of irritation.

"You realize what this means?" Daniel asked her.

Of course she knew what it meant. It meant that he would be making the trip with her all the way to Philadelphia. The thought made Baily queasy. Originally when she had asked him, she thought his presence might mean good company, protection, someone to break up the driving. That was two shared Diet Pepsi's and a walnut debate ago. What Baily had come to understand during their trip so far was that she was much too interested in this man than an-about-to-become-engaged woman should be. She liked him. Even when they fought, she liked him. That in itself was bad, but worse was the fact that every time she gazed into his hazel eyes her heart pounded heavier, her blood raced thicker, and violent flashes of the two of them together naked flashed before her eyes. That was really bad.

The first thing she'd wanted to do when they arrived at Jackson Hole was to get him his own car. She couldn't take the risk that she might have to spend another day with him. Now it appeared that she was going to be spending more than just one more day with him.

"It means," Daniel finished, "that we'll drive to Philadelphia together. That is, if your offer is still open."

"U-uh," Baily stuttered.

"What am I saying? Of course it's still open. You wouldn't leave me stranded in Jackson Hole, would you?"

"No?" Baily asked, not as certain of that fact as he seemed to be.

"No."

Defeated, Baily nodded. She was just going to have to keep a stranglehold on her wayward thoughts and her out-of-control hormones.

The couple backtracked their route just in case Daniel's wallet had dropped out along the way. Since he'd kept his wallet in his back pocket, it seemed unlikely that he could have dropped it, but both of them wanted to be positive, each for their own reasons. After a thorough search, their conclusion was still the same. The wallet had been pinched. Baily suggested that they file a complaint with the police. Daniel agreed and the two went in search of the local cops. The officer on duty quizzed Daniel for details, but Daniel couldn't tell the man much. Equally, the officer couldn't offer Daniel much in the way of hope that his wallet would turn up.

As the two headed back to the motel Daniel reiterated what he had told the police, in the hope that maybe something would spark his memory.

"I thought I felt somebody bump into me a bit harder than one would normally expect. But no way I felt a hand reach into my back pocket. It must have been a pro. A serious pro."

"Heaven forbid that you get ripped off by an amateur," Baily snickered. Typical man. Not just any old pickpocket was brave enough or smart enough to outwit the almighty Daniel Blake. It had to the best pickpocket in the West.

Finally they reached the motel lobby. Daniel held the door open for Baily and graciously allowed her to enter ahead of him. Together they approached the motel clerk.

The young girl with the bright smile and blond ponytail was completely unaware of the brewing storm that had just entered the small little lobby. They looked like two normal people and a cat. She would never know what hit her.

TEN MINUTES LATER an enraged Baily emerged from the lobby holding on to Miss Roosevelt with one hand while she held the door in the other.

As soon as Daniel reached the door, she slammed it backward with intent to kill. Or at least to bump him in the nose real hard.

If Daniel's reflexes hadn't been as quick as they were, Baily might have succeeded. Fortunately for her, he knew her well enough by now to expect the dirty trick. A chilling notion if he thought about it for too long.

"You behaved like a child. I don't see what the big deal is." Daniel fumed under his breath as he trailed her to *their* room. He'd never been so completely humiliated in his life. Humiliation, a heretofore unknown emotion, was now as commonplace to him as breathing thanks to an unreasonable redhead.

"You wouldn't," Baily responded to his muttering. "But trust me, it is in fact a big deal."

"Meow," Theodora concurred.

"See, even she agrees with me," Baily announced.

"Oh, now I'm convinced because the damn cat said so."

Baily lifted Theodora off her shoulder so she could see her face. "Did you hear what he just called you?"

"Meow."

"Clearly the man has no sense of propriety," Baily said, cuddling Theodora once again over her shoulder.

In one coordinated motion, Daniel passed Baily and her cat en route to the room and removed the key from her hand. He had opted not to rise to her previous challenge. Daniel fast discovered that Red took a profound delight in having the last word. If he chose to respond to her comment, he knew there would be more to follow. And between the morning's argument, the afternoon's argument, and the early evening's argument, he simply wasn't ready to engage in a late-evening argument.

Once inside the room, he couldn't ignore the gasp from immediately behind him. So much for détente.

"Look at how small the room is! It's minute, minuscule, miniature, tiny, teeny, weeny—"

"I get the point," Daniel interrupted.

"But you said it probably wouldn't be that bad. You said we'd never even notice one another. You said we would forget the other person was even there," Baily protested, throwing Daniel's words back at him.

"I said we would try to forget the other person was there, and believe me I will do everything in my power to make that true. It would help things considerably if you shut your mouth for more than five seconds at a time. Not that I think you could even if you wanted to."

"You don't think I can keep my mouth shut."

"Yes, I'm pretty positive you couldn't keep your mouth shut for any extended period of time."

Baily closed her mouth, determined not to talk. Which was her misfortune, since she still had a considerable amount to say. It was like shaking up a soda can and then refusing to open it. All her fizz was bursting to get out. Then again, it wasn't as if she hadn't said everything already.

At the registration desk, she had asked for one room for herself and Theodora. She'd then stepped aside so that Daniel could ask for his room.

That was when he reminded her that his wallet had been stolen.

She told him he couldn't share her room. It was unthinkable. She wasn't that kind of girl.

He told her he wasn't that kind of guy, but where in the hell did she think he was going to stay.

She told him she couldn't afford two rooms. It would run up the limit on her credit card too fast, what with the bulk of the trip in front of them. And she had no idea where he was going to sleep.

He told her to get a grip. He was staying with her. Then he added all that stuff about the room being so big they would miss each other.

She told him that she wouldn't miss him even if he were the last man on the planet.

Then he'd tried to walk out on her.

And she'd discovered that she did miss him. That is, she missed the opportunity to punch him right in the nose. So she'd walked out on him first.

Now she sat on her bed, the one that was only a foot away from his bed, and sulked. She threw in a few pouts and sighs every now and again for good measure. But she didn't say a word. He was lying back on his bed, seemingly oblivious to her irritation.

"Uh-hh-hh," she sighed once more, this time so audibly that he couldn't miss it. She waited for his reaction.

Slump. A large white puffy mass hit her square in the face. For a moment she was too stunned to think. Then it hit her. Literally. Why that arrogant, no good, stinking, rotten, conniving…jerk! No, wait. Bastard! He'd just thrown his pillow at her.

Taking the weapon in hand, Baily stood over him astounded that he had the nerve to close his eyes. Didn't he know she would retaliate? She poised the pillow high above her head in attack position ready to bring it down on his face…hard.

It was as the pillow was on the way down that she realized she had made a tactical error. She'd been suckered into a trap. The most obvious trick in the book. The play dead routine. After having used the same ruse on her brothers a multitude of times, she should have been adept at spotting it herself.

In an instant Daniel's eyes were open. His hands sprung up and captured her wrists. Stopping the attack wasn't enough, however. He had to disarm her before he could truly consider himself safe. Keeping a firm grip on her wrists, Daniel pulled her toward him while at the same time rolling so that her natural momentum threw her down next to him on the bed. In a flash he rolled on top of her, pinning her arms high above her head. A quick glimpse confirmed she still had the pillow.

Panting with sudden exertion and blushing with humiliation at having been so easily duped, Baily confronted her conqueror. That was her second mistake. Hazel eyes loomed above her. Their color was extraordinary. But no more so than the man to whom they belonged. His breath blew in little puffs on her mouth. An odd expression suddenly crossed his face. It must have just occurred to him—the predicament he had put them in.

Daniel looked down at his captive. He'd been prepared to taunt his victory over her, but once he saw her eyes and dove into those green depths, he was helpless to stop the rush of desire that crashed over him. Red tresses shot like flames from her head to decorate the whiteness of the pillow beneath her. They demanded to be caressed. Freckles called to him for a kiss, each one individually.

"Red..." he whispered. Then, "Red?"

"Daniel?" Baily replied, not knowing what else to do. Her neck arched ever so slightly, bringing his lips into closer contact. He lowered his head and the touch of his lips was like the brush of a feather across her own.

"Meow!" Theodora chose that moment to launch an attack on Daniel's back. She used her front paws to scrape at his back through his cotton shirt. Apparently, she didn't like the idea of anyone pouncing on her mistress—other than herself, of course. "Me-ow!" she roared furiously.

"Miss Roosevelt! Really," Baily scolded, although she didn't know whether she was grateful, angry, or frustrated with her cat's interference. She'd lay odds on frustrated.

With a groan, Daniel slowly rolled to his side to give the cat a chance to jump. She did and went along her merry way now that her mistress was out of trouble.

"What just happened?" Daniel asked.

"How about dinner?" Baily suggested, completely ignoring his question. Her voice was tense and high-pitched. She bounced off the bed and ran to the bathroom. Her only hope was that she didn't trip in her urgency. "I'm starved. Why don't you check the hotel guide for a restaurant," she called out from the other room.

"Red..." Daniel began, uncertain of what to say. Perhaps dinner was the best idea. They had the whole night to talk about the attraction that had sprouted between them. The whole long night in the same room with their beds mere inches apart. Yes, dinner for now. Later... Well, who knew what the night would bring. He was, however, going to have to do something about that cat. One pussycat in his bed was enough.

In a smooth motion Daniel leapt off the bed and waited for Red to finish up in the bathroom. He felt like a freeloader at that moment. She'd provided him with transportation, shelter, and now she was going to feed him. He was a wealthy man and an old-fashioned one. It wasn't his style to let any woman pick up the tab. What if she demanded sexual favors in return for feeding him?

Hot damn.

He chuckled and told himself that tomorrow would be soon enough to pick up some cash.

Bruce. Daniel needed to call him now if he was going

to be able to get his money by tomorrow. The best solution would be to have him wire the money to their next pit stop. Daniel searched his memory for Bruce's home number then realized that Bruce was more than likely still at the office working on the bid for the Northern California Timber Company.

Red walked out of the bathroom, her hair still a little mussed, although it tended to do that naturally, and her cheeks a little redder than normal. Other than that she appeared to be unscathed from their near miss.

Baily had taken more deep breaths than she could count, yet she still hadn't managed to slow her pounding heart. She could only hope that he couldn't actually see her heart pulsing through the T-shirt she wore. That was impossible. Wasn't it? She waited for him to ask again about what had happened on the bed. This time she was prepared with an answer.

It was a natural reaction after all the tension they had been through that day. They were both looking for release after having fought for so long. *Boy, are you looking for release,* a little voice in her head gibed.

*Stop that,* her conscience warned.

That wasn't part of the answer, Baily reasoned. They were two adults. Nothing happened. Nothing could happen since she was on her way to be with Harry and Daniel was eventually going to be returning to Seattle. Baily was not a one-night-stand kind of girl. Or a one-trip-stand kind of girl, for that matter. That was why when he asked where they were headed tomorrow, Baily naturally assumed he was on another topic.

''Well, we are not headed to bed!'' she stated indignantly.

Daniel laughed until his sides hurt. Which in turn only served to make Baily's skin flush from blushing pink to infuriated purple. "I'm sorry...I'm sorry," he said between gasps. "It's just that you looked so serious."

"I am serious." She stomped her foot to prove it.

"I think the lady is doth protesting too much."

"You're lousy at quoting Shakespeare," she informed him with a sneer. "If you didn't mean what I thought you meant, then what did you mean?"

Daniel had to think about that. She had this way of talking that twisted his mind into knots. He was beginning to think she did it on purpose. "I meant, where is our destination tomorrow? I'm going to call my vice president and have him wire me some money. I'll have him wire it to our next stop so it will be there when we get there rather than wait around here all morning."

"Custer."

"Are we back on the dinner subject?"

Baily closed her eyes. "Not custard. Custer. Custer is where we are headed. It's in South Dakota not too far from Rapid City."

"Can't we just go to Rapid City? It's larger, and we'd be more likely to find a Western Union office." It was a logical suggestion, but Red was shaking her head and looking at him as if he were insane. "Stop shaking your head. Why can't we go to Rapid City?"

"Because then we would miss Mount Rushmore, silly. You know, the presidents... Washington, Jefferson, Lincoln and—"

"Roosevelt," Daniel finished as understanding dawned on him.

"Meow." Theodora, now snuggled on the pillow that had once been used as a weapon against her mistress, lifted her head for a moment to give her opinion.

"Yes, Miss Roosevelt. I promised you we'd go to Mount Rushmore," Baily said lovingly. To Daniel she said, "And you know I always keep my promises. But we'll pass through Rapid City the next day so you can tell your vice president to send the money there."

"Too late. I don't want to wait two days. We'll just have to hang out here tomorrow morning. Sorry about all this." Daniel picked up the phone and dialed nine to get an outside line.

With another shake of her head, Baily dismissed his apology. "You were robbed. There was nothing you could have done."

Daniel smiled, thanking her for her acceptance. His conversation with Bruce was curt and to the point. The money would be there tomorrow. Daniel hung up the phone and turned to find Baily with her hand on her chin as if she were considering something. "What?" Daniel questioned.

Baily shrugged her shoulders. "I was just thinking that maybe you could have realized that the shove you received was more than accidental."

"How was I supposed to tell that? It was a shove. I think there was a guy in a brown hat, and then I felt a bump. How could I have guessed I was robbed?"

"I'm not saying that you should have. I'm merely pointing out that if you had checked your wallet after you were bumped, maybe you would have been able to catch the guy. You could have chased him down into an alley. Then maybe you could have kicked the knife out of his hand—"

"What knife?" Daniel asked incredulously.

"The knife in his back pocket. All professional crooks carry a knife. And we do agree that he was a professional?"

"Damn straight."

"There you go. You would have kicked away his knife and punched him in the nose. Then you would have ripped your wallet out of his greedy little paws and said something macho like, 'Nobody messes with Daniel Blake.' Then you would have returned to me triumphant." Baily sighed. "It would have made a wonderful story."

"What if I turned tail and ran after I saw the knife?"

"You're not the turn-tail-and-run type of guy," Baily assured him.

Amused by her conviction, Daniel thanked her for the compliment.

"But since you didn't do any of that, we'll have to wait until noon before we can leave. I don't mind, but what about your sister? Can we afford the delay?"

*Nobody messes with Daniel Blake.* Would he have really said that? God, he hoped not. A shake of his head brought his focus back to the matter at hand. He'd been grappling with the problem of making the wedding in time all afternoon as he drove Red's Bug. Her worn-down, pitiful little Bug couldn't be pushed past sixty-five without making a fuss. The car wasn't made for a high-speed trek across the country. Perhaps the best thing he could do would be to buy himself more time.

"I have an idea."

"Uh-oh."

Daniel shot her his what-the-hell-does-that-mean look. Baily couldn't decipher it, so he asked her, "What the hell does that mean?"

"Nothing."

Satisfied, Daniel picked up the phone again.

"I just meant that your last idea concerning your sister—offering her beau a bribe—bombed so miserably that maybe you ought to let me do the thinking from now on."

Wolflike growls originated from the back of this throat.

Baily didn't seem to notice. "For instance, I was thinking that maybe you could call Sarah and tell her you are running late. Is it a big-deal wedding? You know, church, reception, that kind of thing.''

"No, she said Pierce didn't want to wait. They're being married at city hall.''

"So ask if she could postpone the wedding for a few days. That way we'll have a little extra time built into our schedule.''

"That was my idea!'' Daniel shouted irritably.

"Okay, okay. No need to get huffy. Make your phone call. Then we'll eat.''

Punching the necessary numbers with a little more force than necessary, Daniel barked a hello. "Oh, it's you, Larson. Listen, get my sister. It's an emergency.''

Baily waited and listened to his side of the conversation.

"What do you mean, she's not there? Where is she? …Out shopping for a gown…. I see… When will she return? …You don't know. She's your fiancée yet you have no idea when she's coming home? …What the hell was that crack supposed to mean? …I am not too possessive… Listen you…''

Baily watched as he became increasingly agitated. If he didn't control his temper, there was no way Pierce would consider postponing the wedding. She jumped up to stop him before he said something stupid. Grabbing the phone out of his hand, she spoke to who she assumed was Pierce Larson.

"Hi, Mr. Larson. You don't know me, but I'm a friend of Daniel's.''

"I didn't know he had friends,'' came the response from the other end of the phone. Baily had already made up her mind not to like him but she couldn't help smiling at the insult.

"Yes, well, he does. He's been having a little car trouble, and wallet trouble, and bump-on-the-head trouble.

What I mean to say is that he's running behind schedule. So we thought since it's so very important that he be at his own sister's wedding that you could postpone the wedding for a few days.''

"I don't know. We've got everything planned already," Pierce said smoothly.

"You're getting married by a judge, aren't you?"

"Yes."

"Then you should have no problem simply making another appointment. Daniel is her brother. He's got to be there."

"I'll tell you what I'll do. I will run it by Sarah. If she agrees, then we'll postpone everything until Daniel arrives."

Baily smiled triumphantly at Daniel who was still trying to contain his temper. "That's perfect. I'm sure Sarah will agree. Goodbye."

"IT WAS ELEVEN O'CLOCK at night," Daniel said to the waiter. It was an odd response considering the waiter had asked him if he would like anything to drink.

"Excuse me, sir?"

Daniel paused for a moment while he attempted to gain his focus.

Baily jumped in with an apologetic excuse. "You'll have to forgive my friend. He was hit really hard on the head today. And his car was trashed, and his wallet was stolen, and…"

With a warning glance, Daniel attempted to shut her up. Fat chance.

"We really don't even know if he has suffered any permanent damage," Baily continued, unaware of Daniel's disapproval. "Head wounds can be tricky."

The waiter nodded sympathetically, but it was easy to

see that all he wanted to know was what the man would like to drink.

"Stuff it, Red," Daniel told her. "I'll have a beer, a cheeseburger, fries if you have them, and a large salad with blue cheese dressing."

Baily nodded approvingly. "Sounds good. I'll have the same. Except no fries. And I'll have a chicken sandwich instead of a hamburger. No cheese on the chicken of course. And instead of blue cheese dressing I would like something low fat if you have it. If not, then I'll take honey dijon."

Daniel shook his head. "That wasn't the same thing at all."

Baily handed the waiter the menus while looking at Daniel in an attempt to decipher what he meant. She didn't notice that the waiter practically sprinted from their table. "What are you talking about? I ordered a beer, too."

"Never mind," he muttered, knowing it wasn't worth what little energy he had left in this day.

"Speaking of not knowing what you are talking about, what did you mean by eleven o'clock?"

"Larson said Sarah was out buying a dress." Daniel had calculated the time difference and realized that it was after eleven at night Philadelphia time when he had called. "What kind of stores are open at eleven at night? He lied. He didn't want me to talk to Sarah. I can't stand that he lives with her in that house. He's got too much control over her that way."

"What kind of control?"

"He can screen her calls, for one thing."

"He has to. He's afraid you'll talk her out of getting married. It's actually a risky gamble on Pierce's part. If Sarah finds out that her calls are being screened, she might call off the wedding herself."

"He's right to be afraid. I'm sure if I could talk to Sarah, I could tell her what lunacy this sudden marriage is." At least that was what Daniel hoped. He didn't want to think about the possibility that his sister was truly in love with this con man.

"Do you think he'll do what you asked? I mean, if he's a true con man he's better off if you don't make it to the wedding."

Good point. He didn't know. "I don't think Sarah would let Pierce rush her down the aisle without me there. And hopefully it won't matter. I still plan—I mean, we still plan to be in Philadelphia on time, right? There's nothing he can do from his end to stop me."

Daniel's eyes were lit with a ferocity that sparked something deep in Baily. She imagined what it would be like to have a man love her with same intensity that Daniel loved his sister. She knew that a man like Daniel would be protective as well as possessive. But he would also be giving and indulgent, much as he was with his sister. Much as her own brothers were with her. If only Harry could be more like Daniel. But Harry was Harry. He was sweet, and lovable, and an absolute pushover.

Their meals came and for the next hour they satisfied their hunger and attempted not to further confuse the waiter. It was while they sipped their coffee after dinner that Daniel decided it was time to talk about what had happened back in the motel room.

"Listen, Red, we need to work a few things out."

Baily's eyes met his over the rim of her coffee cup, and instantly she knew what he referred to. His hazel eyes took on a deeper color and he lowered his voice. He hunched forward in his seat, creating a more intimate atmosphere. And if it were possible, although Baily didn't see how it was, he made himself look sexier.

"Did I tell you about the history of this restaurant? It was named after a famous mountain man." Baily simply couldn't tell this man with a straight face that she wasn't interested in him, which of course she had to say because she was going to become engaged to another man in a few short days.

"You're avoiding the subject," Daniel informed her. Ironic, since he was usually the one to avoid personal conversations. It was why he had never dated a woman for any longer than a couple months. There was only so much sex you could have and so many superficial conversations you could carry on. Once a woman started to talk about a future and family, Daniel bolted. He had no interest in becoming part of another family again. Not when he knew from experience that the pain suffered from the loss of a family could cripple a man. He'd protect Sarah, but that was where all of his family obligations ended. He couldn't say that he ever broke any hearts. Most women never got to know him enough to like him very much, let alone love him.

Red was different. He wanted to talk about the intimate stuff with her. He wanted to talk about what they were going to do with this attraction they felt for one another. And it was mutual. Instinctively, Daniel knew that to be true.

"Did I tell you that this man was the first to cross the Sierra Nevadas? He was. He fought off Indians. He tackled bears. He charted new land. He...."

"...seduced virgins," Daniel filled in, hoping to snare her attention.

"I don't think he did that."

"I do. It must be the air at this altitude," Daniel quipped. Pushing ahead now that he had her attention, he continued. "So about what happened in the hotel earlier…"

"I'm engaged!" Baily shouted, which in turn caused the other diners to turn their heads in their direction.

In a lower tone, but no less menacing, Daniel insisted, "No you are not. Regardless, that doesn't have anything to do with us."

"Of course it does," Baily replied, her tone equally soft.

"This is between you and me. Howard has nothing to do with us."

"It's Harry, and I hope you aren't implying that I'm the type of woman who could promise one man that I was going to marry him and then sleep with another man days before I saw him again." Just because that was exactly what Baily wanted to do didn't mean that he could go around implying it. Besides, it didn't matter what she wanted. She couldn't betray Harry. It would be wrong. No, they weren't married. No, they weren't engaged. They had never even been lovers. Really they were just good friends.

But she had made up her mind that she was going to marry him, which meant that she had to be faithful to him starting now. Never mind that in her heart she had already been unfaithful to him. She wanted Daniel. Was it wrong to want someone when you were supposed to want someone else even though you didn't really want the someone else? She thought so. It was hard to tell.

Sometimes, Baily confused herself.

"I did not imply anything," Daniel countered irritably. In truth though, he had. He wanted Red, and he was annoyed now that he wasn't going to get to have her because of some man that waited for her in New Jersey. A man, he could tell, she didn't even want. "Why are you marrying this man?"

"I've already told you," Baily said as she reminded him

of their conversation earlier that day. That day! Had they only known each other less than twenty-four hours? It didn't seem possible.

"Oh, yeah, now I remember. Security." He might as well have said money for all the disdain in his voice.

"If I remember correctly, you agreed with me."

Daniel shrugged his shoulders as if to pretend he couldn't quite recall what he said on the matter. It had been a long day. Day. Had it only been one day?

"We both agree that love is nothing more than a fancy word for poems, songs and romantic stories," Baily continued. "In real life it doesn't happen the way people say it does. There are no sparks." *Well, there were a few between them it seemed.* "There is no love at first sight." *Okay so maybe she'd been attracted to Daniel at first sight, but that wasn't love.* "And there is no 'happily ever after.'"

And that was certainly true. Even if they did decide to pursue their mutual attraction it would only end in heartbreak. He was going to Seattle. She was going to be with her family in New Jersey. Certainly not a fairy-tale ending. Baily told herself to stop being depressed by that thought.

Daniel wondered what she was thinking that dimmed the sparkle that always seemed to glow in her eyes. He supposed it was her convincing argument that true love, magical love, didn't exist. He wondered why that thought should depress him.

"Go home and marry Herbert. See if I care," he said a bit nastily.

"That's exactly what I'm going to do," she returned haughtily. "Nothing is going to stop me."

*Please stop me. Please.* Shut up, she told her conscience. She was doing the right thing. She had waited all her life for someone like Daniel. She had waited for someone handsome, smart and funny. Okay, so he was a little arrogant. And maybe he could fly off the handle from time to time. But probably only after trashing his car or getting his wallet lifted. A case could be made that he was overly protective of his sister, but that really couldn't go down in the negative column. There was still the whole walnut issue. Frankly, she didn't know if that one was surmountable. Not that she wanted to sur…mount him. But if she was considering him as a potential love interest, it was just possible that he might be the very sort she would fall for. For some unfathomable reason, she wanted to cry.

The meal was over, but Baily wasn't ready to retire back to their small room where the beds practically touched. Instead she had a better idea for the evening's entertainment. "How about a gunfight?"

"You're not still on the room thing, are you?" he asked a little worriedly. Pistols at fifty paces over a motel room seemed drastic, but he didn't put it past her.

"No, silly, it's a tourist attraction. Like a reenactment of a real-life shoot-out. Two men face each other at dusk and stare down the barrel of a gun aimed at each other's heart. Neither one knows if they're going to live or die. It's all very intense." Baily's face was flushed with excitement at the thought of actually being able to see a real-life gun battle. A real-life fake one, that is.

"And very dramatic," Daniel added. "You've seen too many movies."

"That's the point! This will be like watching a movie only live." Daniel knew he wouldn't be able to squelch her enthusiasm so he didn't try. Besides, watching her watch the gunfight would be like watching her watch Old Faithful. For that it would be worth the price of admission.

The two left the restaurant in search of the attraction. They didn't need to walk far. The gunfight was held in the center of town, which, Baily insisted, was the only place to hold it.

Jackson Hole, despite its chic shops and expensive restaurants that catered to the skiers, still maintained an authentic Western atmosphere. All of the storefronts were faced in a dark wood and since the main street was framed by a large wooden boardwalk one could imagine horses tied to the posts out front. The effect was nineteenth-century Wyoming, and it attracted tourists during the summer as well as the winter season.

Finding a place to watch the event wasn't easy. Daniel managed to squirm his way up to the front, dragging Baily with him. He wanted her to have a front-row view. She would enjoy the show best that way, and he would enjoy watching her best that way, as well.

The actors came out and faced each other from across the street at a distance of about twenty yards or so. One began saying that the town wasn't big enough for the two of them. The other replied he was sorry that the other man was going to have to die. The cliché dialogue continued for a few minutes. Then they both fell silent. The crowd noise fell to a hush. Baily reached over, grabbed Daniel's hand, and squeezed it hard. It was becoming a pattern. Daniel understood that Baily was the type of person who couldn't keep her excitement to herself. She needed to share what she felt. Apparently, she did that through touch. Daniel couldn't help but imagine what kind of lover she would be. Then he abruptly dismissed that thought from his mind. It was not going to happen. Not as long as Harold was in the way.

Suddenly the man from the left drew his gun, and then the man from the right did the same. There were several loud popping noises after which they both fell dead. A man in a dark suit and a tall hat came out to measure the bodies.

"The undertaker," Baily whispered in case Daniel hadn't already figured that out.

The undertaker dropped sheets over the two men, essentially ending the play, and the crowd erupted in thunderous applause. Then the two men under the sheets stood to take their bows. Daniel thought it rather anticlimactic.

"They should have stayed dead until everybody left," Daniel complained like a kid who was disappointed to learn that there was no Santa Claus. They headed back to their motel, enjoying the fresh air and the view of the mountains in the distance.

"You're being unrealistic. They would have had to stay under those sheets too long. Besides, they deserved to take their bows just like any other actor," Baily said, answering his compliant, but her mind was elsewhere. Now that the gunfight was over there was nothing to prevent them from returning to their tiny room. Maybe it had gotten bigger in the past few hours.

They reached the door of their motel room. Both were clearly reluctant to go inside. "If this were a date," Baily noted, "this is where I would say thank you for a lovely evening."

"It was a nice night, wasn't it?" Daniel seemed slightly stunned. He couldn't recall a date when he'd had as much simple fun. Innocent pleasure. This must be what it felt like to be a boy on a first date. Daniel was sure he must have felt this way before. If he had, it was too long ago to remember. This night, however, he didn't think he would ever forget.

It was almost perfect. Almost. "You know if this were a date," Daniel continued, "and you did have a nice time like you said you did, it wouldn't be such a horrible thing if I asked for a kiss. Would it?"

"Daniel, I already told you that I can't—" Baily started.

Daniel put two fingers against her lips to stop her excuses. "One kiss, Red. One kiss, then we'll call it quits, go to bed, and never bring any of this up again."

She couldn't refuse him one kiss. She couldn't refuse herself one kiss, either. Tilting her head slightly, she allowed him to press his lips against hers. First he was gentle, tugging at her lips with his own. Then he was playful, darting his tongue out to caress her lips and the seam between them. Then he was bold, pushing his body against hers until her back was pressed against the door and her arms had no place to go except around him. His tongue plunged into her mouth, conquering her with his intensity.

She tasted him and he was wonderful. She knew he tasted her, as well, and groaned with the thought of it. Baily could only hope that she was as pleasing to him as he was to her. Every good intention she ever had was about to fly out the window because she couldn't remember the name of the person she was having those good intentions for.

Daniel chose that moment to end the kiss. He practically had to rip his lips off hers. For a moment they looked at each other and felt their chests beat against each other as their lungs struggled for breath. Baily wanted to tell him to forget Howard, or Harold, or whatever his name was and take her right there against the door hard and fast and so deep that she would never forget it.

Instead she said, "Wow."

"Yeah, wow," Daniel repeated. Then he backed off, leaving her arms empty. "A deal's a deal." He took the key from her hand, opened the door, and went inside.

Numb, Baily could only stare at the open door.

# 5

"ARE YOU ASLEEP?" The soft question filled the dark room. Even Miss Roosevelt, who was sleeping soundly on Daniel's chest, pricked up her ears.

"No," he replied with resignation. How the hell was he supposed to sleep with a cat on his chest and a woman's soft lips on his mind? He told himself a hundred times that he could have taken her, should have taken her. She wanted him as badly as he wanted her. Her lips said as much even if her words did not. But he had done the right thing. He'd let her go and denied both of them what could have been the sexual experience of their lives. Why had he done that?

"You were a real gentlemen earlier," she said somewhat forlornly.

"Thanks."

It wasn't necessarily a compliment. She had rather hoped that he would have proven to be an absolute cad. She would have been seduced against her will, forced to make love with the man, and it would have been beyond her control. No guilt. All pleasure.

Instead he'd gone and ruined everything by listening to her.

Baily smiled at her own silly thoughts. Daniel wasn't to blame; she was. She was the one who put up the hands-off sign. At the time, she had meant every word of it. It was only when he'd started kissing her that things had gotten a little hazy. Fortunately, he'd had the willpower to break away before things had gotten out of hand. And it was fortunate, she told herself firmly. She was too close to reaching her goal and fulfilling her dream of creating a family to be thwarted by something as trivial and transient as desire.

Oh, yeah, he had all the willpower. Baily, however, had needed a good five minutes to recover before she could even walk through the door. Daniel, already out of the bathroom, had snuggled into bed. Miss Roosevelt, evidently having forgiven him for his previous attack on her mistress, had huddled into a ball on top of him. Traitor.

It was the first time Baily could ever remember being jealous of a cat. And what made it worse was that Miss Roosevelt had gaped at her mistress as if she were crazy to pass up the opportunity to snuggle with Daniel. Evidently, he was a very good snuggler.

Now in the wee hours of the morning, Baily was feeling restless and very unsnuggled. It was only right that Daniel share in her insomnia. "So you can't sleep, either," she said, stating the obvious.

As if he could have slept with her only one foot and eleven inches away from him. Did she think he was made of stone? He hadn't been able to close his eyes let alone sleep. Every time he did, he saw flaming red hair. Red hair spread out against a white pillow. Red hair clutched between his fingers. The only way he knew to prevent the erotic, ungentleman-like dreams that would surely come if he slept, was to stay awake.

Awake was no picnic, either. Awake, he heard her soft breathing, imagined the rise and fall of her chest, imagined her soft, full, and well-kissed lips parted ever so slightly. No, awake wasn't any easier than asleep was, and now

Red had just made it harder by informing him that she was having as much difficulty sleeping as he was.

"I see you're having the same problem," Daniel noted with a hint of smugness. The way he saw it, her suffering was of her own making. She was the one who'd established the rules.

"Yes, and it's all your fault," Baily snipped. She was tired and frustrated, feeling lustful and guilty all at the same time. If he hadn't kissed her, she'd be snoozing sounder than Theodora right now. It was definitely all his fault.

"My fault! The way I see it, Red, this is all your fault," he informed her, amazed at her audacity to blame him.

"My fault!" she exclaimed. "You're the one who kissed me."

"And you're the one who said I couldn't do anything more than kiss you. That's why we're both frustrated. I'm a gentleman, remember." Daniel taunted her with her own words.

"I said you couldn't do any kissing before you kissed me," she retorted. "Then you kissed me, anyway. That's why we're both frustrated. Now that I think of it, you're about as far away from a gentleman as as...Miss Roosevelt."

"Meow!" Theodora wailed from her perch, apparently not pleased with the analogy.

"Honey, you may have said no kissing, but your whole being cried out to be kissed. I was simply...helping you fulfill your needs." As soon as the words left his mouth, Daniel had the distinct impression that he'd said the wrong thing.

"What in the hell is that supposed to mean?" Baily

fairly shrieked with rage. Fury vaulted her into a sitting position. "Are you saying that was a pity kiss?"

"I wouldn't go so far as to say it was a pity kiss," Daniel said, attempting to retreat. But he had a feeling that one false move and she would be feeding him his other foot.

"Theodora! Get off him," Baily ordered. The cat, despite her contended position, knew where her kitty kibble came from. She immediately jumped off Daniel and off the bed to seek a safer bed.

Daniel should have seen it coming. Without the cat in the way to prevent a full frontal assault he was left vulnerable to whatever revenge Baily had in mind. The pillow that hit him squarely in the face wasn't a surprise. Nor was the second one. He thought she overdid it when she threw the third pillow, and he laughed out loud when she threw the fourth pillow.

"Why are you laughing?" Baily screamed. Her temper still flared, only now she was weaponless.

"Typical redhead. You got yourself in a snit and now you've just thrown all your pillows away. Looks like you'll be resting your head on the mattress tonight." Daniel chuckled. He had to admit she was entertaining.

After a few deep breaths Baily managed to calm herself. Fighting with a man she had no intention of remembering five days hence was pointless. So she decided to forget her temper, put him completely out of her mind, and drift off into a peaceful slumber. Which was exactly what she would have done if she had a pillow.

"Give me my pillows back," she ordered.

"No," Daniel answered smugly.

"Come on, just one pillow."

"No." Who had the last word this time? Him. Heh, heh, heh.

"If you don't give them back I'm just going to come over there and get them," Baily explained logically. Then she saw the form beneath the sheets move. Suddenly his eyes gleamed at her through the dark, cat's eyes that seemed to see right through her despite the lack of light.

"If you come over here, I can guarantee you won't make it back to your bed tonight. Have I made myself clear?"

The husky timbre of his voice, the gleam in his eyes…yes, his point had been made, and his threat was unmistakable. Baily shut her mouth and laid her head down on the mattress. It wasn't so bad.

"THIS IS HORRIBLE!" The morning sun was harsh on eyes that hadn't been closed for more than a few hours off and on throughout the night. Baily felt as if her whole body was about to burst with annoyance as she stared down at her car. The one with two flat tires. Two. How could anyone get two flat tires at the same time?

"What the hell did you park it on? Glass?" Daniel had exited the room with the cat under one arm and their overnight bags under the other.

"Me?" Baily still hadn't recovered from being furious with him the night before. So it wouldn't have taken more than a sneeze for Daniel to irritate her all over again this morning. He had just given her more than a sneeze. "If I recall correctly, you were the one who parked the car when we drove up to the motel. So what the hell did *you* park it on?"

"It's pointless to stand around here arguing about how it happened. What we need to do is get it fixed. Then we can find the Western Union office. I can't waste a whole day in Jackson Hole, or I'll never make it to Philly in time to stop the wedding."

Baily mumbled something about men never being able to admit when they were wrong, but she let it go at that. He was right. This was more than two flat tires. This was his sister's future. "I spotted a gas station when we pulled into town. Maybe they have a tow truck."

"They'd better."

He turned his back on her then and returned to the room to get the rest of their belongings. As if Baily had any say in whether the gas station had a tow truck or not. She took the opportunity to stick her tongue out at him again. The effect was ruined with the sight of Theodora's tail swishing about from under his arm. Baily was forced to smile and that only irritated her more because the last thing she wanted to do was to dwell on how cute he looked holding her cat.

Better to think of him as a tyrant. Much better. It wasn't as if she wanted to be stuck in Wyoming with two flat tires. She had places to go, people to see, a man to become engaged to. Okay, so maybe there were worse things in this world than being stuck in Wyoming. Still, she hadn't popped the tires herself. Not only that, but if they didn't manage to find two new tires they were going to have to spend another night together in that tiny motel room. She simply didn't have the willpower.

After a short search in the small town, Daniel and Baily first located the Western Union office, then the service station. Luckily, the attendant had two tires available for them and Daniel was able to pay cash as an incentive to speed the process along. The attendant promised to tow the car and change the tires. They could return in a few hours for the car. Baily balked at Daniel's highhandedness for paying for the damage, but he considered it his way of paying for his trip across country. Since Baily secretly believed that the tires were his fault anyway, she accepted.

"We've got some time to kill, what do you say we hunt something down to eat?" Baily suggested. Daniel agreed, and the two took an idle walk about the town until they found a small nook of a restaurant that served breakfast.

Seated in the small diner off the main street, they ate bagels and drank coffee.

"Are you sure Miss Roosevelt is okay in that motel room by herself?" Baily asked the question for the third time that morning.

"Yes," he said for the third time since they had left her. "I don't get it. We left her alone in the room last night when we went to dinner. What's the problem this morning?"

"That was before the slashed tires," Baily told him worriedly. "What if someone is stalking you and the tires were just a warning?"

He hated to admit it, but she wasn't completely out of line this time. A stolen wallet was one thing, but two flat tires were something else. No one had this kind of luck. Not ready to voice his thoughts on the subject and frighten her quite yet, he turned the question back on her. "How do you know our stalker is after me? Maybe he's after you."

"Don't be ridiculous. Who would want to stalk me? You, on other hand, I can see ticking off a lot of people. And you know what deranged psychos do to poor helpless pets, don't you? Bad things, that's what. Not that Theodora wouldn't put up a good fight considering who she is. So you really think she's okay?"

"Yes."

"That's what I thought you'd say," she mumbled under her breath.

With a sigh, Daniel put down his coffee. "You know, Red, I'm going to tell you something, and I want you to listen. Your pet, Theodora Roosevelt, is a cat. A cat with ears and a tail. She is not a child." He only meant to tease her. But he saw an expression cross her face that wasn't funny at all. Her eyes were serious and sad, and a bit stubborn.

Knowing that her eyes would betray too much of her emotions, Baily turned her head away from him and pursed her lips. She didn't trust her voice not to crack with emotion if she told him what she thought of him at this moment.

Daniel was shocked by the reaction. He expected a stinging retort, a sour look, maybe even a gentle kick under the table just to let him know she didn't care for his remark. Instead, silence. Something he could never have anticipated from Red. Reaching his hand across the small table, Daniel placed his fingertips under her chin and turned her face to his. The impact of her moist eyes slammed into his gut with the power of a sledgehammer.

"What did I say?" Daniel asked, not in a defensive tone, but as a legitimate question so he would know never to repeat his mistake again.

Baily shook off her sudden sadness like a dog shaking off water after a bath. To break the contact of his hand she lifted her chin even higher. Then she took a deep breath to calm her emotions. It was ridiculous. Daniel hadn't said anything that anyone who has ever known her and her cat for a length of time hadn't also said. Theodora was a cat. Baily knew that, of course.

Only there were days. Days in Seattle when she felt alone, detached somehow because there was no recipient for all the love she had to give. She didn't have a husband to pamper, or children to watch over and protect, but she did have Madam President. So maybe her treatment of Theodora was questionable. It stemmed from a fear that Theodora would be the closest thing she'd ever have to actually having a baby of her own. That was why she had to marry Harry. Maybe it was wrong to use him for her own ends, but she would make Harry a good wife and she would be an even better mother for his children.

"I'm sorry. You didn't say anything. I was just being a ninny." Baily smiled to back up her words. Her sadness, as always, was a momentary aberration. Life was too short to brood. As a result she limited all brooding episodes to only one minute apiece. Two minutes, max.

He should have just smiled and changed the topic, but he wasn't satisfied with her answer. "No way."

"No way I'm not a ninny?" Baily asked, thinking what a sensitive guy he was to understand that everyone is entitled to an occasional moment of sadness.

"Oh, no, you are a ninny," Daniel clarified.

So much for him being a sensitive guy.

"Tell me why you looked so hurt a minute ago. Surely you know that your cat is a cat. I mean, I'm not driving all the way to Philadelphia with a delusional wacko...am I?"

Baily was about to start shooting fireworks when she caught a glimpse of his lopsided smile. He was attempting to be funny. He wasn't. But the attempt was sweet nonetheless.

"Not a *delusional* wacko," she returned with a wry grin. "Theodora is special to me, that's all. Of course she's not a child. But she's the only one I have to give all my love to. I have this deep endless well of maternal mushy feelings. Sometimes they bubble up on me and if I don't use them I know I'll burst. So maybe Theodora is spoiled more than your average cat. She's my family, and I love her accordingly.''

"Family," Daniel repeated derisively. What was so wonderful about a family? Families were nothing more than groups of people depending on each other and needing each other. When one person in the family failed to live up to all that responsibility, everyone suffered. It was far more advantageous to be independent and free of familial burdens. No letdown. No pain.

''Why do you say 'family' like it's a bad word?'' Baily asked.

''Do I? I didn't notice,'' he said dismissively.

With a shrug and a small chuckle to break the tension that seemed to have formed around the table, Baily concluded, ''Theodora won't be so spoiled once I have my children. That's why I'm going home to marry Harry.''

The image that suddenly formed in Daniel's mind wasn't a pleasant one. Baily was pregnant with another man's child and that man wasn't worthy. ''Harry,'' he muttered as if the word was a curse.

''Harry,'' Baily repeated as if it were final.

Silence hung over their heads. They shared a private look, almost as if Harry was at the table sitting next to them and they couldn't voice their thoughts in front of him. One was a look of longing, the other of regret.

''You think the car is ready?'' Baily offered.

''Let's check.''

Both knew that the car wasn't ready. However their discussion had come to an end, and to prolong it any further would more than likely result in an argument.

Together, but separated by a new tension that flowed between them, the two meandered down the main street of Jackson Hole. Baily let her eyes wander so that she saw everything except Daniel.

Studying the people around her, she noted the obvious tourist wearing the wrong kind of shoes, experienced hikers who looked as if they were off to the mountains never to return, and a familiar face. She couldn't say why the gentleman looked familiar to her. He wore casual brown Dockers and a beige shirt. She wanted to tell him that his color sequencing needed a bit of work. Especially considering that he wore a brown baseball hat to top off the ensemble. He was across the street and a few paces back, so she didn't bother.

A brown hat! She'd seen one like it the other day on their walk to the car rental place. Of course, that could mean nothing. He could be just another tourist taking in the sites as they were. Jackson Hole wasn't so big that it was inconceivable she would run into someone she'd seen last night. Yet something nagged at her. Baily was about to catch up to Daniel to ask him if he recognized the man in the hat, but he was three feet away and walking as if his life depended on getting away from her.

She wasn't sure why he bothered. They were both headed to the garage. Taking her own sweet time, she arrived several steps behind him.

"It wasn't a race, you know."

Coolly, Daniel turned toward her. "I'm sorry. Weren't you able to keep up with me?"

He knew just the right words to irk her. And the thing that galled her most was that he had done it on purpose.

It was obvious that anytime Harry's name was brought up in the conversation, Daniel immediately turned nasty afterward.

"Look, I apologize for mentioning Harry," she apologized. "Clearly, talk of my engagement distresses you. I'll make an effort to avoid further conversations about my future bliss."

"Your engagement does not distress me."

His teeth were clenched, his jaw muscles were flexing, and the veins were bulging in his neck. Nah, he wasn't distressed at all. "Yes, it does."

Astounded at her cheek to even suggest such a thing, Daniel discovered a new muscle in his jaw to clench. "I've only known you the sum total of a day and a half. And from all that I know I haven't even decided if I like you yet. Please don't think I've forgotten how you practically forced me off the road and are the absolute cause of my being stuck in Wyoming, relying on a car with two flat tires, a car that shouldn't even be driven to the market yet alone cross-country. So there is no reason under the sky that I would have any reason to be distressed about you and some wimpy sensitive man named Herman getting married!"

"It's Harry. But you're right. How could I have been so blind?" In the face of his tirade, she had made her point.

Good, Daniel had made his point. "Now that all that nonsense is settled. Why don't we get the car?"

"My car?" Baily asked innocently.

Not in the mood to be toyed with, Daniel simply nodded.

"You mean, the car that isn't fit to drive to the market? The car that so far has taken me across this county once already? The car that has driven over mountains, never not started when I really needed it to, and has already taken us through two states, unlike a certain Mercedes that I know of? That car? Huh?''

Daniel watched her eyes flare and her red curls bounce around her head in absolute fury. She was beautiful at rest. She was breathtaking on fire. A fist of desire slammed him hard in his lower gut. Normally, Daniel didn't consider himself the wildly romantic passionate sort of man. When the need warranted, he could be creative in bed, but for the most part he'd never felt comfortable enough with a woman to completely lose control when having sex. More often than not he watched himself, as if from above, giving his body directions to follow.

Do this now. Do that now. Okay it's your turn. Take your pleasure then let's get out of here. We've got an early meeting in the morning.

Baily, however, was someone who would demand total attention. She was someone you slammed against a dirty wall behind a greasy service station, ripped her clothes to shreds, and took hard and long standing until she was screaming with pleasure and raking her nails deep into your buttocks. She was someone you made love to all night long, waking her up time and time again to sink your body deep within hers because at that moment, when she was lying under you, taking you deep into her womb, she was truly yours.

He had to have her. It really wasn't an option anymore. In his mind he'd crossed some invisible threshold and now he knew that he couldn't leave this woman until she screamed out his name in mindless earth-shattering pleasure. Just once. Maybe twice.

He'd give her back to Harvey when he was done because he couldn't give her the family she said she wanted. But before he turned her over he had to have her.

"That car?" Baily repeated, slightly unnerved by his silence. Not to mention that he was leering at her as if she were the Roadrunner and he was Wile E. Coyote.

"Yeah, that car." His voice was a timbre she didn't recognize. It was low and husky, and he said the words as if they meant something completely different.

"Oh." Somewhere along the way Baily had lost her point. "Let's go get it then."

"I'll get it because I need it. I have to have it. Nothing can stop it now."

Baily was definitely on the wrong wavelength. His eyes were intent on hers and they willed her to understand his meaning. She had an irresistible urge to cover her arms over her breasts. Not that his gaze made her feel uncomfortable. More accurately, it made her stomach clench and her breasts tingle.

He started walking toward her and suddenly she knew how a deer caught in the sites of a hunter felt. His stride was careful and his gaze watchful, and she knew if she tried to bolt, he would catch her.

"Daniel?" Baily's voice quaked with tension and a little fear. Not of what was going to happen, but of what her reaction was going to be when it did happen.

"Daniel," Baily said again, attempting to coax a response from him and break the spell he seemed to be under.

"Daniel!" She used her teacher voice. The one she used to stop spitballs in mid-hurl. Nothing was having an effect.

The tone of her voice did force Daniel to lift his head and survey his surroundings. They were standing just outside the autobody shop's office where anyone walking down the main street could see them.

Needing more privacy, he pulled on Baily's hand and led her down the alley that ran behind the gas station. Without a sound he pushed her up against the brick wall that was the back of the garage, pinned her hands above her head, and leaned his body into hers so that her breasts were crushed against his chest. He took quick breaths as if he had run a mile, only he hadn't. In truth if he stopped to analyze his actions he would be at a loss to describe his behavior. All he knew was that he needed her, and he didn't have it in him to stop himself. Maybe she would.

"Stop me," he told her, his lips now brushing against hers.

Unfortunately, Baily was currently suffering from memory loss and she could not for the life of her recall how she'd got into this predicament. One minute they were fighting about her car and the next he looked as if he wanted to rip her clothes off. Now he was asking her to stop him, only she couldn't. Never before had she found herself caught in such a wellspring of desire. Never had she believed that her body would actually ache to be touched and move of its own volition toward the body she wanted to be touched by.

"I can't."

Daniel didn't let her continue. Crushing her mouth with his, he felt first relief. As if he'd been too long without water and it was only now as he tasted her moist lips that he realized how thirsty he'd been. Their tongues dueled for supremacy. Daniel's won. Slowly he began to control the heat and depth of the kiss. He thrust his tongue in and out of her mouth in a steady tempo that all but hypnotized her with pleasure and forced her to accept him completely.

Baily had no option other than to surrender to him while his mouth made love to hers.

*Throw her on the ground.* It was what his desire ordered him to do. Throw her on the ground and take her before you explode, he thought. It sounded wonderful in theory. But he couldn't do it. Not on the ground, not out in public, not this way. Baily would be his. There was no question about that now. But he didn't want her to look back and regret a moment of their short time together.

Breaking away from her lips, he managed to pull himself together. When he looked at Red he saw that her eyes were cloudy and vacant with desire. As if she were a little girl, he smoothed her hair and straightened her clothes. Then he placed a gentle kiss on her lips and led her back to the street. "Let's go," he prompted.

"The car?" her voice squeaked.

"The car," Daniel repeated. There was no rush. They had all the time in the world.

# 6

"FASTER. Can't you make this thing go faster?" Daniel put his hands on the dashboard as if he could actually push the car to make it go faster.

"I told you not to worry. Mount Rushmore stays open late. And we're not going to miss Mount Rushmore, are we Theodora?"

"Meow," the cat confirmed from the back seat.

"We'll have plenty of time to see it. And my car does not like to be rushed." Her car was doing sixty-two miles per hour and hating every moment of it if the shaking, rattling and coughing were any indication. To push it even further might really upset the car, and she was already displeased after the whole tire fiasco.

"I just want to see the damn car do seventy. Is that too much to ask? My sister's life is still in jeopardy," Daniel reminded her less she had forgotten the whole point of this trip.

"Listen, I said I would get us to Mount Rushmore today, and that's what I'm going to do. Getting us to Mount Rushmore faster isn't going to get us to Philadelphia any faster. Besides, my car is doing the best that she can."

"She?" Daniel queried, then wondered why he had.

"Paulette Revere," Baily stated as if it were a perfectly normal thing to name a car.

"Paulette Revere?" All right, it was semi-cute.

"'Not a man is surely alive who remembers that fateful day and year...' Longfellow," Baily quoted with a smile. "Do you know your history? So many people don't, you know. They all think what's past is past. That's not true. History shaped our today. We could never begin to understand the people we are today if we didn't know who the people of yesterday were."

"You sound like a schoolteacher who teaches history."

"Excellent," she beamed. "Because I am a schoolteacher who teaches history and an assortment of other classes. I worked at a small parochial middle school. We sort of had to make do with the staff we had. So I was the history teacher for three grades, as well as the gym teacher, the music teacher and the art teacher."

"Wow. You must be really talented to be able to teach all that." Daniel was actually impressed.

"Oh, I can't play an instrument or draw a stick figure or jump a rope. I would just teach the history of music, and the history of art and the history of..."

"Jumping rope?"

"No," she said. "The history of sports."

"Of course."

"What about you? What do you like to talk about?"

"Trees."

"Love trees, do you?" Baily was curious about his living. When she thought about it she couldn't recall him mentioning his work. Considering what she had let him do to her that morning, it would be nice to know what the man did for a living. Besides, it would give them a nice safe topic for discussion. A nice long dissertation about trees was as far away from cheating on her soon-to-be-fiancé as she could imagine.

"I love the idea of preserving them," Daniel answered,

unaware of his driving partner's turmoil. "I install computer systems that track growth rate and the rainfall required for maximum health. The software can warn planters of mudslides, et cetera. It's all fine and good to say you cut trees and replant them, but if the replanting isn't done in ideal conditions, the young trees will die. And we run the risk of eventually running out of lumber, not to mention oxygen." Daniel shot Baily a glance. He figured by this time she would be zoned out. Most women went to sleep when he started talking business. Instead she turned her head and smiled. The interest on her face was obvious.

"Go on. Tell me how a Philadelphia native got to be so interested in trees."

It was a story he didn't think about often because when he did he had to think about his parents, and that was usually painful. This time, however, he wanted to tell the story. More accurately, he wanted to tell the story to Red. Why, he couldn't say. Daniel wasn't the type to spill his life story to strangers, unlike Baily who talked about everything as if she didn't have a secret to keep from the world.

So why was it important for Baily to know? It wasn't as if he had thoughts of prolonging their relationship. Daniel was determined to make love to Baily, and he was just as determined to say goodbye at the end of the trip. She would marry Herby and have her family. He would head back to Seattle, alone, unencumbered and free. If that sounded a bit heartless, he didn't dwell on it.

Perhaps he wanted to tell her because she was such a good listener. Perhaps it was because nobody had ever asked him the question before. "I'm rich."

"Oh." It was the only response Baily could think of. No, wait, she had another one. "That's nice."

Daniel smirked. "I'm beginning a story, not bragging. I come from a wealthy family. My father inherited a fortune when he sold the family business. He used his money to run for office. He was a state assemblyman, then a United States' congressman for years. He was planning to run for the senate before he died."

"Daniel Blake Senior. Sure, I've heard of him. My dad used to talk about him a lot. He was into the environment, right? I was pretty young when he was in office."

"He was a politician. Sometimes I think he did the right thing. Other times...well let's just say we didn't always agree. One of the big issues we disagreed on was the environment. He believed in preservation at all costs, even at the expense of jobs and factories. A lot of the kids I went to school with were the sons of high-powered industrialists who didn't like the idea that my father cramped their polluting style. Since it was more important for me to be accepted by my peers, rather than by my father, I sided with them. We used to get in the most awful fights over what seemed a really vague concept for me. All I knew was that the guys at school were on my case because my dad made their dads lose money. Not that they didn't already have millions."

"I like your dad!"

It was said wholeheartedly and so enthusiastically that for a second Daniel felt himself getting a little choked up. He stopped that nonsense at once. "Anyway, when he died I suppose I wanted to find out what we had been fighting about for so long. I wanted to know what kept us at each other's throats rather than out throwing a football around. I went to Alaska. I got a job with an environmentally sound timber-cutting organization. Then I turned my talents for computers toward an environmental cause. The rest is, as you would say..."

"History," Baily finished. It was a wonderful story. Except for one thing. "Why did you have to go all the way to Alaska? And what about Sarah? Didn't she miss you?"

Guilt tore at him. He hadn't been completely blind to the pain he'd caused Sarah by leaving. Technically, if he wanted to be honest with himself, this hasty imprudent marriage could be his fault. He'd left her to fend for herself because he couldn't stand the pain that being home caused him. He and his father fought, that was true. But there was also love. A deep love that never had to be spoken because each knew how the other felt. Love permeated the whole house. And when his parents had died the house had become nothing more than a reminder of that love.

But it didn't bring comfort. Instead, Daniel had felt loss. When he'd left, he'd tried to persuade Sarah to come with him to escape the house and all its memories. Sarah, however, had been resolute. She'd needed her home to feel safe and protected. An elderly aunt had moved in to take care of her until she was able to look after herself, and Daniel had been free to leave. In hindsight, it was a mistake. He was the only immediate family Sarah had left, and he had all but abandoned her. Their aunt Esther was a kind woman who was wonderful to Sarah, but she couldn't replace their mother. And his annual trips home weren't enough to fulfill his duties as older brother. He knew that. But at the time he didn't think he had a choice. The house and the memories suffocated him.

"Where are we, anyway?" Daniel asked, avoiding her questions.

"Wyoming. We've been in Wyoming all day."

"Yes, but where in Wyoming?" In every direction there were open fields that stretched on forever. Not a soul, a house, or even a horse could be seen for miles.

"We passed a town about mile back called Chugwater." Baily couldn't say the name without giggling. She'd been thinking about it ever since they passed the sign. Chugwater. Chuu-ugwater.

"Chuu-uggwater," Baily lowered her voice and added a raspy quality. She sounded like a cross between the Exorcist child and Roy Rogers.

Daniel could only stare at her in amazement.

"What do you do in Chugwater?" she continued, switching back and forth between characters, completely oblivious to the fact that Daniel was already wondering how to get in touch with the nearest mental health facility. "You chuu-ug water. I'm the chuu-uggwater champ of Chuu-uggwater. Oh, look. Up ahead. It's the Chugwater River. I chuu-ugg Chuu-uggwater River water to be the Chug Water Champ of Chuu-uggwater."

"I think you've been driving long enough," he finally said. She was obviously losing grip on reality.

Obviously, he didn't know how to be silly when the occasion called for it. "I was only playing. I'll stop."

"Thank you." Playing was for children. Adults didn't play. They didn't make funny voices, they didn't talk to their cat as if it were human, and they didn't bounce up and down at national monuments. Which served to prove that Baily, despite her almost thirty years, was really just a big child. Where he was a mature, sophisticated and sensible adult.

"Chuu-uggwater!" Baily broke out laughing. "I'm sorry. I had to do it just one last time."

Daniel refused to crack a smile.

Her comedic efforts wasted, Baily turned her attention to a more sober topic. ''We need to talk about something serious.''

''You know how to be serious? I'm stunned.'' It was an intentionally rude comment, and Daniel couldn't be sure why he said it. Perhaps he lied to himself about her being a child. Perhaps he was searching for something that would make her appear less charming, less whimsical, less happy about life.

Slightly affronted, but not enough to stop her from bringing up the subject that she'd been mulling over all morning, she continued. ''Yes, I can be serious, and that time is now. I've been thinking about the tires. I really do think it was your fault,'' she proclaimed.

''My fault! Your threadbare tires go flat because you're pushing them too far and probably haven't had them rotated in at least a year, and it's my fault?''

''You know, for someone who doesn't talk all that often, you have an amazing skill of fitting more words in one sentence than anyone I know. Now shut up and listen. I don't mean that it was your fault they went flat. Although I did not anticipate your considerable weight added to the car load when I started this trip.'' She felt it necessary to get that gibe in. ''What I meant to say was, don't you think it's odd that all these horrible things have happened to you since you've started this trip? The car accident, of course, was completely your fault, but since then, your wallet has been stolen, and my tires have mysteriously developed holes. Not one tire, that would have been easy enough to fix, but two tires at the same time. I know I joked about a stalker this morning, but maybe it's not a joke.''

He refused to buy that. It simply wasn't conceivable. ''Maybe I'm cursed.''

"Cursed? What a ridiculous thing to say. Do I look like the sort of person who would believe in curses? Ohmygosh, look over there on that ridge. It's a tiny graveyard. Hold your breath!"

Daniel watched her as she sucked in her breath and eyeballed the graveyard at the same time to be sure that she didn't breath in again before they passed it. Once the graveyard was behind them, she slowly exhaled and tossed Daniel a satisfied smile as if to say it was tough, but she had done it.

"*You* believe in curses? Of course not! What was I thinking?"

Confused for a moment, Baily debated whether he was being serious or sarcastic, but his expression betrayed him. "That's completely different. One is superstition. You never breathe while driving past a graveyard or the spirits will inhabit your body. Everybody knows that. It's like leaving your shoes on a table, or walking under a ladder or—"

"Meow," Theodora interrupted from her seat in the back with her own suggestion.

"That's right, Theodora. Having a black cat cross your path is also a bad one. There are certain laws of superstition that must be followed."

"Well, Theodora is a black cat. Maybe she is the cause of my bad luck." He didn't just suggest that, did he? He didn't actually believe that a cat had actually caused any of his bad luck.

"Your bad luck started before you met Theodora. Besides, she doesn't count. She's not completely black. She has a little white puff on her belly."

Knowing that she was the center of conversation, Theodora moved up to the front seat and settled on Daniel's lap as if to prove to him that she wasn't the bad luck he thought she was. Daniel patted the animal's head apologetically. He certainly hadn't meant to offend the cat.

Oh! He'd done it again. He'd allowed his mind to think the most ridiculous things. Apologizing to a cat. He had to get out of this car soon.

"Back to our original discussion. If I'm not cursed, what do you think is the cause of my...for lack of a better word, bad luck?"

She didn't know. That's why she brought the subject up. Her hope was that he might have some ideas. After all, it was his curse. There was one idea, but it was farfetched. He probably would laugh her right out of the car. Scratch that—if he hadn't laughed her out of the car by now then she was probably safe. "What if...do you think...maybe...."

"What?" It wasn't as if she could shock him anymore.

"What if it's not a stalker but someone who is deliberately trying to stop you from getting to that wedding on time?" Baily braced herself for his reaction.

Daniel paused. It was better than a curse. But who?

"Maybe Pierce is behind this," Baily offered.

"He's the obvious candidate," Daniel agreed, "but it's impossible. When I called my sister last night, he was in Philadelphia. There was no way he could have been in Jackson Hole to steal my wallet and flatten your tires and in Philadelphia to answer the phone. How would he even know what car was yours?"

"I see your point. It was just an idea," she said.

Daniel hadn't meant to dismiss her theory so quickly. It was only that he'd been thinking similar thoughts and had ruled out Pierce hours ago for the very reasons he mentioned. The problem was that nothing else made sense.

"Do you have any enemies?" Baily could certainly see where he might have angered a few women throughout the course of his life.

"No one has been more hostile to me than you in the last ten years of my life. So unless you snuck out last night and punctured your own tires, which we both know you didn't because we were both up listening to each other breathe, your idea is nonsense." Enemies! People in spy novels had enemies. James Bond had enemies. Daniel Blake did not.

"Simply because I happen to be vocal in my hostility toward you doesn't mean that other people haven't felt it. Like now for instance. I'm feeling very much like your enemy, only you wouldn't know it because I'm being sneaky." Listening to him breathe. How dare he make such a comment? It was accurate, of course, but unfair of him to rub it in her face.

Sneaky. Daniel smirked at that idea. Red didn't have a sneaky bone in her body. Everything she felt was expressed in her eyes. Everything she thought, she said. He was grateful that she hadn't chosen to make her living as a CIA agent.

Unless…

What if she were some kind of actress? Could it be possible that she was working with Pierce? That perhaps she'd followed him and purposefully goaded him into losing control of the car then picked him up so no one else would? The trip to Yellowstone, to Jackson Hole, and now to Mount Rushmore…could they all be ploys to stall him so he wouldn't reach Philadelphia in time? Sarah was worth an exceptional amount of money. Perhaps Pierce, anticipating that money, had hired Red to stop him. Maybe even seduce him so that Daniel wouldn't spot the trap.

It explained everything.

Slowly he turned his head as if he expected Red to realize that he was on to her. Maybe she had a gun. Maybe she planned to kill him before they reached Philadelphia. As he stealthily stole a few glances, he noticed that she continued to mutter the word Chugwater under her breath.

Maybe he was an idiot. Red was no more a hit woman than he was a clown with the circus. He remembered her expression of passion that morning; it was the most honest expression Daniel had ever seen. No one was that good of an actress. Paranoia was setting in and he was succumbing to it.

"Red, I hope you take this as a compliment, but I've decided you can't possibly be a hit woman." That said, Daniel rested his head back against the seat as he settled in for a few hours of sleep. He hadn't gotten much rest the night before. Absently, he stroked Theodora until he elicited a purr from the cat. The animal's soft purr had the soporific effect of a glass of warm milk.

Baily, meanwhile, was still trying to interpret what he'd meant when he'd said she wasn't a hit woman. It was pointless to dwell on it. Daniel's mind, Baily discovered, often went off on the strangest tangents. Much better to concentrate on who might want to stop Daniel from reaching Philadelphia.

It was either that or dwell on the fact that her lips still tingled from where he had kissed them this morning. She was convinced that the devil had sent Daniel to tempt her and lead her away from her dreams of hearth and home. If she succumbed, then what? An affair? Passionate, definitely. Exciting, absolutely. Short, probably. And when it was over she would never be able to look Harry in the eye again. No, she couldn't think about that. She wouldn't.

But it wouldn't leave her. The comparisons between her present and her future bombarded her. Harry made her want to smile. Daniel made her want to laugh. Harry irritated her. Daniel infuriated her. Harry made her nauseous. Daniel made her faint.

Two men. One she could have but didn't want. One she wanted but couldn't have. Boy, life sure could be interesting.

"THERE IT IS! Can you see it? Can you see it!?" Baily was like a rubber ball bouncing up and down and all around in the passenger seat. They had switched driving shifts a few hours back and Theodora had taken that opportunity to use her mother's lap as a pillow. Awake now, she looked to be almost as excited as her mistress about the next attraction.

"We'll get much closer than this. Stop straining your neck. In a few minutes you'll be standing right in front of it." Daniel pointed out the obvious, but he wasn't surprised when Baily didn't listen to him. She couldn't have sat still if her life depended on it.

"But it's so thrilling, and it's right around the corner. Look how big it is." Baily was pleasantly surprised. Everyone had told her that Mount Rushmore was smaller than it seemed in the pictures and on film. They had misled her. It was monstrous. Awesome. It was history and nature combined in a way that would last for generations. And Baily was only five minutes away from it.

Daniel drove up the hill and into a parking lot. The couple emerged from the compact car with the cat in tow. Around them were many families with small children performing the same ritual. First came the I've-been-sitting-in-the-car-too-long stretch, followed by the shared smile of excitement now that the trip was over, finishing with the frantic whine of the children who urged their parents to hurry before the mountain went away.

"Meow!" It wasn't a child's cry, but as far as Baily was concerned it might as well have been.

"It's okay, baby. We'll be there soon. Wait until you see your namesake. He was the handsomest president ever. He had big white teeth just like yours," Baily crooned to Theodora who was cuddled in her arms and sheltered by her soft bosom.

For a moment Daniel envied the cat, but then he pulled himself back from the brink of those lustful thoughts. They weren't getting him anywhere but hard, and that was nothing but uncomfortable. But it was the picture Baily presented to him. In her typical short-shorts and T-shirt ensemble, she seemed to him like a child playing grown-up. Except the way she treated her pet made her seem like a mother.

It made sense to him that she was willing to marry a man without love so that she could have children. She was born to mother, to nurture and to comfort. She was born to love. It bubbled out of her, much like her humor and her charm and her excitement. That being the case, it was wrong for the forces of nature to put Baily and Harry together. A woman with so much love to give shouldn't be stifled in a loveless marriage. A woman like that should be loved passionately in return.

Then again, it was just as wrong for fate to place him with Red. Daniel would never again risk love. At least not the kind of love Baily deserved. Sarah, he had to love. He had no choice. He would protect her as best he could, but that was the extent of what he was willing to give. But with Red he did have a choice. When this trip was over he could walk away from her emotionally as well as physically. At least he hoped so.

"Come on slowpoke, Madam President does not like to be kept waiting," Baily informed him. She hoisted Theodora over her shoulder and marched up the hill that was decorated with every state flag in the union, which Baily knew was called the Avenue of Flags.

Admiring the sway of her behind, Daniel followed, unable to stop himself from comparing them to every couple that walked by with their children in hand. He and Baily might not share true love, they didn't even share the history that Baily shared with Harry, but they did have an easy camaraderie with one another that resembled other married couples that crowded around them. It was a bond formed in a short period of time, and if examined for strength and longevity, Daniel would be hard-pressed to say if it would last. But it was definitely there.

Baily couldn't help comparing herself to the other married women around her. She saw them with their children and their husbands, laughing, arguing and nagging. Family. That was what Baily wanted. She didn't want Harry. Lord knew, she didn't want Harry. She did want that sense of belonging though. She wanted the fulfillment and sense of accomplishment that came when two people produced a loving environment for children.

Maybe she just missed her own family. An insight she didn't necessarily believe, but she was willing to except it as a legitimate excuse for all her recent introspection. Or maybe the truth was that she was falling for the wrong guy. At least, he wasn't falling in love with her. Lust maybe, but not love. That should help her to keep a firm grip on her own heart.

But feelings, as Baily discovered long ago, couldn't be

controlled. If they could, she would be madly in love with Harry. Still, to throw away a future on emotions wasn't practical thinking. Baily had her whole life to consider. And however strong the attraction between her and Daniel was, and however much she might believe that she was falling for him, Baily was determined to deny her own heart. Her children were counting on her.

"We made it." Daniel saddled up behind his woman and her cat. They stood at a railing across from the great monument. There were pay telescopes available, but they were unnecessary. Mount Rushmore was impressive to the naked eye alone. Baily leaned forward slightly on the railing, and Daniel stood beside her and placed a protective arm around her back.

She felt the slight contact on the small of her back all the way to her toes.

Her body began to tingle, but Baily clamped down on the sensation. No, she tried to tell her wayward hormones. But the flesh was weak and wouldn't be denied. Her blood began to hum in her veins and she felt her skin pulse. Hadn't she just decided against feeling anything for Daniel? That such feelings were fruitless and would prove to be harmful to her long-term plans? Of course she had! Apparently her body wasn't listening.

"Impressive."

Baily couldn't suppress a smile. Said in such a stately manner, without much expression, Daniel conveyed to Baily that he was truly impressed with the wondrous sight. It was odd to say that she was coming to know him, but it was true. When he got frustrated with her, his teeth clenched and the big vein in his neck bulged. When he was amused, his lips would twitch ever so slightly, as if he were trying to smother his own smile. When he was aroused, his eyes would darken and his eyelids would droop. And he would touch her subtly, intimately.

Whatever he was feeling, Baily knew that he would show the least amount of emotion possible. Maybe it was because he ran his own company that he had developed such an austere persona, but Baily didn't think so. It was just his way. As though he was trying to stop himself from feeling too much. Presumptuous perhaps, but she could honestly say that she was beginning to understand him.

"Impressive?" she repeated, half serious, half teasing. "That's all you can say. We're standing at the most amazing rock carving ever created and all you can say is 'impressive'? It's magnificent. Outstanding. Inspiring!"

Daniel's lips twitched. "I said impressive, and I meant impressive."

Baily smiled brightly. "See Mr. Roosevelt, Theodora. Isn't he wonderful? Now I told you all about how he was once a police commissioner in New York City, but did I tell you about the time he was secretary of the navy? Or about his first marriage that only lasted a year? It was tragic. The poor girl died in childbed, but it was really meant to be because then he went on to marry Edith who was his true soul mate."

The three of them stood together, inches apart, and enjoyed the great spectacle in front of them. Baily immersed her senses in the smell of fresh pine that emanated from the trees surrounding them. Together they watched in fascination as the color of the rock on the side of the mountain shifted and changed from various shades of orange as the sun passed over on its way to bed. The air, cooler anyway at the higher altitudes, actually became chilly, and Baily was forced to move closer to Daniel.

Okay, so maybe "forced" was a bad choice of words.

No one held a gun to her head. It's just that when he had his hand on her back she felt warm. Without that contact, she was inexplicably cold.

"Cold?" Daniel asked, enjoying the companionable silence.

*More than you know,* Baily wanted to answer, but instead she nodded her head vigorously.

Seeing her need for warmth, Daniel pushed himself off the rail and pulled Baily toward him so that he could shelter her from the cold. His chest blanketed her back, his arms locked her in place against the railing, and his thighs brushed against her bottom. She was trapped and loving every minute of it. She felt his mouth move closer to her neck and she thought all she had to do was tilt her head and—

Again, her conscience kicked into gear. She wasn't supposed to let this happen. With a regretful sigh she told him, "We can't do this again. We both know where it's going to lead. It was wrong the first time. I'm not blaming you, but I don't have the willpower to stop you anymore. That means I'm leaving it up to you to stop for both of us."

It was a bombshell placed in his lap. Daniel's immediate thought was that his waiting had come to an end. He'd backed off that morning because he wanted their first time to be special. Not in public and certainly not on the ground. Now there was nothing to stop him from taking her to a motel room and loving her all night long in all the ways he wanted to love her.

Accept her trust in him, that is. She trusted him to do the right thing for both of them. The right thing, he supposed, was not to push her into something she might regret. But Daniel couldn't let her go. His body craved hers as if she were the very air he breathed. He ached to touch her and to kiss her in a way that he had never known before. If he had once thought himself beyond such feelings, he knew better now. It would be a travesty to lose this part of himself that he had so recently discovered. The part that was Baily.

"Don't make me stop, Red. I need you too much." Letting his actions speak for him, he closed his lips around her soft pink earlobe and tugged it into his mouth. His teeth held the tiny morsel in place while his tongue danced across the tip of the soft flesh. After he felt her shudder with desire, he concentrated his attention to the spot behind her ear where soft wisps of her hair tickled his nose. She intoxicated him.

"I don't want you to stop, but please…" It was a plea, only Baily didn't know what she was begging for. All she knew was that at this moment Daniel was giving her the world.

Blood coursed through her veins. He brought life to parts of her body she hadn't realized existed until now. Again they were in public, although the ledge they had chosen secluded them from the other tourists. Baily was comforted in the knowledge that no one would view her flushed face or her shaky knees. But there was no doubt that someone heard the moan that escaped her lips when he bit the back of her neck ever so gently.

"Ohh-hh." It came from her soul, and it meant Daniel.

The moan stopped him. It was unguarded and completely honest and it made him want her that much more. But the fact that her cat was bawling pathetically in her mother's too tight grip didn't help the mood.

Baily was suddenly awakened from the sexual trance

Daniel had kissed her into. "I'm sorry, Miss Roosevelt. Are you ready to leave now?"

"Meow," the cat replied.

Backing off, Daniel allowed Baily to escape. She shot him a grateful look, and he squirmed with guilt. The only reason he had been so indulgent was that he knew they were headed back to a motel. He couldn't let it end now, not this time. He had managed to convince himself that making love with Baily Monohan was the right thing to do and he was going to do it.

Baily trucked back down the path that led to the parking lot. She thought perhaps if she ran fast enough she could escape the attraction, the lust and the man that wouldn't leave her alone. It was the third time she had escaped his clutches, and deep in her heart Baily knew she wouldn't escape a fourth time.

Not willing to let that happen, Baily cuddled Theodora closer to her and began to weave between the casual sightseers who were strolling back to their cars. It was as she dodged a family of three, practically knocking a little boy over in her haste to get to the car, that she realized one inescapable truth.

There was nowhere to run.

Daniel was walking back to the parking lot when it occurred to him that Baily could possibly get in the car and take off, leaving him to fend for himself at Mount Rushmore. He began to sprint then stopped at the row of parked cars where the Bug should be waiting for him. With a deep breath to express his relief, he casually walked up to the yellow car and gazed down at Baily who sat in the driver's seat looking incredibly disappointed with herself.

"It wouldn't start," she murmured.

"Keys tend to be helpful in these types of situations."

Glancing up at the keys that dangled from his strong hands, Baily knew a sense of defeat and a sense of inevitability. "So what do you think about tube tops and push-up bras?" They were normally the sorts of things a woman who cheated on her soon-to-be fiancé wore, weren't they?

If Baily thought she would shock him with such an off-beat question, she was again disappointed. "Theoretically, I'm for them but only for women who have something to be tubed and pushed. Now move over so I can get us out of here."

Baily lifted herself over the gearshift and settled her seat belt around her.

"I won't sleep with you!" she said emphatically and loud enough for George, Teddy, Thomas and Abe to hear her. She might as well as have told the tide to stop coming to the shore.

Daniel slid into the seat and started the car. He figured he'd better make a speedy escape before someone called the cops and accused him of rape. To her he said nothing.

"Did you hear me?" Of course he'd heard her. She tried again. "I said I wasn't going to sleep with you and I meant it."

Still nothing from him.

"I really mean it. I won't. I won't say I haven't thought about it. I won't even say that I didn't feel a little something while you were kissing my neck...or my ears...or my lips for that matter, but that doesn't mean I want to sleep with you."

Silence.

"It could mean that. I can understand how you might have concluded, what with all my moaning, that I might enjoy making love with you. But I wouldn't. Okay, maybe

I would enjoy it, but I would hate myself afterward. You're everything I don't want for my future.''

Daniel's stoicism began to grate on her nerves.

''You don't believe me. You think I'll cave. You believe in that warped arrogant male mind of yours that you can kiss me on my cheek, and I will fall down at your knees and beg you to make love with me. That's what you think, isn't it?''

There was no point in responding to her questions when they both knew the answer.

A few silent minutes later they were pulling up to a small motel en route to Rapid City. Daniel went to claim a room. This time two rooms were possible, but Daniel viewed it as an unnecessary pretense. He returned with no words for her. Only a key. They drove around to the back of the motel and pulled into a spot in front of Room 110, which matched the number on the key he had given her.

After unloading the car and stretching a bit in the confines of the small room, Baily began to wonder if Daniel would ever speak to her again. Theodora had taken shelter under a bed almost as if she was anticipating trouble. And Daniel was in the bathroom, apparently getting ready for bed. He emerged from the room in a pair of boxer shorts and nothing else, which was enough to stop Baily's heart.

His chest was a work of art of which Michelangelo would have been envious. Soft brown fur matted his upper chest then tapered off in a straight line down to his navel. His muscles were pronounced, and Baily could imagine mighty trees falling at the blows that his massive arms delivered with the aid of an ax. Did people really look that good without plastic surgery?

Baily's tongue felt as if it had swelled in her mouth. Swallowing became a chore, which was unfortunate considering the increased amount of saliva she now had in her mouth.

Not sparing her a glance, Daniel brushed past her and threw the covers off the bed. He tossed himself onto the bed, threw the covers over him, and turned his back to her, as if she were invisible.

"Nope, I definitely won't sleep with you, so don't humiliate both of us by even asking." Proud of herself for making that perfectly clear, she marched into the bathroom and prepared herself for bed. When she emerged dressed in her Snoopy-imprinted nightshirt, the room was dark. She thought about going to sleep, but somehow the idea of getting into the bed all alone repulsed her. Instead she stood in the middle of the room and felt tears well up behind her eyes.

"Red?"

The soft voice called to her out of the dark, and unconsciously she moved toward it. "I don't know what to do," she told him between sobs.

"Come to bed." With that he lifted the covers off his bed and stretched out his hand to her. When the time came, her choice was ridiculously easy.

# 7

THE BOTTOM LINE WAS THIS: she didn't love Harry, but she did love Daniel. Ridiculous. Absurd. No sane, rational-thinking person fell in love in the course of a handful of days. Since Baily on numerous occasions was neither sane nor rational, the rules didn't apply to her. She loved Daniel. In the end she would pay the price for having given her heart away so quickly, so recklessly. He didn't love her. He wasn't thinking of *their* future. He was only living in the moment. Baily accepted that and decided to join him in bed.

Taking his outstretched hand as if it were a lifeline, she allowed herself to be pulled toward him until she was next to him on the bed, his warm arms wrapped around her. Heat surged throughout her body. Baily was aglow with need. She would have believed she was feverish if she hadn't felt this warmth with him before.

Go slowly, Daniel commanded himself sternly. This is important. As soon as that thought came to him he wanted to shake it off. This was sex. A lustful tension that would peak then burst. Nothing more.

*Don't look into her eyes then. If you do, you'll see the truth.*

Again, Daniel brushed away the troublesome thought. Surely, Baily knew what this evening meant. They were two consenting adults who wanted each other. If it felt more like need to him, he rationalized it was just a powerful desire.

His thinking done for the evening, Daniel let himself only feel. He felt the tremors in his muscles, the quivers in his stomach, and the heat in his sex. He felt like a seventeen-year-old virgin with his first girl. He wanted to please her. He wanted her to remember him. He wanted. What he had to do first was wipe the tears from her eyes.

"Please don't cry," Daniel whispered as he kissed her eyes and soaked up her tears with his lips.

"I'm just so…so excited," Baily explained.

It warmed Daniel to know that this was something she wanted as badly as he did. There would be no turning back. He didn't know exactly where they were going, but he knew they were going there together.

"Take off your nightgown," he commanded. He needed to feel her soft body against his. Much like her cat, he simply wanted to rub against her and be caressed by her softness.

"It's Snoopy," Baily returned as she lifted the gown off and over her head with his help.

Daniel said nothing in return. He could sense her nervousness, but was too focused on what was about to happen to ease her anxiety. Her bounty was before him. Halloween never provided anyone with so much sweetness in one sitting.

A taste of her lips revealed they were as ripe as fresh fruit. But Daniel knew that, already having tasted them before. Her neck had fine soft wisps of red hair that brushed against his cheek when he kissed the soft spot behind her ear. Her creamy skin made him think of sweet milk, and when he placed his lips on the swell of her breast he knew that was exactly what he tasted.

A shudder racked his body, forcing Daniel to his knees and away from her so that he could breath properly.

"What's the matter?" Baily was obviously confused. There was no reason to stop now; she had given herself to him regardless of the consequences. In this position, his strong body loomed over her, and Baily, too, surely felt the need to breathe deeply. As if helpless against the impulse to touch him, she lifted her hand and placed it in the middle of his chest, letting her fingers curl in the soft matting of hair she found there. Short sculpted nails raked his skin ever so gently. Daniel tensed. Bolder now, she brought her other hand to match her actions.

Never before had Daniel been so overwhelmed with emotion. Lust yes, emotion never. If he didn't gain some distance, he would have no control over their lovemaking.

Then Baily's hands began to roam down his chest until they rested against his flat stomach. Distance was no longer an option. He felt his muscles tighten and she sighed in response. She moved her hands lower and they shook with trepidation. He saw uncertainty in her eyes. But he couldn't stop her as he was trapped in the spell of arousal. His only recourse was to allow a moan to escape his lips to let Baily know how pleased he was that she wanted to touch him the way he needed to be touched.

Encouraged by his obvious pleasure, Baily pushed the obstructive cotton shorts down over his hips and around his thighs. She sucked in her breath at the sight of Daniel aroused. It wasn't that she hadn't ever seen a man. She'd been raised with five brothers and knew basic anatomy. But she'd never seen a man like this…for her.

Daniel removed the shorts completely and allowed her to look her fill, as if sensing that this was somehow new to her.

He was beautiful in a way that Baily had never understood about men before. Tentatively, she touched him again, this time flesh upon flesh. She felt Daniel quiver at the gentle contact and saw his face tighten. A tension had gripped him. That tension, that fierce expression of pleasure encouraged Baily. He didn't simply enjoy her touch. He craved it.

Unable to be apart from her any longer, Daniel fell down upon her and captured her lips. He thrust his tongue deep into her mouth, wanting to be inside her so desperately but wanting to wait, as well. His hands moved up her body and captured her breasts, and her nipples rose to greet his touch. He tugged softly and felt Baily arch her back in response, pushing her body against his overly aroused one.

His mouth explored her everywhere. He suckled her breasts. He dipped his tongue into her belly button, which made her cry out with sensation. He moved lower and placed damp kisses on her soft mound until she begged for release. But he wouldn't give it to her. He had to know her, all of her. Daniel was consumed with his need. His body wanted to burst after she had first touched his sex. Now it was beyond bursting. He had reached a level of sensation he couldn't name. And it wasn't the end.

Flipping her over onto her stomach, he began his journey again. The backs of her knees were soft and tempting. The small of her back he teased with the tip of his tongue, which caused Baily to arch her body off the bed high enough so that Daniel could caress her breast while his tongue made journeys up her spine.

He didn't stop. Couldn't stop until he heard her sob. Gently he turned her over on her back again and settled his weight against her, his thighs between hers. The soft flesh of her inner thighs caressed his hair-roughened legs and created the sweetest friction. "Sweet, don't cry. Did I hurt you?"

"I can't stand it," Baily cried. She brought her arms around his neck and clung tightly.

Daniel would have been offended at the remark if he hadn't known what she meant. She couldn't stand the waiting. His body, too, clamored for a release. Reaching under the pillow for the condom he'd deftly placed there when he'd first crawled into bed, he quickly tore the wrapper and covered his raging erection. Pushing his hips forward, Baily opened her legs, instinctively wrapping them around his waist.

"Please, Daniel, please." Thrusting her hips against his hardness, Baily was without pride as her body cried out for what it so desperately desired.

"Red," Daniel began, his body now inflamed to the point where he felt compelled to push forward. His hands under her buttocks, he lifted her hips to him and thrust himself into her, driving so deep until…he heard her scream.

A virgin. A thirty-year-old virgin.

"It's okay now," she told him. "It doesn't hurt. Please don't stop."

Not that he could have even if she had begged him. She was so tight and so incredibly hot and wet around him. The further he sank, the better it felt. He took an infinite amount of time to allow her to accustom herself to his size. Her comfort was his pleasure as he wallowed in the luxury of being inside Baily. Moving gently, slowly, Daniel pulled himself away until he couldn't stand it then sank back into her heat. It was a sensation like nothing he had ever felt before.

It wasn't until she began urgently lifting her hips against him that he knew she was ready. His thrusts became urgent, as did her cries. When he felt her tighten around him,

he knew she had found her pleasure. Of course her screaming at the top of her lungs was also a good indication.

He plunged one final time and felt himself spill his seed.
And for whatever reason, in a small corner of his mind he
found himself resenting the barrier that was between them.

DAWN BROKE HARSHLY through the slit in the shade that
covered the motel room window. It took a moment for
Daniel to get his bearings as several things became obvious. One, he had never felt so good in his entire life. His
body throbbed with a sated pleasure that made him wish
time would stop. Two, Baily was cuddled against his chest
as if he were her favorite pillow. And three, Theodora
Roosevelt was standing over him meowing profusely.

"Let Mommy sleep, baby. I'll feed you in a little bit,"
Baily muttered, still half asleep. Apparently, it was a ritual
they performed often as Theodora took to heart her
mother's words and left the bed content to clean herself
while she waited for her mistress to wake up.

"It's getting late," Daniel told Baily. He had no desire
to begin the day, either, but it was time for the morning-
after regrets. Daniel regretted taking Baily's innocence,
and Red, he was sure, would regret giving her innocence
to him.

With an abrupt jerk, Baily lifted her head, momentarily
surprised by the male voice that had awakened her. When
she gazed down at Daniel, however, a dreamy smile came
over her lips. Her body ached with virgin pains, but it had
all been worth it.

"Don't say it," Daniel told her immediately. Sure she
looked happy now, but that was only because she didn't
realize the significance of what she had done. Any second
that realization would dawn and the accusations would
begin.

Before Baily had a chance to say anything Daniel bolted out of the bed.

Baily watched him walk to the bathroom. His shoulders were broad and strong. His buttocks were firm, his legs long. Wow! What a body.

Say what? After being dazzled by the picture he presented from behind, Baily was finally able to concentrate on what he had told her. Not "Good morning." Not "Last night was perfect." No endearments. No soft words. Just "Don't say it." What the hell did that mean?

Don't say that she was thrilled that her first time had been so wonderful? That she had felt safe and comfortable and excited all at once and that was a tribute to Daniel? Perhaps he found it odd that she was still a virgin after all these years. It certainly wasn't the norm. But all through high school and college when most girls were experimenting with sex, Baily was dating Harry. She'd never had the desire to go to bed with Harry. And he'd never pushed her. In her travels, there simply hadn't been anyone she could say she loved well enough to give herself to. The older she got, the choosier she became. Daniel was the first. The first to win her heart, her mind, and now her body.

Is that what he didn't want to hear? Did he think now that he had taken her virginity, or more accurately, she had given it to him, that Baily would demand marriage? She wasn't that old-fashioned! Still it said a great deal about Daniel's intentions. Obviously he had no thoughts of prolonging their relationship. Once he stopped the wedding, he would return to Seattle. Baily wouldn't go back. She was going forward. More importantly, she was going home.

Home was a concept Daniel rejected.

*Don't say it.*

What he meant to say was, "Don't say that you love me because it's not going to work." Wrapping the sheet around her body, she stood, unable to stay a minute longer in the bed they had shared. How had it become so cold when only a few minutes ago it seemed like the source of all warmth and comfort to her? *Oh, Daniel,* Baily thought. *What are we going to do?*

OH, THIS WAS FUN. No tension at all in this car. A quick peek in the rearview mirror revealed even Theodora's hair was standing on end. Baily drove the car, winding her way through the densely forested Black Hills of South Dakota. She couldn't admire the view of the ageless trees that surrounded her. She couldn't appreciate the thrill of the drive that tested her skills around the sharp bends in the road. She couldn't even sneeze.

That would have required Daniel to offer a response. A simple, "God bless you." Baily didn't think he was capable of it. And she knew nothing would hurt more than to sneeze and have him intentionally ignore her. Not that she wasn't hurting already from his behavior that morning, but it would have been the final straw if she sneezed and he didn't offer a lousy "God bless you."

Meanwhile, Daniel was lost in his own thoughts. She was a virgin. A thirty-year-old virgin. How was such a thing possible in today's world? Daniel could only guess it had something to do with Hubert and Baily's obvious reluctance to marry him. That whole relationship made no sense. No one waited around seven years for a girlfriend to return home, and no girlfriend who was in love with her boyfriend left for seven years. Which meant that Baily wasn't in love with her soon-to-be fiancé, which in a weird way explained why she was a virgin. Too honorable to give herself to anyone but her fiancé, but not in love enough with him to give herself to him. Ironic. Baily.

Enter Daniel stage left. Apparently she had no problem giving herself to him. Which meant that more than likely she was, or at least she believed herself to be, in love with him. Ridiculous of course. They had known each other less than a week. Baily had simply mistaken lust for love. Perhaps she didn't even mistake the emotion. Perhaps she knew it was lust, but chose to call it love to assuage her guilty conscience.

Daniel glanced over at his driver's profile. Every time he gazed at her some part of him wished that the spell would fade, that he wouldn't be so captivated by the light in her eyes or the fire in her hair. Daniel studied her in an attempt to find some flaws. Her red hair spiraled out around her head in curlicue flames. Her nose tilted up on her face and her lips were slightly parted as she breathed.

She was breathtaking. Just as she had been last night.

Last night! Daniel would spend the rest of his life trying to repeat the same experience. And he doubted he would ever come close. Last night hadn't been about lust and it certainly wasn't about lies. Red made love with him because she loved him. That much he was sure of. That much he was willing to admit. What he didn't know was what he'd been doing there last night. Did he love her? He honestly couldn't say. He felt something. Was he ready to pick up his life and move back to the East Coast to raise two point five children with her?

Definitely not.

Probably not.

Maybe.

Noticeably, his chest tightened. This was exactly the reason why he'd avoided love. Love meant commitment and responsibility. Love meant depending on another person for his happiness. The risk was that one day he might wake up and Baily would be gone and all his happiness with her. It could happen as fast as a plane could crash. For this reason, Daniel had kept the circle of people that he loved limited to one. Did he dare expand it?

A loud piercing shriek filled the car. Instantly, Daniel covered his ears to protect his sensitive eardrums. Theodora dashed under the seat, terrified at the sound her mother had just emitted. Baily, oblivious to her companions's discomfort, continued to yell. Loudly!

"What the hell are you doing?"

"I just couldn't take it anymore," Baily explained.

"What couldn't you take?"

"You…sitting there…thinking. I'm not a fool, Daniel. I know what's going through that incredibly dense skull of yours. You're thinking about last night. You're thinking about why I was a virgin and more importantly why I gave my virginity to you. If you want the answers to those questions, why don't you just come out and ask me?"

*Because I'm afraid of them. Because I'm simply not ready to hear them.* A smile lit Daniel's face. What was he worried about? It wasn't as if she would tell him the truth. Nobody walked around today blurting out his or her true emotions. It was too risky. No, people today kept everything bottled up inside. It was why ulcers were so common. "All right. Why did you give your virginity to me?"

"Because I'm in love with you."

His heart began to pound, his lungs constricted, and if he wasn't mistaken, his eyes just rolled back into his head.

Baily heard his sudden wheezing and acted immediately. Reaching over she grabbed his head and tried to push it between his legs. It was standard procedure when someone was about to faint. Unfortunately, the dashboard interceded and all Baily managed to do was to give Daniel another sizable lump on his forehead.

"Ouch!"

"I'm sorry! I thought you were fainting so I tried to push your head between your legs."

"I wasn't fainting," he told her irritably.

"Yeah and you're not afraid to fly, either. I know." Baily glanced over at him and tried to weigh the damage she'd done to his head. It was all red and blotchy but she didn't think she'd broken the skin. Just in case, her purse was on the seat behind her. Baily reached into it and began searching for a tissue that she could use to dab away any blood that Daniel might have spilled. As soon as she had her tissue in hand, she made several attempts to pat his wound with it, but Daniel rejected her medical attention.

"Keep your eyes on the damn road. I'm fine," he said as he reached out to still her hand. He took the tissue away and tossed it behind him.

"No reason to shout," Baily complained. After all, she was only trying to help.

It took longer than a minute for Daniel to regroup his senses. By the time he was finished he was convinced he hadn't heard what he'd thought he heard. Absolutely, positively convinced. "I know I didn't hear you say what I think you said."

"I said I lo—"

"Don't say it," Daniel interrupted sharply. Not twice in one day. His heart couldn't take it. Neither could his head. "I can't believe you said it. Don't you know you're not supposed to say it? No one ever says it. You're supposed to keep those feelings inside."

"I'd get an ulcer if I kept everything locked up inside me."

"Exactly!" He was a blathering idiot, but he didn't care.

Nothing had ever shaken him to the core as firmly as Baily's declaration of love had. Maybe because no one had ever said it to him before.

"You didn't let me finish," Baily whispered. It wasn't as if she didn't know in advance what his reaction would be. She had already sensed his unwillingness to become involved. It was the way he spoke about marriage and love as if they were beyond him. Out of his reach. Yes, he had wanted her. But only for a night. A week. Not a lifetime.

"What I meant to say was that I slept with you last night because I love you."

Daniel wanted to interject. To tell her that she mistook lust for a much stronger emotion that she couldn't possibly feel toward him. It was too soon. Too impossible.

Baily refused to allow his interruption. "I do. I know you probably think it's silly. We've only known each for a short time. But what little you know of me, I think you realize that I never would have made love with you last night if that wasn't what it was for me. Making love."

Yes, damn it. He'd known it when she'd come to him. He had seen it in her eyes, but he'd refused to acknowledge it then as if his ignorance would make it all go away. Only it didn't. He should have been the one to walk away. He should have left her and his needs behind. His willpower failed him. Baily was simply too strong of an enticement.

"Anyway, I guess I just wanted to let you know that," Baily continued, her heart breaking piece by piece along the way. "But now you need to listen. I realize that you don't feel the same way. You're far too practical to be swept up by love in such a short time. You're not a fairy-tale type of guy and that's okay. Because the truth is even if you did love me, it wouldn't work."

That comment stunned Daniel.

"When I was a little girl, I used to believe that love conquered everything. Every romantic movie I watched or book I read, the hero and the heroine always triumphed over the odds to be together because they knew that all they needed was love and each other. They were beautiful stories. But that's all they were. Just stories.

"Now I'm all grown up. And I know that fairy tales don't always come true. I know that a commitment needs more than just an excess of emotion. I love you, Daniel, and I'm not ashamed or embarrassed to admit it. But I want certain things for my life. I want a marriage. I want a home. I want children. I want to raise my kids close to their cousins. I want to go to family picnics in the summer and spend Christmas Eve around a huge tree drinking egg nog with all the people I love."

"If I could…" Daniel began, but the words died on his lips. What was he saying? Everything she had just described was everything he had spent a lifetime avoiding.

"But you can't. So accept what I have to offer. Let me cry when you leave, but don't make me suppress my love or keep it hidden because it makes you uncomfortable." Her face was a picture in sincerity. Daniel could see that every time she turned toward him her eyes were filled with tears and truth. This wasn't a ploy to make him admit things he didn't want to admit. This was a serious Baily. And the idea that Daniel had, for a second, removed the laughter from her eyes caused his throat to constrict.

Suddenly defensive, Daniel felt anger spurt to life within him. He couldn't help but feel like a heel for letting her down, for not being what she wanted him to be. But damn it! He never asked for any of this. "All I wanted was a damn ride to Philadelphia to stop my damn sister from marrying the wrong damn man. I don't want your love! Your body, yes, definitely I want your body, but that's it!"

Baily couldn't help but blush at the angry yet complimentary declaration. No one had ever wanted her body like this man did. It was a small consolation for a broken heart, but it made her feel warm inside. And a little frisky, truth be told.

"This is all my sister's fault!" Daniel muttered under his breath. "I'm going to kill her when I get home."

Nothing like dead-sister talk to ruin the mood. Baily decided to change the topic. "Speaking of your sister, we never did get around to deciding how we are going to stop this sham of a marriage. Are you going to pull a Dustin Hoffman or what?"

"What the hell is a Dustin Hoffman?" Daniel asked, irritated that she had the power to confuse him so easily. One minute they were talking about love and marriage, and in an instant her sober face was gone and in its place was the face of a leprechaun bent on mischief.

Rolling her eyes in absolute astonishment, Baily spoke slowly and with little words to help Daniel understand, "Let's begin with the fact that he's an actor. A very good one."

"I know that," Daniel snapped, not amused by her sarcasm. "What does he have to do with stopping a wedding?"

"Obviously you've never seen *The Graduate*. Dustin Hoffman runs to the church where his true love is marrying another. He pounds on the glass and shouts, 'Noooooo!'" Baily pounded on the dashboard for effect. "It was really quite romantic."

He was unfazed by her outrageous performance. He found that he had grown accustomed to them. A scary thought. Dryly he asked, "So what you're asking me is if I plan to run up to a church and pound on the glass and shout the word no over and over again?"

"When you put it like that I guess it does sound a little silly," Baily conceded.

"A little silly?" Daniel wasn't satisfied with such a halfhearted concession.

Baily refused to take the bait, but laughed at herself instead. For now, momentous declarations of love and thoughts of impending heartbreak were cast aside in favor of a lengthy discussion on how to stop a wedding. No brilliant ideas were forthcoming.

After a short pit stop, driver and passenger switched positions.

"Theodora, how about coming up front and sitting on mommy's lap for a while," Baily suggested. She had a sudden urge to touch someone, and since her earlier words had unfortunately augmented the distance between herself and Daniel, that someone had to be Theodora. Theodora, who didn't realize she was being used as a replacement and who would have been highly offended if she had, popped her head up from her pillow in the back seat and made her way onto her mistress's lap, which was softer than any old pillow.

Daniel couldn't help but envy the cat as he looked on with quick glimpses as Baily pet the cat's fur in long full strokes. No, those thoughts were over. He had taken his fill last night and that would have to be enough to satisfy him for a lifetime. The fact that his body still throbbed, in fact still hummed with sexual energy, and that if his body could talk it would say, "More," didn't shake his constitution. If Baily thought she was in love with him after only one night together, who knew what another round of love-making would do to her? It might drive her over the edge. Daniel smiled at his own immodesty.

But it wasn't only a sexual tug that pulled at Daniel. Seeing Baily with the cat, how she held it so tenderly in her arms, he was once again reminded of how maternal she was. Daniel knew that any child who was fortunate enough to have Baily as a mother would be loved and cherished. What if that child were his?

Dear God, he needed to get the hell out of the car!

"Look, up ahead," Baily blurted as she pointed to the view beyond the dashboard. "The Badlands. Wow. Aren't they spooky? All the sharp and craggy white rocks and crevices. A person could get lost in there." Baily shuddered slightly. This place was just a bit too eerie for her.

"Let's stop and walk around," Daniel suggested, suddenly enthralled with the spectacle in front of him. He needed space to run from the vision that haunted him. No, it wasn't just the vision. Baily haunted him. She was an aberration, someone whom he'd met, and whom he would forget. Life would continue. It would be lonely and colorless for a while, but it would continue. Like the white rock dwellings in front of him, Daniel thought. They were desolate and empty, too.

Grimacing, Baily watched as Daniel navigated the car through a toll booth and paid the park admittance fee. "I had to practically drag you to go sight-seeing with me every other time," she reminded her copilot. "Now, the one time I don't want to get out of the car you act like a kid who has just seen Disneyland for the first time."

"How come you don't want to explore? By now I thought you'd be bouncing up and down in your seat with excitement. This is what you love to do."

"I don't like this place." Baily's tone was adamant, as if she'd given it all the time she was going to give it and her decision was made.

Bemused, Daniel asked, "Why? Look at it. There are all sorts of places to search out. Who knows what we might find?"

Precisely. Baily could imagine what they'd find. Snakes. Lots of snakes in all those little crevices. Snakes galore like the ones that were in the movie *Raiders of the Lost Ark*.

"Come on," Daniel urged. "You afraid?"

Yep, they were definitely coming to know each other. Only a comment like that would be enough to get Baily out of the car. And he knew it. "I am not afraid. Stop the car and lets get this over with."

Not commenting on her lack of enthusiasm, Daniel obeyed her directions. There was an actual parking lot for tourists. A few cars were already parked; among them was a beige sedan that looked vaguely familiar to Daniel. Coincidence, he told himself. But he couldn't stop a sudden impending feeling of trouble. He gave the car another look, a longer one this time, but could see no one in it. He'd keep his eyes open. For what, he wasn't sure, but that feeling of trouble wasn't going away.

"Are we taking Theodora?" Daniel asked as he extricated himself from the car. He didn't think it was the best idea. There were too many places a cat could get lost if she happened to pop out of Baily's arms.

"No, I don't want her getting loose in a place like this," Baily answered, confirming Daniel's thinking. "All right, Miss Roosevelt, you stay here. We'll only be gone a little bit." Baily left a window rolled down a crack to give her air, but not enough space to crawl out. She locked her door and followed Daniel.

Stepping gingerly in the same path that he took up the rocky mound, Baily kept her eyes on the ground, totally prepared for unexpected slithery shadows to come sneaking out of nowhere. "If I see one snake out here, you're a dead man."

"Is that what all that fuss was about? The snake is more afraid of you than…"

"…I am of it. I know. I've only heard that line a million times. Let me tell you, I don't believe a word of it, either. I don't come with poisonous venom. There's no reason for the snake to be afraid of me."

Retracing his steps, Daniel came back to Baily. He reached out his hand and offered it to her. "I won't let the snakes hurt you." It was a solemn vow.

It wasn't enough. "I don't want to even see a snake," Baily revised.

After an exaggerated roll of his eyes, he made his pledge once more. "I'll keep all the snakes away from you. How about that?"

The hand promised safety, so Baily took it. More accurately, she latched onto it with a death grip. Then she clung to it, as Daniel brought her closer to his body, until she was practically pressed against his back. He took every step first up the white rocky mound. He found the easiest route with the least amount of suspicious crevices. He talked about the beautiful weather. He talked about the vastness of the land and how he had never enjoyed the trip cross-country as much as he had this time. He even talked about the Philadelphia Eagles' chances of winning the Super Bowl this year. He did basically anything he could to distract Baily from her groundless fears.

Before she realized how they got there, they stood together on a rock that overlooked a valley of more rock. She supposed it was beautiful, but she didn't want to look too long in case she saw something she didn't want to see. She'd rather just concentrate on the feel of Daniel's hand in hers. The roughness of his palm that indicated not all his time was spent at a computer. The firmness of his grip made her feel sheltered. The thickness of his wrist made her believe that she was in the company of a strong man. Yes, his hand was much better than a bunch of rocks.

After he had seen enough, he led a very willing Baily back to the car. When he spotted the car door ajar, he knew that the impending sense of trouble that had been niggling at him had just become more than a feeling.

"Baily, I don't want you to panic."

A surefire way to get anybody to panic. "It's a snake, isn't it." Baily slammed her eyes shut, but visions of curling, sliding, slithering reptiles filled the blackness. Her imagination had to be worse than reality. Baily opened her eyes.

"The car door's open. I think Theodora got out."

With that Baily lost all fear of snakes and felt a most profound fear for her beloved pet. She ran to the car but it was in fact empty. "Miss Roosevelt!" she called. Attempting to make kissing noises, but not able to make her trembling lips obey, Baily scoured the area for any sign of her cat.

"It's not possible. I locked the door."

Daniel knew that. Instinctively he looked for the beige sedan and saw that it was gone. Damn it, he should have followed his gut. "I think you were right earlier. I think whoever slashed my tires might have followed us here."

"What if he took her?" Baily cried.

"It's doubtful. He probably just left the door open. Come on, we'll find her."

Together they combed the area. Soon park rangers were involved, as well as any tourist within speaking distance. Everyone searched for the black cat with a white puff on her belly that answered to a dead president's name.

Daniel watched as Baily, despite her phobia of snakes, crawled in every open crevice she could find. She was relentless in her search. Like a mother bear gone wild for her missing cub. But no Theodora.

Suddenly she stopped. ''I'm going about this all wrong.''

''What are you talking about?'' he asked, standing next to her, out of breath from all the hills he'd been climbing.

''I need to think like she does. Where would she go?'' Baily rubbed her chin for a minute and suddenly it came to her. ''Of course! Follow me.''

She pointed to the highest hilltop and began sprinting toward it, careful to keep her eyes on the rocks so she wouldn't turn an ankle. Using the crevices, she pulled herself up to the very top of the highest rock formation.

Theodora was perched on the summit, looking rather miffed that it had taken her mother this long to find her.

''My baby!'' Baily wrapped her cat in her arms and Daniel was behind her to help her down from the rock.

''I don't get it,'' he finally said after they thanked all the park rangers for their help and were once again secure in the Bug. ''How did you know where she would be?''

''Easy,'' she said holding on to Theodora with a death grip. ''It's where T.R. would go.''

''Where?''

''The high ground. Remember San Juan….San Juan *Hill*.''

Daniel wasn't sure what frightened him more, that he understood what she meant, or that he was beginning to believe that the cat was in fact a reincarnated president.

# 8

"YOU'RE KIDDING ME."

"This has been a very stressful day for us, Daniel," Baily reminded him.

After they found Theodora they had driven through the rest of the afternoon and into the late evening and were currently in a motel just outside of Indiana. Once again, Daniel had decided to do away with the pretense of two rooms. As far was he was concerned it was a little like closing the barn door after the horse had left. He told himself earlier that he'd had his fill of her, but he had lied. He didn't think he would ever have his fill of her if he lived to be ninety.

And since they both seemed to agree that their time together was limited, he figured they should be taking advantage of every minute left together. Which is why he naturally assumed that when he asked for a single king-size bed that they would be sharing it together. Just the two of them.

That was before Theodora curled up in a ball on a pillow smack in the center of the bed and refused to be moved. Or rather, her mother refused to move her.

"But she slept under the bed last night," Daniel reminded her, hating the trace of whininess he heard in his own voice. He refused to be one of those men who whined for sex.

"That was before she spent two hours lost in the midst

of the Badlands. She needs me, and frankly I think you're being slightly insensitive to even suggest that I drop her on the floor so we can romp around on the bed like a couple of..."

"Lovers," he supplied, which is exactly what they were, at least for the next forty-eight hours.

"I was going to say humans, but that will do. The point is, she stays."

"Meow," Theodora concurred, snuggling herself deeper into the center pillow.

Grumbling, Daniel shucked off his clothes and climbed into bed, careful not to disrupt Theodora. He reached over and turned out the light, blanketing the room in darkness.

"You should know I was thinking about you, too. This is going to be one of our last chances to have great sex. Then you're going to have to go home and spend the rest of your life having sex with Harper." Not exactly the image he wanted to take with him into his dreams. Idiot, he cursed himself.

Baily wasn't going to marry Harry. She couldn't now that she understood what it felt like to be in love and to be with the man she was in love with. She and Harry were friends. That was it. A family, no matter how badly she wanted it, needed to be born out of love not compromise. It was wrong to think either one of them should settle.

She chose not to share that information with Daniel, however. It would no doubt only make him feel guiltier for leaving. And if by some miracle he did decide to stay with her, she certainly didn't want him doing so out of guilt.

Instead she said, "Somehow I'll manage."

"Huh. You think so. You don't know how rare last night was. But trust me, I do. That kind of magic doesn't just happen. Last night was special."

She smiled in the darkness and wondered if he even realized what he was saying.

"Good night, Daniel."

"Whatever," he snapped, and turned on his side.

"Good night, Theodora."

"Meow."

The last thought he had before he drifted off was that the cat was mocking him.


"IF I CAN'T BRIBE HIM, maybe I can beat him up?" They were driving through the rolling green hills of Lancaster County, Pennsylvania, only hours away from their destination, and it occurred to Daniel that they still hadn't come up with a legitimate plan to separate Pierce from Sarah.

"You can't beat him up. Sarah will take pity on him if she thinks he is being bullied."

"What if I logically and calmly point out to Sarah that Pierce is only after her money and that to marry him would be the biggest mistake of her life?" Daniel asked.

Again, Baily played the devil's advocate. "How well did that work the last time?"

No answer was necessary.

"All right Miss I-Have-All-The-Answers, what do you suggest?"

Not afraid to voice her opinion on the subject, or on any subject for that matter, Baily came up with the only solution possible. "We need proof."

"Proof of what?"

"Proof that Pierce is a con man out to rob her blind. We both agree that all of the bad luck we've experienced on this trip can't be coincidental. Someone is following us. I'll bet anything that Pierce is somehow behind it. Technically the wedding is supposed to be the day after tomorrow, right?"

"Right, but I asked him to postpone it, remember."

"What makes you think he'll do it? Maybe that was his plan all along, to slow you up so you wouldn't reach Sarah in time to stop the wedding." Baily began to recount the mishaps on her fingers, holding them high so Daniel could see the number had grown. "One, the stolen wallet. Two, the slashed tires. Three, the open car door, and four, the mysterious beige sedan."

"What did you say?"

Jeez! Baily sighed. He wasn't even listening and it was his sister in trouble. "I said, one—"

"No," Daniel stopped her. "What was four?"

"The mysterious beige sedan."

"You saw it yesterday, too?"

"Yes, but I didn't see anyone in the car. I thought there was a man wearing a brown baseball cap in Jackson Hole who looked suspicious, but I didn't see him at the park."

"But the car...the car! Of course. It was the same car outside my condo when I left Washington."

"You think he's been following us this whole time?"

"You think Pierce would go so far as to hire someone to stop me from getting to the wedding?" Daniel countered as if the answer to one question was the answer to both.

"If he did hire someone, we know one thing for sure about his employee."

"What?"

"He's the sort of man who thinks nothing of turning a cat loose in a strange park. A man like that is nothing but pure evil."

"You'll have to come with me," Daniel decided. "To the house in Philadelphia. I'm going to need you to back me up when I tell Sarah."

"If I have to." Baily shrugged and tried to hide her pleasure that this trip they were on wasn't quite over.

IT WAS PAST ELEVEN by the time they rolled into Daniel's upscale Philadelphia residence. Baily had spent the past twenty minutes gaping out the window at the size and the luxury of the homes they passed. She thought she'd come from a big house, but her home was nothing in comparison to these mansions.

Even Theodora was impressed, and she was a Roosevelt.

As they pulled into the driveway, Daniel saw immediately that the garage was open and Sarah's BMW was missing. Where would she be at this late hour? And where was Pierce? With his sister, Daniel supposed, keeping tabs on his meal ticket. Not a problem. He and Baily could wait at the house for his sister to return. "Come on," he said, parking her Bug in the circular driveway.

Daniel took her inside and with a flick of his wrist on the side wall, he seemed to illuminate the whole downstairs.

"Meow!"

"I know," Baily whispered reverently. "Go explore. But remember, you're a guest here," she said, letting Theodora roam while she tried to absorb what she was seeing.

Thick Oriental carpets covered hardwood floors. Paintings were lighted with the tiny bulbs that were attached to the frames that Baily thought only existed in museums. Antiques—real ones, not the ones she liked to pick up at flea markets—decorated the mantel above the fireplace and the end tables in the living room. Or at least she thought it was the living room. It was a huge square room off to her left as she entered the foyer. Perhaps it was only the sitting room for people to gather in before they were escorted to the formal living room. Cool.

"How do you like the house, Red?" Daniel couldn't say why, but he was eager for her approval. It had been so long since he'd seen the house from someone else's eyes. Watching her enjoy it made him appreciate all that he had. But it was more than a renewed love for his home that he was looking for. He wanted Baily to love the house because…

*Don't finish that thought. It begins and ends with "happily ever after."*

"I love the house. Who wouldn't? No wonder Pierce is after Sarah. You guys are loaded."

"I suppose we are. We had parents who loved us. We had each other, even though my sister does test my patience. We were wealthy in all the ways it counts. This house is just icing on the cake."

"Some icing. Chocolate fudge to be sure."

Daniel laughed, but he could sense Baily wasn't all that comfortable. "It's just a house, Red. Bigger than some, smaller than others. Home." And he'd been gone from it for too long. Oddly enough, standing in the foyer with Baily, he wasn't hit with the sensations that normally accompanied him when he returned home. The sense of loss that the house usually conjured was still there, but was less suffocating, less oppressive. In its place was a sense of rightness. Daniel hardened himself against that particular emotion. It was aberrant, he was sure. The pain would return soon enough.

"I guess Sarah's out with Larson. Our best bet is to settle in and make a night of it."

Baily wiggled her eyebrows suggestively and sauntered over to him in what she hoped was a sexy sashay. "A night of what exactly?"

"Oh sure, now you want me," he huffed, even though he could already feel his blood starting to heat.

"Well, you did say that we only had so many chances left. And we have this whole big house to ourselves. It really seems a shame to waste it."

"I suppose," he said, striving for a casualness he didn't feel.

Baily waited until he reached for her before she moved out of his grasp. "Or we could just sit on that couch over there and wait for Sarah."

"They could be out for hours," Daniel noted, moving toward her even as she backed away with a teasing smile.

"Hours, huh? Let me think, what else could we be doing for hours?"

"There's always the library."

"Yes, there is that. Or—" She laughed as she raced over to him and kissed him fully on the mouth. "How about a Rhett Butler?"

"Is that anything like a Dustin Hoffman?" Daniel quipped.

"Sort of. Neither one of those men took no for an answer, if you know what I mean."

Daniel laughed. Then in a smooth motion, he lifted Baily from the floor and carried her up the wide staircase all the way to his bedroom. It was one of the master suites, preserved for him just as he left it. A dark cherrywood bed was decorated with a forest-green comforter and large throw pillows in offsetting shades of green. In front of the bed was a smaller version of the living room downstairs. A comfortable leather couch and matching recliner both faced a wide-screen television. The room once served as his fortress of solitude, he told her.

Since the house was the size of a city block, she couldn't imagine when Daniel ever lacked for privacy with or without the sitting room. Baily let her eyes wander. She saw trophies he'd won in sporting events. Academic awards that had been framed, no doubt by his mother before she'd died. It was a man's room now, but Baily could see remnants from his boyhood. And it warmed her. Daniel had once been a boy. A vulnerable, probably arrogant, probably isolated, little boy.

He laid Baily down on his bed and then backed away. It was the first time he had ever brought a woman to this bed, to this room. It should have alarmed him that he was allowing her entrance so easily, but it didn't. It was right. She was right. Her fiery red hair spread out in waves over the dark green of the cover in perfect contrast. A perfect match.

"Undress for me," he told her, his voice a harsh whisper.

She sat up and with trembling fingers did as she was asked. She started to pull her plain, soft blue T-shirt over her head. But as her arms were caught up in the shirt, Daniel took the opportunity to gently push her down on the bed again. With her arms confined in such a manner she was helpless to prevent his touch.

Not that Baily would ever try to prevent Daniel's touch.

He fastened his lips on her breast and kissed her through the lace of the bra she wore. His teeth worried her nipples into hard nubs that scratched against the lace of her bra, creating a unique pain for Baily that was absolutely delicious.

Her arms still occupied, Daniel realized that if he wanted to get Baily out of the rest of her clothes he was going to have to do it himself. Using his lips as a guide he mapped his way over her full breasts and turgid nipples, down her belly—with a quick stop to tickle her belly button with his tongue—to the top button of her jean shorts. Careful to conceal his fingers that shook slightly, he released each of the buttons from their holes and slid her shorts down her legs until they dropped forgotten to the floor.

Baily should have felt embarrassed or awkward lying

there with her wrists fastened above her head and her body exposed so completely to Daniel's lustful gaze. She wasn't. Instead she felt gloriously free. A woman in love, making love with her man. And apparently, if Daniel's reaction was any judge, she was pretty good at it.

"Mmm," Daniel murmured, unable to prevent the sound that escaped his lips as he lowered her panties down her legs and tossed them to the floor to join her shorts. "You are incredible." Falling to his knees in front of her as if she were a goddess to be worshiped, Daniel leaned forward and placed his mouth right below her belly button where the skin was soft and tight. The ache it caused Baily an inch or so lower was indescribable and the sigh that she believed escaped her lips sounded more like a scream to Daniel's ears.

One of the things Daniel cherished most about Baily was her exuberance. He gloried in her pleasure because it was his, too. When Daniel brought her to her peak, he could sense how much joy Baily felt for life. He shared in that joy. And it became a part of him, as well.

"Oh, Daniel. Please."

There was no reason for Baily to ask. Daniel needed to be inside her as much as she craved for him to be inside her. Standing, he leaned down over her to kiss her lips.

When he released them she ordered on a sigh, "Let my arms free. I want to hold you."

That was fine. Daniel wanted to be held. He pulled the shirt off her arms then undid her bra and tossed them both aside. Immediately her arms were wrapped around his neck. They pulled him closer so that Baily could press her body against his. His clothes, still adorned, made her shriek with frustration. Quick to remedy that problem, Daniel all but ripped the clothes off his own body.

Nude, and as breathtaking as she remembered, he returned to her.

"Do you have any...you know, left from last time," Baily asked breathlessly.

"I bought another pack," he said, removing a condom from his wallet and sheathing himself quickly. He tapped his head with his finger and smiled. "I'm always thinking ahead, Red. It's about time you learned that about me."

She wanted to learn everything about him, she thought dazedly, but didn't voice her thoughts. Declarations of love now would only scare him away.

His legs brushed her thighs apart, and he stood between them. Baily reached for his hands and tugged at his arms until Daniel came down on top of her. His arms supported his weight, but Baily was free now to press her breasts against his hard chest. His faced loomed above hers just out of reach and she was forced to lift herself off the bed if she wanted to kiss him.

After several efforts of kissing him and then falling back onto the bed, she realized he was doing it on purpose. Letting her come to him. The glimmer in his eyes and the curve of his lips said everything.

"You tease," she accused him.

"I want to see how much you want me."

Shyly, she told him.

Daniel shook his head. "I need proof."

Baily was up for the challenge. Once again she wrapped her arms around his neck. With a strength she didn't know she possessed she was able to lift herself off the bed and turn. The sudden change in her motion knocked Daniel off balance. Before he realized what had happened he was on his back, and Baily was climbing over him. She had the look of a tiger on the prowl. A fierce red-hot tiger.

Daniel was in heaven.

"Proof enough?" Baily taunted.

"Not hardly," Daniel whispered.

Encouraged that he approved and enjoyed her boldness, Baily pressed forward.

"I think I found some more proof," she teased. Hard, hot and throbbing proof that when she sat back on her haunches she felt pressed against her soft bottom. To entice herself and to tease him, she wiggled her bottom back and forth until Daniel moaned in agony.

"Want more?" Baily meant proof.

Daniel heard differently. "Yes-ss," he hissed. Then he brought one arm up to capture Baily and lowered her mouth to his for his penetrating kisses. One kiss turned to ten, which turned to twenty. It wasn't enough. He needed more. Her taste. Her sweet richness. Baily was her own aphrodisiac. The more he tasted of her the more pronounced his desire became.

Finally, it was crisis time. He'd let Baily believe she was in control, but now his need outweighed his restraint. With strong arms he clutched Baily's hips in his hands and positioned her over him. His intent was clear.

"Help me," he told her.

Baily readily complied. Reaching down, she stroked Daniel's sex. Baily loved the feel of his pulse beneath her fingers. Life was never so obvious as it was in a man's sex.

"No, inside. I need to be inside you." Another time he would let Baily explore and play. Now he was too far gone.

Since Baily, too, felt a sudden urgency to be united, she did what he asked. As he penetrated her body he also penetrated her soul. Their union was nothing short of magical. Overcome with emotion and excitement, her body could do little more than keep itself upright.

Fortunately, Daniel had enough presence of mind to complete the task at hand. With his strong hands on her hips, he lifted her up and down, forcing himself deeper, bringing her down harder until there was no space, no breath, left between their two bodies.

Together they imploded. Baily felt it start deep in her stomach and for a moment she thought her whole body would collapse in on itself. Daniel felt her muscles tighten around him and he, too, was caught in a whirlwind of pleasure that sucked the air out of him and left him at the same time deflated and rejuvenated.

Baily also struggled to catch her breath. She knew she was a novice in this particular area but the power of their joining seemed almost unbelievable. Something that powerful couldn't be born of two people who merely liked each other, wanted each other. Something that powerful had to come from two people who loved each other. Didn't it? Baily knew she loved Daniel. So that must mean...

"I think there's something you should know, Daniel."

"What?" he asked, still struggling to regain his breath and his senses. She had eased her body off of his and was now lying on top of him, her faced propped up in her hands as she met his eyes.

"I think you're in love with me."

How did someone respond to a statement like that? Not well, he was sure. "Baily," Daniel began gently, "I don't want to hurt you for the world. I won't say I didn't want this. As soon as I saw you I knew that I wanted you as my lover. But love? It's too soon. We haven't known each other long enough to be in love. And as much as I want to get to know you better, I can't stay. I have a life waiting for me." He was trying to escape and he was going to have to do better than that. Then he remembered. "I have a business in Seattle."

"Why can't you move your business to the east coast? Where your home is," Baily pointed out.

"Because my business revolves around lumber. People cut wood in the northwest, not in the northeast."

"So you overcome your fear of flying, and you travel to the places you need to go." It was a practical solution.

Daniel closed his eyes. Baily wasn't going to let this be easy. Did he blame her? He supposed not. She thought she was in love, and she was fighting for that love. That made her courageous, not stubborn. "I'm not afraid to fly. But aside from that, you ask the impossible. You want to make it seem easy when it's not. I know it hurts you to hear this but I don't love you, Red. I can't let myself love you."

For a moment she was quiet. Daniel assumed that she was absorbing the pain of the punch he delivered.

"You might," she suggested.

"But I don't."

"But you might."

"But I don't."

"Maybe."

"No way."

"Possibly."

"Absolutely not," Daniel shouted, tired of playing verbal tag. "And I'm through talking about this with you, Baily."

She smiled joyously at him.

"What are you smiling for?"

"You just called me Baily."

Daniel groaned. It had been a slip of the tongue. Nothing more. Now she was mooning at him as if he had just proclaimed his everlasting love. There had to be something he could say, something that he could do that would convince her. In one motion he rolled Baily off his body and stood next to the bed. "Come on. Get dressed."

Baily blinked a few times in confusion. "Dressed? Why?"

"I'm taking you home. Now. I don't know how to convince you, *Red,* that this was just an affair. That's all. You are too emotional. Probably because I took your virginity. I understand where this attachment comes from, but I can't encourage it. So I'm taking you home and ending it now. Then you'll understand I'm serious."

Like a zombie, Baily rose from the bed and began to put her clothes back on her body. This she wasn't prepared for. It sounded as if he actually meant it. He was going to drop her off at her home and leave her forever.

Have faith, she told herself. What Daniel said and what Daniel was able to do might prove to be two different things. There was a reason for his reluctance to make a commitment. Something about loving her frightened him. If only he would confront his fear instead of ignoring it. If only he would fight that fear.

Soundlessly, Baily followed Daniel downstairs. Theodora had found the most expensive piece of furniture to curl up on, much to Baily's dismay. She lifted her pet over her shoulder and stared down at the mound of cat hair left on the chair. "I'll pay to have it cleaned," she told him.

"Don't worry about it."

"So I guess this is it," she said, sadly standing at the front door.

No, he couldn't let her go this way. It wasn't right. It was late and she would have to drive through the city to reach New Jersey. What if the car broke down? What if she fell asleep at the wheel?

"I'll take you and get a cab back here."

"There's no need..."

"I said I'll take you," he repeated firmly.

Baily shrugged her shoulders and followed him out to

the car. He clearly wasn't ready to leave her yet. Oh, yeah, she thought. He definitely *might* love her.

"I DON'T BELIEVE THIS," Daniel muttered for the twentieth time since the car had come to a dead halt in residential Haddonfield, New Jersey.

"Well, how was I supposed to know we didn't have enough gas?" Baily asked as she steered while Daniel pushed the car from behind. If his expression was any indication, she was pretty darn sure that if he did love her, he was over it.

"The gas gauge on Empty is usually a good warning," he returned, cursing her name under his breath. Thank heaven it was a compact car. He'd complained about that fact often enough in the past few days, but now it was a blessing.

"I thought we could make it. Usually this car can run for miles on fumes." Baily doubted that fact would improve his mood. The truth was they'd been running on fumes when they'd crossed the Ben Franklin Bridge. Baily considered herself lucky to have made it to her hometown.

Haddonfield was a small historical town filled with big homes. It was beautiful; unfortunately, it was also the type of town that closed down early. They were on the main street when the car puttered and died, and there wasn't a soul around. Not a police officer, not a gas station attendant, no one.

Daniel had been pushing the car for the last mile, and they still had another mile to go. "It's not much farther," she told him for what seemed like the hundredth time.

Daniel didn't bother to acknowledge her words or to gain hope by them. Instead he continued to push and curse, with that damn cat staring at him through the rear window the whole time.

A mile later, Daniel pushed the car into Baily's driveway. It was a large Colonial home, and judging by the number of cars in the driveway it was filled to the brim with people.

"My family knew I was coming home. They all wanted to be here to welcome me back," Baily told him by way of explanation for all the cars. "It's almost three in the morning. Why don't you just sleep over, and one of my brothers will take you home in the morning. If that's what you really want."

Daniel closed his eyes in resignation. It wasn't what he wanted. He wanted to leave now while he still had a chance. The last thing he needed to do was to meet Baily's family. No doubt they would suffocate him with their geniality. He saw the whole picture clearly: mother, father, children, all would prod at the still raw scar that marked his heart. They would behave like a…a…family. No doubt there would be questions regarding his intentions toward Baily. It was enough for him to start seeing stars. Or maybe that was exhaustion setting in.

But she was right about one thing. He had no energy to call for a cab. Pushing a car for two miles in the middle of the night could do that to a person.

"All right. I'll stay. But I'm leaving first thing in the morning."

"Sure."

Daniel was too tired to interpret the tone of her reply so he didn't try. He had to hope that Baily would come to accept his decision and see that it was the only rational course of action.

After all, what if he did move back to the east and marry Baily and his company failed? Was it worth risking his business to have Baily in his life? What if he moved back to the east coast and his marriage failed? What if she died?

Daniel felt himself sweating, but he didn't know if it was from the exertion of pushing the car or fear. Considering his sweat was cold, he assumed it was fear.

"I'm afraid all I have is a couch to offer," Baily noted as they walked up the steps to her home.

For the moment Daniel was released from the fear that gripped him. Baily's words penetrated and Daniel found himself gazing up at the large Colonial house. There had to be at least five or six bedrooms in a house this size. All she had to offer was a couch? Whose stupid idea was this to leave his comfortable house and bring Baily home? Oh, that's right. It was his idea.

As if reading his thoughts, Baily began to explain to him as she led him toward the back door. "There's Nick, who is living at home temporarily—I told you about him. He's divorced. Whatever you do, don't bring that up. He's very sensitive about it. He's probably bunking with James. Michael and his wife, Sharon, will no doubt have another room. Their three kids, plus Billy and Donna's baby, are probably in another room. Billy and Donna have to have their room. Sean and his wife Meg are probably bunking in with their new baby in the upstairs den, and of course, Mom and Dad have the master suite. That's all of the bedrooms and roll-out couches. But there is a very comfortable couch in the den downstairs."

Baily lost Daniel's attention after the second brother. Damn, he was tired. The days of driving and the hours of pushing had finally caught up with him. By the time Baily let him in the house he was already half asleep.

She steered him through a few rooms to the couch that would be his bed. He crashed, and she came down next to him with a blanket that would keep them both warm.

His last thought was that they probably shouldn't sleep

together under her parents' roof. It was discourteous. He told her as much.

"It's okay. We'll just wake up before everybody else does." With that, she settled against Daniel's chest. Baily loved the closeness she felt when she was with him like this. She loved the sound of his heart, the strength of his body, the scent of him that would fill her senses all night long. Just as she started to get ideas though, she heard a faint snore from above. In an excited whisper she told a sleeping Daniel, "I can't wait for you to meet my family. They're going to love you."

# 9

DANIEL HAD THE DISTINCT impression that Baily's brothers were not going to like him. Upon waking that morning, he was greeted by the sight of six large, scowling men standing over him. One man, the oldest of the group, spoke first. "Would you like us to begin by ripping off your arms, or would you prefer if we started with your face?"

Great, he had options.

"His face, Dad. I would bet my Corvette that he's never even had his nose broken." This was said by the blond bruiser with the fiercest scowl.

Daniel took pride in his unbroken nose.

The smallest of the six spoke up. "You know, if we break his nose we'll be taking Baily's wrath all day long."

At last, a reasonable voice among the barbarians.

Another brother with red hair and a wide smile continued, "Yeah, breaking his nose would be stupid. We've got to hit him where the bruises won't show."

Clearly this one was not an ally.

"Shut up all of you," the oldest one said. "She's waking up."

Baily stretched gloriously. Not quite ready to face the day, however, she cuddled even closer against Daniel's strong body. Then she realized that they didn't have much time before the house woke up. They needed to be up before her father and her brothers were aware that they had spent the night on the couch together. "Daniel," Baily mumbled as she nudged Daniel's ribs. "We better wake up before the family realizes we slept together." Caressing her hand down his strong chest, Baily quickly changed her plans. "Of course, we might have time for a little…"

"Red, if you value my life, you will not finish that sentence," Daniel warned her.

Confused by his words, Baily opened her eyes. "Dad! Nick, Michael, Billy, Sean and James! You're all here. Isn't it wonderful! I'm so happy to be home!"

The men in her life were not currently sharing her excitement. "Baily, is there something you want to tell us?" her father prompted. "For instance, who is this man with his arms wrapped around you like you were his own personal teddy bear?"

Out of spite, Daniel hugged Baily closer to him. He refused to be treated like a teenager who'd just got caught kissing their precious little girl on the patio.

If it were possible, the brothers Grimm plus one father deepened their scowls. Sensing the tension in the room and knowing only one way to appease them, Baily spoke up, "Dad, boys…it's okay. Daniel is my fiancé!"

All at once their attitudes changed. It was as if someone had waved a magic wand and transformed them from lions to pussycats. "Well, why didn't you say so?" Baily's father chastised her.

Reaching down, Nick Senior pulled Daniel off the couch and onto his feet. Before he knew what was happening, Daniel was shaking the man's hand and trying not to grimace at the strength of his grip.

"Welcome to the family, son."

Had anyone heard him gulp? At least a noticeable gulp was better than a fearful squeak, which was what Daniel felt like emitting. Instead he did the manly thing and accepted every good-natured slap on the back and handshake that was offered to him, even though the slaps on the back practically knocked the breath out of him and the handshakes threatened to break his fingers.

"Okay, guys, enough of the macho stuff. Give us a minute so we can wake up and prepare to greet the rest of the brood."

"Sure thing, sis," Billy said, the only rational brother as far as Daniel could tell.

En masse, the men left the room. Daniel couldn't help but be amazed at the size of all of them. Even her father, who must be over sixty, still looked as if he was capable of playing linebacker for an NFL team.

"Now, Daniel, I don't want you to be angry," Baily began hesitantly.

With a look of mock surprise, Daniel replied, "Angry? Why should I be angry? Because I had to push a car for two miles until the wee hours of the morning? Because I was awoken by six men whose sole goal when they saw me was to inflict the most physical damage they could without leaving visible evidence? Because now you've told these men that I've asked you to marry me when I specifically told you last night that was not going to happen? Is that why I should be angry?"

Nodding sheepishly, Baily answered, "Yeah, I thought that might upset you…a little."

"Well you're right!" he shouted. "Why the hell did you have to tell them I was your fiancé? I could have survived the beating I was going to get for sleeping with you on the couch. I won't be that lucky when I become the man who broke his engagement to you."

Baily could have said that he didn't have to break the engagement if he really didn't want to, but she thought that might be pushing it a bit, especially after the rough morning he'd just had. "You're just cranky because you didn't get enough sleep. How about we meet the family and sit down to breakfast? It's Sunday, and if I know my mother, there will be eggs, bacon, scrapple if you're lucky, and English muffins.''

Only because his stomach growled madly did Daniel allow Baily to docilely lead him out of the den and into the kitchen. What followed was more shouting, hugging, screeching, kissing and crying than he could possibly imagine. Children bounced up and down trying to gain Baily's attention. Babies in walking gizmos bumped into Daniel's legs from all angles. Wives screamed with delight at the idea of Baily being engaged, and the men stood off to the side with their suspicious gazes trained on Daniel.

In the middle of this was one tiny woman who had been standing by the stove with a spatula in hand. She parted the crowd like Moses parting the Red Sea. ''So you're the man who is going to marry my daughter?''

Daniel had to say that he was more intimidated by this woman than he was by all the brothers and the father combined. And she only reached his chest. He found himself not wanting to lie to the woman, but he also didn't want to know what she would do with that spatula if he told her the truth. Still, he wasn't a liar. ''The truth is, Mrs. Monohan…''

''The truth is he's crazy about me, Mother!'' Baily interrupted. She rushed to Daniel's side and slid her arm through his. She did this so her family would know how much she loved him. She also did this so she could pinch the sensitive flesh on his upper arm. It was her way of warning Daniel not to mess with the woman wielding the spatula.

''I am crazy, that's for sure,'' Daniel said, completely truthfully.

''It's a good thing,'' Mary Ellen began. ''I didn't know

how I was going to tell you this, sweetie, but it doesn't matter now.''

"Tell me what?'' Baily asked, concerned with any news that her mother didn't want to tell her.

"Harry eloped last week with a showgirl from Atlantic City.''

"He did what!'' Baily was stunned. Harry was supposed to wait for her. He was supposed to be in love with her. She had almost been faithful to him! Then realizing how ridiculous she was being, she burst out laughing. "Harry with a showgirl. Well, good for him!''

Everyone joined in with jokes about Harry while they sat down to more food on one table than Daniel had ever seen. He wasn't sure how he felt about the Harry situation. On the one hand, he was grateful Baily wasn't going to settle for someone she obviously didn't love. On the other hand, this meant that when he left she would be alone. Would she miss him? Or would she start her search for the replacement Harry?

Maybe if he stayed for a little while, let Bruce handle things for a month or two, he could...what? No, Daniel thought, shaking off a sudden pain that had gripped his heart. There was only one way to deal with this. He was going to have to rip Baily off of him like a bandage.

"I have to go.''

Baily ducked her head so her family wouldn't see the hurt in her eyes. After all, she was the only one who knew Daniel wasn't coming back.

The rest of the group started to protest. One breakfast wasn't nearly enough time to get to know a prospective family member. Mrs. Monohan would need hours to properly grill her future son-in-law and said as much.

"My sister needs me,'' Daniel explained pathetically.

Baily came to his rescue and filled her family in on

Pierce, his treacherous tactics and the peril Daniel's sister was in. By the time she was finished Daniel thought he'd been living in the middle of a soap opera for the last week. He did notice that Baily failed to mention that she'd only known Daniel for less than a week. The story she told made it seem as if they had planned this trip cross-country all along. Obviously, she knew her family wouldn't understand her becoming engaged to a man that she had known for six days. Daniel wanted to shout, "See, I told you so. We can't be in love." But he didn't.

Baily's family immediately understood Daniel's predicament as well as his concern for his sister. All of them would do the same for Baily if they thought she was marrying the wrong man. Confronted with the power of family, Daniel was hard-pressed to remember his reasons for rejecting it. He'd forgotten the sense of belonging and fellowship that came with being a member of a family. For the first time, he actually missed it.

"So what are you going to do about it?" This from Nick, who wasn't much for discussion, but was ready for action.

"My plan was to boot the guy out of the house and lock Sarah in her room until she learns some common sense." The Monohan men nodded in unison. They liked the way Daniel thought.

The women shook their heads and Baily sided with her sisters-in-law. "I told him that wouldn't work. Unfortunately, I haven't concocted a better solution. We need proof that Pierce sabotaged our trip, but I can't see how we'll get it."

"Talk to your sister, Daniel," Mary Ellen Monohan ordered. "You can't know how she feels until you talk to her and listen to her. Sometimes it's the listening that's the hardest part."

Daniel agreed. So much so that he wanted to hear Sarah's voice immediately, rather than wait for the time it would take for him to return home.

Baily escorted him to a private phone in the den. Daniel punched the numbers he knew by rote. Finally, he heard a familiar voice answer the phone.

"Sarah?"

"Daniel, where are you? I thought I saw that you had slept in your bed, but I couldn't find you this morning. I didn't know where you were. The wedding is tomorrow. I didn't think you were going to make it. And you're the only family I have."

Guilt smacked Daniel hard in the face. He was her only family and he hadn't been much of one. So distant from his own sister, he didn't even know what was in her heart. Then something she said hit him.

"Tomorrow? You call that postponing a wedding!"

"What are you talking about? I told you the date when I left the message."

Obviously, she hadn't gotten the message he'd left with Pierce. "Forget the date, Sarah. The most important thing is that we need to talk about this before you go ahead and get married. You don't even really know this person."

For a moment she was silent. When she finally replied her voice was chilly. "Are you going to make it? For that matter, where are you?"

"I'm close, Sarah," Daniel said, not taking the time to elaborate. "Listen to me. You don't know Larson as well as you should. Do you know that I called him from the road? He told me you weren't there."

"It's entirely possible that I was out, Daniel."

"Yes, but I asked him to postpone the wedding. I was having all kinds of problems, and I needed more time. Did he tell you any of that?"

"He must have forgotten," Sarah said justifying her fiancé's actions. "Pierce does have a lot on his mind, after all. He's getting married tomorrow."

Not if Daniel could help it. "Sarah, please, just listen. The problems I've told you about, they weren't normal problems. Tires slashed, wallet stolen and I think he tried to kill Theodora."

"What are you talking about? Who is Theodora? Are you saying that Pierce has something to do with all of this? Are you accusing my future husband of attempted murder?"

"Well, of a cat, yes!" Daniel took a deep breath and tried to make some sense to his sister. "I think that Pierce hired someone to stop me from getting to the wedding. I think he's after your money."

Baily, who stood in the doorway quietly offering support, grimaced at that last comment. It had been a tactical error on his part.

Sarah's voice blasted through the receiver and Baily had no difficulty understanding the gist of the conversation. "How dare you! Don't you think anyone could love me just for myself? No, only someone who is short on cash would have anything to do with Daniel's flaky sister. Well, I've got news for you—you're crazy if you think that Pierce is out to sabotage you. He's not that kind of man. He loves me, and he wants to marry me. If you would like to be a part of that, you can meet us at city hall at noon tomorrow. If not, don't bother ever speaking to me again."

Daniel heard the resounding click in his ear then the dial tone. That hadn't gone the way he'd wanted it to go.

"Never tell a woman the only reason anyone wants to marry her is her money. It tends to put her on the defensive."

Daniel turned and looked to Baily for advice. "You're right. So what do I do now?"

There wasn't much left to do. "You go to the wedding. You offer her your support, and you hope she makes the right decision."

"Or you go get her now and lock her away." This suggestion came from Nick, who stood behind Baily in the doorway.

"She's a little steamed at me right now. I don't think she would let me anywhere near her. Maybe I should give her a chance to cool off?"

"Okay," Nick nodded. "Your second option is to get to the wedding early and cart her off before she makes a mistake she'll regret forever. I'll go with you if you want."

Daniel looked toward Baily, then toward Nick. "Thanks. I'll need your help to keep Pierce busy while I get Sarah out of there. City hall at noon."

Baily could only sigh with frustration. Men. They didn't know anything about women. "I'll go, but for the record I oppose these guerilla tactics."

Daniel would spend the rest of the day with Baily's family and then leave first thing the next morning for city hall. Hopefully, he could simply talk Sarah out of the wedding. If not, Daniel would simply haul her off over his shoulder and leave Nick to keep Pierce occupied. It was a perfect plan. Which naturally made Daniel nervous.

Dinner that night began with grace. It ended with funny stories about Baily's youth as the only girl growing up in a family of boys. Daniel laughed at her expense and loved it.

As for Baily, she was more than willing to submit to the humiliation if it meant that Daniel would be more at ease around her family. Early on in the day he had acted more withdrawn than she knew him to be. He wasn't comfortable with the abundance of people that occupied the house. That much was evident. What puzzled Baily was that if she had to describe his mood and temperament she would have called it cautious. As if he were afraid of something that even he couldn't quite put his finger on.

Family was a stumbling block for Daniel. She knew that. But Baily had believed that Daniel's reluctance for a family stemmed from his unwillingness to make a commitment. It wasn't as if he would have been the first man who feared marriage and babies and all the strings that came with them. Only now she was beginning to understand that Daniel's fear was altogether different. How strong that fear was remained to be seen.

She would need to find a powerful weapon to overcome it. She had one particular weapon in mind.

Lingering over after-dinner drinks, Baily and Daniel watched as each couple eventually grew too tired to maintain their end of the conversation and headed up for bed. It finally came down to Baily's parents and Nick, who'd found that he had a great deal in common with Daniel. Then Nick yawned.

"See you both early tomorrow," Nick said as he headed up to his room.

Now it was down to four. Baily silently pleaded with her mother to head upstairs so she could have private time with Daniel. The way she saw it she had bought herself one more day with Daniel, but time was definitely running out. Tomorrow he would be occupied with Sarah all day. Once that situation was settled there was nothing to keep him in Philadelphia.

That left Baily one night. Her mother, however, was an interference that Baily hadn't counted on.

"I meant to ask you Daniel, where is Baily's engagement ring?" Mary Ellen asked out of the blue. So out of the blue that Baily had almost forgotten that she told her parents she was engaged to Daniel. It seemed like a casual question, but Baily knew better. Mom was suspicious. As well she should be, considering Baily had lied about their engagement. Her mother could always catch her in a lie.

"The ring?" he repeated. Daniel did not have a clue how to answer that question.

"You know, the diamond that tells all the world that Baily belongs to you."

"I haven't picked it out yet, Mom. Daniel didn't want to buy me something I wouldn't like." It was a good cover story.

"A shame then."

"What do you mean?" Baily asked, not liking the tone in her mother's voice.

"You know the rule, Baily. No ring, no room."

Daniel didn't quite know what that meant. But Baily did. "But, Mother, we're engaged."

"Not until there is a ring on your finger. I've set up a cot in the kids' room. You can sleep with them. Daniel takes the couch." Her mother's voice was commanding and Baily knew better than to argue.

Daniel finally understood what "no ring, no room" meant. It was just as well. If they slept together, he would want her. And it didn't seem right making love to their precious baby downstairs while the family slept upstairs. Especially when he planned to leave her the very next day.

"But..." Baily protested. It only took one look from her mother to silence her on the issue.

Her mother and smiling father stood and headed toward the stairs. They paused at the bottom and waited for Baily to join them. Daniel stood, too, and lifted Baily to her feet. He took her face in his hands and kissed her softly on the lips. "Good night."

Pouting, she met her parents at the stairs. They both backed off so that she could go up ahead of them. Suddenly, Baily knew how Juliet felt being spirited away from Romeo by her evil family.

"'Night." She waved to him one last time.

"Good night," he said again.

"I love you."

Evil, he thought, saying it in front of her parents like that. He couldn't not respond, but he would be damned if he used the words. Scowling, he muttered, "Ditto."

Baily smiled at his cagey answer and climbed the rest of the stairs.

Settling on the couch, Daniel tried to keep his mind off his mock fiancée. Instead he tried to concentrate on his approach for the upcoming confrontation. All possible catastrophes aside, Daniel believed that it was really going to be quite simple. As long as everything went according to plan.

NOTHING WAS GOING to go according to plan. Daniel instinctively knew that. Any day that went awry at 12:01 a.m. was bound to be disastrous.

It had started with what Daniel believed to be an erotic dream. He felt warm kisses on his chest and warm hands that massaged the muscles beneath his skin. He could feel himself harden, and to his utter delight he could feel a soft, warm hand reach into the sweatpants he'd put on earlier that night and caress him almost to the point of explosion.

Grinning outrageously, Daniel forced himself to open his eyes before he lost complete control. That was when he realized it wasn't a dream. He lifted his head and saw flaming red hair spread out across his belly. Red! Baily dipped her tongue into his belly button, and the sensation caused him to gasp.

"What are you doing?" he rasped as he reached down to still her hands before it was too late.

With a bemused expression on her face, Baily's eyes met his. "What is the matter? Aren't I doing it right?"

Daniel remembered her innocence and tried to take into consideration that this was all new to her. She was vulnerable, and he had to be careful how he handled the situation. Unfortunately for her, now that he knew fulfillment was going to be denied to him, he was a little testy.

"Hell, yes, you're doing it right. But why are you doing it?"

Baily was a little thrown off by the question. She thought the answer was obvious. "I was achy."

Daniel wanted nothing more than to soothe her ache and his own in the process. But he couldn't. He wouldn't. Not in her parents' house. Not when they had placed their trust in him. Daniel couldn't specify why that trust was important for him to keep; he only knew that it was. Needing to deal with the problem at hand, or in her hand as it were, Daniel reached down and yanked his sweatpants back up over his hips. Only to have her yank them back down again.

"Red, stop it. We can't do this."

Baily huffed with frustration. She was achy! Since she had just discovered what it meant to have that ache satisfied, it only doubled her frustration. "Don't be such a fuddy-duddy. They'll never know if you keep it quiet. Although you do like to groan." Baily smiled wickedly and then went back to her task of removing the offensive sweatpants.

"Me? Groan? Listen, Little Miss Whimper, I'm not the one with the vocal problem. But that is beside the point. I'm not going to make love to you while your parents are upstairs asleep. It wouldn't be right. Besides, I'm too old to be sneaking around like this." Daniel had to capture her hands to get his point across.

"But this may be our last time!" Baily screeched.

Last time. The words registered with a huge impact. And they hurt so much that Daniel fought against them. "No, Baily. Last night was our last time. You knew that."

Cut to the quick, Baily sat up on his lap, her hands still within his. Her choice was to burst out into tears or to get mad. "Oh, you stupid oaf!" Baily lifted herself slightly and sent her bottom crashing into Daniel's stomach. "I love you and you may very well love me...."

"But I don't," he insisted.

"But you might. Only you're going to lose me and then what will you do?"

Since all the air had been forced out of Daniel's lungs, he had no response. Unfortunately for Daniel, who was trying to be noble, there was nothing sexier than watching Baily not get her way. If he could have seen her crackling eyes, her rosy cheeks, or her pouting lips, he might have been helpless to stop himself.

Then he did.

Light illuminated the room suddenly. Daniel only had Baily's expression to go by as the door and the light switch were both behind him, but he had the distinct impression that one or both of her parents were standing in the doorway.

*Please don't let it be her mother. Please don't let it be her mother,* Daniel silently chanted. That woman's wrath frightened him more than any of her brothers or her father could.

"I came downstairs for a glass of warm milk, when I thought I heard something," Mary Ellen said from the doorway.

Daniel groaned silently. He picked Baily up and off his

lap and set her on the floor. Then he rose and stood behind Baily to try to calmly and rationally explain to her mother what happened.

"It was all her fault." Not the bravest course of action, he had to admit, but the truth nonetheless. In case Mrs. Monohan didn't get the reference, Daniel actually pointed to make his point clear.

Baily turned and shot him a scathing look. "Rat fink."

Daniel simply winked at her and desperately tried not to smile at her predicament.

It wasn't necessary for her mother to say any more. Lifting her nightgown a bit, so as not to trip on her way out of the room, Baily marched regally out of the den and back up the stairs. It wasn't until her back was turned on her mother, that her mother cracked a smile.

"Kids," she sighed, then followed her daughter up the stairs.

Daniel didn't think now was the time to point out to her mother that Baily was almost thirty years old. Plopping himself back on the couch, he tried to get back to sleep, only images of Baily stayed with him all night long.

*You're going to lose me and then what will you do?*

"I don't know," Daniel told a dark empty room early that morning. It wasn't until almost dawn that he finally drifted off to sleep.

Which was why he blissfully slept through the children at play early that morning. He also slept through the smell of bacon and coffee. He would have slept through a thousand alarm clocks if they had all decided to go off at once. What he couldn't sleep through was the glass of water that was spilled directly over his head.

"What the heck?" he sputtered. He tried to jump off the couch to avoid getting any wetter but tripped over the blanket and instead ended up sprawled on the floor. When he was finally able to dry his face, he opened his eyes to find one evil-looking redhead standing over him with an empty class.

"Wake up, rat fink. You're late."

Like the dog Baily currently believed him to be, Daniel shook the water from his head, thoroughly disgruntled with the untimely bath. It therefore took a moment for Baily's words to register.

"Did you say I was late? Late for what?" Daniel asked, still dazed.

"Helloo-oo, you drove three thousand miles to stop your sister's wedding. Now you're about to sleep through it. It's already eleven o'clock."

Eleven o'clock! The wedding was at noon. "Why the hell didn't you get me up earlier?" Daniel shouted. Hurriedly, he scurried around the room, throwing on his discarded shirt over his head.

"I hope you don't believe I'm the type of person who would resort to water without first attempting other means to rouse you."

Daniel paused only long enough to send her a look that said he completely believed she was the type of woman who would resort to the water trick first.

Naturally, he was right. Baily had let him get as much sleep as possible before she'd filled her glass. Hell hath no fury…and all that jazz. Now, however, was the time to put those petty revenge tactics aside and stop a wedding.

"Nick has got the car ready. Mom has a cup of coffee for you to go. All we need is you."

Throwing on his sneakers, Daniel looked at Baily. "What is that you are wearing?"

Theodora poked her head out from the baby cozy that Baily had fastened to her chest. "Meow!"

"She's coming with me."

"Why?"

"I almost lost her and I'm not taking any chances. And Michael's youngest has got quick hands and an affinity for cat tails. Besides, it's only right that Theodora get to see this through to the end, too."

Since he didn't have time to argue he followed Baily out of the den and into the kitchen, where Mom Monohan gave him the coffee and a kiss on his cheek.

"For luck," she told him.

In a flash Daniel was out the door. The foursome headed back across the Ben Franklin Bridge to city hall to stop a wedding.

"WELL, THAT ONLY TOOK an hour," Daniel huffed. Now he knew where Baily had inherited her slow driving habits. Nick had driven his car, a Corvette no less, the proper speed limit the entire way.

"I told you, I'm a police officer," Nick responded. "As an officer of the law it is my job to obey the law at all times." Nick was a stickler for the rules.

"A waste of a good car as far as I'm concerned," Daniel mumbled.

"Enough about the slow trip. We have a couple to find. What chambers are they in?" Baily asked. The rescue team stood just inside the city hall lobby. It was one thing to know city hall at noon; it was another thing to have to guess what judge's chambers they were getting married in.

Frustrated and impatient, Daniel barked, "You think there would be some kind of list or something."

Nick calmly walked up to the clerk seated behind the main desk in the lobby. "I'm here for a friend's wedding. I know they're being married here at noon, but I don't know what judge is marrying them."

With a friendly smile, the pretty young clerk on duty began to aid Nick in his search.

Daniel, too agitated to make himself understood, stood back and watched the whole process. He couldn't help but be irritated by the smooth way Nick handled everything. Then again, it wasn't his sister getting married. His sister would never be at the mercy of a con man. Baily would drive a con man crazy long before he could get hold of her money.

Staring at Baily now, she seemed so innocent. She wore a cute little dungaree jumper with a T-shirt underneath and a cat attached to her. She could have been twelve. But she wasn't. She was a woman. A woman who wanted to marry and begin a family. The thought made Daniel's stomach clench.

Not my family. Not my marriage, he reminded himself sternly.

In a few hours Daniel could conceivably be back on the road and headed home. No, not home. Seattle. There was a difference. A difference that was more pronounced now than it ever had been.

If Daniel did succeed in stopping this sham of a wedding, what was he going to do with Sarah? Leave her brokenhearted and alone with no one to comfort her? It didn't seem fair. He could ask her to come with him to Seattle, but he doubted she would leave her home. It was when things got tough for her that she clung to that house and its memories. But a house filled with nothing more than memories could get awfully lonely. Is that why she had turned to Pierce?

"I should have been around more," Daniel muttered to no one in particular.

Baily heard him anyway. "Hard to be around when you

live three thousand miles away. Especially when you're afraid to fly.''

"I am not afraid to fly," Daniel corrected her for the umpteenth time.

"You ran away from home, Daniel. It was your choice. Now your sister has made her choice, and you have to respect it. Just like she respected yours.''

Had he run away from home? Yes. But not from home. He'd run from the empty hole left by his parents' deaths. It was a harsh truth to recognize. Daniel didn't like the idea that he'd run away from anything.

*Aren't you running away from Baily?*

Nick approached the suddenly somber-looking couple. "Come on. There's a noon wedding being performed in Room 310. We have to hurry, though. It's past noon, and Nancy said that Judge Morgan is prompt. The ceremony might have already begun." Nick led the way, and Daniel followed, nearly jumping out of his skin in an effort to reach the elevator before it closed. Baily barely managed to squeeze in as the doors closed behind her.

"Have you thought about what you're going to say?" Baily prompted, knowing Daniel hadn't.

What to do with Baily? What to say to his sister? How to stop a wedding? Did the questions ever end? "What did Dustin Hoffman do again?"

"He pounded on the glass and said no over and over again," Baily reminded him.

"That's sounding better every second."

The elevator bell dinged to let them know that they had arrived at the third floor. Room 310 was just off to the left. Upon approaching the glass-windowed door, and although the glass was textured, Daniel could clearly see a man and a woman dressed in wedding gear turn to one another and kiss.

They were too late. It was all he could think of. The kiss came at the end of the wedding ceremony. Three thousand miles, two national parks, flat tires, a missing cat, and they had missed the wedding. Not knowing what else to do, Daniel threw open the door and shouted, "No!" as loud as he could. The rafters shook with his fury. A step behind him, Baily and Nick stood on either side of him and stared at the shocked expressions on all of the faces in the room. When Daniel finally ran out of breath and was able to look at the couple himself, he noticed one very significant detail. The woman in the white dress wasn't his sister.

"Oops."

"Oops?" Baily questioned.

"Oops?" Nick asked.

"Oops," Daniel repeated, a bit more sheepishly. "You're not my sister," he told the bride who was still too shocked to reply. "And you're not Pierce Larson." The groom had the presence of mind to nod in agreement. "And I'm at the wrong wedding."

"The wrong wedding!" Nick and Baily chimed in together.

Daniel didn't have time for embarrassment. Stepping forward between the recently married couple with a polite, "Excuse me," Daniel queried the judge. "My sister, Sarah Blake, was supposed to be married here today at noon. Do you happen to know what happened to that wedding? Is she next in line?"

The judge paused for a moment, and then answered, "Blake, you say? Yes, I had Blake in here earlier. Their wedding was scheduled for eleven. Actually they were originally scheduled for noon, but the groom called this morning and bumped up the time."

A wave of crushing disappointment crashed over Daniel.

Now he really was too late. He felt Baily come up behind him and grab hold of his hand in a gesture of support.

"I didn't marry them," the judge added, just in case that was pertinent information.

"What do you mean, you didn't marry them?" Daniel asked hopefully.

"The bride called the whole thing off. Something about a message she didn't get. Then she left. And then the groom left."

Smiling brightly, Baily began to bounce again. It was a bounce-worthy event.

"Meow!" Theodora shrieked in protest.

"Sarah didn't go through with it." Daniel had to repeat it once to be sure that he wasn't mistaken. "Ha ha!" Grabbing Baily's face he planted a large kiss on her lips. It was while he was kissing her that he felt a tap on his shoulder.

"Hey, buddy, do you mind?" This came from the groom.

"Right. Pardon me. We should really go and let you get back to your wedding."

On their way out the door, Baily shouted over her shoulder, "Congratulations." It was the least she could do.

"So what next?" Nick asked once outside.

"If they didn't get married, I can only assume that Sarah would have gone home."

"Men," Baily sighed in resignation. "The last place she would go is home. She just left her groom at the altar. She's distraught and confused and probably wondering whether or not she did the right thing."

Following her train of thought, Daniel prompted, "So where would she be?"

"An ice-cream stand," Baily told him affirmatively.

Both men dropped their jaws. Nick was about to ask his sister to explain herself, when Daniel stopped him by holding up his hand. "Don't. I know what you're thinking. Trust me on this one. I've been down that road. Before you know it you'll find yourself in the middle of an argument on whether or not there should be walnuts in chocolate-chip cookies. Let's do this. You go search the streets for an ice-cream stand. I'll take Baily with me back to my house."

Daniel held out his hands, and Nick handed over the keys. "The speed limit is…"

"Yeah, yeah. Got it. Hand over the keys." Keys in hand, Daniel sprinted toward the car pulling Baily behind him. Baily offered one last bit of advice for Nick. "Chocolate ice cream, Nick. Look for a stand with chocolate ice cream."

Nick watched the couple take off and shook his head. "Walnuts," he muttered under his breath. "Who the hell likes walnuts in their chocolate-chip cookies?"

# 10

"SO THIS IS IT." It was a little on the dramatic side, but since Baily herself was a little on the dramatic side it seemed appropriate.

Daniel, who was concentrating on breaking the all-time speed record across the city of Philadelphia, paid little attention to Baily's sighs of fatalism.

"Yep, definitely it," she repeated.

"Okay," Daniel finally replied. "What's it?"

"This is the end of the line, the final stop, the last call, the climax, the zenith..."

"I get the point. This is about me leaving. You're angry."

"I'm not angry," Baily corrected. "Sad. This has been the best trip I've ever had. Like one great big roller-coaster ride. I'm just sorry the ride has to end. Of course, if you continue to drive at Mach 10, this trip will probably end a lot sooner than we expected."

Horns blared as Daniel continued to weave the Corvette in and out of traffic. Nick would be furious with him for disobeying the speed laws, but Daniel had other considerations. If his hunch was correct, now that the wedding had been called off, Pierce would be on his way out of town and Daniel wanted the satisfaction of booting him out of town himself with a nice swift kick in the— Enough said.

A quick glance at Baily, her face white with tension,

and her arms wrapped protectively around the feline bundle attached to her chest, Daniel eased up on the gas. Slightly.

"We've been over this, Red. I have to go home."

"No, you have to go back to Seattle. This is home. Sarah is home. Seattle is…" Baily scrunched up her face and tried to think of something really awful.

"Where my life is," he finished.

"Home is supposed to be where your heart is."

His heart. As if he could trust that. It was telling him that Baily might actually be right. That he might actually be in love with her, which was absolutely impossible to do in six days. Wasn't it?

"You're right, Red. This trip has been a roller-coaster ride. Exciting, passionate, fun and temporary. I can't trust that you love me the way you say you do. I certainly don't trust my own feelings toward you. The sensible thing for me to do is to return to Seattle. Work things out in my head."

"Whatever you think is best," she said sadly. "You have to make the right decision for yourself."

When did the right decision become such an elusive thing to find? Then again, maybe there was more than one choice. "Come with me, Red. Come back to Seattle with me. Let's be together for more than a week. Then we can decide if what we have is a lifetime's worth of love." Somehow Daniel knew it was wrong to ask her to leave. Especially since he'd seen her reunited with her family and seen how important those people were to her.

Baily felt her heart leap at his suggestion. He wanted her with him. It was the first time that he'd given her any indication of how he truly felt. But as happy as she was about that admission, she couldn't be happy about what he was asking her to do.

"I can't."

Daniel had known her answer before she said it. So it surprised him that he felt such a kick in the stomach when he actually heard the words. "Why is it that you have no problem asking me to sacrifice everything so I can stay with you, but you refuse to leave your family and come with me?"

"Daniel, I know you might think I'm being selfish by not wanting to leave. And you probably aren't going to understand what I'm about to say, but the truth is I think you need to stay. It's time you came home. I've been away for a long time, and now that I'm back I understand what home means. It's a sense of belonging and connection that you get nowhere else in the world. You left home to forget the fact that your parents weren't there waiting for you in your house like they should have been. You're afraid that if you build a home and put people that you love inside it, that one day they might not be waiting for you, either. It's a risk, Daniel. And it's one that you have to decide that you are ready to take."

Baily was finished. Everything that needed to be said was said. Since Daniel had no answer for her, the car became very quiet and the remainder of the drive seemed endless. Each was left to think about what the other had said and to decide for themselves where the future would take them. Each was frightened of the idea that their time together may soon be coming to an end. Each began to feel the stirring of the pain that would only intensify when they were actually separated.

Daniel pulled into the long driveway that circled in front of his spacious house. Home. Family. Fear. He swallowed audibly though his mouth was dry.

"Look!" Baily screeched. She reached over to yank on Daniel's arm, which caused the car to swerve up the driveway. Only Daniel's quick reaction saved them from heading into the shrubbery.

"What do you think you are doing? Do you want to kill us?" Daniel slammed on the brakes and stopped the car halfway up the driveway.

"The car. It's the car."

"Whose car?" Daniel asked, trying to follow Baily's ranting. Then he saw what Baily saw.

"The man in brown," Baily whispered.

"Or at least his car," Daniel finished.

"What should we do? Should we call the police? Do you think they are armed?"

"One question at a time," Daniel told Baily in an attempt to slow her down. There was no point in getting excited. After all, it wasn't as if Pierce was a criminal. Just a con man. "I don't think he's armed but I think you should stay in the car while I walk up to the house and investigate."

"Yeah, right!" Baily had the door open and one foot on the ground before Daniel could say otherwise.

"Okay, you can come with me, but let's do this quietly. We don't want to let them know we're here."

"Sure thing," Baily agreed. "Quietly."

As stealthily as two people who had absolutely no idea what they were doing could, Baily and Daniel crept up the driveway using the azalea bushes as cover. They followed the half-moon driveway to the top of the arch until they were directly opposite the front door. The beige car sat between them and the house.

"What do we do now?" Baily queried in a hushed conspiratorial tone.

"We wait."

For how long Daniel couldn't say. And exactly what

they would do when they saw Pierce and his hired thug Daniel had no idea.

And he wasn't given much time to contemplate it. Pierce burst out of the front door carrying a huge duffel bag, which he threw into the back seat of the beige car. "Come on, we don't have much time," Pierce called to the man, who now exited the house with a large painting in his arms.

Baily recognized the second man immediately. His face, although nondescript, was very familiar. Sandy-brown hair, boring features, average height and brown clothes. It was no wonder he managed to blend into crowds so often.

Pierce was a different sort altogether. Tall, with dark wavy hair, he looked like a candidate for the next James Bond film. He still wore his tuxedo from the almost wedding, and Baily had to force herself to blink. No wonder Sarah had fallen for him.

"Easy with the painting. It's worth a fortune," Pierce told the man in brown, as he tried to force it into the back seat of the car.

"Hey, I'm tired of listening to your orders," the man retorted. He threw the painting into the car, causing Daniel to wince. "Before I do anything else, I want my money."

The man in the tuxedo snarled back, "I told you, there is no money. I couldn't get the dolt to go through with it. So we're taking the antiques instead. They're worth a fortune."

"I don't want this stuff! I want cash. I did everything you asked, the wallet and the tires. I let the cat out of the car. And now I want to get paid!"

"Meow!" Theodora squawked, and scrambled out of her nest on Baily's chest intent on exacting revenge on her attempted kitty-napper.

Daniel couldn't act quickly enough to prevent Baily's outburst. "Theodora!"

Pierce and the man in brown spotted Daniel and Baily behind the bushes. And both watched as the cat leapt onto the man in brown's leg and began scratching.

"Ow!" he shouted as he tried to shake the attacking animal off of him.

So much for subterfuge. Daniel was about to rush him when Larson reached down and snatched the cat up in his arms.

"Don't move or the cat gets it!"

Daniel and Baily froze in their tracks. "Great," he muttered to Baily.

They all turned in the direction of the sound of another cab pulling up. Nick got out and behind him was a shorter, prettier version of Daniel in a wedding dress. She flew into her brother's arms, oblivious to the stand-off. "Oh, Daniel, I'm so glad you're here," she cried. "Nick told me on the way over that Pierce really did try to stop you from getting to the wedding."

"And I was this close to succeeding," Larson said bitterly. "But now that there isn't going to be a wedding, I'll just take these few pieces as my alimony and be on my way. And I'm taking the cat just in case any of you try anything. Get in the car," he told his partner. The man in brown got in the driver's seat and pushed open the passenger door.

Sarah turned and saw Pierce clutching a cat to his chest. "Daniel, why is he holding a cat?"

"If you hurt her, I'll hunt you down to the ends of the earth," Baily shouted passionately as Pierce slowly made his way to the car.

Daniel looked to Nick and nodded his head in the direction of the car that was still at the bottom of the driveway. Casually he tossed Nick the keys, making his message clear, and turned back to Larson.

"You don't actually think we're going to let you leave here with a fortune in antiques. I mean, it's just a cat."

"Daniel!" Baily shouted. "How could you?"

"Yes, Daniel." Larson smiled slickly just a few feet away from the car now. "How could you?"

"Let him have it all," Sarah told her brother. "It doesn't matter just as long as he's gone."

"Sarah, he's got the Degas. Baily will understand."

"I do not understand! Are you saying that a stupid painting is worth more than my precious Theodora?"

"Meow!" Theodora protested, putting her two cents in.

Daniel turned and saw that Nick had successfully made his escape back to the Corvette. He sighed heavily and put his hands up in surrender. "Fine, take it and go. Just leave us the cat."

"I'll let it go after I'm convinced you're not following us," Larson said, and got in the car. He tossed Theodora onto the back seat not realizing that the back window was open. Instantly, Theodora made her escape, leaping out the back window.

Pierce looked behind him in time to see the cat jump to safety. "Step on it."

The man in brown hit the gas pedal. He checked his rearview mirror to see if anyone chased him and relaxed slightly when he saw that the man and the two women stood rooted in place. He was so concerned with what was behind him he neglected to see what was in front of him.

"Stop!" Pierce shouted. But it was too late. The man in brown looked up to see a Corvette parked smack across the driveway, preventing their escape. At the last moment he tried to swerve, but it made little difference. The beige sedan smashed into the back end of the Corvette. Both

men, neither wearing their seat belts, were knocked sense-
less on the dashboard.

All that was left for Nick and Daniel to do was to call
for police backup.

"I KNEW HE WAS A CON MAN," Daniel said later that night
in the comfort of his living room. The group had ordered
pizza and drunk enough beer to overcome the excitement
of the day.

Baily smiled as Theodora slept soundly in her arms.
"You were right all along. And you were so brave, too."

"You were ready to rip my head off when you thought
I was willing to sacrifice Theodora."

"Yes, but then I understood you were just stalling. Very
clever of you. I should have known better, too. You could
never do anything to hurt Madam President."

"Okay." He shrugged, taking her word for it.

"It certainly was a daring plan," Sarah commented. To
Nick she said, "And it was awfully nice of you to sacrifice
your car like that."

"That's okay. I've always seen myself in a Mercedes.
Black was the color, wasn't it, Dan?"

Catching onto the conversation, Baily turned to Daniel.
"You gave him your car?"

"It seemed only fair," Daniel told her. There had been
nothing left of the tail end of the Corvette. "Nick's going
to fly out to Missoula, pick it up and drive it back."

"But what will you do?"

"I'm going to rent a car here. Then I'm driving back to
Seattle." It was said without emotion, but Baily knew what
he meant. His decision was made. He was leaving.

At least that's what he thought.

IT WAS THE NEXT MORNING, in front of Baily's house, and
Daniel stood in front of his rental car and tried to convince
Baily for the final time that he was in fact leaving.

"I'm going." Daniel didn't know how to say it any plainer.

Baily stood on the driveway with him, her arms folded in front of her. "You only think you're leaving."

"No, I know I'm leaving."

"Okay," she said. But she didn't believe it. They had spent last night together making love over and over again. In her heart she knew a man couldn't touch her like that or love her like that and not be in love. At least, that was what she was counting on. She had hoped he would realize it before he left, but now it looked as if he might actually go. So she just had to hope that he would come to his senses somewhere along the trip and come back.

"I wanted to tell Nick that I appreciated his help yesterday."

"He's at work. You can thank him the next time you see him," she said with what she hoped was a confident smile.

With a resigned sigh, Daniel tried again. "I'm serious, Red. I'm going. I'll be in Indiana by the time your brother gets home."

"Okay."

"You're never going to see me again," he said once more, hoping to impart the significance of this moment.

"I might see you again," she tried.

"You won't," he insisted, although even as he said it he wasn't exactly sure.

"Maybe."

"Not going to happen."

"It could. You never know. And if you do change your mind somewhere along the way, promise not to drive like a maniac getting back to me." Baily turned and walked up the driveway without a backward glance.

He was stupefied. No kiss goodbye. No tears. No "I'll always love you, Daniel." Nothing. Fine, he thought bitterly, getting into the car. If she wanted to live in her little fantasy world, so be it. He was going back to Seattle. Back to sanity, which as far as he could tell was about as far away from one Baily Monohan as a person could get.

Baily watched the car pull away from her driveway and decided that absolutely under no circumstances was she going to cry. She might feel the water build behind her eyes. Her nose might be getting a little stuffy, but she wasn't going to cry. No sirree, not her. She had faith.

He would be back within the day.

She hoped. Okay, maybe she was going to cry just a little.

DANIEL WAS TIRED and cranky from driving so long. All he wanted to do was to pull off to the side of the road and sleep for the next year. Instead he made it to a moderately seedy hotel in Indiana. The atmosphere didn't help his mood. After a day in the car without Baily's witty banter, he felt starved for companionship. Something that he'd never had a problem with before. The only thing to greet him in the hotel room was a television and a bunch of reruns.

A cat. That's what he would do when he got home. He'd get a cat and name it Georgette Washington. Perhaps that would make him miss Baily just a little bit less.

No, he couldn't think that way. If he began thinking about how much he missed her, he would consider doing something stupid like turning around and going home.

Ah! There he went again thinking that Philadelphia was

home. It wasn't. Seattle was his destination. That's where he was going.

"WHERE IS DANIEL?" Baily's mother asked. It was just the three of them, Baily and her parents, who sat down to dinner. Nick was pulling a double shift, something he did often since his divorce, and James was off on another business trip. Baily wasn't happy about the fact that there wasn't anyone around to cushion the blow she was about to give her parents, but she guessed they deserved the truth.

"Right now?"

"Baily Christmas Monohan." Mary Ellen's tone said it all.

She couldn't help but wince at the use of her full name. Her father, she noticed, winced, as well.

"I would guess he's in Indiana."

"Indiana!" This from her mother and her father at the same time.

In her calmest tone Baily explained, "Don't worry, he'll be back. He thinks he's leaving me, but he won't be able to go through with it. I don't think I gave him enough credit for his stubbornness though. It might take him more than a day to come to his senses. I give him until Wyoming."

DID THE STATE of Wyoming ever end? The barren landscape was grating on his nerves. When he looked in front of him all he saw were waves of beige grass. When he closed his eyes, all he saw was Red.

He missed her. He missed her so damn much!

Suddenly, Daniel brought the car to a screeching halt in the middle of the road. Normally that might have caused a multicar crash. But since Daniel was convinced that no one actually lived in the State of Wyoming, he wasn't worried about the consequences.

Looking up, he spotted the sign that had caused him to stop. Chugwater was only ten miles ahead. Chugwater. Her voice filled the car. Her laughter rang in his ears. Her face swam in front of his eyes. He loved her. The circle he'd worked so hard to keep so small had expanded despite his wishes, and it wasn't going to get any smaller. He loved her. He loved her cat; he was even beginning to love her family. There was only one thing left to do.

It was time to go home.

The problem was how the hell was he going to be able to return to her and still maintain a little pride? Daniel weighed the options in his mind.

A little pride.

Red.

A little pride.

Red!

No contest. With a quick jerk of the wheel, Daniel managed to make a U-turn in the middle of the road. What he didn't manage to do was to avoid the large cow that had wandered into the middle of said road while he'd done his mental weighing.

"Mooo!"


"HEY, SIS, don't fret it. He'll be back or he won't. You've got to stop worrying about it." Nick leaned back on the couch with a beer in hand.

Baily heard her brother's words and knew how right he was. The last thing she wanted to be was some clinging woman who was waiting for a man to make her happy. She would get over him if he never returned. She would have to. It's just that she didn't want to.

"I'm not worried," she lied.

Nick chuckled then stood and headed up the stairs for bed.

Baily resumed her vigil in silence. She was staring so intently out the window that she almost missed the phone ringing. It was after eleven at night. Who would be calling now?

Baily leapt from her position on the love seat and winced as her body protested the sudden movement.

"Hello?"

There was a pause. "Meet me at the damn airport tomorrow morning. Delta. Flight 701."

A click followed the sentence, and for a moment Baily wasn't sure what had just happened. And then she did.

"He's coming back! He's coming back!" Baily shouted it as if from the rooftop.

Nick came rushing down the stairs, after hearing her shout. When he reached the bottom, he spotted Baily standing in the middle of the living room sobbing.

"What is it? What happened?"

Choking back her sobs she told him. "He's coming back."

"Yeah. And you're crying because..."

"He's flying," Baily told him, expecting her brother to see the significance of that statement. He didn't, and Baily only cried harder.

SHE WAS PACING back and forth by the gate when the flight was announced. She spotted him walking toward her and her heart jumped into her throat. His skin was pale, his mouth drawn. The man was terrified.

Then he spotted her and his eyes signaled relief mixed with joy. Baily jumped the rope that held her back from the exiting passengers. Banging into several disgruntled travelers, she threw herself into his arms.

"I didn't know. I hoped, but I didn't know for sure if you would be back," she told him, while she placed kisses all over his face and chased away the demons that still haunted him.

"Yes, you did," Daniel said, wrapping her in his arms and kissing her until her knees gave out from underneath her.

"I flew," he said wanting to explain.

"Yep." Baily didn't want or need explanations.

"I'm afraid to fly. I have been ever since my parents' death."

"That I knew."

"I love you."

"I'm pretty sure I knew that, too."

What Baily wanted to know was what was next. "Where to now?" she asked, breathless and anxious. She had a wedding to plan, children to create, a home to fill with love. She was pressed for time.

Daniel wrapped his arm around her and tucked her close against his body. He could have sworn he heard the sound of them clicking together.

"Home," Daniel said. Then because it sounded so good, he said it again. "Home."

# 1

---

"So you and young Eddie didn't hit it off, huh?" Her father's question echoed with blatant disappointment.

Thankful that phones still lacked video capability, Wendy Marek rolled her eyes. "We didn't have time to, Dad," she said, trying to be patient, though she couldn't help wondering where even this level of interest had been when she'd really needed it. "He was already blasted when he picked me up at eight. By ten o'clock, he'd passed out."

"That's too bad," was the only sympathy Wendy's father gave her wasted Saturday night. "Well, I noticed a new electrician's apprentice at the 'Lyssian Fields's site Friday. I'll ask—"

"Dad!" Wendy quickly cut him off. Holy hubcaps, his matchmaking obsession was driving her crazy! "Please— no more blind dates."

"But, sweetie," her dad protested, "you're—" *beep* "—wenty-four years old. Do you want to be a secretary for the rest of your life?"

"No-ooh," Wendy said, feeling her temper slip a notch and stifling a yawn at the same time. Eddie fiasco aside, she'd spent most of the weekend working and reworking her budget. Trying to squeeze dollars out of nickels. "That's why I applied to the Paris Design Institute, remember?"

She'd been accepted, too, but she only had a few more months to scare up the tuition money.

"Paris!" Her dad dismissed the city—and her dream of

studying fashion design at P.D.I.—with a sound that would earn the admiration of her friend Robin's nine-year-old son Max. *Beep* "—rong with getting married?"

Wendy rolled her eyes again. Ever since her brother Patrick had outed himself at a neighborhood block party, Dad had been pushing her to marry and to give him grand-kids.

Didn't he know? Hadn't he learned that marriage was no substitute for creativity and kids weren't enough of an outlet for an artist who needed to express herself in con-crete terms?

Well, Wendy knew—and she was determined not to re-peat her mother's mistake.

"Hold on, Dad," Wendy said wearily. "I've got another call."

She'd never trade the creative career she craved for a family she'd abandon a few years later. "Let me see who it is."

Ruefully wishing her father would support *her* dreams instead of his own, Wendy clicked over. "Hello?"

"Is this Wendy Marek?" The caller's monotone sounded almost computer-generated.

"Ye-es."

"Sorry to disturb you on a Sunday evening, Ms. Marek." The flat voice didn't sound particularly regretful.

"That's okay." As long as whoever this was didn't try to railroad her into marriage, she'd be happy to talk to him.

"Are you employed by a university there in St. Louis?"

"Who, uh, who wants to know?" *Please let this not be a bill collector.* It had taken her six months to save up the P.D.I. deposit. One unexpected additional expense and her checking account would self-destruct.

"This is Agent Rudolph Roland," the voice rattled off, still as flat as western Kansas. "I'm with the U.S. Immi-gration and Naturalization Service in Chicago."

Immigration? Nuts. Her parents had been here five years

when her older brother, Patrick, had been born—and she was three years younger than him.

"What's this about, Agent Roland?"

"Are you expecting a Peter Havel?" The agent's tone remained unchanged.

"Oh!" Sheer relief had her babbling. "Yes, yes! He *is* scheduled to arrive tonight—I'm picking him up at his hotel in the morning."

Agent Roland managed to contain his excitement. "For the record, then, this individual is known to you?" he droned. "His arrival is expected and you are anticipating his visit to this country?"

The only thing Wendy was anticipating was going to Paris. If her dad would get over his obsession with her getting married and help her with the tuition. Otherwise... There were no scholarships for Americans—and although she'd never seen the document to read the fine print, she'd always been told that she couldn't touch her share of her grandparents' trust fund until she turned thirty.

"Ms. Marek?"

Oh, yeah. The Havel guy... "We haven't actually met in person," Wendy admitted. "Just over the Net."

"Over the—" The unflappable Agent Roland uttered a Federal Communications Commission infraction. "But you are expecting him—this Dr. Havel?" he asked after a moment of disapproving silence.

"Heck, yes!" Her boss, Dean Leippert, and Dr. Boroni, one of the antiques in the math department, were beside themselves over the brainiac's visit. "With bated breath," she assured Roland cheerfully.

"Very well," the agent said—taciturnly, of course. "We just needed to confirm that. Thank you and have a good evening."

"You're welco—"

The guy hung up before she could finish the syllable.

Wendy committed her own F.C.C. offense as she

clicked back over to her father. Was this Self-Absorbed Males Make Phone Calls Night?

"Thanks for waiting, Dad. I'm back."

"Was that Eddie?" her father asked eagerly. "Maybe you should give him another chance, honey. Mechanics make good money and—"

"I don't care if he's a gazillionaire, Dad! I don't want to get married. I want to go to Paris to study fashion design."

Phooey on this "want to" stuff, Wendy thought, looking across the room at the chaos of fabric, pattern paper and sketching materials left over from her application portfolio. She *was* going to Paris. She *was* building herself a career in a creative field. She was *not* getting sucked instead into that marriage/baby-carriage thing. It led straight to discontent.

And to innocent people getting hurt.

But she needed a financial windfall to pursue her dream.

She either had to start playing the lottery or to figure out a way to wean her father from his grandbaby fixation. Or wait six more years. Or change the date on her birth certificate.

*Bet I'm the only woman in America who can't wait to turn thirty!*

"I've got to go, Dad," she said, again interrupting his renewed plea for an heir. As if her brother couldn't take over her father's plumbing business just because he was gay. "But I'll make you a deal. You think about me going to Paris and I'll think about getting married."

She would, she thought as she hung up. The same way she'd think about volunteering to be trapped on a desert island with a serial killer....

PETER HAVEL NODDED farewell to the flight attendants, then doggedly followed his fellow passengers out the jetway and down the carpeted terminal. Hoping they would lead him to the baggage claim area. Otherwise, he admitted as he adjusted his grip on his carry-on, he might not find it.

His eyelids felt like coarse sandpaper and the letters on the airport signage were jumping around too much to read.

After more surgeries than he cared to remember, the vision in his left eye was still blurry, the hearing loss in his left ear around eighty percent—and that was under the best of circumstances.

Which *now* wasn't.

*Now* was a midnight arrival in the mid-American city of St. Louis, hours later than scheduled, thanks to that delay at Customs and Immigration in Chicago.

He still didn't know what the problem had been. He'd explained his changing the Czech spelling of his name—"Petr"—to the more American "Peter" on correspondence, but they wanted something else explained, too. He'd tried to bluff his way through their questions, but finally had been forced to hand over his letter from the university.

Peter growled. He hated accommodating his handicaps and he despised asking for help. But it had worked. After copying the letter and making a phone call—to his supervisor, Peter guessed—the dour bureaucrat had filled out another form, then stamped his passport and allowed him to complete his journey.

Almost. He still needed to reacquire his suitcases. Then find the hotel.

He supposed he could ask someone about luggage—if he swallowed his pride *and* remembered enough English to form the question properly.

But between the cavernous, arching space of the St. Louis airport and his damaged ear roaring with the pounding-surf sound that always accompanied fatigue, understanding a response would be impossible.

Perhaps he *should* have accepted the assistance offered in the letter....

Bah! He was not helpless. Damned if he would act that way.

That's why he'd spent the past year in remote southeastern Siberia, Peter conceded as he trailed his guides past a phalanx of phone booths, most of them occupied even at this ungodly late hour.

He'd been holed up in the Altai Republic like one of its snow leopards retreating to its den to lick his wounds. Swallowing the disappointing results of the last operation. And avoiding any more of his ex-fiancée's relentless smothering. They'd been engaged two years, neither of them in any hurry to settle down.

But he'd broken the engagement three months after the operation—when Katrina'd tried to wipe his nose for him.

*Hovno!* He'd wanted to get married, not be coddled like an egg.

The next person who tried to baby him would see those swirling cartoon stars, Peter vowed silently, moving past a wall of backlit fast-food ads.

A voice suddenly blared from the overhead speakers, further exacerbating the fatigue-worsened damage caused by his collision with an opposing player, the goalpost and the boards in the last game of his Olympic hockey career.

Peter's steps slowed momentarily as the memories flooded through him. The capacity crowd, on its feet, cheering as his Czech Republic teammate stole the puck and dished it to him in the final minute of the gold-medal game. The satisfying rush of adrenaline as he'd swooped down the ice, then Fortisev's check…the blinding flashes, the exploding pain as his head hit metal. Blackness. And more pain….

*Stop,* he ordered, resuming his pace. *The past is over.*

At twenty-eight, he had a new life. After the accident, unable to pursue the surgical career he'd planned, he'd turned from medicine to chemistry and mathematics. He'd found solace in the elegant complexity of crystalline-structure matrices and nonlinear differential equations.

A few months ago he'd conceived a new approach to Gandel's Anomaly and had consulted Emil Boroni, one of the world's leading authorities in this branch of higher mathematics, by e-mail.

As a result he'd been invited to St. Louis to work on the Anomaly with Dr. Boroni and to review a project within his field of expertise for some of the chemistry faculty.

*And then?*

Peter shrugged. After St. Louis, he was scheduled to collaborate with Wilkersen at U.C.L.A. Then there was the contract to deliver a series of lectures in Guadalajara.

Yes, this was his life now: nomadic mathematician.

"Is fine," Peter muttered fiercely. He didn't need to be settled. He didn't need a wife and family. He didn't need anyone.

*No one needs you, either,* whispered a little voice through the roaring surf in his head.

Peter ignored it, since it never had anything useful to say.

The herd of travelers wheeled left. Peter did, too, but that set the wide walkway spinning. Muttering under his breath, he halted until the walls went stationary again, then hurried to catch up.

Maybe he *should* have allowed someone from the university to meet him tonight....

"No," Peter growled as his guides turned right into another long hallway and he carefully followed their lead. He could find his own way out of an airport!

Minutes later, the crowd left the last gate behind and split apart. Some headed directly for doors set in a towering wall of glass arches now black with night. Trailing the others, Peter ascended a short ramp to—

At last. Baggage Claim.

He joined the clumps of people to stare at gleaming

stainless carousels. One of which eventually disgorged his luggage.

Moving slowly to avoid upsetting his equilibrium again—*that* legacy of Fortisev's cross-check worsened with fatigue, too—Peter claimed his bags, proved they were his to the luggage guard, then carried them out to the taxi stand, where he showed his itinerary sheet to the nearest driver.

When he pointed to the hotel, the cabbie nodded, threw his suitcases into the trunk and motioned Peter into the back seat.

Leaning back and closing his eyes as the taxi pulled away from the terminal and threaded its way onto a highway entrance ramp, Peter made himself think in English. *You see? I need no help. I am care to myself.*

Twenty minutes later, after paying the cabdriver—at least they'd let him use the Automated Teller Machine during that delay in Chicago—he pantomimed his way through registering at the hotel. Waving away the yawning bellman, he hefted his two suitcases and the carry-on containing his laptop and set off to find his room unaided. Finally, exhausted but triumphant, he used the card key and dragged his suitcases inside.

A king-size bed filled the room.

*A king-size,* lonely *bed,* whispered that little voice as Peter closed the door with his hip and shoved the luggage against a wall.

*Not lonely, dammit, just empty. Unoccupied.*

"Correct that I will," he murmured, stripping off his shoes.

Fatigue and blurred vision slowed the process, of course, but eventually he had the bedside clock's alarm set.

Peter turned the volume as high as it would go. He hoped it would be high enough.

Straightening, he rubbed the damaged side of his face, then removed his shirt, socks and slacks. With the last of his energy, he pulled back the dark floral bedcover and aimed himself at the mattress.

*Ahh...*

He was asleep by the time his cheek hit the pillow.


WENDY HALTED just inside the hotel's imposing entrance until her eyes adjusted from bright morning sunlight to refined dimness.

Then she headed for the bank of elevators on the far side of the lobby's rug-strewn, gleaming-marble acreage—to pick up the latest genius too brilliant to find the campus by himself.

After punching the up-arrow button, Wendy rocked back on her heels to wait.

Her dad had one thing right, she decided, tucking her hair behind her ears with a sigh. Much as she loved her boss and colleagues, she did *not* want to be a secretary the rest of her life.

So why couldn't her father just support her plans for her life instead of searching out every employed single male in St. Louis?

Wendy tucked again. Expressing her creative flare in a career in fashion design would give her all the emotional satisfaction she'd ever need—and without the risk of a broken home.

She had to come up with that tuition money.

*Ding!* Three elevators signaled their arrival simultaneously. Wendy momentarily abandoned her search for a solution to her financial crisis. Time to collect Dean Leippert's visiting genius.

*I hope the old guy speaks* some *English,* Wendy thought as she waited for six chattering nametags to exit before stepping into the nearest car and punching the button for the eleventh floor.

The doors closed, the elevator achieved liftoff; after a few irritating bars of saccharinized heavy-metal music, it stopped and opened its doors again. Getting off, Wendy began reading room number plaques along the silent, anonymous hallway. Eleven-seventeen—wasn't that it?

Mentally crossing her fingers, Wendy knocked on the so-labeled door and waited. She could remember colors, textures and complicated garment construction techniques, but numbers slipped her mind like silk from polished marble.

Another knock, another wait.

Wendy sighed as she recalled the last visiting professor they'd had. Lifzmeier. Frail, elderly—and so preoccupied with neutrinos he couldn't keep track of his sweater.

More knocking. More waiting.

Darn it, she didn't have time to baby-sit another absentminded genius! "So don't," Wendy advised herself. "Tell the brainiac to watch his own sweater." Pleased with her assertiveness, she raised her hand to knock again.

Just as her knuckles contacted the surface of the hotel room door, it opened....

Wendy felt her throat dry and her jaw slacken as she stared at the massive, muscular, golden expanse only inches away.

*It's a chest,* she realized finally, her fist still suspended in midair.

*A hard, naked,* magnificent *male chest.*

"S-sorry. Wrong room," she croaked—just as The Chest, incredibly, expanded even more and a deep, husky voice purred, *"Dobré ráno."*

# 2

*"DOBRÉ RÁNO,"* Wendy echoed mechanically, still glazing—er, gazing—at the cloud of dark gold crinkly hairs that sprinkled across the muscular expanse of chest then coalesced into a line traveling down its center to the leading edge of—she swallowed—a *very* well-filled pair of black-cotton, thigh-hugging boxer briefs.

Quickly she jerked her eyes upward. The greeting was the only Czech she'd learned from her grandmama Ana, who'd come to stay with them for a few months after her mother split. Once Wendy'd proven she could cook and keep house well enough to keep the Marek men alive, Grandmama had returned to Florida.

"Good morning," Wendy repeated in English, her feeble hope that she'd knocked on the wrong door dying as it formed.

Even a math midget such as herself knew that the odds of two Czechs in the same St. Louis hotel were not good.

"You are from the university?" The Chest asked in that deep, deliciously accented voice.

Wendy nodded slowly.

*Get a grip,* she ordered herself.

So Leippert's latest guest professor worked out a little.

*Yeah, like Bill Gates is slightly rich.*

"I, uh… Yes. I'm Wendy Marek," she managed to finally say, rousing herself from her contemplation of the most magnificent male torso she'd ever seen. The cotton-covered part of his anatomy seemed pretty, er, *magnificent,* too. "Welcome to St. Louis, Dr. Havel."

"Americans are not so formal," the lightly clothed Czech declared.

Wendy felt her jaw drop again. *Answering the door in your underwear—even if it resembles bike shorts—is formal?*

"You are calling me Peter and I will call you Wendy. Okay?"

Her gaze threatened to slide downward again toward that intriguing black-cotton region; she forced it upward to the face that topped all that magnificence.

And stifled a groan with difficulty.

Peter Havel's face and body were a perfect match: hard, sculpted, ruthlessly masculine. From his deep-set, smoky-blue eyes—one of which was bracketed by faint lines that disappeared into his thick, golden hair—to his strong, straight nose, to the chiseled mouth, to the hard jaw and planed cheeks wearing a dangerously sexy shadow of beard and... *Pillow creases?*

"Don't tell me, let me guess," Wendy blurted in an effort to fight the heat licking through her body as she stood so close to this so-undressed babe magnet. "You just woke up."

"Yes, I have just awakened," Peter admitted, then clamped his mouth shut. Why was he about to blurt excuses to this little... *little enchantress, spitting fire like a cranky kitten?*

*Blbec!* he chided himself. *No woman affects you this way.*

Until now. And it did not require perfect vision to discern the charms of this feisty female who barely reached his chin. Her silky brown hair probably danced with coppery highlights in the sun, her eyes were as green as a May meadow and, when he'd first opened the door, her hint of a smile warmed his insides like brandy on a winter's night.

"I'm here to drive you to the university," the little tigress proclaimed in barely slow enough English. "But you'll have to humor me and get dressed first."

She took a step forward.

*Mmm, patchouli.* Peter's primary erogenous zone responded vigorously to her subtle, arousing scent.

He turned, hoping to distract them both from his body's erotic enhancement. The half spin allowed him to hear her mutter, "I expected you to be ready by now."

He was ready all right. Readier than he'd been in years.

She was correct, though. He should already be dressed. Judging by its display, the alarm clock had been buzzing almost twenty minutes before he'd awakened. He'd just turned it off and begun to grope his way to the bathroom when he'd heard a small, intermittent sound. With his damaged ear, it had taken him three tries to localize it as knocking on the door.

"You are to forgive me," he informed her, coolly arching an eyebrow. *Be smart, Havel.* His foolish and unexpected attraction to the unimpressed Wendy Marek would doubtless lead nowhere—except, perhaps, to the one thing he could not tolerate: pity. "I do not sleep fully clothed."

"I'm sure that's your wife's concern, Dr. Havel, not mine," she snapped, her eyes flashing like emeralds in sunlight.

"I am not married," Peter replied, covering a flicker of regret with more ice. Not that he missed Katrina's insulting treatment. He'd simply always expected to live his life *with* someone rather than alone. Isolated.

"And I'm not interested."

Humph. Judging by the thorough way she'd inventoried his body, Wendy's words were not strictly accurate.

"Because *you* are married," he ventured, his curiosity as aroused as his masculine interest.

"Not even. I've got other things to do with my life besides sign up for the ol' ball and chain."

Peter didn't understand most of that, but the message

was clear. Wendy Marek might look him over like a vegan eyeing a ripe peach, but she was not shopping to buy.

For a moment the challenge tempted him....

But he did not wish to see sympathy replace sensual interest in this woman's lovely green eyes. *Hmm.* Had Katrina's post-accident pity battered his self-confidence so severely he was afraid to flirt? If so, he would correct that, but not now. And not with a colleague.

*So stick to business, Havel.* "How am I late?"

Wendy blinked. A little furrow appeared between her brows. And Peter felt an urge to smooth it away with a fingertip.

Instead he tried another sentence construction. "I am late how much?"

Her brow cleared, her lips curved upward. They looked soft and sweet. He wanted to taste them, wanted to cover her mouth with his, wanted to—

Bah. Was he so eager to recoup his male pride that he would volunteer for certain rejection?

"Dean Leippert is expecting you in—" Wendy looked at her watch.

While she did that, Peter studied *her,* turning his head slightly to the left to minimize the input of his weak eye. A long, loose jacket with an eye-catching asymmetrical opening hid most of her body, yet hinted at delightful curves.

"...about half an hour."

Mmm. The matching short skirt might be skimming a pair of long, enticing legs. He tilted his head a bit more.

"And since the university is twenty minutes away—"

"You worry I could arrive late." Peter concluded the mathematical exercise.

"If you don't get a move on," Wendy agreed.

As he tried to make sense of *that,* Peter took a backward step. He still hadn't gotten a clear view of her legs.

Wendy followed him forward, her hands making shooing motions. *As if I am a goose to herd,* Peter thought, grinning at his reaction to her lack of interest in him. He should be insulted—but found it too refreshing to be offensive. And *her* as attractive as hell. An almost irresistible combination. Guaranteed to stimulate his competitive spirit. And one already-aroused body part.

*Unless…* Putting his hands on his hips, he frowned. Had he already released the cat from its box concerning his limitations?

Wendy waggled her hands again. "Anytime today," she suggested, her slightly impatient tone making the phrase's meaning clear.

With a low growl, Peter turned, stalked over to his largest suitcase and hefted it onto the bed with one smooth motion.

He unzipped the bag with two imperious flicks of his wrist as Wendy closed the door behind her and sidled over to the TV, where she stood tucking her hair behind her ears while raptly studying a framed flower print.

She was nervous?

*Continue dreaming, as they say in English. More likely, she is irritated with your slowness.*

"I will require only few minutes—*a* few minutes—to shower and shave," he announced, determined to halt the inner voice now that it had begun to nag again.

"Are you an associate of Dr. Boroni, Wendy?" he asked while he retrieved underwear and socks.

"I'm a secretary," she replied. "I work in Dean Leippert's office."

"How is it you speak my language?" Peter wondered out loud as he located his shaving kit.

He looked up in time to see her tuck her hair again.

"I don't. My grandmother's Czech. She came to live with us for a while after—when I was twelve…." Gripping her elbows, Wendy moved over to study the other floral picture.

There was more to the story—even *he* could see that. But Ms. Marek did not wish to share it with him.

"I understand some Czech," she continued, still not looking at him. "Not much, though, and *dobré ráno* is about all I can say...." Wendy looked at her watch and Peter took the hint.

"After shower, I am dressed. How?"

"How what?" Wendy asked, glancing around at... something, anything, to avoid ogling the rumpled bed. Or the massive, magnificent torso so perfectly visible above the suitcase on it. Not that she *needed* to look at either one. Her imagination was already in overdrive, working up exquisite combinations of cool, cotton sheets and taut, hot skin—

"How am I to dress?" he asked patiently.

*Quickly,* Wendy thought in desperation. *Cover that incredible physique with some clothes.* Any kind of clothes. The more, the bulkier, the better.

"I wish to make proper impression when first appearing at university," the hunka-hunka raw Czech sex appeal declared as he dug deeper into the suitcase.

*That shouldn't be a problem.*

For a mathematician, Peter Havel was killer attractive. Tall, but not outrageously. Six-one probably—lean and muscular, narrow hips, wide shoulders, powerful thighs. Not to mention that chest with its enticing cover of dark, crinkly hair!

Jeez Louise—any woman with a pulse would be lusting after those sleepy blue eyes, those golden pecs...*that bulging black cotton!*

"I have come from the Altai."

Even his accent sounded erotic—er, exotic—wrapped in that deep, velvety voice. "There is not much..." He paused, obviously unable to complete the sentence in English.

And apparently unwilling to test her Czech comprehension. That boded well, Wendy thought with relief. No baby-sitting.

"Perhaps my wardrobe is not..." Peter paused again,

rubbing one side of his beard-stubbled jaw as he searched for a word. "Appropriate?" he offered.

Wendy groaned silently. Vulnerability peeked from the depths of Peter's smoky-blue eyes, which were framed— she couldn't help noticing—by thick lashes *exactly* one shade darker than his longish, disheveled, dark gold hair.

It disappeared as quickly as a snowflake would on this already-hot, late-August morning, of course, but the damage was done.

Empathy bubbled through her like yeast through warm bread dough as Wendy considered the situation from Peter's standpoint.

Gorgeous, nearly naked hunk or not, the man was alone in a strange culture, preparing to meet and work with some of the best minds in his field, while having to grapple with the weirdest language on earth. On top of which—

"You flew in last night, all the way from this Altai place?" she asked.

Peter nodded slowly. "From Barnaul to St. Petersburg is—" he rubbed one side of his face "—five hours, three time zones. From St. Petersburg to Copenhagen, then to Chicago, then St. Louis is nine more time changes, twelve more hours in plane flying. Plus waiting between flights and going through customs...." He lifted and lowered one huge shoulder.

No wonder he'd had trouble waking up this morning. "You're jet-lagged," Wendy declared.

"Excuse?" When he cocked his head like that, one long strand of golden hair brushed over an adorably crooked eyebrow.

Oh, nuts. She'd been listening to her dad's matrimonial brainwashing too long. Women focused on a career didn't classify eyebrows as adorable—even though Peter's definitely were. "Never mind." Wendy shook her head briskly. "About your wardrobe... St. Louis swelters this time of year, and the math department—"

"Chemistry," Peter interjected in purring, velvety English.

*Heck, yes, there's chemistry going on here!* Wendy expected spontaneous combustion to occur any minute now. "C-chemistry?" she croaked.

Methodically, Peter removed items from his luggage, stacking them neatly on the bed. "I will be working with some of your chemistry faculty, also."

"Oh." Wendy struggled to corral her wayward thoughts. "Well, they're not exactly a hotbed of fashion forwardness, either. The whole faculty's pretty laid-back—about everything except the sci-fi channel, that is."

Silence. Then, "Excuse, please?"

For a second Wendy actually considered trying to translate the whole speech into Czech. Gave it up in favor of getting that magnificent male musculature covered. A.S.A.P. Her hormones were surging again—like a bunch of lemmings heading for the nearest cliff at warp speed.

"Do you own a coat and tie?" she asked grimly, curling her fingers into fists.

"Yes, *milenko,*" he assured her with a sexy chuckle that somehow clearly defined the word's sappy meaning.

"I'm not your *mil*-whatever," she corrected him instantly. She wasn't anyone's sweetheart—smooth-talking Czech geniuses included—and she intended to stay that way. She was going to Paris. To study fashion design and to fulfill her need for creative expression *before* risking the complications romance could cause. *If* she could scrape together the dinero.... "Wear whatever you want," she suggested, pivoting and heading for the door. "I'll wait downstairs."

"First, you are making coffee, please?"

Was this persistent self-interest thing a sex-linked genetic defect? Wendy wondered, spinning around to straighten out the... *Ooooh!*

But Peter didn't give her the chance. "I ask big favor, I know," he purred with a sweet, lopsided, freaking *irre-*

*sistible* smile as he indicated the small coffeemaker next to the TV. "But only to rescue, no—*save?*—time while I am within the shower. The lagging jets..." he added, shrugging one broad shoulder and smiling crookedly again. "My head stays in the Altai."

Well, shoot. When he put it that way.... Wendy retraced her steps, thunked her purse onto the counter, lifted the carafe from the warming plate and began filling it at the sink.

"*A* shower is more correct? I cannot keep straight." Peter's deep voice slid over her skin like smooth, heavy satin....

Cold water overflowed the carafe and soaked her sleeve.

"Either way is fine," Wendy said as she twisted the faucet shut and turned around. "And it's 'save.' Time, that is."

"I will remember," the math whiz hottie promised in that plush voice, twinkling those smoky-blue eyes and flashing a smile that could melt steel plate at ninety paces. "And I will be wet only short time," he added as Wendy marched herself past him to clunk the carafe down beside the coffeemaker.

"Take your time," she suggested, picking up the foil pouch containing the coffee filter pack and shaking it energetically. "It's your impression."

After a short pause Peter gave another wickedly alluring chuckle, then disappeared into the bathroom.

Finally.

Wendy's relief died a quick death. At the sound of cascading water, heated images pulsated through her head. Steamy images of slick, golden skin and silvery droplets of water beading on that crinkly mat of—

Ripping open the coffee prepack, she dropped it in the brew basket, slid that into place and poured the water through.

*Calm down,* Wendy told herself, reclaiming her purse

while the coffeemaker hissed and dripped its dark brew into the pot.

*So the guy's sort of—hot.*

*Yeah. Like a habanero pepper. In Death Valley. In July.*

Well, once she delivered him to Dean Leippert and Dr. Boroni, her dealings with Peter Havel would be limited to public places and academic issues.

Another half hour with the Czech Chest wasn't going to kill her.

She actually believed that, too—until he emerged from the bathroom, one totally inadequate hotel towel wrapped around his flat abdomen, his hair gleaming wetly, his firm, newly shaven jaw glistening smoothly, a few random drops of water sparkling from his torso....

Huh. Any woman immune to that much masculine appeal would automatically have her femininity revoked.

Holding the towel carelessly low on his hips, he padded toward her. She caught a whiff of soap and clean male as he reached past her to snag the carafe, pour himself a cup of java juice and lift the steaming coffee to his lips.

"Thank you for brewing the coffee, Wendy." After taking a sip and sighing with pleasure, Peter strolled across the room and bent over the clothes he'd laid out on the bed.

Mmm, even the man's walk was pure pleasure to watch—a lithe, graceful cross between a stride and a swagger that made her knees go weak.

Wendy staggered—er, retreated—toward the door.

*Get. Over. It.* She was heading to Paris to develop her God-given talent for design, not going ga-ga over some sexy math prof. She hadn't met a guy yet who'd tempted her enough to forget what she'd learned from her parents: that love and creativity didn't mix—and Peter Havel wasn't going to be the exception.

"I don't mean to nag," Wendy said through clenched teeth when he swayed toward the suitcase as if reconsidering his clothing selections. "But hurry up and get dressed!"

Peter straightened, a devilish twinkle brightening his incredible smoky-blues. "Are you sure you wish me to dress this fast?" he asked, grinning as he loosened his grip on the towel, threatening total disclosure.

"What do you think you're doing?" Wendy cried, whirling around, telling herself to keep her eyes on the door panel, unable to keep her mind there, though.

He hadn't revealed a thing, of course, but—what if the item-formerly-covered-by-black-cotton *did* match the magnificence of the rest of his body? Her breath lodged in her throat.

"I am obeying orders," Peter replied blandly. "You are so in much hurry..." His deep voice tapered off as he puzzled over the mangled English phrase.

"In such a hurry," Wendy supplied, determinedly staring at the plaque on the door.

"I must say I do not find much pattern in your language," Peter informed her over the crackle of starched cotton being unfolded.

"There is no rhyme or reason to English," she agreed, glancing at her watch. "We should be leaving soon."

"I am almost dressed," Peter assured her, the words a sexy rumble within the sounds of rustling fabric.

Wendy resisted the urge to personally determine the state of his clothing. Instead, she forced herself to read the tiny type expounding on maximum room rates, checkout times, what to do in case of fire....

The *zzzt* of a metal zipper, then Peter's deep voice announced, "Ready for exhibition. I hope I am appearing appropriate."

Wendy turned—and sagged back against the door.

In such a classic, staid outfit—khaki slacks over those black boxer briefs that still bulged—er, burned—in her memory banks, a white shirt covering that incredible chest *with* an effort and a gold-buttoned black blazer—Peter Havel should have looked dull. Boring.

But with that mane of hair like silken sunlight, those knockout blue eyes, the rugged attractiveness of his face *and* the sculpted, masculine beauty of his body… "Fine," she croaked, swallowing a groan. "You look…fine."

A slight understatement.

*Like calling Einstein's intelligence "above average."*

"Then we shall go?" Peter asked, strolling toward her.

Wendy tore open the door and threw herself out of the room.

*Okay,* she thought dazedly as she sped down the hallway to the elevator, *so he's gorgeous and brilliant and… and…gorgeous.*

Her dad would go wild over this guy's potential gene pool contributions! Wendy pressed the down-arrow button. *But I'm not interested.* Except maybe in the donation process….

Frantically, she jabbed the already lit button again.

"After you, Dr. Havel," she breathed when the elevator doors finally split open.

"This is not right, also," Peter said, holding the door with one hand, sweeping his other in a gallant arc to usher her into the elevator first.

"Thanks," Wendy murmured as he took his place beside her and pressed the button for the lobby. "Although completely unnecessary."

Sir Galahad pretended not to hear her.

TWO MINUTES LATER, as Wendy disappeared around a fountain surrounded by large plants, Peter stuffed his hands into his pockets and scowled at her retreating back. He supposed he could have chased after her, asked her to repeat what she'd said just before veering away as they crossed the lobby, but…

All he'd heard clearly was, "Wait here."

So here he waited. Recalling his enjoyment of the last half hour. And reminding himself of its pointlessness.

So Wendy Marek had admired his body. And she'd almost snapped at him a time or two.

That didn't mean she liked him.

It just meant she didn't know about his flaws. When she did... Peter growled.

But until this woman, this morning, he'd forgotten the fun of flirting, the joy of matching wits with a smart, attractive woman. His struggle to heal was not over, he realized. The damage done by Fortisev's cross-check and Katrina's coddling was deeper than the loss of sight or hearing. It had affected his confidence, his very spirit, his competitive drive. Until now.

*Hovno,* how his heart had leapt when Wendy had marched out of his room just now, ignored him in the elevator, as if— *Oh.*

Now he understood. She couldn't wait to get him beyond her hands.

Out from her hands? Away of—?

Bah. She was not interested in him.

And who would blame her? Peter thought heavily as he watched the checkout frenzy at the nearby reception desk.

Whatever she'd said to him just now had been lost in the jumble of noise around him.

And that was his reality now.

The last operation had produced no measurable improvement. His balance was unreliable; his hearing and vision impairments permanent.

As was the loneliness that came with being isolated by such physical limitations.

Bah. He was not lonely. He was alone—and would stay that way before he'd accept pity as a substitute for love and mutual respect.

Wendy reappeared around the indoor jungle—and his body didn't care about respect. It responded to the sexy sway of her hips, the coppery highlights in her hair, those incredible legs....

*Blbec!* He *was* a fool. He knew this woman would not want him the way he was now—and he desired her anyway.

In an amazingly primitive, elemental way.

God help him, he actually wanted to stride across the figured carpet, closing the gap that separated them. He wanted to carry her back upstairs and down, down, down onto that unmade bed. Take her mouth with his. Then slide a hand under that enticing, camouflaging suit and discover the exact shape of her curves, explore her feminine secrets with his fingertips. Teach her his—

Muttering a Czech oath unsuited for mixed company, Peter wheeled toward the hotel's glass front, seeking to anchor himself in his surroundings before she returned and those green eyes saw too much.

Once the world stopped spinning, he caught a glimpse of water between the buildings across the wide, traffic-filled street. A lake? No, St. Louis sat beside a river. What was its name?

"Peter."

He spun around without thinking—and wobbled as the lobby canted.

Wendy surged forward to put her forearm under his to support him.

And he burned.

He jerked away. *Stop! Accept what is possible for you now.* The gathering of knowledge and the respect of colleagues, not the pursuit of an attractive woman with silky hair and sunshine smiles.

But he looked down at her. Wendy's eyes were a soft, rain-soaked moss green now and for a moment, he didn't wish to accept such a limited life. He wished to dream, to seek, to be completely the same as other men.

"Here," she said, extending her hands. One held a capped container of coffee topped with a muffin; the other cradled an apple and a banana. "Breakfast buffet," she added, as if that explained something. "You can eat while I drive."

Without another word, she exited the hotel.

Peter followed her across the parking lot. Folded himself into the passenger seat of her small, battered car. Caught another whiff of her scent—and *wanted....*

*America is the land of opportunity,* his foolish inner voice reminded him as he hooked the door closed with his elbow, then juggled the food and coffee to fasten his seat belt.

*Forget it,* he ordered himself. *You will only open basket of snakes.*

"What is the river's name?" he asked, waving the fruit in its direction before turning to face forward.

Wendy muttered something as she cranked the engine. Damn, she was on his left. The damaged side.

He thought about asking her to repeat what she'd said, but.... No. He could not bear to humiliate himself in front of this woman.

*And in only a few more minutes, I will not have to.*

So he gazed upward. Pretending he was not listening instead of unable to hear.

The engine sputtered, then roared. A tune-up it needed. And a new clutch. Gears ground as Wendy wrestled the transmission into reverse then gave it some gas and released the clutch.

The apple flew into the windshield. Peter managed to block it with the coffee container as it rebounded, but a jerk, a turn and sudden braking sent the fruit ricocheting into his still sensitive lap.

Gingerly, Peter reclaimed the apple and waited for both pain and vertigo to pass.

Pulling out of the parking lot, Wendy guided the car around a stalled delivery van and joined the heavy traffic flow, muttering the whole time. Was she talking to him about the river or offering opinions on the other drivers' skills?

Out of habit, he didn't ask. Not asking left him ignorant, maybe, but not embarrassed. Still pretending to ignore his surroundings, Peter took a bite of muffin. Chewed. Swallowed. Uncapped the coffee, took a sip. And nearly spewed his drink when their front bumper missed hitting a van with no brake lights by the diameter of a cat's whisker. It had stopped for no reason and now it spurted away again.

Wendy Marek just might be the best driver he'd ever ridden with, Peter thought admiringly. What other talents did she—?

"Say, are you interested in any of this or should I have saved my breath?" Wendy's question penetrated the pounding of Peter's heart and the low, residual foaming-surf sound filling his left ear canal.

He twisted on the seat so he could face her. Taking a deep breath, he told himself to confess his flaws. To explain his hearing loss in the very ear facing her.

But when he opened his mouth, masculine pride muscled aside conscience. "Sorry," his ego lied. "I am not listening."

*Hovno,* even her little snort of disgust stirred him. Challenged him.

And for the first time since the accident, Peter wanted to accept the challenge.

Wendy rolled her eyes. "I was answering your question. Then I threw in some background on St. Louis. Sorry, I didn't realize you were deep in thought." Her ironic tone indicated a possible lack of respect for the process.

Peter sipped his coffee as he contemplated his unusual reaction to this woman. The more she acted upset with him, the more she attracted him. Simultaneously, apparently, he'd prefer she think him dull or boorish rather than damaged.

Wendy waved a hand forgivingly. "I should have

known. The geniuses I work with do the same thing. Drift off on some distant mental cloud without warning.''

The stoplight at the corner turned yellow; instead of gliding through the intersection, she stood on the brakes.

This time, Peter braced a hand against the dashboard, still facing Wendy.

"So," she asked while the car dissipated its inertial forward momentum, "what secret of the universe were you contemplating while I played tour guide?"

Was it the condescension he expected to hear in her tone that made him do it? The lagging jets she'd accused him of earlier? Or the simple, age-old male drive to conquer, to possess, what he desired?

Peter had no idea.

But with a swift, smooth motion that surprised even him, he leaned across the narrow console between the seats, cupped her chin with his palm...

...and kissed her.

Her lips stiffened, then melted beneath his. She gave a soft moan, low in her throat.

Instinctively, Peter deepened the kiss.

And discovered that Wendy Marek kissed the way C-4 exploded.

A car honked. Then another.

Wendy pushed him away—weakly, though—as she let out the worn clutch.

"That is mystery I contemplate," Peter murmured while she drove as steadily as possible in stop-and-go rush-hour traffic. What she wanted to do was to pull the darned car over to the curb, kill the engine and start running her hands all over that rock-hard Czech chest. While she kissed the sweet syntax out of him.

How, she wondered, could four lips and two tongues generate that much pulsating, white-hot sexual need in, like, one-point-oh-oh seconds?

It didn't matter, Wendy reminded herself as she let a

bus swerve around her, then signaled a left turn. She wasn't interested.

*Yeah. Like Swiss bankers don't care about money.*

"N-never do that again," she stated, hoping her voice wouldn't crack and reveal just how much she foolishly, insanely, totally wanted him to kiss her again. Or vice versa. *"Ne-ver."*

The visiting math genius merely grinned.

Still shaking from the magnitude of her response to Peter's kiss, Wendy turned down a tree-lined street and into a parking lot, then headed for the far end where she slotted the car against a short, yellow pole.

"My first American kiss," Peter rumbled in his dark, seductive voice as he calmly brushed muffin crumbs from his coat sleeve. "Very…nice."

Nice? Wendy's jaw fell again. He thought that earth-shattering experience had been *nice?* Holy granola, what would a "great" kiss be like?

*Like a meteor colliding with earth.*

She'd seen that movie.

"But no cigar." Wendy added as she shut off the engine and removed the key from the ignition. Although for the first time, she could see some merit in getting seriou— No. She was going to Paris. *If* she could find the money to go.


FROM THE PARKED CAR, they followed a wide sidewalk, bordered by tall, leafy trees with mottled, creamy bark, to a three-story, Gothic Revival building of gray stone.

Inside, Wendy's heels clicked against the polished, stained-cement floor as she led Peter down a hallway lined with classrooms to a door whose top half was frosted glass.

Gold lettering on the glass announced College Of Arts And Sciences. Smaller letters below that stated The Office Of The Dean.

Wendy halted in front of the door. When she turned to look up at him, flames flickered in her green eyes—and again, Peter burned.

"I will now introduce you to Dean Leippert and Dr. Boroni." She issued the words in short bursts. "Then you're on your own."

Swallowing a sigh, Peter nodded. He certainly didn't regret that impulsive kiss, but he accepted the probability that it had damaged the opinion of this tantalizing woman who, he suspected, would not cater to his disabilities. Not that he wished to get seriously involved with Wendy—or anyone else—but to win her interest would be incontrovertible proof that his ex-fiancée's pity had been misguided. That he *could* bring something of value to a relationship with a woman.

Pulling open the door, Wendy motioned him inside.

Two women looked up as they entered. A third desk—belonging to his guide, no doubt—fronted a closed door in the far wall.

Wendy indicated the older woman, who sported a pencil above one ear and two pairs of glasses on cords around her neck. "Mrs. Malone, meet Dr. Havel. Mrs. M. coordinates faculty issues."

Peter murmured. Mrs. Malone smiled her greeting.

His escort pointed to the other woman, who was Wendy's age. Bright blue hair spikes extended from the top of her head at incongruent angles; the rest of her hair was black and about a centimeter long. "This is Robin Donahue. She handles the students."

Peter thought Robin said, "Rowrrr, baby," but she was on his damaged side, so perhaps he misunderstood.

After they exchanged greetings, Wendy asked, "Is Dean Leippert in yet?"

"Yeah," Robin said with a slight frown. "Dr. B.'s in there, too."

"Great. Come on, Peter." Wendy tugged on his coat sleeve and headed for the dean's door. Eager to get this sexy mathematician delivered before tempting images of his buff body and echoes of that awesome kiss stored themselves in her long-term memory.

"They, uh, they're not alone," Robin warned, fingering her eyebrow ring.

Wendy paused with her hand on the doorknob of the dean's office. Chemistry profs, probably. Whatever. She had work to do. Finances to locate. Fashion design skills to hone.

Mostly, she needed to put immediate space between herself and this man, the first to curl her toes with a kiss. Nice, indeed!

After rapping on the door of the dean's inner sanctum, Wendy turned the knob and ushered her companion inside.

"Good morning, gentlemen," she said with a bright smile, following the brawny brainiac into the office. "Allow me to present Dr. Peter Havel, the Czech Republic's mathematical pride and joy."

She gestured toward the portly, silver-haired man rising from his desk. "Peter, this is my boss, Dean Leippert."

The two men nodded at each other. Wendy's eyebrows squinched together. Why was the dean fiddling with his tie? He only did that when potential donors threatened to take their money elsewhere.

With a mental shrug, Wendy continued her introduction. "And the gentleman next to him is Dr. Emil Boroni."

Peter shook hands with the elderly mathematics professor, who looked like one of Santa's elves: small, wizened, and normally full of cheer.

Only, this morning his expression indicated someone had broken into Santa's workshop on Christmas Eve and snagged all the toys.

"I'm pleased to meet you, Dr. Havel," Dr. Boroni said loudly, casting a furtive glance sideways. "Your visit is an amazing coincidence."

Huh?

"Yes. Nice of Wendy to bring you by," Dean Leippert boomed, also glancing at the chair beside his desk.

Wendy blinked. What was going on here? She followed Leippert's gaze to the man seated on his right.

Oops. Not a chemistry prof. *Not one of ours, anyway.*

The stranger was small, narrow-shouldered, with thinning hair, a long, pointy nose and close-set, beady eyes behind thick black-rimmed glasses. All he needed was a tail to look rodential.

He wore a short-sleeved white shirt, drip-dry pants in a nondescript color and a clip-on bow tie that emphasized his scrawny neck: the universal uniform of the petty bureaucrat.

Wendy suddenly had a *very* bad feeling.

Apparently, Peter did, too; he took a step closer to her, as if silently offering support. Not that she needed it, but the heat radiating from his powerful frame did seem to counter the chill radiating from Mr. Rat.

"I, uh, don't believe you've met Francis J. Worthington." Dean Leippert's voice sounded weird. Strained.

So strained that for a second, she actually did lean back against Peter. Who wrapped his hands around her shoulders. And kept them there, as if they belonged, even when she regained her sanity and unleaned.

"Mr. Worthington's with Immigration and Naturalization," the dean continued, flapping his tie again.

"Pleased to meet you, Ms. Marek. Dr. Havel." The rat-resembling bureaucrat didn't even look up as he removed a piece of paper from the battered briefcase he held on his knees.

"It's a conspiracy! A conspiracy, I tell you!" Dr. Boroni cried before pressing arthritic fingers against his lips.

Worthington frowned at the nutty professor's outburst, then nudged the bridge of his glasses with his index knuckle.

"He's here about Peter," Dean Leippert blurted. "Your, uh, your fiancé."

# 3

*"FIANCÉ?"* Wendy's inflection expressed her opinion of the idea.

It did not sound flattering. And apparently it needed elaboration.

"You must be—"

"Pleased," Dean Leippert inserted. "Happy for you."

"Thrilled," Dr. Boroni contributed. Both men were nodding anxiously, like the little dolls with movable heads Peter had seen on TV during an American football game beamed into Barnaul last January.

"Determined," Worthington pronounced in ringing tones, "to prevent a miscarriage of justice."

"Are you all on club drugs?" Wendy asked, stinging his pride.

And confusing him, Peter conceded, because instead of answering, the others began protesting. Loudly. Wendy responded. Simultaneously.

*Hovno,* the woman was a puzzle he itched to solve. For now, however...

Peter stepped back, crossing his arms over his chest, unbothered this time that sounds and syllables had melded into pure cacophony. His handicaps weren't to blame; even with perfect hearing, his English comprehension couldn't keep up with their conversational speed.

Yet. But his mind still worked, even if some of the data it received came in garbled.

Peter set aside his chagrin at Wendy's rejection of him

as fiancé material in favor of seeking information on the more immediately pressing issue.

"Miscarry-ed justice?" he asked in a voice that sliced through the others' babble like so much lunch meat.

"Yes, indeed," the officious immigration official agreed through the ensuing silence, giving the piece of paper he held a sly look.

"Explain, please," Peter commanded of the smirking bureaucrat.

"To put it simply, Dr. Havel, the U.S. government does not recognize intentions," Worthington said solemnly— and slowly enough for Peter to follow. He waved the sheet of paper as if it were a yacht pennant in a stiff wind. "This was faxed to our office this morning. It's a translation of the letter you supplied our agents in Chicago last night as proof of your visiting status. It doesn't mention any engagement. It offers you *employment*."

The man made it sound like illicit drug dealing. Peter shrugged, still mystified. "It is illegal to work in U.S.A.?"

"In your case, yes!" Worthington crowed. "Because you, Dr. Havel, are here on a tourist visa. So, engaged to Ms. Marek or not—" his expression doubted it "—you're still banned from working at this university."

"It's a plot, I tell you," Boroni shouted. "A plot! Michel and Sternbridge... They'll do anything to prevent us from solving Gandel's—"

Cacophony erupted again.

Peter decided to give them three minutes. He turned to his right, pretending to study the bookcases lining the side wall; the ranting and raving became part of the foamy ocean sound filling his bad ear.

With his good ear directed toward the outer office, he could localize a phone ringing there—once, then someone answered it.

His bad eye caught movement. He turned back in time to see the little immigration official stuff the sheet he'd been waving into his briefcase, remove a stack of papers

from it, slap them on Leippert's desk and snap his
satchel shut.

"As long as you—assuming *you're* an American citizen, of course, Ms. Marek—and this foreigner are not legally married," the pompous Worthington informed
Wendy while shooting Peter a narrow-eyed, suspicion-
filled glare, "he can't work. Period."

"But if they were?" Leippert asked, his tie wiggling
like a teen idol's hips.

"Then he could be granted a conditional work permit
while we process his application for resident alien status,"
the petty official admitted reluctantly. "But until I see
proof of a bona fide marriage, it is my duty to enforce INS
regulations. I'm warning you—any infraction will result in
your deportation, Dr. Havel. Good day."

With that, the little man scurried from the room. The
others looked at each other, then burst into simultaneous
chatter again. Boroni waved his arms. Wendy tucked her
cinnamon hair. Leippert shook his tie.

Bah. He was sick of standing on the sidelines. If he
meant to avoid being babied, he must take charge of his
life. Beginning now—even at the risk of revealing his
flaws to the enchanting Ms. Marek.

Stepping around her—to put his good ear in the best
position to hear them all—he summoned his most author-
itative voice. "Please. Cork your bottles!"

Through the sudden silence, he heard a phone ring again
in the outer office. Then even it stopped. *Good. Now we
are arrived somewhere.*

"Please, one person only explains. Am I working here
or not?"

Dean Leippert sputtered and fluttered his neckwear. Dr.
Boroni resumed his arm-waving, shouting again about con-
spiracies.

Only Wendy responded helpfully. And luckily, slowly
enough for Peter to follow. "Apparently, the university's
legal department screwed up your paperwork and some-

how, the INS thought you were coming here to see me. Dean Leippert threw out the engagement ploy as a stall tactic.''

Leaning closer, she said, ''I think he panicked.''

She tucked her hair behind her ears with a frown as she continued. ''You see, your appointment's created a real political problem for us. The chairman of the board of trustees wanted it to go to one of his pet physicists and unfortunately, he's a rather unforgiving old man. If you don't perform *all* the contracted duties—starting with an appearance at the welcoming reception tomorrow night—Chairman Moss will undoubtedly veto the funds we need for new classrooms for the math department.''

''This is Dr. Boroni's conspiracy?'' Peter asked, enthralled by the distress visible in her green eyes. Perhaps to have a woman worry over him would not be so unpleasant after all. Perhaps it depended on the woman as much as what worried her....

''What? Oh. No. *He's* just got a little more hole than donut,'' Wendy whispered as Robin appeared in the doorway to the outer office.

Peter held his hands out, palms up. Intrigued by the colorful phrase but uncertain of its meaning.

''He thinks everyone's out to keep him from reaping the fame he deserves,'' the little tigress explained, rolling her eyes. ''Like anyone would get that excited about the mumbo-jumbo math you guys do.''

Peter couldn't help grinning. Truly, this would be the ideal woman to test himself against. Wendy Marek even held his *abilities* in disregard!

Yes, convincing this woman of his romantic appeal would prove past—no, *beyond* to doubt that he was fully capable of winning any heart he chose.

Of course, courting her might be as difficult as solving the Anomaly. But not impossible. Nothing was impossible to a determined man. *Except healing an optic nerve with willpower*, Peter amended ruefully.

One hand leveraging the door frame, the blue-spiked Robin leaned into the office. "Uh, Wendy?"

But courtship required access.

In that instant, the solution came to him, complete and fully formed, the same way his crystalline-structure designs did.

"Your chairman of trustees cares," Peter pointed out. "And your dean. And Dr. Boroni. So marry me."

"Don't be silly." Wendy's tone communicated her opinion that it was already too late.

Perhaps he *was* crazy—to be attracted to someone who thought him silly. *Is better than "poor baby."*

Peter recalled their kiss. Repeating that experience seemed eminently un-silly.

"It's a simple, elegant solution," he said, one corner of his mouth lifting.

"Wendy," Robin repeated from the doorway.

It's a recipe for disaster, Wendy thought as she wheeled to regard her friend. Peter had the sex appeal of six Hollywood hunks combined. And a half dose of that freaking irresistible smile was as effective as the full deal. Not that *she* couldn't resist him.

"What is it, Rob?"

"Line one's for you," Robin said, fingering her eyebrow ring. "Claims it's an emergency."

Another one? What a morning! "Can you—?"

Dean Leippert punched the blinking light on the phone on his desk. "She'll be right with you," he boomed into the receiver.

Wendy smothered a sigh. Typical Leippert. Always being helpful in the most unhelpful way.

Next to the dean, Dr. Boroni stood wringing his hands. Poor guy. He'd been on cloud nine ever since they'd gotten Peter's visit approved over the chairman's protest. Solving this Gandel thing was his life's goal. And darn it, she knew how important dreams were to the people who dreamed them.

Spinning around, she jabbed a finger into the Czech Chest. "What did you tell them to make them think you were a tourist?" she demanded.

Okay, she'd probably confirmed their assumptions, unintentionally of course, but still... "Where'd they get the idea you were coming to see *me?*"

Peter shrugged one massive shoulder. "They offered to send for a translator, but it was late." He stuffed his hands in his pants' pockets—which reminded Wendy of the black, formfitting cotton beneath the khaki. "So I showed them your letter and just—" he shrugged again "—agreed with whatever they said.

"I still agree," he declared. "For you to be my wife is best plan."

The dean and Boroni started looking hopeful and bobbing the hollow spheres growing at the end of their necks.

Blue eyes gazed deep into her soul. "Say yes, Ms. Marek."

Wendy couldn't say a word; she tucked her hair instead. And tried not to look at Boroni or Leippert or Peter's chest. Or the washboard abdomen it tapered into. She sure as heck wasn't letting her eyes drop to his beltline—or below it.

Which left those smoky-blue eyes, those thick lashes, those beautiful cheekbones—and those warm, skillful lips.

*No, no, no!* She didn't want to marry anyone, even as a useful ruse! She was going to Paris. To make herself a life nobody could take away. To create her own happiness—one that didn't depend on anyone else. That didn't hurt anyone else....

"I—I've got to answer the phone." She indicated the instrument the dean still held.

"First you will answer my question, please," Peter said in his darling accented English.

Wendy frowned as she moved toward the phone. *Heavily* accented, that's what she meant. There wasn't anything darling about the man. *Except everything she'd seen so far—which was darned near* everything.

"I can be good hobby for you," he insisted.

She halted in midstride. He thought marriage was a recreational pastime? Men. Unbelievable.

"Look, I know you're supposed to be some kind of certified genius," Wendy exclaimed, jamming her hair behind her ears. "But try to concentrate. We're talking about immigration and work permits, not...not stamp collecting!"

"I am concentrating" he assured her with a laugh. "A fiancé can be deported. Hobby cannot."

From the doorway Robin giggled. "I think he means 'hubby.' As in husband. Right?" She directed the question at Peter.

Who nodded. "Yes. Huzband," he said carefully. "Huzband can work. Attend reception. Marriage prevents deportment."

I'll show you deportment, Wendy thought, reaching over to take the phone out of the dean's hand. I'll refrain from screaming, no matter how provoking you are.

"Would only be for a short time."

As if even one minute married—even to the gorgeous Peter Havel—wouldn't seem like an eternity! Why did he think it was called the Theory of *Relativity?*

"It takes three days to get a license in Missouri," Robin offered. "That's why my roommate eloped to Vegas."

Wendy shot her soon-to-be-former friend a withering glance, which bounced right off her blue spikes.

"I'd never ask such a personal sacrifice of an employee," Dean Leippert said, obviously wishing he could. "But...remember what happened when the drama department wouldn't stage the play Moss's granddaughter wrote?"

Wendy shuddered. They'd lost half their budget, most of the faculty and all of their reputation for excellence. She wasn't a heartless witch; she knew Boroni was counting on Peter's help to solve the Anomaly. And she'd do anything for the dean, who'd hired her right out of high school, let her take a drawing class during working hours last semester, even allowed her extra time off—with pay— when her father had his mild heart attack last year, but...*marriage?* "Glarrrgh!"

Peter shoved his hands deeper into his pants' pockets. Made himself shrug. He wasn't familiar with that word, but he could guess its meaning. And who could blame her?

"I understand," he said stiffly. "You do not wish to marry me."

"Bingo!" Wendy cried, then added, "But don't get your ego bruised—I don't want to marry anybody!"

Such a spitfire! So wonderfully unsympathetic.

Capturing *her* interest would be the ultimate challenge, Peter mused. And he'd enjoy exploring further the sensual promise in that kiss....

"Then I am perfect choice."

Wendy shook her head to clear it. Between that metal-melting smile and the proximity of that fantastic male body, who could think, let alone follow Peter Havel's idiot-savant logic and fractured English?

"The phone, Wen?" Robin reminded her. "He did say it was an emergency."

"Oh, right." Wendy put the phone to her ear, hoping the "emergency" required immediate space travel or deep-sea cave exploration. *Some* escape from the lunacy surrounding her right now. "This is Wendy Marek. How may I help you?"

"I just talked to an apprentice electrician," her father gushed. "His name's Bart. What night do you want to go out?"

A red haze blurred Wendy's vision. *If I was a camel, this would be the last straw.*

She cupped her hand around the mouthpiece. "I am not dating an electrician's apprentice," she hissed.

Without missing a beat her father said, "They're installing cabinets down the street. I'll check out the carpenters. Tomorrow night okay?''

In the painful years after her mother had bailed on them, Wendy's dad had been distant and disinterested. Half the time he acted as if he didn't remember she existed. But now—clearly, he'd gone bonkers since his brush with mortality and Patrick's closet-exiting revelation.

Neither of which gave him the right to meddle. Uncupping the phone, Wendy summoned her firmest tone. ''No, Dad. Not tomorrow, not ever. I know you want a grandchild, but I'm not getting married just to give you one.''

Peter's mouth twitched into that hot half smile.

''Now, honey…''

''No.'' Wendy tried to ignore the heat building in her. ''You have to stop matchmaking!'' Then she smiled. Her father prided himself on his ''reasoning'' ability. ''Unless you can convince me that there's something in it for me, of course.'' Besides dirty diapers.

Wendy's dad had the audacity to chuckle. ''Well, how about thirty…maybe forty thousand dollars?''

''Wha-at?''

''Your share of your grandfather's trust fund. Make a nice down payment on a house.''

It would pay for Paris, but… ''I don't get that until I'm thirty.''

''Thirty or married,'' her dad countered. ''Read the fine print.''

How could she? She'd never seen the actual document. Just heard about it, mostly from Patrick. No wonder he'd never mentioned the marriage option.

''I just have to get married?'' she asked to be absolutely sure. ''Not stay that way?''

''That's all the folks in the Union Federal's trust department need, but naturally—''

Why, that old-fashioned— Wendy covered the phone and looked at Peter. ''Okay, Dr. Havel, I'll marry you,'' she told him. ''On two conditions.''

His blue eyes deepened to navy. "Name them."

She had to push the words past suddenly dry tonsils. "I wo— We're not... I mean, no—"

"No consummation?" Peter guessed. At her nod, he shrugged one shoulder. "I'm devastated, of course, but I do not enjoy making love to unwilling women."

Because, Wendy would bet, there were plenty of the willing variety.

She glanced from the Czech babe magnet to Robin catching flies in the doorway, then to Leippert and Boroni, who looked like puppies begging for a bone.

But it *was* a simple solution. To Peter's problem—and hers. Tapping the trust fund would give her the money she needed in time to enroll.

"Second condition?"

"Once you get your work permit, we file for divorce. No fault."

Peter gave her a look so intense it made her toes curl. Then he did that very European, one-shoulder-shrugging thing—he probably held a patent on it.

"If you wish," he said quietly. "Anything else?"

"I'm not going to Las Vegas. Too cheesy." And that's where her mother had gone when she'd left them.

When he nodded, Wendy uncovered the phone. "Forget the carpenters, Dad. I'll find my own husband."

She listened a minute, then said, "Oh, you'd be surprised how fast I can locate a man with marriage on his mind."

Hanging up, she told their audience, "Okay, we're going to make the INS very happy."

Dr. Boroni gave a triumphant whoop.

"And royally tick off Chairman Moss," Wendy added, flashing a smile that raised Peter's testosterone production—and his determination to captivate her. Somehow.

The blue-spiked woman waggled her eyebrows. "Rad, bad and mad!" she exclaimed, grinning. "But if you've nixed Las Vegas, where're ya gonna go to get hitched before tomorrow night?''

Peter understood one word out of ten. But the difficulty of conquering Wendy's language—*and her,* he vowed—would only make his eventual victory sweeter.

''But you could be married by Elvis in Las Vegas,'' Boroni protested.

''How about Reno?'' boomed Dean Leippert.

''Sawn Taffy,'' Peter declared, hoping it was not far away.

Why did they all stand there, looking blank?

''Well, candy's dandy,'' Robin said finally, ''and sugar, you are eye candy at its best, but—''

Wendy frowned her to silence. Peter wondered if anyone understood the blue-spiked woman or everyone merely humored her.

He tried again. ''Iz capital for Nude Mexico.''

Robin giggled. ''There's a mental image!''

Rubbing the damaged side of his face, Peter struggled to explain. ''On airplane, I read magazine article about Sawn Taffy Indian Market—and also it says weddings there require no tests or waiting.''

Robin snapped her fingers. ''Santa Fe!'' She glanced over her shoulder. ''Uh-oh, students,'' she said, and disappeared into the outer office.

Peter looked at Wendy. ''Okay?'' he asked.

Say no, she counseled herself. Say, ''What was I thinking?'' Tell them to make the school's lawyers fix his damned visa. Go hold up liquor stores to fund your Paris fling. Do *not* enmesh yourself in any way with this temptation in magnificent male form.

Wendy ignored her own advice. ''Sure,'' she said, carefully aligning the phone with the corner of Dean Leippert's desk. ''Santa Fe sounds great.''

PETER MADE the arrangements using Wendy's computer. *Click, click*—plane reservations. More clicks, a couple of quick e-mails and presto! Lodging and wedding package booked.

Then Boroni drove him back to the hotel where they conversed in halting Italian while he downloaded his latest work on the Anomaly and handed it out—no, *over*.

After the elderly professor left, clutching his Zip disk as though it were a holy relic, Peter went to the coffee shop and ordered lunch by pointing at pictures. Then he walked down to the brown river and around the bases of the towering silver arch rising above it. He wanted to nap but didn't dare risk oversleeping the way he had this morning. Eventually, he returned to the lobby to wait for his pretend fiancée.

Wendy stayed at the office wading through classroom assignments, mediating textbook delivery problems between professors and the campus bookstore and helping Robin with last-minute student scheduling crises.

Then she went home, packed an overnight bag, called the Union Federal Bank & Trust to make an appointment to get her share of the Marek trust—and mailed off her deposit to the Paris Design Institute.

She'd dreamed of studying fashion design since middle school, when she'd had to wear the "who cares about cool, these are practical" clothes her father bought her. Ironic that getting married was the only way to achieve her dream, since it was the one thing she swore she'd never do—ever since that day in seventh grade, when she'd come home to find a note on the kitchen table and her mother gone for good....

THEY FLEW NONSTOP to Albuquerque, where a van picked them up and delivered them an hour later to their hotel in the heart of Santa Fe, a quaint, all-adobe town nestled at the foot of the Sangre de Cristo Mountains.

The ceremony was scheduled for early the next morning, with a return flight to St. Louis arriving in midafternoon.

After checking in, they followed the instructions left for them and walked one block up, two blocks over to the Santa Fe county clerk's office. Ten minutes and twenty-five dollars later, they emerged from the low, cream-colored abode building with an official license to wed.

The concierge advised them to dine at a café around the corner, run by the chef credited with inventing southwestern cuisine. When he mentioned a curving flight of green stairs, Peter quickly suggested the hotel restaurant instead. How was he to discover what chance he had of beginning a relationship with Wendy when tonight, still "jet-lagging," he could hardly walk without bumping into walls?

Luckily, his fake fiancée agreed without argument.

She ordered a glass of wine before dinner—but Peter was the one who felt drunk. Between the last two days' travel and Santa Fe's altitude, he knew he'd be unable to hide his disabilities unless he hid himself.

So he yawned theatrically through the appetizer; by the time the waiter cleared the entrées, his act was genuine. "Perhaps an early night is good idea, *milenko.*"

Wendy signaled for the bill. "Not for me," she said, tucking her hair and not meeting his eye. "I want to look around town a little. Santa Fe's supposed to be a hotbed for art."

Peter shrugged off his disappointment. He was not so handicapped that he thought she'd fall into bed with him just because they were alone together in a charming village, surrounded by cool mountain air filled with crystal moonlight and the perfume of exotic—at least to him—flowers.

He yawned again behind his napkin.

*A man could wish, though.*

If he wanted to waste his time.

She figured out the tip and added the total before handing over the charge slip. Was she trying to take care of him? Why? Did she think a mathematician could not determine percentages? Scowling, Peter scrawled his name on the line, then stood as his ''fiancée'' excused herself to see the sights of Santa Fe.

He staggered up to their suite, to the bedroom that didn't contain Wendy's suitcase. *And another empty bed,* pointed out the nagging little voice.

*Don't start,* he told it as he dragged off his clothes. *Not tonight.* He fell asleep brushing his teeth and only managed to reach the bed unscathed because there were no obstacles between it and the bathroom.

SCENTED STEAM WAFTED upward from the hot, bubble-topped water. Carefully, Wendy stepped into the deep oval tub, then let herself sink beneath the foam until her head rested against the tub's rim.

*Mmm.* Closing her eyes, Wendy let the hot water ease her aching calf muscles.

She'd walked for hours, refusing to return until almost midnight.

Because no way she was encouraging the erotic fantasies starring the gorgeous, sophisticated, *male* Czech Chest that had reared their enticing images as soon as Peter had started talking about going to bed. Dangerous enough just being here in this romantic, picturesque artist's haven, reveling in these luxurious surroundings—with said heartthrob snoring lightly in the other room.

Huh. Right about now, a matrimonial-minded woman would be *so* dreaming of the ceremony tomorrow and a life of wedded sex—er, bliss. Conjuring up a warm, close-knit family and a laughter-filled home.

Wendy plucked a thick, pink washcloth from edge of the tub and dropped it into the scented foam.

*She,* on the other hand, was contemplating the handcrafted jewelry, art and clothing she'd just viewed in numerous shop and gallery windows. Because Wendy knew that a fulfilling career offered the only true security—emotional, financial or otherwise.

Her mother had fallen in love and been so horribly unhappy when she'd had to choose between her painting and family obligations that she'd eventually made another choice.

A career never abandoned you without warning. *Never left you wondering what you'd done wrong....*

"Paris," Wendy muttered as she reached for a little bar of French-milled soap. "All I need is Paris."

To get there, she'd marry the devil himself—even if he was as handsome as sin and she had to wallow in the lap of luxury to do it.

FOR A MEANINGLESS legal fiction, it was a lovely wedding.

Beneath a sweater to ward off the morning chill, the bride wore a calf-length, swirly skirted sundress in a cream-and-green print with matching green anklets. She carried a translucent plastic craft-supplies box as her purse.

The groom simply wore his black sport coat over an oatmeal-collared knit shirt. And jeans.

*Okay,* Wendy thought, telling herself to breathe instead of producing excess estrogen, *so Peter looks sort of sexy in denim.*

*Yeah, like Miss America's sort of nice-looking.*

A young, ponytailed man from the wedding-package company drove them through town, then up a narrow winding road lined with little adobe houses converted into art galleries.

A right at a school, then left at a church—and up into the hills above town.

Finally the driver pulled into a tiny graveled parking area. Across the road, behind an eight-foot adobe wall topped by red Spanish tiles was the wedding site, a private estate.

After handing her a bouquet of shell-pink silk roses and Peter a matching boutonniere, the ponytailed rep directed them through a door set into one of the massive wooden gates that served as the estate entrance.

A sigh escaped her as they stepped inside. What a picture-perfect setting for a wedding! *Or for presenting a fashion collection,* Wendy corrected herself as she looked around.

On the left side of the flagstone courtyard, a fountain splashed brightly from a stone pedestal. To the right, more water trickled softly from a blue-tiled niche in the wall forming the north end of the property. In the center of the patio was a silver-leafed Russian olive tree surrounded by a lush flowerbed.

The celebrant waited to perform the ceremony in front of the trickling blue fountain, which was flanked by terraced, tile-edged flowerbeds filled with more colorful blooming plants.

After introducing herself, the Reverend Judy, wearing a self-designed vestment featuring fuzzy orange suns on purple lamé, insisted on arranging them in accordance with the earth's magnetic field. The actual wedding took less time than the alignment—even though Peter made Wendy repeat everything Reverend Judy said and made his vows in English *and* Czech. When it was her turn, he cocked his head and leaned closer, as if suspecting discrepancies between Judy's prompts and Wendy's recital.

In no time at all, the Reverend Judy was intoning, "By the power vested in me by the State of New Mexico, the County of Santa Fe and the messages received from intelligent beings throughout the universe, I now pronounce you husband and wife."

Then the magnetic, purple reverend started the you-may-kiss-the-bride part and Peter grinned as he swooped toward her.

Unable to stop him, Wendy attempted to let the kiss land on her cheek, but Peter, reading her intentions and reacting with lightning speed, captured her head with his large, strong hands. Swaying as if trying to synchronize their movements, he pressed his lips to hers.

Holy cow! The same molten-bones, off-the-Richter-scale earthquaking sensation as the last time.

With much difficulty—and the resistance wasn't coming from Peter, either—Wendy broke the kiss.

"Didn't I tell you," she asked in a hoarse whisper, because her voice was weak and shaky and so were her insides, "to never do that again?"

The Reverend Judy opened her mouth, then closed it, clearly amazed at probably the quickest time to a newly-wed spat she'd ever witnessed.

"I promised to love, honor and cherish," Peter purred, his smoky-blue eyes now crackling with flames of desire... For her? Or just any old female? And it didn't matter, did it? "Not to obey. Especially when your lips and your body do not agree with your vocal cords."

Before she could sputter out...*something* to correct his false impression, Peter added softly, "I also promised never to bed you against your will, *milenko,* but whenever you wish to explore what we are now legally sanctioned to enjoy, I will be happy to accommodate you."

And with that outrageous offer, her short-term husband turned to shake Reverend Judy's hand.

Wendy retreated to the car. And while Peter completed the paperwork with the divine Purple One and the pony-tailed witness, she sat there reminding herself that a fairy-tale wedding to a gorgeous Czech hunk who kissed the way Mozart wrote music wasn't going to affect her one little bit.

The deal included breakfast, so their guide dropped them at a hole-in-the-wall he claimed was another award-winning Santa Fe restaurant.

As they sipped fresh-squeezed orange juice and Peter ate every bit of his gourmet quesadillas—whole-wheat tortillas folded around mounds of scrambled eggs, cheese, sliced avocados and apple-smoked bacon—Wendy toyed with her seven-grain hot cereal and tried to deep-six the memory of that hot ceremony-sealing embrace.

Damn, the man could kiss! And if the rest of the process was even half as steamy— *Come on, connubial consummation!*

"W-when does our plane get into St. Louis?" she asked, desperate to get a grip on her nearly departed sanity. Before she did something stupid. Such as jump his bones. Right here. Right now.

"Before reception."

*Did that XY chromosome make guys genetically disposed to self-centered thinking?* "I've got a four-thirty appointment at the bank."

"Why?"

"To get things rolling," Wendy said, smiling at turning the tables on her father with the help of Grandpa Marek and his outmoded beliefs. "I want to access my share of the lucre as soon as possible."

Peter's fork clattered to his plate. "That's why you marry me?" he asked, the syllables suddenly harsh. "For money?"

Her eyes narrowed. "Don't go all shocked and innocent, Havel. You're the one defrauding the U.S. government."

Bah. Despite the revelation of this mercenary streak, his green-eyed tigress of a wife still turned him up—no, *on*. Like a porn star affects a teenage boy.

"And hey, it's *my* money," she said, tucking her hair behind her ears. "At least it is now that we're married."

Peter stood and tossed some bills onto the table—all but one of which Wendy scooped up and tried to return.

"Keep," he said roughly. "As you say, it's yours now."

Her laughter penetrated even his damaged ear. "No, silly," she told him, using a tone normally reserved for old, stupid pets. "I was talking about *my* money. My share of a family trust fund. Now that I'm married, I can claim it and I need it—to study fashion design in France."

"Oh." He wanted to turn and run, but he knew that what would happen would only embarrass him more: he'd lose his balance and fall in a heap at her feet. "I must go," he mumbled, stepping away slowly.

Wendy cocked her head. "Where?"

"Shopping," he muttered, easing around a high-backed chair blocking the narrow aisle to the café's door. "For souvenir. I will meet you at the hotel. In one hour."

PETER ROAMED THE SHOPS lining the plaza and the little alleyways leading off it, berating himself for hopping—no, *leaping* to conclusions, which no scientist did!—until a window display caught his eye.

Later, when the tray tables were returned to their upright and locked position and the plane descended over the wide brown river whose name he still didn't know, he slipped his purchase—a zigzag ribbon of black opal set in a stippled gold band—out of his pocket and onto Wendy's third finger, right hand.

He expected questions or protests or a blunt rejection, but after staring at it a minute, all she said was, "Helluva souvenir, Havel, but this is America," before moving it to her left hand.

"WOULD YOU LIKE ME to drop you at your hotel?" Wendy offered as they stepped off the plane in St. Louis. Not that she could be bought, but the ring *was* a nice touch, especially for her appearance at the bank. And it *was* beautiful. Fit perfectly, too, which told her plenty about this hottie's level of experience with women. Up there in the big numbers.

"Not necessary," Peter replied, something glimmering in his blue eyes.

Wendy told herself to resist the urge to figure out what that something was. Her part in this little play was over. They'd gotten married and filled out the stack of INS forms on the plane. The hotel could courier them to Worthington, so Peter could show at the reception tonight and start working on the Anomaly tomorrow.

She'd leave the other certified copy of their marriage license with the Union Federal bank folks and be on her way to being on her way.

Or whatever.

"Okay, then." Wendy held out her hand. After a brief hesitation Peter's mouth quirked, but he took it, rubbed his thumb along the inside of her wrist, then let go, thank God. "I'll see you," she said. Meaning around campus—fully clothed. With a couple thousand chaperones between them.

"Oh, yes," he purred, the smoky blue of his eyes deepening to navy. "And right now you will kiss me, too. A long, deep, hot kiss."

Wendy felt her jaw drop. Just *imagining* that kind of kiss with this man was frying her brain cells and sending swirls of desire to her lower abdomen. "W-why should I?"

"Because, *milenko,* the little bureaucrat—"

*Worthington J. Rat?* Wendy groaned.

"—is playing peep-Tom behind newsstand."

In this deep already, what else could she do? Wendy let Peter's strong, muscular hands curl around her shoulders, let him pull her close. She even lifted her mouth to be captured by his. It was, after all, just kissing.

*Yeah,* she thought dazedly as the fireworks started again. *And an orgasm is just nerve-receptors firing.*

Once Worthington was satisfied and they got out of this infernal airport, it had to stop, though. *Married or not—* Wendy moaned as her husband's lips and tongue played hers like Yo-Yo Ma played Carnegie Hall—*Peter and I must really not do this again....*

# 4

WENDY STEPPED from the revolving doors into the cavernous interior of the Union Federal Bank & Trust.

The place was a true cathedral to money: soaring columns and a high, barrel-vaulted ceiling; gleaming marble and dark wood; tasteful guards loitering near the ditto artworks dotted around the joint.

Since her brand-new husband was still pulling some kind of gentlemanly "after you" act on the sidewalk, Wendy moved out of the traffic path to wait. She still felt slightly floaty that he'd offered to come with her as Exhibit A. Floaty and secretly grateful; his commanding presence would give her the extra courage she'd need to get through this last bit of make-believe.

After which, they'd part company. Wendy frowned. Shouldn't she feel a whole lot happier anticipating his departure? Even a little bit happy?

Okay, so Peter kissed like Warren Buffett made money, had a body that would send Michelangelo's *David* whimpering to the gym and handed out kindness like Halloween candy.

She still shouldn't want to hang with him any longer than it took to pry some bucks out of this trust department.

Wendy refused to feel guilty about this marriage charade. Her reasons for participating in the ruse, she reminded herself as Peter continued to play doorman, were complex but not unworthy, ranging from loyalty to the dean to exasperation over her father's refusal to accept, let alone encourage, her interest in fashion design.

All she wanted to do was to study in Paris so she could eventually design unique, exciting clothes and support herself doing it.

And it wasn't as if she was stealing from the trust fund. The money had been set aside for her. Was it her fault her grandfather had antiquated ideas about women?

Ideas her mother had certainly disproved. Wendy tucked her hair against the memory.

*Finally!* Peter emerged from the glass-and-brass contraption—and stumbled. Briefly, lightly, he clutched Wendy's shoulder.

And heated tingles seared through every one of her female locales.

Okay, so his touch affected her a little.

*Yeah, like Moses and those plagues made a slight impression on Pharaoh and his Egyptians.*

"Sorry," Peter said, jerking his hand away, then rubbing the side of his face, as if...embarrassed?

Sympathy tugged at her. Wendy tugged back, warning herself against letting Peter Havel distract her from her goal. And lordy, was he distracting—even to a woman dedicated to her career.

"No problem," she said, smiling briskly. "We've got, oh, thirty seconds before we're officially late."

Peter actually looked at his watch.

Stifling a giggle, Wendy led the way across the polished marble floor to a desk discreetly labeled Inquiries. As she gave her name to the woman sitting there in a neat, boring navy suit, she could feel Peter's male presence behind her.

Apparently Ms. Prim could, too: she just blinked.

Too busy to hear Wendy's question or to respond. Busy fluffing her hair at Peter...crossing her legs to hike her miniskirt into a belt...fluttering her eyelashes and licking her lips.

Wendy felt a strange urge to break something over the woman's head. What was that about? She didn't remember ever feeling that way before. Of course, since meeting Peter she'd been feeling lots of things she'd never felt before. Wonderful—no, confusing, inexplicable things…

"And you, sir?" The receptionist smiled at Peter.

*Like a barracuda grinning at raw bait.*

Crossing her arms, Wendy waited for Mr. Bait to smile and purr at La Primbo the way he had at her yesterday when he'd opened that hotel room door in all his bulging-black-cotton glory and sent a herd of sensual tremors stampeding through her with his velvety *"Dobré ráno."*

"We are expecting," he said in a cool, neutral voice.

After a blank blink at Wendy's waistline, the woman murmured, "Uh, congratulations."

"He means expect*ed*," Wendy heard herself explain over more strange, knee-weakening feelings. "I have—"

Peter circled her shoulders with his arm as he corrected her. "*We* have."

Again, Wendy's hormone levels skyrocketed. She tried to ignore them.

"Uh, yes. We have an appointment with…with…" Fudge balls. Names, like numbers, rarely stuck around her memory box long. "Ah, someone in the trust department."

As the receptionist communed with her phone console, Wendy made herself wiggle out of Peter's embrace.

Rather than protest—though he wanted to—Peter shoved his hands into his pockets. Certainly he understood Wendy's message, but she could not deny the facts. They were legally husband and wife. By her choice as well as his.

He would see that she remembered it.

Not that Peter wished Wendy to begin fawning over him….

His internal nag snorted in disagreement. *You get hard just remembering her responsiveness to your kiss, the way she fits in your arms. Fawning with Wendy is exactly what you—*

*No!* Peter rubbed the damaged side of his face. He'd learned his lesson. No woman would be allowed to insult him again with her pity, to turn from lover into nanny. He might enjoy an affair with Wendy, but he would walk away. First.

Covering the microphone wand of her headset with her palm, the receptionist said something as she swiveled to point out a pair of elevators in the far corner behind her.

All Peter heard was ''—floor. Someone there will direct you.''

Refusing to betray that he'd missed the one vital piece of information, Peter pressed fingertips to the small of Wendy's back.

She leapt at his touch, so rapidly that her foot slipped on the polished marble.

Peter's reflexes forgot about his shaky equilibrium; he sprang forward to break Wendy's fall. Nearly caught her, then lost his balance....

They headed floorward together, since, as Galileo demonstrated a few hundred years ago, they fell at the same speed.

Landing in a very promising tangle of body parts—at least it was promising until, in scrambling to her feet, Wendy pressed the heel of her hand down on Peter's most sensitive appendage.

Blinding pain replaced his interest in remaining entangled. *''Hovno,''* he breathed as his hands briefly cupped the crushed area. ''You are a walk to disaster,'' he informed Wendy a second later as he rose slowly, carefully, and managed an almost-upright position.

''Oh, Peter! I—I'm so sorry!'' she gasped, her eyes telegraphing distress.

''Apology accepted,'' he replied.

''I'm sorry,'' Wendy repeated. ''I hope I didn't...'' She turned away pink-cheeked. After a second she turned back. ''Um, by the way, the correct phrase is 'You're a walking disaster.'''

''Walking disaster—I will remember,'' Peter promised

as he mentally filed the correction. Not that it made any more sense than his version....

He lost interest in language variances when Wendy suddenly leaned forward, her eyes sparkling bright green even in the bank's subdued light. To seal her apology with a kiss?

Wishing to be cooperative, Peter carefully angled his body toward her. Just as he got close enough to inhale her enchanting patchouli scent, Wendy straight-armed him, palm to chest, elbow locked.

"Then remember this, too, Dr. Havel," she said in a low voice. "We may be married, but we are not, repeat not, going to talk, act or think like it. I don't care how attractive you are, I do not have time for...for—for anything." With that, she spun around and marched off toward the elevators, hair swirling like cinnamon-colored silk.

Peter stared after her. She'd just admitted and rejected their mutual attraction in one sentence. Did she think any man could resist such a challenge?

*He* couldn't, Peter decided. Though he intended to guard his heart, it *was* time to test his abilities. To prove that his handicaps were inconvenient but ultimately inconsequential. That a full, normal life, including a wife and family if he wished, could be his.

Wendy would be the perfect subject for such an experiment. So independent, so driven that she wouldn't get hurt if he convinced her to revise her attitude about their mutual attraction.

As he followed his wife across the bank lobby, he did not fool himself. Pursuit and conquest of Wendy Marek would be as difficult as solving Gandel's Anomaly.

In true scientific fashion, Peter pondered several possible approaches to his campaign as they took the elevator to the third floor, where she grappled with another receptionist whose deck, he easily observed, lacked several cards.

He had not yet formulated a workable plan by the time

they were ushered into a small office containing a large desk—and a stereotypical banker: tall and slender, fastidiously groomed, wearing a dark suit and gold-rimmed glasses.

America, Peter mused as the man rose and tweaked the cuffs of his snow-white shirt, was not as he'd expected.

Where were the cowboys? The loud, hearty salesmen? The spoiled rich kids trying to look poor?

"Good afternoon." The banker extended his hand, first to Wendy, then to Peter. "I'm Darren Dinwiddie, manager of the trust department here at Union Federal. Please, have a seat."

Even Dinwiddie's diction was neat and precise. He probably ironed his underwear.

After shaking hands, Peter stepped back to give Wendy access to the chairs squeezed in front of the desk.

Once she was seated, he claimed the other chair, turning it slightly to increase his chances of hearing the conversation. Not that her money was his business, but he must remain alert for any opportunity to dismantle Wendy's resistance to her attraction to him.

Clearly, the first requirement was time together. Something for which Wendy would probably not volunteer.

"Thank you for seeing us on such short notice, Mr. Dinwiddie." Eager to get this over with, Wendy began digging into the depths of her purse as she added, "I'm Wendy Marek and this is Peter Havel."

The Czech Chest emitted a deep grumble.

Oops. She'd forgotten how hyper these academic types were about their titles.

"Uh, *Dr.* Havel, that is."

Peter touched her shoulder.

Sensual heat and serious longing lanced through her. Again.

*Forget it.* She wasn't falling for some guy just because he curled her lashes. She wasn't falling for…*anything!*

She was going to Paris.

*Because you can't count on anybody staying around to catch you. And falling just hurts when you land.*

She forced her attention back to the banker and her mission.

Behind his glasses, Dinwiddie's expression was polite but remote. *As in far-side-of-the-galaxy remote.*

Folding his hands atop the desk and briefly exhibiting a set of cosmetically perfect teeth, he asked, "How may I help you today?"

Nobody this side of a funeral parlor would call that tooth display a smile. Still, Wendy flashed a polite smile of her own. "I understand you administer the Dominik Marek family trust."

Dinwiddie's hands unfolded to clutch the knot on his tie, then vanished behind the desk. "What is your interest in the trust?"

"Well…" Wendy dug deeper, shoving aside her checkbook, calculator, a card of buttons, some fabric samples….

Aha. Locating the document authenticated by Reverend Judy, she pulled it from her purse, unfolded it and laid it triumphantly on Dinwiddie's polished mahogany.

"I'm one of Dominik's grandchildren and this—" Wendy twirled the marriage license around on the glass-smooth desktop and pushed it toward him "—is proof that I'm now eligible for my share of the trust."

Wendy tucked her hair as she sat back. Okay, she felt sort of sleazy—er, uneasy—marching in here demanding money.

But she wouldn't be in this position if her father would be supportive instead of unreasonable. Dammit, fashion design was an honorable pursuit. Instant grandbabies were his fantasy, not hers.

Oh, someday she wanted to have children, but she didn't need a husband for that. Not these days.

And she didn't think she wanted one. Why risk that their differing needs would tear them apart and scar their kids' psyches forever?

Safer for everybody if she avoided the whole thing. Which was why she was here. Doing what she had to, to achieve *her* dreams.

Wendy lifted her chin. "So, um, how soon can you write me a check?" she asked, trying not to notice the Czech hottie beside her, silently dispersing masculine charm the way fresh potpourri gives off scent.

*Stay focused,* she counseled herself. In a few minutes she'd be out of here, check in hand.

Then she'd drop Peter at his hotel, putting an end to the shortest-lived marriage this side of television.

Surely she could hold out that long against the desire bubbling inside her for one more bone-melting kiss.

A manicured hand peeked over the edge of Dinwiddie's desk, then crept forward far enough to touch the certificate gingerly. The banker's brow furrowed as he pulled it closer and studied it.

"Let me get this straight," he said a moment later, releasing the paper to smooth his palm over his immaculate hair. "You're alleging that you got married—today—in New Mexico and now you're here expecting a distribution from the Marek trust?"

Hmm. Dinwiddie appeared to be somewhat suspicious of their fake marriage.

*Yeah, like the Sierra Club's a little skeptical of the oil industry's environmental claims.*

"Is there some reason I shouldn't?" Wendy banished another twinge of guilt. "The way my father explained Grandpapa's trust, I qualify for the money when I'm thirty years old—or married. I picked Door Number Two."

Glancing at the certificate again, Dinwiddie pursed his lips. "Well, Ms. Marek—or should I say, *Mrs.* Havel?— your summary of the eligibility provisions of the trust is correct. However…"

*Attitude,* Wendy thought faintly as a block of shock bopped her over the head. *He's giving me attitude.*

The banker smoothed his hair again. "I'm afraid it

would be quite…premature to release any funds without first confirming both your relationship to Dominik Marek and the legality of this…this…'' A finger waggled at the marriage certificate.

Peter cleared his throat and Dinwiddie hurriedly displayed his showcase teeth. ''I'm sure you understand. We must follow certain procedures.

''For one thing, we'll need notarized birth certificates from you and your father, Mrs. Havel. No hurry,'' he assured her. ''You can drop them by…oh, after you've returned from your honeymoon.''

Wendy was still organizing her first protest when the Peter calmly declared, ''We have no time for a honeymoon now.''

Then he smiled at the banker for his unwitting assistance. ''But we will have a small party for family and friends. A—'' he turned to Wendy and spread his hands in appeal ''—receipt?''

''Do you mean, a reception?'' Her voice gave nothing away, but her eyes flashed alarm.

Peter grinned. This was going to be fun. ''Yes. We must have a reception party for me to meet Wendy's family and friends.''

Her eyes widened, those soft lips parted and rejoined several times—an amazingly accurate imitation of an astonished fish, he thought.

''We— Wait— Reception? What are you talking about?'' Her voice rose with each question.

''I have idea!'' Peter exclaimed, trying to sound spontaneous. ''Let's invite Mr. Dinwiddie to celebrate our nuptials, too.''

For a long moment Wendy stared at him as if he had sprouted a second head.

Finally she asked in a faint voice, ''When exactly were we having this party?''

''In one week?'' he suggested, then addressed the

banker. "If you attend, it will help you confirm our marriage, yes?"

Dinwiddie was silent a moment before reluctantly conceding, "I suppose it wouldn't hurt."

Peter beamed; he'd just secured his first necessary requirement: more time with his intriguing wife. "We will call you to confirm." Rising, he smiled down at Wendy. "Shall we go, my dear?"

"Let's," she agreed, her green eyes telegraphing too many messages for Peter to comprehend. "I'll get you those birth certificates," she promised Dinwiddie as she got to her feet. Then, with another significant glance at Peter, she marched out of the office.

THE ELEVATOR WAS PACKED with employees exiting the daily grind, so Wendy remained silent. No way she was broaching the party thing in front of an audience. Sheesh, the nutty mathematician would probably invite them, too!

Finally. The doors opened and they emerged on the main floor.

Grasping the brainiac's arm and digging in her heels, Wendy pulled Peter aside while the rest of the crowd flowed around them and dispersed.

"Are you bananas?" Wendy croaked when they were relatively alone, willing herself to stay on topic—despite the electricity sizzling between her palm and his rock-hard bicep. "A wedding reception? To meet my family? And you want Dimwit—er, Dinwiddie to come?"

Peter cocked his head to one side, as if thinking about his answer.

"Never mind," Wendy sighed. "Where do you geniuses get this stuff?"

Suddenly, without any warning at all, Peter cupped her face with his large, masculine hands—and kissed her.

And with the same high-voltage results as before. Spinning head, heart rate climbing, skin heating, body begging to melt against the hard planes of this magnificent male—

*No! It's just lust and lust is just another detour that sends you off course.* Wendy fought free of Peter's embrace. *Like love and family.* "What is it with you and this public kissing thing?"

Peter grinned at her. "Missouri is Show Off State, yes? So let's show we are married. Come…come back into my arms," he murmured with such seductive, velvety warmth that Wendy started toward him.

Halting, she shook her head and clasped her hands behind her so they wouldn't do something stupid. Such as reach for her Czech mate. "I don't think that's a good idea, Peter."

But she couldn't deny that part—several parts—of her thought it was.

"I helped you with your banker," Peter whispered. "Now help me with Immigration."

"I already helped you with that," she pointed out. "I married you, remember?"

Peter twinkled his smoky-blues at her. "I remember," he assured her in his smooth as twenty-year-old-Scotch voice. "But Agent Worthington does not."

"Huh?"

Peter gestured with his chin, then closed his eyes. For a second it looked as though he was swaying to music only he could hear. "He lurks behind the second column on right."

After a quick check Wendy stepped into Peter's arms and did as he asked. Under duress, she told herself.

*Yeah, right.*

Peter bent his head, angling his mouth over hers.

And she was sliding her hands up and around his neck. Burying her fingers in his thick golden hair. Pressing her soft breasts to his hard chest. Opening to let his tongue stroke into her moistness. Learning his taste in return.

It's just for appearance's sake, she told herself through the haze of desire enfolding her like a cashmere pashmina.

It did *not* feel like coming home.

She'd learned the hard way not to trust that feeling anyway. Because it hurt too much when you got left there alone.

"What are we to do?" Peter breathed the question in her ear.

*Find a motel…the back seat of a car…a deserted office or rest room or rooftop. Anypla—*

"…if Worthington continues to follow us?"

Wendy jerked her mind out of the bed—er, gutter. "Why don't you invite him to the party, too?" It was harder to jerk herself out of temptation's arms, but she did it.

"Good idea!" Peter exclaimed. "That way, all eggs sit in same bag."

"Basket," she corrected absently, pivoting to check on Worthington, hoping he'd split—so she could just take Peter back to his hotel and then go somewhere to have a nice, private nervous breakdown. "You put all your eggs in one basket."

She felt the heat of Peter's powerful body first. Then a certain large, firm cotton-brief-covered aspect of the man came into contact with her backside.

Wendy groaned silently as her libido revved into high gear again. She'd never been this interested in physical intimacy before.

But she'd never been married to the sexiest man ever to visit the Midwest before, either.

"Paris," she muttered the reminder to herself. "I'm going to Paris."

"Now, *milenko?*"

"No, Peter," she said wryly. "But soon. And I'm not your sweetheart."

Did he murmur "yet" before he moved around her to stalk toward Worthington?

A hot 'n' spicy thrill raced through Wendy at the thought of Peter applying that magnificent chest and the bulge behind the black cotton to seduce, beguile, entice her—

Oh, wake up, Cinderella. All Peter Havel wanted from Wendy was her cooperation with the INS.

Anything more was beyond the scope of their agreement. And too close to a danger zone Wendy refused to enter. Even though, she admitted, she was finally beginning to understand the powerful appeal that getting involved could have.

An odd sound—half squawk, half squeal—claimed her attention.

*Uh-oh.* She started across the marble floor. Peter had the INS clerk backed against one of the crowd-control ropes set up to protect the tellers from those awful, intrusive customers.

As she neared the two, Wendy greeted Bow Tie Boy with a loud "Hello, Mr. Worthington. Fancy meeting you here."

"I—I'm just doing my job, Miss Marek."

Over the agent's head, Peter aimed radiant blue eyes at her. They spoke volumes—and she understood their meaning perfectly.

"That's Mrs. Havel to you," she corrected. "And we've got the papers to prove it."

Francis J.'s pointy nose actually twitched. "Marrying for the sole purpose of obtaining resident status is a federal crime," he proclaimed officiously. "And the last time I checked—which was ten minutes ago—Dr. Havel was still registered at his hotel. Therefore, you'll have to pardon me for thinking that you two are attempting to commit fraud against the United States government!"

If he hadn't been so self-righteous, Wendy might have remained rational. But Worthington's monomania was too much like her father's. And, like her, Peter had done nothing to deserve this persecution.

She went ballistic.

With a furious glare, she informed the bureaucratic rodent lookalike, "Sorry, buddy, but you've leapt to the wrong conclusion.

"For your info, we got married this morning in Santa Fe. Upon our return, we had an appointment here at the bank. Now we're headed to Peter's hotel to pick up his luggage and check him out. The next stop is my apartment, which from now on, of course, will be *our* apartment.

"And in case you're interested," she went on, "at seven, we'll be attending Peter's welcoming reception at the university. After which, we'll return home. Together. 'Cuz that's what married people do, isn't it?"

Worthington knuckled the bridge of his glasses. "D-don't think I won't check up on you," he huffed. "Enforcing the immigration laws of the United States is my sworn duty."

"You may also check up on us by attending our married reception next week," Peter added. "Now, if you will excuse us."

Flashing Wendy a smile that turned her knees to mush, he swept one hand in an arc in front of him. "After you, my dear."

Wendy ignored the endearment this time. What the hell, they had bigger problems than semantics. "Thank you, darling. Later, Worthington."

As she wobbled her way out of the Union Federal Bank & Trust, she wondered, Could it get any worse than this?

She didn't see how, but dire warnings about being stupid-stupid-stupid pounded—er, sounded—in her head.

PETER STILL COULDN'T decide if Wendy was unbelievably skilled or incredibly lucky, but by the time they'd loaded his luggage into the virtual trunk of Wendy's car and set off for her apartment, he was a wreck. The other drivers swerved and veered with reckless abandon, jumped lanes, sped up when the traffic lights turned yellow and stopped—*when* they stopped—with their bumper kissing hers.

Wendy remained calm, oblivious to the dozens of accidents they barely escaped.

No thanks to anyone else, Peter thought as she turned down a street lined with the mottled-bark trees and cozy-looking, four-story, red-brick apartment buildings—and a BMW sedan that started racing her to a parking place along the curb.

Wendy won by the diameter of a carbon molecule.

She exulted in her triumph. Peter missed the words, of course, but guessed the meaning from her tone.

"You have a lucky cat," he agreed as he climbed from the little car and folded the seat forward to get to his luggage.

Wendy tucked her hair, frowning at him. Then she smiled.

And, as before, he *burned*.

"Don't you mean I'm a lucky dog?" she asked as she took his laptop and started up the sidewalk to a nearby building.

If she said something more, he didn't know. And he would not ask. But these stupid handicaps would *not* dictate his life!

"No, cats are the animals having nine lives," Peter said, following her into a tiny vestibule footing a narrow staircase.

Without answering—he thought—Wendy mounted the stairs.

Grimly he kept pace, climbing, turning, climbing…. His vertigo was in full spin by the time they reached her apartment. On the top floor, naturally.

Keying open the door, Wendy motioned him inside.

He tried to comply, but waves of dizziness and nausea swept over him. Dropping his suitcases, he grabbed the doorjamb for support.

Closing his eyes, he swore under his breath. No matter how much time passed, his inability to control the effects of his injury incensed him.

"Hey, it's not that bad!" Wendy cried before adding sheepishly, "Well, I wasn't expecting guests."

Grateful for her misinterpretation of his behavior, Peter opened his eyes.

"I had a deadline to meet."

"Deadline?" he asked, looking around.

"For my application portfolio."

He raised an inquiring eyebrow.

"To the Paris Design Institute?" Wendy rolled her eyes. "That's why I need the trust money. I'm going to study fashion design." She frowned. "And teach my father that I run my own life."

Interesting information, but Peter couldn't process it right now. The apartment still spun; he closed his eyes again. *Better.*

"Your home is very charming," he said, giving his vision another try. Success: the walls remained stationary.

"Thanks," Wendy said, laughing as she picked up one of the cases he'd dropped, "but there's no need to be polite."

Peter thought of some very *im*polite things they could do together.

But not yet. "You've been busy," he commented, looking around as he followed her into the apartment's spacious main room. "I admire people who can create, who think originally."

*Who don't care about tidiness more than inventiveness.*

That difficulty with Katrina had nothing to do with his injuries, Peter realized as he continued to study Wendy's home.

Scraps of fabric and trim, spools of thread and large pieces of brown tissue paper drifted over a worn carpet and lapped up onto equally worn furniture. Sketchpads, pincushions, markers and a sewing machine sat on a large table at the far end of the room. Tall windows that overlooked the street had their curtains tied back to let in golden rivers of late-afternoon sunlight.

To his left were three doors. The closest one stood open, revealing a painted iron bed. Large enough for two people, as long as they were willing to be quite friendly.

Moving cautiously, Peter picked up the rest of his luggage. "Where shall I deposit my things?"

"Check your bags wherever you like," Wendy said. "One of us will be sleeping there." She pointed to a sofa that had seen better days. Decades of them.

"I'll take it," Peter said with a shrug. If—no, *when*—he convinced Wendy to release him from his promise and they shared a bed, they would not be sleeping.

"Bathroom's through there." She pointed to the center doorway. "It also opens into the bedroom, so remember to close both doors for privacy. Last door's the kitchen, but good luck finding anything edible in there. I don't cook." Not since she'd moved out on her own.

"I do." Peter strolled slowly through the living room. Like some lithe, golden-maned lion. "But tonight…"

Oh, yeah. Now that he mentioned it, she was starving. Wendy fished the phone out of the swatch pile in the armchair. "Pizza or Chinese?" she asked. "They both deliver."

The Czech Chest rubbed the side of his face absently, considering his choices, she guessed. "Pizza," he said finally.

As she hit the speed dial for Lombardo's, Peter strolled to the windows overlooking the street. Silhouetted against the sun, he glowed like a golden statue of a Greek god.

"Should we order something for our INS friend?" he asked.

"Don't tell me—"

"Yes. Worthington waits below."

With a groan, Wendy ordered one medium and one small deep-dish pizza, extra pepperoni, extra cheese.

When she'd hung up, Peter said, "I wish to wear a suit tonight. Shall I take shower first or press my pants until the pizza arrives?"

*I'd like to press your pants.* Before she could stop herself, Wendy was picturing Peter, naked, in her shower. Her pulse shot into Mach numbers.

Get a grip, she told herself. It's just a simple case of lust. So this Euro hottie packed gorgeous looks and oozed masculinity. So what?

"Y-you can probably do both," she said. "Pizza takes thirty minutes." She looked blindly at her watch, telling herself to stop imagining intimate interpersonal interaction with Peter Havel.

*Yeah. Then make the Mississippi River flow north.* She focused on the numbers on her wrist. "You're right, it's almost six. We should start getting ready."

After providing Peter with a fresh towel and demonstrating the shower controls, Wendy threw herself out of the bathroom. A tad tardily—a mere glimpse of crinkly dark gold hair sent her hormones jumping like waterdrops on a hot skillet.

To distract herself, she relocated the ironing board— three times—filled the iron and dampened a dishtowel for use as a pressing cloth.

Then she dug through her closet for something to wear. After throwing on the lapis silk she'd designed with the fishtail hem and semi-plunging neckline, she traded places with the towel-wrapped, water-beaded hunk; he ironed and dressed while she put on makeup that melted right off again when she noticed his toothbrush nuzzling hers in the wall-mounted holder.

Maybe familiarity will breed contempt instead of increasing her desire to attempt breeding, she thought hopefully a few minutes later as she pretended to watch TV while Peter tied his tie.

By the time the food arrived, she doubted her hope had a hailstone's chance in hell: Peter looked too magnificent to ignore in a custom-tailored suit that Dinwiddie would probably drool over.

To make matters worse, after her first bite of pizza, Peter

leaned forward to wipe a dab of sauce from the corner of her mouth, then sucked the sauced finger clean, his eyes never leaving Wendy's face.

Somehow she finished the slice—without tasting it— then fled to the kitchen to apply dampened paper towels to her forehead and neck. Trying—damned unsuccessfully, too—to douse the heat her Czech "hobby" had generated with his seductive motions.

At six forty-five she ditched the quilted paper products, donned a short lime-suede jacket with lapis-colored soutache along the front and bottom edges and charged out to her car. Actually looking forward to an evening of stodgy professors, deadly dull academic speak, bland punch and tasteless cookies.

She hoped that observing Peter in the company of his peers for a couple of hours would prove that he, too, was as boring as old toenail clippings.

Provided any of his peers remembered to show up.

PETER FOLLOWED WENDY across campus to the student union, where she halted at the foot of the stairs leading to its entrance. To warn him, he discovered, to lower his expectations.

"I'm sure everyone—except Chairman Moss, of course—wishes you well, Dr. Havel, but…" She tucked her hair. "The beginning of the semester is always busy and…well, I'm sure you realize that experts are only interesting to, uh, their own field."

*Had she misinterpreted diffidence as arrogance?* A sobering thought.

"What I mean is…tonight's just a reception. Don't be upset if there isn't a big crowd in attendance, okay?"

Upset? Peter rubbed the side of his face wryly. A week, a month, a year ago, he'd have been happy with a small turnout. He'd been resigned, then, to his isolated state.

But now… Now he wanted any attention, any accolade, that might improve Wendy's opinion of him.

"I understand," he said. He knew it should not matter what this American woman thought of him. But it did. "Your Chairman Moss...he expects me, yes?"

"Yes. And Boroni and the dean, of course."

"Then let us get cracked."

After a second Wendy said, "Cracking," then led the way inside to the multipurpose room in which the reception to welcome this year's visiting expert was to be held.

She pulled open the door—and stopped so suddenly, Peter's chest collided with her back. He let his hands curl around her shoulders as his legs caught up, then simply stood there, measuring how well they fit.

Perfectly. Oh, yes, Wendy's opinion of him must be upgraded—and soon.

The little tigress remained motionless. Speechless, too.

Dipping his head, he chuckled softly in her ear. "Relax, Wendy," he advised. "It's only a small reception."

Ha. The room was, he noted with a thoroughly male surge of satisfaction he hadn't experienced since his accident, a moderately large meeting venue.

And it was packed.

# 5

PETER'S SENSE of gratification at Wendy's reaction lasted about three point two milliseconds. Just until a wall of incomprehensible noise hit him.

"I can't... Heavens, there are even video setups!" Wendy exclaimed, her green eyes wide. "Were you expecting this?"

"I do not expect." Not anymore. "It leads only to unpleasant surprises."

Wendy nodded. "You can say that again."

"Why?" Hope surged. Hope that his tigress might have some flaws of her own. Then perhaps he could admit his and with truth between them, who knew what might happen?

So. He did long for connection with someone. With Wendy? What had changed to make him flirt with the idea of intimacy—real intimacy, without falsehood between them like a mask?

*Wendy is what happened,* snorted the little voice upstairs.

Shaken by this crack in his self-sufficiency, Peter silently followed his wife into the room.

As the cacophony of dozens of people speaking at the same time rose in volume, Wendy touched his arm. Again he burned—until she started laughing. "It's just an expression," she said, her eyes dancing with amusement. "It means I agree with you."

Of course it did. Peter sighed. Sometimes colloquial English left him upriver without a bridge.

*So stop using it.*

The voice had a point. Though charming, Wendy's laughter edged too close to pity, which he didn't think he could tolerate. Even from her.

Absently, Peter rubbed his hand along the damaged side of his face as he tried to figure out how to deal with this crowd without revealing his flaws.

Wendy's grip on his arm tightened. And he wanted her gripping other parts of him—while he gripped her right back. Their relationship might be doomed to brevity, but with chemistry such as theirs...

"Dr. Havel!"

A rock could hear that booming salutation. As Peter slowly pivoted, seeking the face that went with the boom, he remembered his agreement not to consummate the marriage.

An idiotic promise, he now thought as the florid, white-haired dean emerged from the crowd like a lotto ball popping out of the shoot.

But only Wendy could release them from it.

"Welcome, welcome!"

*Perhaps if he gave her a persuasive reason to do so, she would...* Yes, he had not promised to refrain from *that*.

"Hello, Dean Leippert!" Wendy greeted her boss enthusiastically, hoping he'd snag Peter for photo ops or something. Anything. She needed space, perspective, a few dozen tranquilizers. Why now? she wondered. Why Peter? Why did she feel like a preteen going through her first crush?

Because she'd never had time for crushes as a preteen. Too busy being the family's housekeeper. And when she'd come to work at the university, the only guys interested in her had been looking for a meal ticket. So she'd just given up the whole dating thing. "Q-quite a crowd, sir," she told the dean.

"Wonderful turnout, isn't it?" Leippert's tie wouldn't flap tonight; P.R. duties always made him happy.

"Looks like the whole faculty's here," Wendy agreed. She hadn't seen this many profs in one place since graduation.

"We've got newspaper coverage and a couple of TV crews, too. Seems everyone's eager to meet the fastest rising star of the scientific community."

It didn't hurt that said science star had movie star looks and a lock on that European charm, Wendy thought wryly.

Then she noticed a couple of physics emeriti—the pair ranked as the two worst knowledge snobs in St. Louis—doddering this way. Only one conclusion could be drawn from their presence: the Czech Chest's genius truly encompassed more than kissing.

After a short disconcerted moment, Wendy told herself to feel relieved.

Because an academic hotshot with Peter's apparent international reputation had to be devoted to his career. Which meant he wasn't looking for emotional entanglements, either.

*So maybe we can just enjoy the ride, then go our separate ways.* He certainly had some attributes she hadn't seen in her family before. Consideration, interest in her work, support at the bank…

Leaning close, Leippert dropped his boom to conspiracy level. "Well? Are you married?"

Wendy nodded while Peter turned his head slightly away. Another good sign, she told herself firmly over a twinge of disappointment. Logical he'd be more interested in his numerous admirers than in their phony marriage.

"That Worthington from INS was waiting at the airport when we got back," she reported to the dean in a low tone, "and he's been following us ever since. We even had to move Peter's stuff into my apartment!"

If she expected brownie points for making such an above-and-beyond sacrifice, Wendy thought when Leippert stroked his chin then shrugged, she also believed those multimillionaire basketball players when they insist they're just guys doing a job.

The dean suddenly flapped his tie. "Chairman Moss!"

"Where?"

Dropping the neckwear as if it had burned his fingers, her boss aimed a used-car-salesman's smile past Wendy's left shoulder. Then, shoveling geniality the way bulldozers push dirt, Leippert went into host mode. "Come meet our Czech genius, Mr. Moss! Won't it be a coup for the university if he and Dr. Boroni claim the next Fields Medal?"

"That *would* be a prestigious achievement for us," the trustee, a sour-faced, stoop-shouldered, seventy-something in a gray suit, agreed reluctantly.

Leippert's tie points twitched.

Peter—who'd ignored the whole exchange in favor of surveying the room—bent to murmur in Wendy's ear, "I see a friendly face. Your colleague with the pointed blue hair is here."

"Robin?"

As she rose on tiptoe to peer over the sea of heads, Peter's adorable purr stroked her ear again. "I think also I see Worthington slinking around."

Before she could locate friend *or* foe, her boss clamped one hand on Peter's elbow, the other on Chairman Moss's shoulder and began manhandling them both toward a miked lectern at the far end of the room where the university seal would act as background. "Come on, gentlemen. Let's go have ourselves a press conference."

Several journalists clutching small recording devices and the two TV news teams—cameramen shouldering their equipment and reporters holding microphones like scepters—clustered around the lectern.

*Excellent,* Wendy thought. *Now I can slip away and grab a little breathing room.*

Or not. Peter twisted out of the dean's grip long enough to crook a finger at her. "You come, too," he commanded.

"Didn't anyone tell you, darling?" Wendy's sweet tone

didn't match the ice in her moss-green eyes. "We abolished slavery a while back."

Peter stepped closer. "*Please* come with me," he said softly. "My English...if some jets still lag...well, I don't want to say something incorrectly."

It was as close to begging as he'd allow himself.

Fortunately it was close enough. Though she tossed her tawny hair, his tigress let him capture her hand and drag her to the front, where she stood on his right—his good side, but tantalizingly just beyond reach.

After booming the room to silence, Dean Leippert launched into a long-winded introduction speech, most of which Peter could not hear clearly enough to comprehend but doubted he needed to.

He *needed* to ignore the erogenous effect of his wife's perfume, the curve-hugging dress she was wearing, her delectable long legs and the unwitting mercy she'd just shown.

Carefully, he crossed his hands in front of him to shield his physical response from any prurient onlookers—while trying to distract himself by working one of the more difficult nonlinear differential equations in his head.

When a low, surflike sound in both ears and the audience's hand movements signaled the end of the dean's speech, he took a step forward.

Wendy stopped him with another heat-generating touch that displaced his mathematical musings the way a properly proportioned mixture of potassium nitrate, sulfur and charcoal, when ignited, rapidly expels a bullet from a gun barrel.

"Boroni's first, then you."

Giving her a grateful smile, Peter shook the professor's hand, then stepped back to reflect on the only math his mind now wished to consider: when this welcome reception ended, one him would take one her home, where the two of them would be alone.

Though she seemed unaware of the sensual allure that

clung to her like plastic wrap to itself, Peter was profoundly aware of it. Living together, sleeping together—at least, in the same apartment...conditions for exploring their mutual chemistry had to occur. They'd dress and undress and shower there. Eat, keep house, relax. Together. For no less than a week, thanks to two suspicious bureaucrats.

With the slightest encouragement, Peter intended to indulge his desire for Wendy. With Wendy. To see where it led. Or to get her out of his system.

Anticipation coiled through Peter; impatiently, he turned his head to gauge Boroni's progress from his body language.

Uh-oh. The old man's fist waved in the air and Peter's good ear now captured a portion of his speech. It had become a harangue.

"—unrelenting! Unprincipled! Such deviousness must—"

Peter had already taken a step forward when Wendy jabbed him. For once, his vertigo proved useful. Losing his balance, he stumbled against Dr. Boroni who, once his tirade was disrupted, recalled why they were there and sheepishly but promptly introduced Peter.

Who'd faced microphones and crowds many times in the past. In several languages. But he'd never been less interested in doing so.

As he began to speak, Peter hoped to avoid lengthy questioning, prevent disclosure of his flaws—and to go home as soon as possible.

Carefully, he made flattering references to Chairman Moss, expressed gratitude to Leippert and Boroni and assured the chemists that he looked forward to working with them, as well.

He finished by declaring his pleasure at visiting St. Louis, the Gateway to West. As applause broke out, Wendy touched his hand.

And his mind went blank.

*Hovno,* if one contact deleted his thoughts like so many corrupted files, what would a night of hot, sweet sex do?

A journalist pushed forward to ask a question.

Momentarily ignoring him, Peter raised an eyebrow at Wendy, who jerked her chin toward the left.

Where a faintly scowling Worthington lurked behind a potted plant, scribbling in a notebook.

So. The little man still sought to unmask their deception.

"Dr. Havel?"

Peter turned his attention to the reporter, who asked, "What will solving Gandel's Anomaly mean to ordinary people?"

"Americans," Peter noted with a smile. "So practical always." Shrugging one shoulder, he added, "Perhaps it will assure them we are earning our money."

The audience laughed. Wendy didn't join them, too busy staring at Worthington, who watched her just as closely.

Like a cat and its mouse, Peter thought. But which was which?

He'd put his money on Wendy.

Another reporter asked a question. Peter pretended to be formulating his response, but once again, Wendy had claimed his attention. In that dress, with that body, she must claim the attention of every male with a working circulatory system. Peter growled under his breath.

"Dr. Havel?" Dean Leippert's boom penetrated his damaged ear. "Can you tell us your plans for the future?"

*Wendy and I will go home. We will be alone.*

*And I will still wish to hide my flaws.* Peter frowned. "I work next with Wilkersen in Los Angeles, after which I lecture in Guadalajara."

True, his life now had no room for a woman. But before he left St. Louis, he'd like to get the one he'd married out of her skimpy dress—if only to satisfy his male itch for her.

*And find out if you can trust her with the truth about you.*

As another reporter spoke up, Peter shook his head to silence the voice of loneliness—and had to grip the lectern until the room stabilized. A sure sign he'd reached his limit for today.

"Please forgive me," he interjected impulsively. "Today is my wedding day. My thoughts are not of Gandel..." The look on Wendy's face turned his smile into a grin. "...but of my new bride."

Peter pulled her close. "Please meet the woman of my dream—"

"Your worst nightmare, you mean," she breathed into his right ear.

He pressed his lips to her temple. Interesting to learn that the hesitancy he'd felt around Katrina after his injury disappeared around Wendy. "My wife."

Her heart rate accelerated at the pride Peter purred into those two words.

Until she remembered he was just acting for Worthington's benefit.

Dammit, this adolescent reaction to the man was plain foolish.

Peter didn't want to be married any more than she did. Or he would be already.

And just because there was some slight attraction between them... *Slight, right. About as small as Texas.*

Wendy growled silently. Where was the hard-won wisdom she'd gained from her mother's abandonment? Attraction faded, passion died. People who burned got left with ashes. Smarter to go to Paris than to stick your hand in the fire.

A flurry of questions rose from all sides. For a moment Wendy considered making Peter answer every one, but she wasn't sure he wouldn't trip himself up and Worthington was taking down every word.

She wanted to visit Paris, not Leavenworth.

"Thank you all for your kind wishes." Wendy held up

her hands, palms out, and flashed a politician's smile. "But we'd prefer to keep our personal life private."

She glanced at her brainiac hubby; he was massaging the side of his face again. Did the gesture indicate irritation or boredom—or plain old fatigue?

Whatever. Maybe his jets really were still lagging, as he'd so cutely—er, colorfully—put it.

"If you have any more questions concerning the Anomaly, perhaps Dr. Boroni can address them."

The antique mathematician accepted the limelight's return with a pleased bow. This time, Leippert glued himself to Boroni's side, ready to respin the interview if the elderly nutcase began spouting his conspiracy theory again. Moss moved in to flank the professor from the other side—he loved media attention, too.

"Come, *milenko,*" Peter murmured in Wendy's ear. "Let us split this scene apart."

"Are you kidding?" Wendy smiled wryly. "You're the guest of honor. You can't bail until everybody who wants to meet you, has."

So Peter let Wendy propel him from one knot of people to the next while he tried to solve a compelling mystery. After the way their kisses detonated, why was she so reluctant to return to her apartment with him?

*Leave it for another time, Havel.* Even without the distraction Wendy posed, this crowded reception was a minefield.

Names were only half heard. Most faces he saw too imperfectly to recognize later. He protected his balance by moving like an old man under water. And so far, it seemed, his secrets remained hidden. But every minute that passed increased the odds against him.

He'd had enough pity to last a lifetime.

"Va-va-voom!" Wendy's blue-haired friend—Robin—skidded to a halt in front of them. "Congratulations, kiddos. This is the first fuddy-duddy function I've been to that rocks!"

Peter held out his hand. "Pleased to see you again."

"Likewise." Robin slapped his hand, then held hers out palm up. "How was 'Nude Mexico'?" she asked with a giggle.

"Beautiful," Peter replied, guessing he was supposed to return the slap. As he did so, he tried to keep his one fully functional eye on both women.

"Max is gonna be crushed," Robin told Wendy with a grin. "You know he wanted you to wait for him."

Everything—*everything*—inside Peter stilled. "Max?" he asked softly.

"My son," Robin explained. "He's nine. He thinks Wendy hung the moon."

Peter touched the side of his face. Didn't that phrase mean something one didn't do unless drunk and a student?

"Only because I helped him learn to ice skate," Wendy said, "so he could play hockey."

Robin's eyebrow ring jiggled as she nodded. "I couldn't make the transition from boards to blades," she confided to Peter.

His confusion must have been apparent.

Wendy translated. "She means she can ride skateboards but can't stay upright on frozen water."

Peter gazed at his wife intently. "But you can." Interesting. Another commonality. Or was it? He hadn't been back on the ice since the accident.

With a giggle, Robin snapped her fingers over her head. "Poof!" she cried. "Donahue disappears from Czech radar!" She cupped her hand around her ear. "Hear that? It's my ego crashing."

Nobody understood her, Peter decided. Because she made no sense.

Before he could design a safe rejoinder to such insanity, Francis J. Worthington wormed his way into the group.

"You're not fooling anybody," he warned, squinting his eyes. Which only enhanced the image of a myopic rat. "Especially not me."

The little bureaucrat's bow tie quivered as he poked one bony finger at Peter, then Wendy. "Justice will be served!"

The dramatic effect of Worthington's declaration was spoiled when he spun on his heel to leave—and found himself eye-to-eyebrow ring with Robin.

His mouth sagged open, his spectacles glinting as he tilted his head. Up to view her blue spikes, then down past the yellow camisole and matching shrug, past the gauzy flower-print skirt, to the red-banded sweatsocks folded down atop her chunky black lace-up boots.

Worthington clutched his bow tie for a second, then swallowed visibly before solemnly addressing her. "Sorry, m-ma'am. J-just doing my job." He sounded like someone on helium trying to imitate John Wayne.

Peter and Wendy exchanged amused glances that quickly became shared smirks.

When they started choking back laughter, the INS clerk pulled himself up with a sniff, gave Robin a dignified nod and stalked off.

A few seconds later Robin excused herself to, as she put it, "See if I can get a buzz off the oatmeal cookies."

She'd gone two steps when she turned back, wrapped a hand around Wendy's wrist and tugged. The movement propelled them both closer to Peter's good ear. "You lucky schmuck," he heard Robin say. "Getting to go home with a babe like that!"

Peter pretended to scan the room, straining for Wendy's reply.

Bah. A murmur only. But, he noticed, the crowd had thinned. Meaning he would soon find out through observation.

"Let us go," he suggested, cradling Wendy's elbow in his palm and urging her toward the door.

His good eye still had phenomenal peripheral vision; with it, he tracked Worthington, who again followed them like fate's messenger.

"We have to say good-night to Leippert, Moss and Dr. Boroni first," Wendy insisted, but since she didn't dislodge his hand, Peter acceded. Plenty of night remained for seducing his wife.

And once he'd thoroughly explored her soft mouth and lush body, once he'd tangled his fingers in her silky hair, once his body had intimately mingled with hers, the power of her allure would dissipate like steam rising in cold air. He'd be free. *Still alone—and lonely.*

*No,* Peter told himself firmly. *Still safe from others' pity.*

WENDY GRITTED HER TEETH to keep smiling. Her cheeks ached.

Farewells to the big three were dragging on. *Like that Florida recount.*

Moss voiced more sorrow over his unchosen physicist; Boroni lost another pancake from his stack—this time, he claimed the refreshments proved the conspiracy had spread to the university food service—and Dean Leippert plugged in a platitude disc and downloaded about a million clichés.

Finally, Wendy just said goodbye again, pivoted on one of the heels that had been torturing her feet all night and walked away.

She could feel Peter behind her. *Feel* him—when he was at least eighteen inches away from the outermost layer of her skin.

And *see* him—mentally, as she'd first seen him: smooth skin over hard muscles and distinctly male bulges. Magnificently nearly naked.

She must be crazy, voluntarily taking such a tempting male specimen into her apartment.

Especially since she wasn't taking him into her bed....

Not that she didn't want to. Any woman who'd been through the past twenty-four hours she had would already be half in love with Peter Havel—gorgeous, generous, kind and, if tonight was any indication, professionally a superstar, yet perfectly modest about it all.

So Peter happened to be a little more attractive than any other guy she'd ever met.

*Yeah, like the mother of those septuplets was a little more pregnant than her husband.*

But Wendy still remembered the pain she'd felt reading the note her mother had written about needing room for her artistic nature to breathe.

She wasn't giving anybody a chance to hurt her like that again.

She and Peter would stay married, as agreed, until she got her trust fund payout and he got his green card. But that didn't mean they had to act as if they were on *Temptation Island. We're in St. Louis; we'll act conservative.*

A NONDESCRIPT American-made car with government plates followed them home.

Wendy didn't have to be a superbrain to know who was driving it.

"The man is a bulldog," she muttered as she slotted into the only spot left on her side of the street. Four buildings down.

Naturally, as soon as she shut off her engine, a primer-heavy Buick pulled out and Worthington snagged its place—directly across the street from the entrance to her building.

"It appears our Immigration friend is settling up," Peter commented as they entered the vestibule.

"In," Wendy corrected with a sigh. "And yes, dammit."

"He cannot come inside, can he?" Peter asked. When Wendy shook her head, he shrugged. "Then don't let him chat your butt."

Wendy giggled. There's a picture Robin would enjoy!

"Let's forget bureaucracy now," her brawny brainiac purred. "Let us go upstairs and celebrate our wedding night."

Not even the negligible wattage of the dim bulb overhead hid the undeniable desire smoldering in his smoky-blue eyes. Her own primitive brain started to smoke and smolder, too, brewing up a desire almost too strong to resist. To get naked. With her husband.

Wendy raced upstairs before she burst into flames. Or did something stupid. Something one of them would surely regret.

"I'll bet you're still tired from your trip," she babbled when Peter appeared. She vaulted across the living area in an attempt to put mucho distance between herself and the oh-so-tempting male with whom she was supposed to live—for a week, anyway.

"You are ready to go to bed, *milenko?*"

Could a woman with any heterosexual tendencies resist that velvety male voice? Let alone the golden man behind it?

"Yes! I mean—" God only knows what made her recall that she'd never, on any of her not-that-many mornings after, regretted a night before. For some reason, despite the desire heating her veins, Wendy didn't want to risk breaking that streak tonight. "No. That is, not here. Forget the couch—you can have the bed. I'm spending the night at Robin's."

If she hoped for an argument, she didn't get one. Only a question. "Won't Worthington be suspicious if you leave?"

"I, uh, I'll slip out the back."

After speed-dialing her friend, Wendy rounded up her toothbrush and contacts case and headed for her bedroom, Peter following. Scooping up a nightshirt, she crossed to the window. As she climbed out onto the fire escape, he stopped her with a touch. "Is this safe?"

Safer than staying here with the Czech Chest and an available bed.

"I read that, in American cities, it is dangerous to be a streetwalker at night."

Wendy stifled another giggle—and an urge to climb

back through her window to spend her wedding night the traditional way.

"It's only a couple of blocks. I'll be fine." Unable to halt the glow sparked by his concern for her safety, Wendy eased down the iron steps, then jumped the last two feet to the ground.

She'd spend tonight folded like origami into the extra bunk in Max's room. Because a hockey-mad, nine-year-old kid was about all the man she could handle right now.

"I'll be back in the morning," she called up softly. "Worthington will never know."

WITH THAT, his wife disappeared down the alley. Peter stayed at the window until he saw her emerge into the light at the far end of the alley, then cross the street and pass out of view.

"Some wedding night, Havel," he muttered as he turned on a lamp and studied Wendy's bedroom.

No girlish frills or stuffed toys here.

Instead, richly colored ethnic prints and the creativity evidenced by such things as a chrome teakettle holding dried flowers spoke of a woman with the imagination of a true artist and a strong sense of self.

She deserved a strong and confident man. Was he whole enough?

How, he wondered as he returned to the living room, was he to find out—or, alternately, remove Wendy from his system—if they were never together?

After a moment Peter smiled. *The reception.* Of course!

"No doubt," he told the TV, which just looked back blankly. "Planning and preparing for it will provide the format I need to solve the Wendy questions."

With a yawn, he left the TV blank and prepared for bed. A unique wedding night, capping an equally unique wedding day.

The groom would sleep in his wife's bed. Alone. But not, if he had anything to say about it, for long.

LUCKILY FOR PETER, he was lying on his left side the next morning so he heard Wendy's return. Actually, he heard a thud and a whispered curse, then footsteps past the bed, a door clicking closed, followed by...what?

Ah, running water. She was taking a shower.

Peter's body came fully alert as his mind pictured Wendy's slick, rosy-complexioned female curves beneath the warm spray.

Carefully leaving the bed, he pulled on some drawstring pants and began working out the square root of nineteen to avoid wasting precious bodily fluids. He preferred to save them until *he* was what made Wendy's female parts wet and slick.

WHICH, HE REALIZED over the next five days, might not happen before he left for L.A.

Boroni was determined to monopolize him; every morning at seven, he arrived to collect Peter for endurance math meets. The chemistry professors must have had some sort of extensive surveillance ability: every time he slipped away from Emil, one of them swooped in and dragged him off for marathons of chalked diagrams and long-winded speculations concerning possible applications for crystalline structures nobody had yet produced.

As for Wendy—smoke in a typhoon remained in one place longer than she did. Work took up her days, of course, and whenever he managed to stop by the dean's office, she disappeared within minutes on some mysterious but urgent errand.

They'd married on Tuesday. The little tigress had spent Wednesday evening in the art building, Thursday watching television as intently as brain surgery and Friday doing laundry somewhere he wasn't invited.

She'd spent the weekend with Robin and her son Max, who must have had a science project since, according to

Wendy when they met in the kitchen the following Monday morning—*and he asked*—the three of them had gone to a market for fleas.

Worthington still skulked outside, checking on them, so Wendy ate breakfast and dinner with her husband and occupied the apartment until 10:30 p.m., when she'd stop fidgeting with her dress designs and perform her disappearing act down the fire escape. Every night.

This stalemate gained him nothing but frustration, Peter decided, and clearly, nothing would change unless he changed it.

So that Monday evening, he became proactive in his search for answers to the questions his injury and Katrina's pity had left him. When Wendy came home after work, pizza awaited. A bottle of red wine breathed on the table, along with plates, glasses, silverware and paper towels folded as napkins.

Wendy merely raised an eyebrow, tucked her hair and disappeared into the bedroom to change her orange-and-gray gored skirt for slashed-and-painted jeans that caressed her hips and clung to her long legs.

Then, mumbling something, she headed for the door.

"Embrace your horses!" Peter called—and was pleasantly surprised when she halted in midstride to turn and gaze at him, her lush lips parted. Peter's heart—and another organ located in his southern hemisphere—experienced a rapid increase in blood flow.

"Excuse me?"

"We must talk, *milenko*." Peter spread his arms, palms up. "Come have some wine before dinner."

When Wendy tucked her hair behind her ears, he twinkled his eyes at her. "I won't bite you. I promise."

He wished to promise the opposite, in fact, but...*one step at a time.*

Those smoky-blues exerted their magic power. Wendy walked over and sat down. Telling herself she was starving—and too tired at the moment to sneak around avoiding their personal INS spy. Which reminded her...

"I'm afraid we're going to actually have to do that reception thing," she said as Peter filled her wineglass.

"We're on the same wavelength!" he exclaimed, flashing one of his toaster-oven-on-high smiles. "This is my conclusion, too. And we must invite some people to join the doubting bureaucrats."

"Better put my father on the top of the list," Wendy said ruefully. "He tried to arrange another blind date for me today."

Peter cocked his head as he handed her a pizza-laden plate. "You date men who cannot see?"

Weird—he looked almost…hopeful?

"Blind dates are people who don't know each other."

His hand seemed to squeeze his wineglass. "Haven't you told your father of our marriage?"

"Yes, I did," Wendy replied—then pressed her lips together before going on. "He said he won't believe me until he meets the victim—er, husband."

"How can he not believe his own daughter?" Peter asked softly.

His genuine concern brought tears too close to the surface. Wendy fought them back. "Long story. Too boring to tell."

After a quick bite of dough, sauce and fat, she rushed on. "We need allies. Let's see—we'll have Dinwiddie, Worthington, my dad and my brother. Patrick's probably neutral, but still…"

Peter topped up her glass.

Was he trying to get her drunk? The man could do that without alcohol.

"Dr. Boroni and Dean Leippert?" he suggested, fingers gliding up and down the side of his face. He gave her that half grin that made Wendy not care if it was specially for her or just instinctive flirting.

Flirt or not, he'd shown her more concern and care in a week than her father had in years.

But he hadn't once protested her nightly reverse-Rapunzel thing.

"Let's ask Robin and Max, too," she suggested, determined to deny the sharp disappointment *that* reminder delivered. "Kids make good buffers." Sometimes. She and Patrick hadn't....

"Perfect," Peter agreed. "Now to discuss time, date and menu."

"Menu?" Wendy groaned.

"I've been thinking," the Czech Chest confessed seriously. "A dinner party might be best. A meal is finite—and guests stay seated where we put them."

Hmm. Good thinking. But as far as Wendy was concerned, domesticity held only bad memories—ones she didn't revisit voluntarily.

"Okay," she said as she pushed her chair back from the table. "But I'm not slaving away in the kitchen for Dinwiddie, Worthington or anybody else." *Meaning you, Peter Havel.* In spite of her nightly dreams to the contrary.

She expected an argument. Or an avowal of helplessness, with a side-order plea for rescue. Any of the usual behaviors for getting other people to do what you want.

Instead, Peter beamed at her. Positively beamed. Then he rounded the table and closed the distance between them. His big, hard hands book-ended her face.

And he kissed her.

Their tongues mated.

The sun blew up.

Earthquakes jolted off the Richter scale.

"How can they doubt the reality of our marriage?" he murmured against her mouth. "When you treat me like an ordinary husband. Perfectly normal husband."

Wendy thought she detected a trace of smugness in his declaration, but he kissed her again and she got too busy with tingling inside and tangling her fingers in his rich, golden hair to think about it. To think, period.

Even when he ended the kiss, she couldn't think. Just

feel. And want. And ponder some increasingly insistent needs throbbing through her most feminine places.

"You choose the date for our dinner party," Peter said. "And if you invite the guests, I will shop for the groceries. I can do it tonight."

A vague sound of protest escaped Wendy's lips. *Forget food. Kiss me again....*

"No, no, I need no help. This pony tricks many people."

As the door closed behind him, Wendy drifted to the sofa and sank onto it, her fingers slowly tracing her mouth. He means a one-trick pony, she thought. And what a trick. She could still feel the pressure, the heat of Peter's kiss.

For a warm and extremely pleasant eternity, she just sat there, thrumming with the emotions and sensations Peter had ignited in her. If only he'd—

Wait a minute. The Czech Chest? On the loose with only that fractured English and cocky smile?

With a groan, she snagged her keys, grabbed her purse—and booked.

# 6

WENDY SCREECHED TO A HALT in the brass-mailbox-lined vestibule. What was she doing? Running after *a guy?*

No way. Not even Peter, who, in addition to being hotter than the star of that gladiator flick, had actually been pretty cool the past week. No nosy questions, no intrusive demands, but continued quiet interest in her opinions, her goals, her dreams.

In fact, he'd engaged her in conversations about herself all week. He'd heated up boxes or brought home take-out dinners; in the morning, he'd made coffee and breakfast for her. Didn't toss his clothes all over the way her dad and brother did, either.

Her art and sewing supplies had magically organized themselves, too.

And until tonight, he'd always acted like a total gentleman—aside from tossing heated-interest looks her way.

Not that she'd tossed any back. Despite a *ton* of urges to do so, Wendy still questioned the wisdom of seeking a more up-close-and-personal relationship with her hunky Czech husband.

Because there was danger in getting physical, even if it was mutually declared to be purely recreational.

Sex with a gorgeous, golden, purring hottie sounded fine—unless it led to emotional entanglement.

Which could lead to derailing personal plans.

Of course, she and Peter weren't the bohemian painter and the traditionalist plumber her parents were, but she'd read her mother's farewell note.

Marriage and motherhood had left her mom feeling strangled, choked, dying for lack of creative outlets.

*I'm not willing to gamble innocent children's futures on the possibility my marriage could be different.*

What Wendy had never been able to understand was why her folks had gotten hitched in the first place. Let alone had kids....

Although, thanks to Peter Havel—whose sexual attraction quotient was up there in the stratosphere—she finally had a clue. Desire could exert a powerful force!

Especially when the man also washed dishes, made the bed, never left the toilet seat up, cleaned the sink after shaving and actually seemed to care about her thoughts, her likes, her wishes.

With a sigh, Wendy slumped on the stairs. Okay, so the Czech Chest might be decent mate material.

*Yeah, like Tiger Woods makes a decent living.*

"But the only mate I'm in the market for right now is a roommate," Wendy muttered. *And face it—no woman worth her estrogen could stay platonic around Peter.*

That's why she was racking at Robin's. Not that her husband seemed all that disappointed. She usually left him reading or staring into space, which he called "thinking."

Wendy rose and began to march back upstairs. Babysitting Peter was not her job.

She halted at the first landing. *But acting married to him is.* At least while intrepid INS Agent Double-O Worthington lurked around, eager to right wrong and save the world for democracy by deporting Czech mathematicians.

*That's* what had sent her careering downstairs thinking rescue thoughts.

If Worthington's crusade to deport Peter succeeded, her own plans went down in flames, too. Which made her temp husband's activities definitely her business. Wendy redescended the stairs.

Left to his own devices, who knew where the self-assured genius might end up. What if he went off into one of his intellectual fogs and got lost? And even if he broke male code and asked for directions, would he understand them?

Jiggling her keys, Wendy headed for her car, nodding at Worthington as she passed. Why didn't the university research squads investigate real-world mysteries—such as how *did* the INS spy guy always snag a great parking space?

Wendy started the engine, but didn't immediately put the car in gear.

Since the day she'd moved out of her father's house, Wendy had rejected all things domestic. Meaning she'd spent about as much time in grocery stores the past six years as rappers did at the symphony. She couldn't remember where the nearest one was....

*Let's see.* Yesterday at breakfast, Peter'd said something about Boroni stopping to buy snacks on the way to work.

Okay, Wendy admitted while she pondered her route, she loved schmoozing with her well-traveled, cosmopolitan husband. Was it a crime to take pleasure from a little exhilarating conversation—not to mention cinnamon-kissed coffee in the morning and herbal tea at night?

She couldn't sneak out of the apartment until after dark and had to be back there practically before dawn. They had to pass the time together somehow. She couldn't stay away or busy all the time.

Putting the car in drive and aiming toward the university, Wendy continued to rationalize—er, fight feeling guilty for liking Peter as much as she did.

Despite Max's innocent observation that she was doing her climbing act earlier and earlier every morning and lingering here longer and longer every night, she was *not* pursuing a flirtation. It was more along the lines of not freeloading more than a bed from a cash-strapped, single-mom friend—

*Whoa!* She was passing a large brightly lit store, its windows plastered with posters hawking Weekly Specials.

Red neon letters spelled out "Schnuck's"—St. Louis's leading grocery chain.

Since she'd seen no sign of Peter so far, Wendy entered the lot, parked and went inside.

She was checking out the checkout stands when she heard sounds of a scuffle coming from the back of the store.

And, within the cacophony, Wendy discerned a deep, adorably accented, *familiar* voice.

She raced toward it, hoping she was wrong. Praying she was wrong.

Rounding an end-of-aisle soda pyramid, she stopped dead in her tracks.

There, surrounded by produce, stood her husband.

Or rather, he sprawled over a pile of fruit, his arms bent behind him. A burly, balding guy in a uniform was snapping handcuffs on him.

Powerful emotional concerns that had nothing to do with her personal Parisian agenda blazed through her.

"No-oo!" Wendy stormed through the bins of raw food like a downhill slalom racer who'd overwaxed her skis. "Stop!" she cried. "There's been a mistake."

Yes, Peter thought ruefully as he struggled to an upright position and widened his stance for better stability, the biggest one being his overwhelming relief at Wendy's arrival.

He should be embarrassed at being found handcuffed, accused of…something by the middle-aged woman he'd approached. But he wasn't. He was simply glad to see his wife. For any reason.

"What's going on here?" Wendy demanded as she skidded to a halt in front of the trio.

Peter's anxiety disappeared like the little signs in the pop-up videos he'd watched while he told himself to work on the Anomaly, instead of foolishly plotting methods to get her into his arms.

"Should I call your embassy or something?"

Her green eyes were winter-forest dark, her silky hair glinted cinnamon—and her teeth nibbled on the edge of her soft lower lip.

*Sakra,* Wendy's unexpected—and unexpectedly welcome—concern warmed his heart and put his reproductive region on high alert.

Interesting that her distress over his difficulty didn't make him feel ashamed, as Katrina's had. Perhaps the empathy mattered less than who felt it. *And what you feel for the empath,* suggested his inner voice.

"Ah, Wendy," he exclaimed, before it said any more, "the sight of you hurts my eyes!"

"Huh?" grunted the guard, whose shirt patch read No-Fear Security Force.

"My eyes are sore from seeing you?" Peter suggested.

"I-is he trying to say you're a sight for sore eyes?" the pink-faced midlife shopper asked Wendy.

"Yes! Thank you." Peter smiled at the woman, who stepped backward, clutching her purse.

Wendy crossed her arms over her chest. "Could somebody please explain what's happening here?" she asked as patiently as possible—which clearly wasn't very. Peter grinned, once again imagining that fire in bed. What man wouldn't wish to be with such a passionate woman?

The No-Fear guard gripped his gadget belt. "You know this perp, lady?"

*Perp?* "This is no lady," Peter corrected solemnly— while twinkling his eyes at Wendy. "This is my wife." How he wished to have her twinkle back!

Or at least stop glaring.

Still… For the first time since his accident, he felt no hesitation about explaining himself. "I am shopping, but some items…" Peter shrugged. "I don't know one ahead of the other's tail. I wish everything perfect for our party, so I seek information."

"Information?" the shopper cried. "You made lewd suggestions!"

Wendy's gaze traveled to the plump, middle-aged woman, then back to Peter. His heart leapt when she flashed him an intimate smile of connection before raising an eyebrow.

"No offense, ma'am," Wendy said flatly, "but no way."

Peter leaned a hip against the display of mangoes, actually enjoying this fiasco now that his tigress was here, roaring on his behalf.

"He did," the woman insisted, strangling her purse with both hands. "He said h-he wanted to t-touch my...my chest."

Wendy clamped a hand over her mouth. Peter swallowed his own laugh. Not that the older woman wasn't generously endowed, but...

"We are newlyweds," he announced. Gently but firmly. "The only chests I wish to—"

"Peter." Wendy pressed a finger to his lips.

Despite his earlier wariness about romantic involvement, one touch had him weak and wanting more.

"You asked if you could squeeze m-my melons!" the lady blurted.

Looking around, Wendy muttered something. Then pointed. "Is that your basket?" she asked the woman.

"Yes. Why?"

"Because it's parked by the—" she waved at the beige balls laced with green veining "—cantaloupes." Wendy fisted her hands on her hips as she turned to address Peter. "Is that true? Is that what you said to this woman?"

Peter couldn't help himself. He grinned at his wife who was acting like a stern mother admonishing her child.

*Hovno!* The image of Wendy with a child, with *his* child, struck a powerful, primitive chord deep inside.

He cleared his throat, hoping to banish the image and the longing it provoked. His nomadic life had no room for longing, but certain parts of him, including his heart, were not listening to that truth. Had not been listening since he'd met—and married—this woman.

*Who will not even sleep in the same building with you.*

"I wish to buy a cantaloupe melon," he said carefully, "but how to choose one that is ripe, I don't know." After pausing to raise and lower one shoulder, he went on. "Always I hear Americans are friendly, so I ask her help."

Wendy closed her eyes. "Havel," she said with a sigh, "you need a keeper."

Peter's gut clenched. He wanted this woman to see him as a man, not as a broken child to be monitored.

"Cut me my slacks, *milenko*," Peter growled. "I can keeper myself."

After a couple of blinks Wendy gave the guard a helpless, palms-up gesture. "See? It's all a misunderstanding. The guy's a professor, but he's just off the boat from the Czech Republic and his English sucks." She turned to the shopper. "I'm sure he didn't mean to be insulting."

Then her green eyes pinned Peter. "Did you, darling?"

When he apologized, the woman agreed to forget the whole thing, then stalked off muttering about learning English *before* you came to this country.

Old biddy, Wendy thought, trying to hide her immense relief at Peter's release from the handcuffs. *Probably calls in to Rant Radio.*

"Glad we got that straightened out. No hard feelings, eh, bro?" The security cop tucked the cuffs in his belt, urged them to have a good night and ambled off.

Leaving Wendy where she'd…okay, yes, wanted to be for a week now: with Peter.

And even here, in this public, floodlit, totally unromantic setting, surrounded by the most mundane food and sundries, she couldn't think of anything but the sweet taste of his kisses, the hard beauty of his body and the sexy gleam in his smoky-blue eyes.

*Is it him I don't trust—or my own dedication to my goals?*

"This is like a modern fairy tale, yes?" Peter smoldered his eyes at her—while his mouth quirked into the patented smile that always set off a firestorm torching her insides. "The princess rescues the prince." He brought her hand to his lips. "Thank you, Wendy."

She blinked in amazement. Two seconds after that near disaster, he's calmly flirting?

"You're not welcome," she informed him, reclaiming her hand. "Do you realize if you'd gotten arrested, Worthington would have had you deported before your fingerprints dried?"

"It's very flattering, Wendy, how you are worried for me," he said softly, cupping her face.

She spun out of reach, trying to be angry at him. And not aroused by his slightest touch.

But the only person she was angry with was herself. For feeling so scared for him. And aroused. For feeling anything at all, darn it.

*Anything? Try everything.* Peter Havel made her feel everything she'd spent the past twelve years of her life vowing never to feel. And it had only been two weeks. How deep would she be in by the time this was over?

"I'm worried," she lied through her teeth, "about losing my trust fund monies.

"Why on earth did you have to talk to anybody?" she wailed, playing on—no, *into*—his hands.

"Because you were not here," he said simply. "So I must ask a stranger about her melons..." Peter paused, rubbing the side of his face to dislodge from his brain a picture of Wendy's "melons" filling his hands.

Too late—he was already hard for her. Again.

He swore under his breath. Before he left St. Louis, he must know how she had penetrated his protective barriers—before he found his heart truly at risk.

Wendy brought his thoughts back to the present. "Well, I'm here now. So let's shop."

WITHIN A VERY FEW MINUTES, it was clear she found no joy in the vast array of groceries surrounding them.

"Why?" Peter asked as they rolled down an aisle lined with snacks. In all his travels, he'd never seen more items offering less nutrition. He stopped to stare at one. Rice *Doodles?* Wasn't that…a waste by-product of the digestion process?

"Why what?"

"Why do you dislike food?" He understood that many women had traded the role of full-time homemaker for a career and financial independence. But everyone had to eat.

"It's not the food," Wendy protested. "It's the preparation. To me, cooking's just part of a whole chauvinistic enslavement process. Not gonna happen to this girl."

Peter shook his head at her vehemence—then had to grip a nearby shelf as the rows of snacks dipped and whirled.

"It's only rendering food edible," he said when the groceries quit moving.

"Not to me," Wendy replied, her eyes filled with pain and grief, sorrow and bitterness. "My mother got so tired of the whole thankless homemaker role, she left when I was twelve. Grandmama came and helped out for a couple of months, then I took over. Until the day I turned eighteen and followed my mother's example."

Stifling a soft sob, she strode away. He followed slowly, processing the information she'd divulged and considering the conclusion she'd reached.

Very unscientific. She'd extrapolated a theorem from the explanation of a woman who could not be completely rational. How could she be, leaving her children? And, from Wendy's still raw reaction, apparently without warning.

Peter stopped in his tracks. Her mother's departure had hurt Wendy deeply, had twisted her attitudes about love and marriage and family.

But her kisses, the passion they revealed…. Did a desire

for intimacy without inequality burn in her, too? And if so, could he rouse her to leave another woman's mistakes behind and embrace her own femininity on her own terms?

He wanted to try. To feed her soul and to expand her world to include taking joy and pleasure in everyday tasks. *And me.*

He hurried to catch up with her. Then backtracked them to the produce department, where he fed her a toothpick sample of fresh pineapple. And groaned silently as she closed her lips around the thick piece of pale yellow fruit and pulled it off its little stick.

"Mmm-mmm," she said, eyes closing as she swallowed. "Delicious."

The sensuality of her response tested Peter's control, but he continued the torture, making Wendy sample everything the store offered—from salsa to crab dip.

"Look!" he exclaimed when they reached the bakery department. "Chocolate chops."

Plucking a tidbit from the tub holding cookie pieces, he held it to her lips. Keeping his own response to her pleasure under control, until, after accepting the cookie morsel, Wendy licked a crumb off the tip of his finger.

*Then,* he had to open a freezer case and stand there, pretending to read labels, until he cooled down. Literally.

But the results of his experiment were clear. *Such passion* must *be freed. And enjoyed. Preferably by both of us.*

But not tonight, it seemed.

Once home, Wendy helped Peter put away the groceries, then donned baggy knit pants and a tattered T-shirt, tonight's sleeping attire—neither of which did anything to hide her delectable body from his hungry one.

He tried to stall her with questions about the party, but she just said, "Let's shoot for Friday. I'll call everybody tomorrow."

Then she climbed out the bedroom window and descended the fire escape like a damned cat burglar—leaving him alone. Something he no longer desired. Especially tonight.

He lay awake and aroused for hours, until a fact pushed its way through his physical discomfort. A fact that eased the difficulty of lying here in Wendy's bed, without Wendy.

At the dinner party, she must act happily married.

Peter smiled in the dark. He would be ready, then, to strike when...*something* heated. *Iron? Steel? Soup...?*

WENDY REJOICED when a long-simmering squabble between department heads erupted into open warfare, keeping her busy the rest of the week. Too busy to do more than make the calls inviting their chosen audience to Friday night's marriage charade.

Dinwiddie and Worthington accepted with poorly concealed skepticism, Boroni with glee and Dean Leippert with the reluctance he felt for any non-fund-raising event.

She had to bribe her brother with Rams tickets to keep her dad leashed until Friday. No way did she want to face him before then. Or without backup.

Especially when she knew how guilty she'd feel for smashing his grandkid dream once the truth—and the divorce—came out.

ON THE MORNING of the big day, Peter met her with a mug of coffee as she came through the window.

"Drink," he ordered, his eyes flickering over her tousled hair and damp skin still flushed from the shower she'd taken at Robin's.

Electricity sizzled through every one of Wendy's female cells. Her cheeks felt as if they were the color of a lawn flamingo. What would it take to be unaffected by this man? she wondered as she sipped the java, then attempted to move past Peter to safer ground—like the living room. Or better yet, Mars.

"Boroni works alone today," he announced, blocking her escape with his big, hard body. "And I am cutting short today's session with the chemistry professors, so I'll be home early to start cooking."

His smoky-blue eyes studied her a moment. Could they see the naked desire blooming in her like a red tide?

Without a word, he plucked the coffee mug from her fingers and set it on the dresser.

*The cooking's already started,* Wendy thought dazedly as his hands began caressing her shoulders. "I-is Worthington here, in the apartment?" She pushed the question past parched tonsils.

"No. No audience. Only you and me," he whispered huskily. "*Milenko...*forgive me. I cannot resist any longer."

Then his lips captured hers.

Captured, hell. With a soft moan, she surrendered, her mouth molding itself to his, opening eagerly to let his tongue explore her depths, her tongue returning the favor.

It was glorious. Mind-blowing. Earth-shattering.

It wasn't enough.

Threading her fingers through the thick gold hair at the nape of his neck, she urged him closer. It still wasn't enough.

Then his hands began to move, as if just kissing wasn't enough for him, either. Smooth, hypnotic strokes sliding up her arms and down her back. Circling her waist and slipping under the loose cotton of her T-shirt.

She sighed when the heat and hardness of his palms pressed against the bare skin of her rib cage and began to ease upward.

Just as the ache in her breasts became unbearable, the pads of his thumbs brushed the tips of her nipples, peaking them instantly. Wendy moaned—and Peter groaned deep in his throat.

Then her shirt flew across the room. And she arched eagerly as his mouth and hands, tongue and teeth and fingertips returned to tease and touch, to nip and suck, to lick and abrade her sensitive mounded flesh.

*I'm flying apart,* she thought, drowning in the sensual pleasure of his touch. *I'm going to shatter—and it's going to be wonderful.*

Proof of Peter's own readiness to explode pressed against her. Then he was turning her, still caressing her as he walked her backward to the bed.

Wendy cooperated because, oh, yes, she wanted him. Wanted to take his hardness deep into her core. Wanted him to fill her, to take her, to possess her. She wanted to lose herself in—

"No!"

The hoarse syllable hung in the air until Peter carefully, slowly—as if handling spun glass—set her away from him.

After a moment spent breathing deeply, eyes closed, he raked his hands through his hair.

Were they shaking? Wendy wondered before she swiveled around to locate her shirt, the coffee, anything to avoid looking at the only man who'd ever made her tremble. The only one who, for one long, magical moment, had made her feel loved and completed and safe.

*Oh, Wendy!* The only person who could keep her safe was herself.

"I should apologize," the Czech brainiac said as he moved toward the bedroom door. "I am not sorry. But a man keeps his promises."

And then Wendy was alone. Slumping onto the bed, then falling backward, her head landing on a bunched-up pillow. Peter's own unique male scent wafted into her nostrils.

With a groan, she bent a forearm over her eyes. Which was crazier? she wondered as she lay there, trying to calm her racing pulse and to slow her raging desire. Starting something like that with Peter—or not finishing it?

*Either way, it's too dangerous,* she told herself. *So don't repeat it.*

But, oh, how she wanted to.

Eventually, Wendy pulled herself to her feet, threw on some clothes and went to work, acknowledging—though not appreciating—the irony that she was looking forward to having company tonight.

Imagine feeling grateful for disbelieving bureaucrats. *What next? Start believing that love can conquer all?*

AT FIVE-FIFTEEN that afternoon, she made the last turn and began looking for a parking space through the bundle of nerves that had been growing all day.

*Just keep it simple,* Wendy advised herself. Go upstairs, be cool, be distant and get through the next few hours. Then go hide out at Robin's again.

She couldn't decide what to fear most, anyway—blurting out the truth, thus blowing her chance at Paris, not to mention letting down Leippert and Boroni *and* her father, or unleashing a long-dormant part of herself on a gorgeous man who acted like he cared. *But did he?*

Entering the apartment, she dished out a little irony, "Hi, honey, I'm home."

The irony sailed right past the Czech Chest, who emerged from the kitchen with a tender smile that jolted her sensual receptor sites into overdrive. "Ah, Wendy! How was your day?"

"Fine." She sniffed the air for distraction. "Something smells wonderful." Almost as wonderful as Peter looked.

"Dinner, silly one."

Before she could frame a reply, he swooped close, gathered her in his arms and lowered his mouth to hers.

Longing and lust streaked through her like lightning, obliterating rational thought. At least until an eternity—or two seconds?—later, the downstairs door banged. Reluctantly, Wendy extricated herself from his embrace.

"We...shouldn't...," she began weakly, but Peter stopped her with a finger to her lips. She felt the touch in the deepest part of her deepest feminine part. Which was damned tired of resisting Peter's potent sensual advances, caring behavior and adorable smile.

"We must," he purred, his hand sliding along her jaw, tracing a path down her neck, then trailing lightly down the sides of her dress before curving around her waist and pulling her closer. Her breasts ached where his hard, muscular chest almost touched them. Where he *had* touched her this morning....

Wendy closed her eyes. No amount of willpower seemed to cool her response to this man. He made her ache, made her laugh, made her breakfast.

And he could make her forget Paris, forget her*self* with just a touch. *But how long would the magic last?*

Just long enough for somebody to get hurt. "Give me one good reason," she challenged, wrenching herself free.

"To convince our guests that we truly are in love," Peter said softly, his eyes hot smoky-blue. The faint lines beside the one stood out paler than usual. "Remember?"

"That's right." Wendy couldn't hide her regret. "It's just an act, isn't it?"

Faintly calloused fingers smoothed her hair off her face. "Only at your insistence, *milenko.* I want you. When you are ready to deepen our relationship—just let me know."

"I—" Wendy stared at him. "I've got to change. Uh, clothes."

Fleeing to the safety of the bedroom, she closed the door behind her and leaned back against it. She wanted to accept his offer—and its unspoken promise.

Thank heaven, they'd have company soon—even if it *was* an INS agent, a banker and her father. She needed a dose of dull reality to balance prince charming out there.

Wendy through her closet, ending up in a lemon tank dress and matching ankle-wrap sandals, a hand-painted silk scarf and beaded earrings.

After brushing her hair, she patted an oil-blotting sheet over her face and applied a coat of mascara to her lashes.

There—she was good to go.

Except the only place to go was back to the living room to wait.

It took a few rounds of pacing to realize she was alone. A few more to send her to the kitchen.

"Need any help?" she asked from the doorway.

At the stove, Peter flashed his spine-melting smile. "Ah, Wendy, your lookings are good enough to chew."

She was still trying to rearrange that one when he said, "Would you open the wine? It needs to breathe."

*Me, too,* Wendy thought as she backed out with a sketchy nod.

She was twisting the cork off the corkscrew when a knock sounded at the door. Putting down the wine paraphernalia, Wendy gave the scarf a tweak as Peter appeared from the kitchen.

Lordy! Even the dish towel tucked into his waistband only enhanced his aura of sheer, potent masculinity.

As she reached the door Peter reached her. He bent to butterfly kiss her neck. Then his warm, clean-scented breath tickled her ear. "Time to display how happy we are."

"Right. Curtain up." Wendy told herself to appreciate the reminder: their marriage was pure show.

Okay, so maybe it wouldn't be all that hard to be happy with a man like Peter—sexy, sensible, sensitive...sexy— if she wasn't going to Paris.

But she was. To build a happy life of her own that nobody's departure could destroy. It was the only sure way to avoid being hurt.

Taking a deep breath and hoping for Robin and Max, Wendy opened the door.

"Hi there, honey!"

She summoned a weak smile. "Hi, Dad. Hey, Patrick. Come i—"

"You sly thing! Why didn't you tell me you already had a fish on the hook." Wendy's father hugged her breathless, then pushed past her into the apartment.

Stefan Marek was stocky, dark-haired, maybe fifty, with working man's hands. He wore a short-sleeved blue shirt and a ten-year-old tie. Stopping in front of Peter, he opened his arms wide. "Welcome to the family, son!" he cried.

After giving Peter an exuberant bear hug, Marek handed his daughter a small package done up in white paper and tied with silver ribbon. "Your wedding gift," he explained as if she were brainless. "Open it."

While introducing a younger version of Marek as her brother, Wendy pulled off the ribbon and ripped an edge of the paper free with a fingernail.

With only one perfectly functioning eye, Peter couldn't observe Wendy, their guests *and* the present at the same time. He focused on his tigress.

Who frowned as she removed the wrapping paper. Then—

Her eyes flashed green fire. And hurt. Peter's fingers curled into fists.

The door reverberated with another knock; Wendy thrust the wedding gift into Peter's hands so she could answer the summons.

He cocked his head to identify it—a home pregnancy test?

"Here's hoping you'll be needing that soon," Mr. Marek said with a laugh.

*Hovno*, women weren't broodmares! This insensitive blockhead must also carry some responsibility for Wendy's aversion to involvement.

Could a man with his flaws undo damage that went so deep?

Peter didn't know, but Wendy was like a brightly feathered bird. She deserved to fly.

"Hey, hot stuff." The blue-spiked woman had arrived with a normal-looking kid. "What's shaking?"

"Hands?" he guessed, holding his out.

As Robin introduced her son Max, Peter set aside his

personal concerns. For now, he must persuade the bureaucrats to believe a lie he wished could be true.

Leippert and Boroni arrived as he was polling the guests for drink requests. Max and Patrick opted for soda; Stefan Marek wanted beer. The rest accepted wine.

Peter poured, Wendy served—and Worthington and Dinwiddie sidled into the room together, then immediately separated. Almost like wolves surrounding a herd of deer.

Some of whom were inexplicably suspicious, he thought as he watched Wendy's brother and the banker meet, stiffen for a moment, then carefully circle away from each other.

Hmm. Everyone here, except the bureaucrats, knew Wendy well. Peter sprinted to the kitchen and back with some hot appetizers. He didn't wish to miss a minute. In such a gathering, he might discover more keys to understanding his wife. His flaws might be revealed, too.

But suddenly that was a risk worth taking.

BY THE TIME she got the group safely seated, Wendy decided she'd have to call the evening a riot rather than a dinner party.

Her dad cornered her and Peter in turn, demanding to know how soon he'd be a grandfather. The dean had backed the banker around the living room, interrogating him about estate gifts. Even at the table, Boroni mumbled to himself almost continuously. The only word Wendy clearly heard was "conspirators." She prayed nobody would ask the professor a leading question.

Worthington watched her and Peter like a hawk trained by marines—until she seated him across from Robin, who, with a wink at Wendy, launched into a provocative discussion concerning the Constitution and dirty rap lyrics. Francis appeared to be as fascinated as he was outraged. His mouth hung open all night, except when he remembered to eat.

She'd placed Max on Peter's right for safety's sake; the

two of them talked all through dinner. Knowing the nine-year-old, they were discussing hockey.

A lull in the other conversations proved her right. She heard Max mention stickhandling, then her Czech answer in a low voice.

"Would you?" the boy asked shyly.

When Peter assured him he'd help him work on his hockey skills, Robin stopped ranting long enough to beam at him. "You get my next million," she promised.

"Un-needed," Peter replied. "I have already."

The response puzzled Wendy until she was distracted by seeing her brother Patrick surreptitiously exchange business cards with Dinwiddie.

What was that about? she wondered. Again, not for long.

*"Paris?"* Her father's volume grabbed everyone's attention. His dismissive tone knifed Wendy's heart. "Why? She's married now. She's gonna settle down and have kids!"

"Dad, please!" What a monomaniac. There were other things she could do besides produce heirs, weren't there? A vision of a blue-eyed, golden-haired baby made her heart lurch. *Why couldn't I have both—kids and a career? Was it possible, with the right man...?*

As if reading her thoughts, Peter stood and grinned at her. "My love, will you help bring me from the kitchen the dessert?"

While Robin giggled and Worthington shoved his glasses upward, Wendy followed her husband into the kitchen.

"I'm sorry," she said after the door swung shut. "My dad's obsessed with his mortality."

"Your father makes mistake." Opening the refrigerator, Peter began removing bowls of this and cartons of that. "Marriage offers many benefits."

"Such as?" Wendy's heart pounded. He sounded so sure!

"Companionship, *milenko*. Not just someone to share your bed, but your joy and tears, too. Someone to encourage you, to believe in you." Peter smiled. "To love you for being you."

Something—a dam—broke inside her while her hubby calmly set out plates and began to build skyscrapers of cake, fruit and whipped cream.

Had the problem with her parents' marriage been... *them?*

Not marriage itself. Not her and Patrick, either—but two people who'd never bothered to find out that their expectations were totally incompatible?

*Could* two people share the same life vision?

The very concept left her breathless...and admitting that she did want everything Peter had listed, everything marriage ideally offered.

*But how often does reality realize the ideal?*

Not very. That made her cranky; she took it out on his dessert. "Why're you going to all this trouble?" A finger flick indicated the caloric towers. "A scoop of ice cream would have covered it."

Peter shrugged as he continued sculpting the final masterpiece. "Another effort to convince the bureaucrats—and your father—that our marriage is real."

"All it has to be is legal." And who was she reminding, herself or Peter?

"The two officials remain suspicious."

"What more do they want?" she moaned, unable to disagree. She'd seen Worthington writing on his hand between courses!

Smoky-blue eyes caressed every inch of her. "Proof that we are in love, I think."

Love. The one thing she was afraid to trust.

Was it also, Wendy wondered suddenly, the one thing she'd never be satisfied without, now that she'd met Peter?

*That* scared her spitless. "Bull pucky!" Wendy exclaimed. "They can't possibly—"

Door hinges squeaked.

Light winked on Agent Rat's lenses; she flew into Peter's arms, morphing potential tirade into breathless declaration. "—know how much I love you, darling."

In the shelter of his arms, Wendy could almost believe it was true.

"You make me so happy, *milenko*," Peter proclaimed as he scattered light kisses over her face, "I want to shout at roofs."

Worthington's pointy nose twitched. "Then you won't mind if Mr. Dinwiddie and I continue to drop by occasionally, will you? Since you have nothing to hide…."

"No," Wendy agreed faintly, her heart sinking. How much longer could she resist Peter's offers? And what would happen if she didn't? "Nothing to hide. Stop in anytime.

"Here." She shoved a dessert tower into Worthington's hands. "Enjoy."

# 7

"I GIVE UP!" Wendy exclaimed with a laugh the following Wednesday night as she tossed Max her handset. "You *are* the PlayStation king."

"If only there was a pro tour for video games." Robin's mock complaint came from the corner, where she was standing on her head. "Why can't my son be one of those skaters who do nine hundreds off the ramp?"

"Don't worry, Mom." Max began putting away the game equipment. "I'll support you in your old age." He sighed theatrically. "Somehow."

Wendy racked her brain. Thinking up silly professions was another game they played frequently. "Maybe you could vegetable dye dogs to match their owners' décor. Market them as camouflaged guard animals."

While Max suggested selling personalized cat litter boxes over the Internet, the phone rang.

Since it was on the floor beside her, Robin answered. "It's your hot stuff hubby," she said a second later, awkwardly tossing Wendy the cordless from her inverted position.

Wendy made a face at her friend, who returned it upside down. "Hi, Peter."

"Hello. My name is Peter." The Czech Chest wasn't purring; he spoke stiffly—as if addressing a trigger-happy bank robber.

Wendy prayed he wasn't about to give the prearranged signal.

"I wish to order the usual."

Damn. The prearranged signal. "Again?" This was the third time since the party that either Worthington or Dinwiddie had showed up at the apartment. Her father had been over almost every day. Even Patrick had dropped in on Sunday; he and the banker had watched football for hours.

*Unbelievable. I move out and my apartment becomes party central!*

What did that say about her social life? Maybe she *could* use a little more balance.

"Please double the order."

Both surveillance nuts were there?

"My wife exercises in the bedroom. She hungers enough to eat houses."

"That's 'a horse,'" Wendy informed him, looking around for her shoes and sliding them on. "Or 'out of house and home.'"

The phone emitted confused silence.

"Never mind," she said with a sigh. "I'll be right there."

"Thank you. Goodbye."

"I'll be back when I'm back," she told Robin who rolled out of her headstand as Wendy headed for the door.

"You know you're certifiable, right?" her blue-headed *amiga* asked, following Wendy out to the landing. "Totally nuts to pass up a sweet deal like your hot Czech. No other woman on earth, married to that hunk, would be sleeping here."

Though she tossed a "fuhgettaboutit" over her shoulder, Wendy had to agree with her friend. Sleeping with Peter *would* be great sex—er, fun. But what if, afterward, he went all traditional on her and wanted to get serious?

Men were, after all, notoriously unpredictable when it came to matters of the heart.

And Peter had one. How else to explain his patient handling of Dr. Boroni's paranoia, his courtesy toward her father, who *said* he dropped by to practice his Czech but spent all his time expounding—in English—on the joys of grandparenting?

Wendy crossed the street and turned down her alley. Okay, her husband possessed a thoroughly admirable character, one as attractive as his appearance and his willingness to perform domestic duties.

Bottom line: Peter's insides matched his outside.

Hmm. If marriage partners could be like that, could *stay* like that… Wendy ascended the fire escape, eased open the bedroom window and crawled through. Who wouldn't want to sign up, then?

Only…how did you know the person you married wouldn't change? Wouldn't leave? Why weren't there any guarantees?

Crossing the bedroom, she caught a whiff of Peter's scent. One deep breath set her heart—and other, sex-differentiated organs—singing.

Which, when she threw open the door and jogged into the living room, gave her little puffing and huffing act a realistic edge.

"Whew! Good workout! My, look who's here—Francis and Darren. Howzit going, guys?" Wendy greeted the bureaucrats like long-lost friends; tucking her hair, she prayed for patience.

She wanted some privacy. Enough to discover whether Peter really was crazy about her, as he'd claimed the night of the dinner party, or was just protecting his resident alien status.

She also wished the Spy Twins would get lost and stay that way for an even simpler reason. She was sick and tired of migrating. How did birds do it?

YEAH, WELL, if wishes were horses, we'd all be rodeo stars, Wendy thought a couple of weeks later. The parade of visitors continued unabated. Which meant her treks between her apartment and Robin's did, too. Last night, she'd made two trips!

"Who needs a stair-climbing machine?" she muttered as she squeezed toothpaste onto her toothbrush sometime after midnight. She was wearing a short, purple cotton-knit gown she'd borrowed from Robin because she'd poured chocolate sauce on her lounger while making Max a sundae. "At this rate, my knees'll wear out before Dinwiddie ever gets around to writing that check."

But the Paris Design Institute had sent a receipt for her deposit; she needed that trust money before the semester was over. *Because I'm going to gay Paree then,* she told her reflection. *I'm really going.*

Funny, the woman in Robin's bathroom mirror didn't look as excited about that as she used to.

Wendy spit toothpaste and rinsed. Well, it was late, it was only Thursday and it'd been a long day. The chem profs had burst into Boroni's office during the morning Anomaly session, raving about some breakthrough in their crystalline composition quest. When they'd dragged Peter off to consult on it, Dr. B. had come complaining to her. And nobody complained like an old man whose elevator no longer went all the way to the top.

*Brrrrrrrrng!*

Robin and Max had already crashed, so Wendy wiped the last of the blue-green foam from the rim of her mouth and raced to the phone. Who the hell was calling this late? "Hello?"

"I wish to order the usual—and please hurry."

Silently employing one of those words certain cable TV comedians love, Wendy hung up. She employed it again a few minutes later when, halfway home, thunder rumbled a belated warning and the skies opened.

What's wrong with this picture? she asked herself. Here she was, climbing the rain-slicked fire escape, totally drenched, her borrowed knit gown clinging to her like icy plastic wrap—to convince *somebody* that she and Peter were really married.

*There are better ways to do that,* she decided as she

sneaked into her own apartment, toweled off and changed into a dry nightgown, her teeth still chattering Ravel's *Bolero*. Rainy nights in late September were too cool to wander around soaked to the bone.

After wrapping her hair in a towel, Wendy made her entrance—and spent the next twenty minutes assuring her dad there was nothing wrong with Patrick just because he stared into space and sighed occasionally. He only left when she suggested his presence was interfering with the grandkid instigation process.

Through it all, Peter sat rubbing his face. He always massaged the same side, didn't he? Wendy shook her head to clear it; she had more important things to do right now than tabulate his habits.

"Okay, that's it," she announced. Dry-mouthed at what she was about to propose. Living 24/7 with a man whose proximity spurred her sex drive to whatever pace was faster than a gallop was undoubtedly as safe as playing with live grenades, but... "That's the last straw."

"Excuse?"

Wendy tucked her hair behind her ears. "I'm through with this to-and-fro nonsense. As of right now, I'm moving back into my apartment. Deal with it."

Peter's hand fell away from his face. She was answering his prayers!

"So." She put her fists on her hips. "Who's taking the sofa—you or me?"

Bah. He should have known. *Easy, Havel. Remember, description is the better part of value.*

"I will sleep on the sofa," he offered, hoping gentlemanly generosity would help to change that arrangement. Soon.

Not yet, though. After showing him how to convert the contraption and helping him apply sheets, she said, "See you in the morning." And padded off to the bedroom.

Oh, yes. Peter grinned. And he would see her. From there...possibilities grew exponentially. Something else grew exponentially just thinking about them. "Good night, *milenko.*"

With the aid of still-enthused chemists and very cold showers, Peter remained gentlemanly for almost thirty hours.

But when she entered the kitchen Saturday morning clad only in little plaid shorts and a striped, midriff-baring T-shirt, Peter knew a January dip in a Siberian lake would not discourage his desire. Or lessen his arousal.

He also knew that before they took their relationship to another level—and more extensive physical contact—he should confess his flaws. Honesty formed the only solid basis for affection or sex. If he held hopes for either, he must tell her the truth.

Because that's what he desired most: to know with certainty whether a woman, *this* woman, could ever want a man with his impairments.

He choked on his orange juice as Wendy rose on tiptoe to get a cereal bowl and her waistband dipped to expose her navel, then her pelvic bones....

For a moment everything gentlemanly slid away. Male, primitive need took its place. "Hold on," he rasped. "I'll get it for you."

His hand shook, his conscience throbbed as he handed her a yellow bowl from the top shelf. Something else throbbed, too.

He started to reach for her—then curled his fingers into fists and stuffed them into his pockets. Certainly a well-pleasured woman would be more likely to accept a man's flaws. But even attempting to seduce Wendy broke his promise and destroyed the status quo. And if she turned him down, she might do something reckless. Something that would compromise her dream of studying in Europe.

So he must wait. He must be sure any potential losses were acceptable.

BY TWO-THIRTY that afternoon, Wendy had lost it.

Need proof? She was scrubbing the bathtub—on Saturday!

Well, it was raining too hard to go anywhere and what else was she going to do? Ogle Peter some more? She'd already done plenty of that while they'd straightened the rest of the apartment together.

By now, the sexual tension around here was so thick, you could cut it with a knife.

Knuckles rapped on the apartment door.

Happily abandoning the tub, Wendy rushed to answer it. Peter remained motionless, sprawled in the armchair, immersed in a stack of graphs. Some chemical malarkey, he said.

Huh. She could think of some chemistry she'd like to—

"Patrick! Don't you ever phone first?" She looked more closely at her brother, then opened the door wider. "Come on in."

"You—you're not busy?" Without awaiting an answer, he shuffled in, gave Peter a halfhearted greeting and slouched through the apartment to slump at the dining table, propping his elbow on its top and his chin on his palm.

"So how's it goin', sis?" he asked with a sigh.

So much for the gays-are-sensitive stereotype, Wendy thought. Her brother seemed oblivious to the atmosphere in the apartment. Which was charged.

*Like that bunny's batteries.*

She followed Patrick to the table. "What's up, bro?"

Instead of answering, he buried his head in his hands.

Her gaze met Peter's. *He* quirked an eyebrow; *she* nodded minutely. A second later he announced his need to shower and shave. "Then I am pottering within the kitchen," he said. "Don't think—no, don't *mind* me."

Patrick had started talking before Peter finished excusing himself; he was well into his monologue before Wendy dragged her attention from the disappearing Czech Chest and his thoughtfulness.

"—don't know if I should make the first move or what. I mean, I'm not even sure…"

Ohmigod. "You're not asking me for dating advice, are you?"

Wendy sighed with relief when Patrick shook his head. She wanted him to be happy, of course, but she didn't feel exactly qualified to discuss her brother's love life. Or anyone else's, for that matter.

"Smart move, bro. 'Cuz I wouldn't be any help."

"Why not?"

She shot him a "you're kidding, right?" look. "We grew up in the same house, Pat. Neither of us has had good relationship models."

Her brother freed his chin. "You mean Mom and Dad? What've they got to do with it?"

Were men born obtuse when it came to relationships? *Were NASCAR drivers adrenaline junkies?*

"Mom *left*, remember?" Wendy said. "Dad insisted Mom give up her art to be a wife and mother. And ultimately, she couldn't stand it enough to stay."

Patrick made a *phfffff* sound. "She couldn't stand being cut off from money to gamble with."

Wendy blinked blankly. "G-gamble?"

"Do boats-in-moats mean anything to you?"

She nodded. Initially allowed only on riverboats cruising the Mississippi, gambling was now legal anywhere water surrounded it; most St. Louis area casinos were built on solid ground—inside shallow ditches that held the $H_2O$.

"Mom started going to the boats with some other women. She got addicted to gambling. Wouldn't or couldn't stop. Finally, Dad took her off the bank accounts and credit cards. *That's* why she split for Las Vegas. It wasn't her art that meant more to her than we did, it was slots and poker."

Wendy looked around, expecting to see a grinning cat or a large, white hare. *Hel-lo, Alice!* She felt as if she'd just fallen down a rabbit hole and entered an alternate universe. "I knew where Mom went," she said finally. "But not why."

"Well, now ya do."

Yes. Now she knew. It wasn't a stifling marriage or a family repressing her creativity that had driven her mother away, but a sick need to gamble and a husband who wouldn't ruin his life—or his children's—to support her habit.

Someone knocked on the door. At the same time Peter emerged from the bathroom, wet hair slicked back, a towel around his waist.

Forget her world just being turned upside down. Wendy instantly focused on discovering exactly what that towel concealed!

"I'll get it," Patrick offered. "I probably oughta be going, anyway."

But when he opened the door to Darren Dinwiddie, Wendy's brother apparently forgot he'd said anything about leaving.

From initial bland pleasantries, the two nonresident men segued to…everything. After a few moments of being a passive audience, Wendy winked at Peter, who again took his cue and interrupted to offer the banker a drink.

"A soda would be nice," Dinwiddie said, primly folding his hands in his lap. Surprise—Patrick wanted one, too.

Smelling opportunity, Peter invited Wendy to join him in the kitchen. Where, when he closed the distance between them to nuzzle her ear…jaw…neck, her patchouli scent filled his lungs.

"Ah, *milenko*," he murmured when she sighed against him. "Let us dispose of our company."

"How? Just throw 'em out? I'd love to, but I don't think so."

*Why not?* "Perhaps if we go into the bedroom and pretend we are making love—loudly—they will leave for embarrassment."

"Ours or theirs?" Wendy asked, but didn't wait for his

answer. *Ah. Rhetorical.* "I doubt it'll work, but I'll try anything once."

Peter hoped they would try more than once. "Let us kiss here first. To begin pretension."

"That's preten— Oh, never mind," Wendy said. And then she kissed him. Enthusiastically.

Arousing every iota of male essence in him. Also the front of his towel.

As they ended the kiss—slowly, sweetly—Peter became aware not only of his surroundings again, but of a startling development. He wanted Wendy's body.

But that was not all. He wanted more. He wasn't sure just how much more, but it was time to find out.

His wife was a woman worth taking risks for. Strong-willed, yet open-minded. Kind and patient, but never condescending. Tenderhearted and independent. With Wendy, he wouldn't have to worry about being *perfectly* capable. *She will not need me to carry all the weight if I cannot.*

"Come." He entwined their fingers. His voice got huskier, something else got harder—which he hadn't thought possible. "Let's go to bed. I mean, the bedroom."

With a nod, Wendy pushed open the kitchen door.

Then stopped. Peter's, uh, towel fit against the center back seam of her soft, faded leggings. He closed his eyes to savor an image of their bodies fitting together so. Without cloth separating them.

"Where did they go?"

"Who?" He looked around. Then looked around again. "Oh."

A note lay on the dining table. "Gone out for a drink. Thanks." It was signed "Pat." But the apartment was empty; obviously the banker had gone with him.

Peter bent his head to continue tasting Wendy's soft skin. His hands cupped her hips.

"Well, that was a close call, wasn't it?" Wendy chirped, leaping out of reach.

With a smile as bright and phony as the game-show

ladies on TV—and without looking at him once—she trotted toward the door. "Think I'll go see how Max's hockey practice went." Grabbing her keys and purse, she called over her shoulder, *"Hasta la vista."*

Peter stared at the door as it closed behind her. What had just happened?

He never did figure it out for sure, but his internal nag—not to mention what still saluted behind his towel—remained disgruntled for hours.

WENDY KEPT UP her evasionary tactics through the rest of the weekend. She didn't return until suppertime that evening and only then with Robin and her son in tow, keeping them there playing cards until late and shutting herself into the bedroom—alone—as soon as they finally said goodnight.

On Sunday, she went to mass with her father, then went shopping.

Having received the message, Peter met Boroni at the university. But he refused to be held at bay forever.

Tomorrow, he promised himself later that night as he shifted on the sofa, trying to align his skeleton with its lumps. Tomorrow, he would try again. In public, he decided. Judging by experience, romancing his wife seemed to be safer there.

ON MONDAY, then, after working out one of the remaining subsets of Gandel's Anomaly, he suggested an early lunch. Boroni, tired from the hours of intense concentration but refusing to admit to it, agreed with alacrity and headed for his favorite nearby deli for split-pea soup.

Peter sought out Wendy. Encountering her in the hallway outside her office, he positioned himself so that his good ear and eye were closest to her. This put his back to a cross hallway, but classes were already in session at the moment. At least the ones down the main hallway were, judging by the low drone filling his left ear.

"Darling! Just the woman I am hoping to meet. May I buy you some lunch?"

"And to what do I owe this unexpected offer?" she asked with one eyebrow arched. Her eyes held a smile, so he grinned back. "Oh, good morning," she added.

"Yes, it has been," he returned, perfectly willing to retrace his steps, to follow approved conversational structure. Anything—as long as it led where he wished to go.

To bed with Wendy. And maybe to opening up to her completely.

"How are you and Dr. Boroni doing on the Anomaly?"

She appeared to be looking past his shoulder, but perhaps that was only his imagination—and the monovision effect of standing at such an angle to her.

"Most of it, yes." He answered her question readily, though he wondered about her sudden interest in his work. It was pleasant. "We expect final success quite soon."

"And the chemists say you've given them invaluable guidance on their project to develop...well, whatever they're working on."

Her expression remained that of determined politeness, but her eyes kept darting beyond him, then back, again and again. Did Wendy have a nervous tic he'd never noticed before?

"They're making progress toward a new data storage medium," Peter said, losing patience with this beating at the shrubbery. "Building off my computer chip patents. I wish them success. Let the wealth spread."

He waved his hand negligently, dismissing math and processing chips, academic honors and monetary rewards. "I've enjoyed my work here, but work is not why I have stayed, Wendy."

"Oh, isn't it?" The sharp question cut through the residual buzzing in his damaged ear. It came from the direction in which Wendy's eyes had been darting. He should have known, he thought with a sigh. He should have trusted her.

Slowly he turned around. "Chairman Moss. Hello."

"I don't appreciate being ignored, Dr. Havel." The man bristled. "But now that I have your attention, would you mind answering my original question?"

Peter's heart sank. To think this was how Wendy would learn of his flaws.

"It's my fault, Chairman Moss." Wendy smiled at the trustee. "I find my husband's work so fascinating, I didn't give him a chance to answer you."

Peter rubbed the side of his face, but it took no time and no genius to understand what had happened. *He's been talking to me. Wendy saw him. I didn't. Nor hear him, either.*

"And he always refers these things to me, anyway," Wendy continued. Obviously, *she* had heard Moss's every word. "So allow me to accept your kind personal invitation to the physics department open house. Thank you so much. We'll be looking forward to it!"

Apparently her act satisfied Moss, who favored each of them with a sharp nod before marching off.

He should depart, too, Peter thought. Damned if he'd lie to her, but he wasn't ready to reveal the cause of his odd behavior yet. Not until he worked out why he hadn't trusted her just now—and if he ever could.

"Uh, I must ask that you check the rain for lunch. Excuse me," he added when the—*oh, rain check!*—look on Wendy's face didn't unblank. "I have remembered an appointment." This was true: he remembered a particularly awful dental appointment occurring when he was eleven. His stomach held the same lump of discomfort now.

"And tonight I will be helping Max with his hockey skills." Because until he understood the real reason for his reluctance to confide in her or trust her, he must remove himself from her scrutiny. Wendy was too observant to fool for very long.

He only hoped the boy was available. "Don't expect me until I am late."

WENDY TOLD HERSELF to close her mouth and stop admiring Peter's tight, sexy backside as he strode away. She reminded herself he was crazy or consumed with his work—or both. How else did you explain his ignoring Moss like that?

She mulled Peter's behavior and her regret at the lunch cancellation as she drifted back to the office. Mulling continued while she sorted the dean's correspondence, compiled final registration and financial aid figures and got back to the romance languages department on their request to renumber the Spanish lit classes next semester.

Sometime around four, a toe-tingling answer glimmered faintly.

*Like the Hope diamond in equatorial sunlight.*

What if, beneath Peter's glam package of sculpted body, smoky-blue eyes and dark gold hair was a man who cared more about her than his work? And tonight, he was keeping his promise to a child that wasn't even his! What woman wouldn't be happy to love someone like that? Handsome, sexy, honest, trustworthy, kind, thoughtful— and he could iron!

And if you counted chemistry and math, he was apparently the creative type, too. Making the old "different interests" theory a nonstarter, too.

"Okay, so he's perfect husband material," Wendy muttered to herself as she cleared her In box. "And we're physically compatible and technically, he's mine for the moment. Does that mean we should have ourselves a fling before we go our separate ways? What if one of us wants to turn it into a more permanent arrangement? Is marriage ever worth sacrificing your lifelong plans and dreams for?"

She must have been muttering louder than she realized. Robin had strolled over to lean against her desk. Now she fingered her eyebrow ring. "Better ask one more question," she advised, her rueful smile reminding Wendy that she'd gained her wisdom the hard way. "Does *he* have any long-term plans—and how do you fit into them?"

That was a showstopper, Wendy conceded. Because although Patrick's revelation about their mother's gambling problem had put a new spin on the whole marital thing, she wasn't about to risk flushing the Paris Design Institute and her goal of a career in fashion design.

She loved design work—and her past wouldn't let her put all her eggs in Peter's basket. Especially when he hadn't exactly offered it yet.

*But if we're both just looking for a short, no-strings relationship...*

"Good one, Robin. I'll ask."

She would, Wendy thought hours later. If he ever came home.

"THAT'S RIGHT," Peter called across the rink to Max. "Keep flat side stick parallel to your skates. Now drop it to the ice and sweep. Hold wrists straight. Good, good."

While the boy practiced the stickhandling drill from blue line to blue line, Peter made another circuit of the rink.

They'd been here for hours, but, *sakra,* he'd missed skating! This was the first time since the accident that he'd stepped back on the ice. And he was managing to stay upright.

At first, he'd wobbled, but unwilling to go home and too cold to stand still, he'd kept up his efforts. Soon he'd regained his footing and his balance seemed to improve with every lap. It felt good to exercise his body, too. He and Boroni had followed their long, hard morning with a longer, harder afternoon attacking the last extensive section of the Anomaly that defied their proposed solution. They'd made some progress—perhaps even a breakthrough—but his brain felt like a wet rag in the hands of a Russian babushka.

A group of men wearing either red or black hockey sweaters clumped into the rink area from the locker rooms. Laughing and talking, they removed the guards from their blades and came onto the ice to warm up.

"Time to go, Max," Peter said, skating over to the boy and stopping in a spray of ice shavings. "The teams are here and you've done enough for one night."

"Thanks, Dr. Havel." The youngster was still bubbling when they'd exited the rink and changed back into shoes. "I really appreciate what you showed me about blocking shots and reading the puck. I'm feeling better about our first game."

"You are ready," Peter assured him as they headed outside, where Robin waited to pick them up. She drove so recklessly that he was gripping his seat belt before they reached the first stoplight.

"Will you come watch me play?" Max asked.

Peter smiled at his half-eager, half-shy invitation. "If I can," he answered. "When is your game?"

"Saturday morning. At ten."

"I will be there," Peter promised just as Max's blue-spiked mother stopped the car in front of Wendy's apartment building.

"Here ya are," she said. "Home sweet home—with my thanks."

After exchanging goodbyes, Peter climbed out of the car—and nearly pitched onto his face.

And when his companions said something, he heard only garbles. "Stepped on a rock. No sweets," he assured them. Incorrectly, judging by what he could see of their expressions.

*Hovno,* had he let Elvis leave the edifice? Peter braced himself for questions.

"Whatever," Robin called. "Later!" Max just waved as she drove off.

Momentarily relieved, Peter staggered up the sidewalk into the building, then climbed the stairs slowly, like a snail on tranquilizers, because the risers seemed to twist and buck with every step.

Great. Mild physical and great mental fatigue had joined forces to worsen his handicaps.

*Be careful,* he admonished himself as he entered the apartment. Damned if he wanted Wendy to learn of his flaws this way, either. Flopping around like a drunken fish.

"Good evening, Dr. Havel."

Expecting the kitten's soft, sexy voice, Worthington's squawk surprised Peter. He jerked, the walls tilted. He grabbed the nearest protruding object to keep his balance. Unfortunately, that object was the INS clerk's head.

"N-nice shape," he muttered, releasing his Vulcan death grip to pat Francis J.'s cranium. "Good bones."

Wendy narrowed her eyes as she watched Peter practically fall on Worthington and then throw himself backward to end up sprawled on the sofa beside the man. Had he been drinking?

Maybe. Now he was leering at the little spy. "Tell me, Inspector…you are still investigating marriage or you visit my wife for nepoti—no, *nefarious*—purposes?" A strand of golden hair fell over his crooked eyebrow.

When he tried to rake it back, his fingers jabbed his eyebrows!

What the heck was wrong with him? Wendy wondered as Worthington squawked a denial. And how could she keep it from Mr. INS?

"Uh, honey," she said while he continued to try to make contact with the errant hair strand—with continued lack of success. "Dr. Boroni called while you were out. Do you want to call him back?"

*Please. Before you get yourself deported.*

Peter flung his hand through the air until it plopped onto his kneecap. "Bah. Tomorrow is soon enough for talking with Baloney. Tonight we will visit entertainers—no, we entertain visitors. Yes?"

*No way!* Protectively, Wendy put her hand on Peter's

forehead, brushing the silky rebellious strand back into place in the process. "I, uh, don't think that's such a good idea, darling. You'd better go to bed."

His killer smile appeared. "I am ready, *milenko*," he drawled. "For you, always I am—"

"Feverish. He feels feverish," Wendy hurriedly informed Worthington. "I'm afraid he's coming down with the flu."

Curling her fingers around the hard muscles of Peter's upper arm, she squeezed a warning as she tugged the big lug to his feet. "Come on, sweetheart," she coaxed sweetly. "Rest is the best thing for fighting off illness."

Jeez, she sounded like Mrs. Brady sharing saccharine wisdom with one of the Bunch. But it felt kind of good to take care of Peter, she realized. Maybe because he never acted helpless when he wasn't. "Let's get you under the covers."

Peter opened his mouth to protest. Wendy was this close to calling him a poor baby!

"You oughta listen to the missus, Havel," Worthington advised pompously. "The ladies generally know what they're doing in these matters."

Dammit, he was sick and ti—

*Wait.* He stopped in his tracks. *She's sending you to bed. In her bed.* He was only pitiful if he didn't go!

"Very well, my love. But I can find my own way there." Removing Wendy's hand, he passed Worthington with a grateful smile. Though his assistance was unintentional, it was still appreciated. "Good night, Francis."

As Worthington murmured something, Peter crossed the living room. At the bedroom doorway, he clamped a hand on the molding framing it and turned carefully. "Now, remember, darling—" he focused his good eye and his will on Wendy "—come to bed soon. I can no longer…'sleep' without you."

The flicker of green flames in her eyes assured him she understood his inflection. Now he could only hope she accepted its invitation. Pretending to yawn, he entered the bedroom and closed the door behind him.

If she came, he must be ready. Peter gazed around the room. First things first, he advised himself as he staggered over to the window that opened onto the fire escape and latched its lock.

Then he went into the bathroom and brushed his teeth. He should shave for her, but tonight he didn't trust himself with a razor. Better to be careful applying his stubble to Wendy's skin than put a blade to his own.

*Yes, be gentle,* instructed his internal voice. He hoped he could keep his passion under tight rein while he brought her to pleasure's peak, but—*sakra!*—this woman set him on fire and he wanted to dance in the flames.

Tonight might be his chance, he thought as he thrust his toothbrush at its holder, to truly begin a new life. With Wendy.

# 8

ON HIS SECOND TRY, Peter got the toothbrush docked, then returned to the bedroom. Now, how should she find him? In bed or out? Naked or clothed? Completely clothed or wearing only an essential or two?

He chuckled at his adolescent concern for stage-setting. Ordinarily he never thought much about that or any other part of the process. He'd simply begin, be stopped in mid-seduction or proceed to the finish. That's all there was to sex. Even with Katrina, it had just been a physical activity leading, hopefully, to satisfaction for both parties, period.

But not tonight. Because this time was with Wendy. A woman unlike any other he'd ever known. And so, like her, tonight must be different. Beginning with the surroundings.

Some articles of clothing lay discarded on the floor; he kicked them under the bed. Then he straightened the bedclothes, turning down the top layers like a hotel chambermaid. He located a book of matches Wendy was using as a notepad, apparently, and lit the candles atop the dresser and chest of drawers. When he noticed a shallow basket filled with potpourri, he stirred the dried botanical debris, releasing its faint scent to filter through the room's darkness.

Then he studied the results of his efforts.

Hmm. Did the candles provide enough light? Too much?

*Hovno.* Not even for his ex-fiancée had he gone to such lengths. And though what he felt for Wendy was, he realized now, more than he had for Katrina, what he needed to know most was that she could accept him as he was.

So perhaps he should not cloud her answer with romantic gestures....

*Bah. This gets too complicated. Just get ready and stay that way.*

With a growl, Peter pulled off his clothes, kicked them under the bed with the others he'd relocated there and threw himself between the sheets—then he had to grab the headboard and hang on until the room stopped twirling.

When it did, he folded one arm beneath his head and shifted to find a comfortable position, praying for the vertigo to abate while he waited for his wife to join him.

And waited. The faint candle glow, the stillness...Peter felt himself relaxing.

He yawned a couple of times.

And he waited... His eyelids grew heavier. Perhaps there was no harm in letting them close for a minute while he waited....

"THAT'S JUST SO American, don't you think?"

Huh? Wendy blinked. Darn it, she'd lost track of Worthington's topic of conversation again. Too busy daydreaming about losing herself in Peter's smoky blues. Mmm, they'd be hot with desire and so would she.

No, she already *was!* So who cared about whatever being American?

Who cared about Paris, either? Or losing her "self"?

Right now, she was more interested in losing the company, then her clothes, then awareness of her surroundings due to focusing every particle of attention on the sensual experience awaiting her in the bedroom. In Peter's arms.

Yeah, Paris could wait—tonight.

"I'm sorry," she said, not very sincerely. What *was* Worthington going on and on about? He'd been yadda-yadda-yadda-ing for thirty or forty minutes already! "What's so American?"

And why was Francis getting so excited about it? she wondered, unable to think of anything with a greater "wow" factor than a certain Czech Chest—and the adjacent body parts.

"Robin's attitude," the INS clerk gushed. "Your friend's so...so comfortable being herself. So brash. So...independent. So—"

"She's had to learn to be," Wendy cut off Señor Worthington. "'Cuz some jerk got her pregnant when she was fifteen and promptly split. Her folks are deeply religious rednecks from the Bootheel, so they decided the 'christian' thing to do was to kick her out. And since Robin refused to give up her son, she's had no choice but to become strong. Self-reliant. Tough when necessary."

"And I think it's wonderful!" Worthington exclaimed. "Exactly the can-do spirit that made our country great. Is...is she seeing someone?" he asked abruptly, knuckling his glasses.

Wendy's mouth fell open as she pictured Robin Donahue with her blue-spiked club hair dating Francis J. Worthington, government drone, who even at this late hour still wore a short-sleeved white shirt and bow tie.

Where would they go on a date? The mosh pit? Or bingo?

"I—I really don't know." Which was true. She doubted Robin had any more of a life than she'd had herself before Peter, but as her good friend, she didn't think she should encourage a dweeb like Francis, either. Talk about a mismatched pairing!

Or maybe the dull, by-the-book bureaucrat was exactly what Max's mom was looking for. Wendy realized she couldn't begin to guess anyone else's dream date. Not when, in the past few weeks, after years of rejecting all things marital and domestic, she'd begun thinking about her own life in terms of dream *mates*.

"You'd have to ask Robin," she confessed with a shrug. "I'm clueless."

Wendy did know one thing. She was tired of simply pretending for the sake of the university and her trust money. While she was married, she wanted to *be* married. To see if she and Peter had a better shot at happiness together than her parents had.

How did her fake hubby feel about legitimizing their ruse?

Well, he'd certainly seemed ready to celebrate the honeymoon tonight. *She* sure as hell was. *And if* that *works out, we can go from there.*

Which made it definitely time to evict this bureaucrat/spy.

Wendy turned a one-eighty on the interference question. "D'you want me to ask her?"

Francis J. reddened. His hands started clinging and wringing each other. "I, well…that is, ye—uh, no. I couldn't."

"Couldn't what?" she barked. Then apologized with a pat to his twining hands.

She was just frustrated. In the best worst way.

"Couldn't anything, Ms. Havel," Worthington said with a dejected sigh. His hands parted company and dropped to dangle limply between his knees. "What's the point? I know what people think. Especially someone as bold and daring and free as Ms. Donahue."

Before she could manage even a pro forma protest, Francis went on. "Everyone thinks I'm just a boring clerk. A…a paper-shuffler…. A clock-watcher…. Pencil-pusher—"

"I get the idea," Wendy cut off his lament.

She did it absently, her mind again preoccupied with images of the very unboring Peter Havel. His smoky-blue eyes, his heart-stopping smile, his massive chest…*those intriguing bulges.*

All of which were only a few feet away and available for closer, hands-on scrutiny.

"Everybody does," Worthington agreed, heaving another mournful sigh. "That's…well, that's why I've been following you and Havel so diligently, even though I had to take personal time to do it."

Personal time? *That* distracted Wendy from her sexual fantasizing! Reluctantly, though. Very reluctantly.

"Hold it," she said. "Hit the rewind button. Are you saying that you've been dogging me and Peter—on your own time—because people think you're boring?"

Worthington sighed again. "I don't think I'd put it exactly in those terms, but…yes." He knuckled his glasses upward and scooted to the edge of his seat, his nose twitching eagerly. "See, I'm only clerical support staff right now. I thought if I could nail you and Havel—you know, for something big, like committing a fraudulent marriage—then I could apply for an agent position and they'd give it serious consideration.

"I hope I haven't inconvenienced you—"

"You are now," Wendy muttered under her breath. *Go home and let me commit the act that will* defraud *this marriage,* she added silently, while Francis J. kept talking. Damn, the little guy was like that pile of baking soda after Max poured vinegar on it. Just fizzing merrily away.

"I really do want a more exciting job," Worthington explained earnestly, "but it has to be useful, too. And I don't want to lose my benefits and pension time."

Wendy tucked her hair behind her ears as she thought about it. Worthington's goal didn't float her boat, but she supposed it wasn't any dumber than…*sending yourself to Paris so you won't fall in love—because you might get hurt later?*

Hmm. Preventing possible future pain by avoiding happiness here and now wasn't exactly the most brilliant idea a human ever had, was it?

"Look, Francis." She fought to hold on to her patience. The guy could still make trouble for Peter. Meaning she had to be diplomatic about getting the bozo out of here so she could hustle herself along to the "honeymoon suite."

"If it's excitement you crave, why not apply to the Border Patrol? They're hiring—I saw a thing on TV about it yesterday. And catching smugglers has got to be way more exciting than catching newlyweds being celibate.

"Which we're not, of course," she added quickly, mentally crossing her fingers. Well, it wouldn't be a lie soon. If Mr. Immigration would just get it together and *bail!*

"Border Patrol?" Worthington's nose twitched again. Behind the thick lenses, his eyes glistened. "You mean the guys who patrol the U.S. border?"

*Duh.* "Uh, yeah," Wendy drawled. "I think that's them."

Worthington didn't act as if he even heard her. "D'you think I could qualify?"

He would if she had anything to do with it.

Unless she went to jail for justifiable homicide after discussing the possibility from every angle—including Robin's likely reaction—for twenty more minutes.

Enough already. Subtlety was going nowhere. Wendy pushed a fake yawn to its limit and on over into parody land as she stood.

"What do you say, Francis—can we continue our analysis of your fitness for boundary guarding tomorrow?"

"Huh?" The INS clerk looked at his watch. "Oh, right. It is late, isn't it?" After popping to his feet, he ceased moving. "I'm sorry. I just...well, it really—"

"Right. I know." Resisting the urge to grab Mr. Dense by the collar and drag, Wendy herded the Immigration pest to the door. "Good night, Francis," she said firmly. "We'll talk tomorrow."

Pushing him into the hallway, she shut the door behind him. Just to be sure, she put on the security chain.

Then, with another yawn—dammit, this one was real— she retraced her steps, reluctantly discarding the idea of a sexual romp with Peter. Tonight at least. The guy was probably racked out by now.

And she should be, too. Her marathon chat with Worthington had worn her out. Morning came obscenely early and work always followed right on its heels.

She looked down at the sofa and contemplated opening it up, putting on sheets, casing a pillow, dragging out a blanket…

*Hel-lo! You've got a perfectly good husband—er, bed—all ready and waiting in the other room,* she reminded herself. *And even if the scheduled activity's canceled, why crash anywhere else?*

Unable to refute such a persuasive argument, Wendy quickly brushed her teeth, undressed and pulled on a nightshirt, then tiptoed into the bedroom and around the bed, blowing out candles as she passed. Lifting a corner of the covers, she faced the window wall and slid into bed backward.

One minor wiggle and she was in perfect, spoonilicious position. Though Peter's breathing indicated he slept, his warmth immediately enclosed her—and then his arm moved. Wrapped around her, pulled her even closer, fit her back against his front.

As if *we're* made for each other, she thought as his breathing changed. And so did something else, something south of his diaphragm.

Through the darkness surrounding them, with Peter's masculine scent filtering into her olfactories, Wendy's heart made an astonishing suggestion. *If this works out, why not take Peter to Paris with you? What better place to have a lover?*

"Whoa," she murmured, shocked—no, intrigued—by the very thought. *Get real,* ma'moiselle. Then Peter's lips skimmed the back of her neck—and that article south of his abdomen nudged her behind.

And Wendy instantly, eagerly jettisoned rationality, future plans, even her childhood fears. Leaving but one fervent desire. *To get really,* really *intimate.*

Turning over to face him, she smoothed her hand across the planes of Peter's face, then down the taut column of his neck until finally her palm rested against the crinkly hair and the hard muscles under her Czech Chest's warm, smooth skin.

"*Milenko,*" he breathed, brushing his thumb gently across her lips. "I'll make it good for you." She could see his white teeth as he smiled. "Do you want me to use protection?" he whispered. "Or should we give your father a chance to achieve his wish to be a grandfather?"

His words flashed through Wendy's head like slides at high-speed. Grandfather. *Click.* Chance. *Click.* Baby. *Click.* Family. *Click.* Old Fear. *Click.* Go there?

Hell, she *was* there.

Of course he should use protection. This was sex, not reproduction. Wasn't it?

Wendy gazed at her husband. They lay on their sides, face-to-face, inches—or less, in one very germane instance—apart.

Why even ask? Was he simply too eager to get it on to take the time to use protection or did Peter want children? With her? Now?

She couldn't read his expression. "Um…" She stalled, peering through the faint light, trying to gauge his true feel—

Light? What light? The curtains were drawn and anyway, she was lying on her left side, her back to the windows. Facing the doorway to the rest of the apartment.

Dammit. There was a definite glow coming through there.

She must have left a light on somewhere. The part of her still hesitating, still scarred by the past seized on it as an opportunity.

"Peter," she whispered, loathe to break the mood but needing a moment, just a moment. To be sure she wanted to go through with this. To choose consequences she could live with. "Would you mind going to turn off the light? I—I'm feeling a little shy here for some reason."

His lips moved over hers. "You will not be subfreezing

for long,'' he promised with a sexy—er, husky—chuckle.
''I will warm you up long before a turn of the night, *mi-lenko.*''

What?

Flinging back the covers, Wendy catapulted from the
bed. What the *hell?* Was he making fun of her? Having a
brainiac attack?

He'd better not be hallucinating—or reliving an intimate
encounter with some Altai chick. *That* would be a little
ego-deflating.

*Yeah, like having your first novel critiqued by Steinbeck.*

''Never mind. I'll get it myself.'' Wendy stalked out of
the bedroom, through the living room and across the dining
area. Uh-huh—a line of bright yellow glowed below the
door to the kitchen.

Squinching her eyelids together, she pushed open the
door just enough to slip her hand through and swipe downward. Ah, blessed darkness replaced the bright strip of
light trying to slice its way through her optic protection
flaps.

As she padded back to the bedroom she contemplated
Peter's odd responses. Was there something more to it than
the eccentricity of a genius?

If so, what? Hmm. Maybe she ought to find out before
they took the relationship much further.

That would be wise, she decided reluctantly, pausing in
the doorway of her bedroom. Against the room's blackness, a blacker outline revealed that Peter had switched
places with her. Now he lay on his left side, on the far
side of the bed, facing her.

''Everything is okay now?'' he asked, his voice a deep,
velvety purr.

Her bones melted, though her bafflement lingered. She
was awake, but no longer interested in puzzle-solving.

''Everything's just fine,'' she said, then muttered, ''as
long as you don't shout out another woman's name during

what I hope are going to be some highly sexual festivities.''

''Another woman?'' Peter chuckled. The lush, sensual sound smoothed over her like fur—fake, of course.

Suddenly she didn't care if he shouted out ''Larry!'' as long as he was holding *her*. Kissing *her*. Touching—

*''Milenko,''* he said solemnly, ''since the moment I met you, there has been no other woman in my mind, on my tongue or inhabiting my life.''

Wendy still hesitated, one bent knee resting on the edge of the mattress. Then Peter extended his arm, the palm of his hand up. He waggled his fingers. ''Come, darling,'' he coaxed. ''Let me show you how I concentrate on you.''

She laughed, relieved by his reassurances. And more than willing to set aside the conundrum of his strange behavior until later. Right now she had other things to think about.

Such as the scary but strangely thrilling possibility that she might be falling in love with her husband.

Such as the determination that even if she was, she wouldn't give up her career plans.

And most importantly, that her husband, naked, ready and in her bed, had just made her an attractive offer. *Let me show you...*

''Oh, yes, we're in the right state for that,'' she agreed, taking a handful of bedclothes and lifting them, tossing herself under them, then moving close, closer, closest to him. ''Missouri's the Show Me State. So you show me and I'll show you.''

Being a model husband, Peter, ah, rigidly adhered to the letter of her instructions.

In the beginning, he was ahead in the fewest clothes category; Wendy quickly caught up. And then his hands were everywhere, tracing curves, stroking skin, arousing nerve endings she never knew she had.

His mouth followed the path his hands had blazed— teasing the same nerve endings, laving her breasts until she moaned with pleasure, then working its way down her abdomen, through the curls at the apex of her legs, to the damp, honeyed entrance to her most feminine place.

He plundered, he pleasured. Bringing her again and again to the brink of release…letting her slip back, then driving her higher again—until she thought she'd die of near ecstasy. Loving every exquisite sensation he elicited from her along the way.

*Wait—who says men get to have all the fun?*

Working an arm free, Wendy sought his arousal. Now *she* traced outlines, *she* stroked. Mmm, he was thick and long and hard. A hot, steel rod sheathed in softest skin. Curling her fingers around him, she moved her hand up and down his length.

A groan of pleasure escaped his lips when she concentrated her attentions on the tip of his penis, running a fingerpad along its delicate rim, swirling her thumb across and around its head….

"Wendy, please…" he whispered, his supplication ending in a rough sound of agonized delight.

"Yes," she whispered back. "Please, Peter." Her hand guided him into position. "Please now."

His mouth came down on hers and as their tongues frantically mated, he plunged home, filling her completely. He held himself still a second to let her adjust to his size, then began to move in her—in an ancient rhythm made new by this man, burying himself in this woman. Pulling back, plunging into her sweet, hot tightness again. And again. Then deeper, harder, faster….

Her hips rose to meet him, carrying them both higher and higher, until he cried her name and she moaned his…. One last driving thrust into her slick heat and together they exploded—like a star going supernova, pulsing, pulsing, gloriously pulsing out the very essence of life, like radiating waves of energy filling the universe.

After an eternity of floating through heaven, their breathing slowed, their senses began reporting on external stimuli again, their intimate organs disengaged. Peter still held her, though, his fingers absently moving over her abdomen in slow, swirly figures. Their legs remained twined like tendrils of a vine.

Wow, Wendy thought when she could think again, that was perfect. He was perfect.

"It will be even better," Peter purred against her ear. "Next time."

Holy cow! "H-how?" How do you improve on perfection?

"Next time you will be on top," he whispered huskily, sending dark ripples of anticipation down her spine. "Riding me."

Wendy swallowed. Well, if she must, she'd do her marital duty. "Just say when," she breathed.

A moment or two passed in silence, then—she could actually feel his smile through the darkness. "I say now."

And as predicted, she was. She did. And it *was* more perfect than perfection.

So perfect, Wendy didn't remember until three o'clock the following afternoon that she ought to get to the bottom of Peter's odd, erratic behavior before things went much further.

She had no idea how to manage that little feat until, on Saturday morning, she and Peter dropped Boroni off at the university, then swung by to collect Patrick, who for some inexplicable reason had invited himself along to Max's first hockey game.

THOUGH TRAFFIC WAS HEAVY, Peter paid no attention to Wendy's slow driving—or to her brother's ragged attempts at conversation. He'd turned sideways, not to hear Patrick but to look at his wife while she threaded her way through the weekend traffic.

"You know where the rink is located?" he asked. Just to see her head swivel, her lush, talented lips press together.

"Duh." She slowed to let a city bus that had just roared past them cut in front to pick up a passenger the driver hadn't noticed. "Robin's a wreck. Don't tell me you're nervous, too?"

Nervous? No longer. His questions had been answered. Now he could allow his feelings to develop unrestricted. He could make long-range plans if he wished. The past few nights had delivered not only hours of the most exquisite sexual release and sensual pleasure, but proof. Proof that, flaws or no flaws, he, Peter Havel, could make a woman happy. Even a woman as wonderful, as incredible, as Wendy.

Now, with proof that he could trust her with his body, he could, if he chose, trust her with his heart. Love and marriage were real possibilities now.

Knowing that gave him more satisfaction than winning ten Fields Medals would. By a factor of $n$ to the tenth power.

"Oh, you mean, nervous for Max? No. He has worked hard and I am explaining hockey is only a game for now. He enjoys himself."

"Not as much as I did last night, I'll bet," Wendy said softly. A glance showed Patrick was on his cell phone in the back seat. "I didn't even know that could be done with maraschino cherries."

Peter leaned slightly toward her. "Do not worry, *milenko*," he advised with a grin. "We have not exhausted our repertoire—or our pantry—yet."

Ah, her green eyes widened, sparkling in the afternoon light. "Really?" she breathed, then stomped the brake pedal as a car full of teenagers ignored a stop sign and pulled out in front of her.

"Really," he assured her, letting momentum send him toward Wendy, close enough to inhale her patchouli scent.

*Sakra*—despite the unparalleled intensity and frequency of their lovemaking, he wanted her again. Here. Now. And something told him that would never change, no matter how many years they were together.

As they turned down a driveway toward a sprawling red brick building, Patrick gave a strangled cry and covered his eyes.

"What was the sign saying?" Peter asked as the speeding motorcyclist swerved, blocking the white letters carved into the rough redwood. If they kept St. Louis as a base, he'd buy her a big, safe car. Something that would survive a crash since one looked inevitable, despite her excellent reactions.

"'Welcome to the Edna Washington Community Center.' This place has a swimming pool, tennis courts, jogging trails, soccer fields and—" they reached a parking lot where other adults were congregating or strolling toward a low building "—tah-dah!" she caroled as she avoided wandering pedestrians, slotted the car between white lines and cut the engine. "Home ice of the Fighting Jackhammers, sponsored by Schlichtemeier's Contracting and Excavation—and starring left winger Max Donahue."

Without a change in tone, Wendy said, "Holy guacamole! Look who's a hockey fan."

Peter followed the direction of her gaze. "Disbelievable," he agreed, watching Worthington emerge from his car. Two spaces down, surrounded by SUVs and minivans, sat a similar midsize, midprice, nondescript sedan.

Which, it turned out, belonged to Darren Dinwiddie.

Patrick, the banker and the INS clerk went right inside to sit at the north end of the last of four rows of benches that flanked one side of the rink.

Peter waited with Wendy in the lobby for Robin, who had to be thrown out of the locker room, after which they strolled into the rink area and found places at the south end of the third row, behind the Jackhammers' players bench. The other three then drifted over to sit behind them.

Brief, civilized greetings were exchanged. Kept that way because, when Wendy started to ask the banker about her check, Peter put his arm around Wendy's shoulders and kissed her. Now was not the time to be asking about money. Money she'd use to leave him.

He ended the kiss only when Max tottered up the bleachers in full uniform.

Robin gave her son a fierce but mercifully short hug, then wiped suspiciously damp eyes. Peter's gaze traveled up and down the boy, then he solemnly declared, "You look like a natural."

"I hope I don't mess up too bad," Max confessed with a nervous smile.

"Envision the other team wearing diapers," Peter suggested. "And skate as you do in practice. You will do well."

The smile of approval he received from Wendy— Ha! He felt able to beat the Russian national hockey team. Single-handedly.

Dinwiddie broke off a low conversation with Patrick to lean down and pluck at Peter's sleeve. The right one, luckily, so he heard the man's question. "Is that sweater Versace?"

"Zegna," Peter said. "I bought it in Milan last year."

The banker made an appreciative sound, adding, "I didn't know math professors were paid so well."

"I'm not strictly a teacher," Peter replied with a shrug. "I invent, too. Holding the right patents can be quite lucrative."

"Really," the banker mused. "How lucrative?"

Peter rubbed the side of his face, but Wendy was deep in conversation with Robin and Worthington; Patrick and Max studied the ice pensively. Still...he kept his voice low. "Let us say only that my pockets are lined up very, very well."

Dinwiddie smoothed a hand over his perfectly moussed hair. "If, as I assume from what you've just said, you can easily afford to pay her way to that Paris Design Institute, why is your wife's request for her trust fund portion so urgent?''

Shrugging one shoulder, Peter ended the conversation with, ''Who can understand women? Especially Americans.''

*She* wouldn't *need the bank's money if you stayed together.*

Ah, his internal nag was back. Interfering again. Was he supposed to bribe Wendy? How would that help him build a true and lasting relationship with his tigress?

It wouldn't, he thought glumly. However, Dinwiddie's question served as a timely reminder. He would be more than happy to share his life with someone as bright and sexy, as beautiful and sexy, as clever and sexy as Wendy.

But he knew she remained committed to Paris. And after his experience with Katrina, he simply couldn't give away his own heart until he knew he—just he himself, as is— was not Wendy's second choice.

That was the question that nibbled constantly at the edges of his mind now, much the way Gandel's Anomaly had all those months he'd spent in self-exile. Well, they had the math solution nearly completed now; perhaps he'd find an answer to this personal quandary, as well.

He'd have his answer if, when he left St. Louis, Wendy left with him. Paris could wait a few weeks, couldn't it? Her classes didn't start for, what? Two months?


''YOU'LL BE FINE,'' Wendy assured Max for the tenth time—while Worthington held Robin's attention.

The boy tapped the back end of his skate blade against the cement riser, unable to remain still for a second.

''Tell her that,'' he suggested, jabbing the toe of his hockey stick in his mother's direction. ''She's wiggin'.''

She was. Just since they'd arrived, Robin had chewed the cuticles on one hand down to the quick. As Wendy watched, she started on the other.

''What's up with her?'' she asked. Robin wasn't the

kind of hyper mom who got banned from Little League games. She couldn't care less about Max's performance as long as he had fun and got some exercise.

"It's your husband's fault," the boy said, now adjusting his shoulder pads by hitting them repeatedly with the stick butt.

"Peter's?" Wendy glanced sideways at his glorious, sexy profile. "How do you figure that? Did he teach you how to play dirty or something?"

"Nah, she's just bein' paranoid. Says she's afraid I'll hurt myself permanently—like Peter did when he slammed into that goalpost at the Olympics."

Wendy opened and closed her mouth several times, unable to pick a place to start. Olympics? Goalpost? Hurt?

"Even if I did," Max went on, "so what? I mean, the dude's like a genius, right? An' rich, too. Messin' up his eyesight and his hearing on the one side didn't ruin his life," he proclaimed with childish logic. "Mom should chill."

She still hadn't formed a single word of a single question designed to wring even one byte of information out of Max when a whistle blew. The teams began to gather on the ice.

"Gotta go!" Dodging his mother's kiss, the boy clattered away, nerves apparently as gone as good taste on cable TV.

Sometime during the next twenty-two minutes, the hockey game started, Patrick and Dinwiddie began holding hands unobtrusively and Worthington squeezed his way between Wendy and Robin.

But Wendy couldn't have sworn to any of it in court.

She was a little preoccupied.

*Yeah, like Picasso was sort of artistic.*

She was no math whiz, but by the end of the first period, she'd put two and two together. Max's report and Peter's…oh, let's see—his behavior at the welcoming reception, his response to her request to turn off the kitchen light, even his habit of rubbing one side of his face when tired or pondering something.

Before she took the word of a nine-year-old as gospel, though, Wendy decided a little personal investigation was in order.

As the second period started, she scooted close to Peter's left side and looked straight ahead. "Let's have sex right now," she said softly. "Meet me in the parking lot."

Then she climbed down the bleachers and waited outside the rink area. When the Czech Chest didn't show, she visited the ladies' room and went back inside to sit on his right.

Pretending to stare at the ice again, she murmured, "I could really use something to drink."

Immediately Peter was on his feet. "Lemonade?" he asked, already on his way to the concession stand run by the team's parents.

"Sure." Wendy nodded sadly. "Thanks."

She watched his tall, athletic figure descend the bleacher steps. Well, she had her answer. The man she'd married, the man with whom she'd shared the most intimate act two people could, had a secret—a big, basic one he'd kept from her. Why hadn't he told her? And what else had he hidden?

"How'd you find out about Peter's hockey accident?" Wendy leaned over Worthington and asked her blue-spiked friend, who ignored her until Max skated off the ice. Changing lines, she called it.

Fingering her eyebrow ring, Robin shrugged. "They showed the tape of it a million times when Peter was selected as this year's expert. Didn't you see it?"

Wendy shook her head. "No. And Peter never told me." Lordy, was that petulant voice hers?

Another shrug from the Goth-ish mom. "He was training to be a surgeon before the accident. Maybe he just doesn't like to rehash the whole dramatic life-alteration thing. Can't blame him."

Robin spoke from experience; maybe she had a point. Wendy frowned at the scratched-up surface of the skating rink as she tried to put herself in Peter's place.

It wasn't hard for her to imagine his shock, his pain, his despair when his world turned upside down without warning. One minute he's a brilliant Olympic athlete with plans to be a great surgeon and the next he's coping with devastating handicaps and shattered dreams.

But instead of feeling sorry for himself and hunkering down in a defensive posture, he'd gotten on with his life. *Unlike me. I let my mother's sick choices taint my dreams and hold me hostage.*

When Peter returned with the lemonade, Wendy gave him a tender squeeze and ditto smile.

What a guy she'd married! A gorgeous, hardworking, successful man who'd learned to live and cope with physical difficulties for which his intelligence couldn't always compensate.

Wendy felt a heavy burden lift from her psychic shoulders. That's how you avoid feeling trapped, she thought, her smile unconsciously broadening. Not so much by standing alone, financially or emotionally, but by knowing that you can face whatever life hands you without bailing on yourself.

*"Milenko?"* As his inflection turned the word into a question, Peter's hand rose to the side of his face.

The side with the faint lines. *Surgical incisions.*

And that's what she had to offer such a man. Peter had courage, but she could—choose a military image: take point, cover his back, protect his flank… Her support and sensitivity could help Peter keep his handicaps hidden, as he apparently wished.

She laughed to realize how much she wanted to tell him she'd help. How much she wanted to be needed. By Peter. Did such eagerness to shed her previously absolute self-sufficiency mean she was in l-o-v-e?

"You are thinking of joke?" the man beside her queried.

Wendy frowned as her long-standing doubts assailed her again. This wasn't just some great-sex-induced, euphoric fantasy, was it?

"You forgot punchline?" Peter suggested.

Hmm. Had she? He *hadn't* told her about himself. Until he did, maybe she shouldn't commit herself to anything as serious as the L-word. She sure as hell shouldn't abandon her own life, no matter what. "N-no," she assured him quickly.

Too quickly, Peter decided. Some wheels turned in his tigress's head, but where they took her, he couldn't guess.

She must have read his concern; she patted his hand.

"Don't worry," she said, smiling gently at him. The way one smiles at a beloved but befuddled elderly relative. "Everything's all right."

Peter rubbed the side of his face, pretending to watch the game.

But only his eyes followed the action. His brain was too uneasy to join in.

*Everything's all right,* she'd said.

Then why did everything suddenly feel all wrong?

# 9

IN THE DAYS FOLLOWING Max's hockey game and Wendy's declaration that everything was "all right," Peter's concern increased rather than faded away. And though he tried, he couldn't chalk it up to a new lover's imaginings.

Something *had* changed between them, but he could not put his finger on precisely what.

It was a maddening puzzle for someone with an inquisitive mind and scientific training that demanded supporting data. He had none.

Their lovemaking remained intense, frequent, inventive and always mutually satiating.

They met for lunch every day, at Wendy's suggestion. They shared food, fascinating conversation and long, hot kisses for dessert. How could he complain about that?

He couldn't—and didn't. But his uneasiness remained, like a silent current moving deep beneath the ocean's surface.

When he shopped for groceries, his tigress volunteered to accompany him, though once they returned home, she exhibited no interest in helping him transform their purchases into meals.

Twice, he attempted to open a discussion on their relationship, hoping to discover what had transpired—in the stands or in Wendy's head—while he'd purchased the lemonade she'd requested.

The first time he suggested talking about "us," she'd recalled an emergency errand she had to run for the dean—

and promptly became incommunicado for the rest of the day.

His second attempt to bring out—no, *up* the subject resulted in Wendy claiming she needed a haircut. Immediately.

That was on a Sunday, just before noon. She was gone for six hours.

Her obstinate avoidance frustrated Peter, but after the months of rehab he'd endured, the post-op recovery cycles, the endless tests and retests... Wendy might not know it yet, but she was outmatched when it came to stubbornness. They *would* discuss their future.

Except that time was running out and, so far, no matter how he tried to broach the subject, to discover what had happened, what had changed between them, Wendy continued to place a wall of stone around it.

AT LAST, late on Friday afternoon, Peter found himself wandering through the chemistry building—looking for someone, anyone to stormbrain—no, *brainstorm* with, merely to provide himself a mental distraction from the increasingly perplexing puzzle of his wife.

"If she does not reveal the problem soon," he muttered to the chalk-dust-filled air, "I may go postage!"

He trudged upstairs and down another hallway lined with classrooms, labs and faculty offices. Looking for a student upset over distillation factors or a nice, soothing out-of-control chain reaction. Anything.

But of course, the place was deserted. As empty as a politician's promises. As a looted pyramid. As a dotcom's offices. As—

Bah. Faculty, students, even most administrative support personnel seemed to have begun their weekend early. Dr. Boroni, too, was gone, called to Detroit to authenticate the arrival of his first great-grandchild.

Leaving Peter at loose ends, watching dust motes dance golden in the sunlight streaming through the tall windows.

Outside, a brisk autumn wind piled up fallen leaves against the building.

Peter frowned, unable to dispute the seasonal message. Time was passing. His stay in St. Louis— *Say it.* His marriage with Wendy was nearing its agreed-upon ending. The paperwork delay couldn't last much longer, even with dedicated bureaucrats working on it night and day.

How would the relationship end? Happily? For whom? And what constituted a happy ending? The questions simmered through him, but now he wondered if he was being foolish to pursue Wendy's answers to them.

*Don't ask if you don't want to know.* He'd overheard that wise tidbit while returning to Boroni's den after lunch yesterday. Perhaps he should take the unintentional advice.

But the marriage worked—at least, for him. Wendy gave him loving—and responsibilities he could fulfill. He satisfied her in bed, could provide for her financially and supported her independence. It seemed clear that the best way to end the relationship here was to continue it elsewhere.

He'd always expected to live with someone. Why not Wendy?

Because she, on the other hand, had never considered marriage an option. Peter rubbed at the buzzing in his bad ear. Was that why she seemed…different? Had her attitude about matrimony changed for some reason?

Dammit, he had to know—before his heart went and fell in love. It was, he thought, dangerously close already. So, he would ask his wife to keep his name. Tonight.

If she said no thanks—Peter shrugged mentally—he knew he would live.

He looked at his watch: 4:37. Twenty-three minutes until Wendy's workday ended. Knowing the situation would soon be settled filled him with relief. And if she said yes…

Exhilarated by the possibilities stretching before him, Peter headed for the stairs. Perhaps the computer science—

"There you are!"

At the sound of his wife's voice, Peter turned eagerly. Then had to sag against the nearest wall while the hallway pirouetted.

"Yes, *milenko*," he agreed as the environment returned to normal. "I am here." He could feel his smile grow goofy as he watched her approach. The sunlight behind her burnished her hair and teased the outline of her figure through the silky blouse she wore.

*You want her to say yes.* His internal voice only affirmed what his racing pulse had already announced.

Not that another person could be his reason for living—but Wendy enhanced everything he experienced as no other person ever had.

She brought joy to his life. It was that simple.

And that profound.

"I am very glad to see you, my love," he admitted as she came near. He'd been living in a black-and-white world until Wendy had colorized it.

"Yeah, well, Chairman Moss is going to be royally ticked off if *he* doesn't see *you*—and pronto." Taking Peter by the arm, Wendy guided him through a slow, gradual turn until they faced the right direction.

"Chairman Moss?"

Wendy sighed. It wasn't fair. There was no way she could stay irritated at a bewildered, purring Czech Chest. "The physics department?" she hinted. "The open house? The one Moss specifically invited us to?"

Finally. Comprehension lit his smoky-blue eyes.

"It is today?"

"Give the man a cigar."

The little rebel strand of hair glistened like pure gold as he shook his head. "You make this offer often, but you know I do not smoke."

"Silly, it's a cliché or idiom or whatever." Wendy dismissed technical terms in favor of action. "It means you guessed right. Now—the open house started at four, so let's get over there and make our attendance known. Then I vote we go out to dinner.''

As usual, Peter agreed with every part of her plan. Frankly, his immediate, amiable acquiescence to her every suggestion was beginning to perturb Wendy. Was this geniality—or an indecisiveness she'd never noticed before?

Or was he just placating her because he didn't care what they did outside the bedroom? Aside from an active sex life, did Peter want any relationship—or any future—with her?

Maybe he was only behaving in this pink-cloud, early phase romantic way because he knew the relationship wouldn't, couldn't, shouldn't last. Maybe that's why he'd kept the truth about his injuries to himself, too.

If so, when did the pink cloud turn black?

Not that it mattered. She was still going to Paris. She had to—if only to ensure no regrets later. *Not to mention that Peter hasn't offered an alternative.*

Tucking her hair thoughtfully, Wendy led the way across the quadrangle to the physics building. As long as they were together, though, she could still do her part to keep his handicaps a secret from others. Odd to feel so protective....

''Have you met these physics guys yet?'' she asked as they neared the departmental offices—where, judging by the chatter level, most of the partying was happening. ''They're too far out for me, but I'm sure you'll find common ground.''

''I will?'' Perhaps he would—if he understood what she was saying.

''Of course. You speak scientific and so do they.'' Her hand touched her hair, but she refrained from tucking. ''So I'll just, um…hang with you and, um…listen. Okay?''

There it was again. That something he could not define.

''Okay,'' he murmured, vowing to get to the bottom of this—and soon. ''Let us hang together.''

MATHEMATICIANS SEEK pattern and order. Men who find themselves unexpectedly if still semi-unconsciously in love seek understanding.

Being both, Peter naturally sought both and he did so using the methods in which he'd been trained: observation, speculation, investigation and extrapolation from data thus gathered.

During the hour following their arrival at the physics faculty fête, he applied those scientific techniques to the mystery of what had changed between him and Wendy and what it meant to their future.

First, she dragged him through the crowd until they located the man who'd personally invited them.

"Chairman Moss!" Wendy cried in tones more likely to be used by European soccer fans spotting their team's star player. "Nice to see you!"

She pulled Peter forward—until the old man practically took a shirt button in his nose. "Look, Peter, it's Chairman Moss!"

"It's good to se—" he began.

"Yes, it is," Wendy chimed in loudly before he could finish. "It's very good to see you, sir. How are you today?"

"Fine, young lady. Just fine." Moss retreated a step, re-Americanizing the space between them.

Ignoring the body-language message, Wendy shoved Peter toward the chairman again. At the same time, she pitched her voice even louder than before, as if now communicating with someone a block away. "He's fine. That's great, isn't it, Peter?"

What could he do but murmur agreement?

"Great turnout today, isn't there?" Wendy shouted, smiling broadly at both men. They took turns producing sickly smiles and echoing her assessment.

After a few more meaningless exchanges, during which the tigress stridently parroted what each man said, the trustee excused himself.

"Of course!" Wendy replied, still as if she was talking

over crowd noise at a championship basketball game. "You have to leave now. We understand. Right, Peter?"

With a pained nod, he bade Chairman Moss goodbye. And nearly lost his footing when Wendy jerked on his arm.

"Slowly, *milenko*," he begged. "How far is the fire?"

"What?" Well, at least she quit pulling on him as though she were leading a recalcitrant donkey. "Oh." Without warning, she started emoting again. "The phrase is, 'Where's the fire?'"

"I am corrected," Peter conceded before changing the subject. "How soon may we leave?" Despite her bizarre behavior, he twinkled his eyes at her, hoping to elicit a sign that she, too, wished to go home and enjoy some, uh, privacy. Once there, he would get to the truth.

"Are you tired?" Wendy asked. "Do you need to sit down?"

Was she teasing? Peter cocked his head to look more closely at his wife. No, concern pleated deep lines between her brows. "I am not a grandmother," he reminded her.

And frowned when she looked ready to dispute him.

Why was Wendy suddenly acting like a tour guide for the terminally baffled? What was circulating through that creative but sometimes misdirected mind of hers?

He'd opened his mouth to bluntly ask her for an explanation when a group of chemistry professors hailed them. Relegating confrontation to another part of the space-time continuum, he allowed Wendy to herd him the three steps needed to reach the clump of chemists.

"Hello, gentlemen," Wendy greeted the professors. Then she turned to Peter. "Look, Peter!" she shouted. "It's Dr. Schmidt...Dr. Lee...Dr. Ja—"

"I know their names," Peter interrupted quietly. "Gentlemen." He gave each professor a nod of greeting.

"D'ja hear about Carpenter?" one of them asked in a confidential tone.

"No." Peter shook his head carefully. "What about—"

"What about Dr. Carpenter?" Wendy yelled.

Five pairs of eyes turned to stare in her direction.

*Sakra,* she was beautiful with her skin flushing peach. Peter sighed. But she *should* be embarrassed—treating a grown man like a deaf imbecile.

Didn't she know how denigrating such treatment was? How humiliated its recipient felt?

Probably not. His wife was a generous, openhearted person; she'd have the best of motives for her actions—and never think to consider them from another's more self-conscious perspective.

Which meant he'd have to bring up the uncomfortable subject himself if he wanted her to stop doing…whatever she was doing.

*You know what she's doing,* insisted his internal voice. *You just don't know why.*

For now, Peter chose to ignore the whole thing. Or to at least try.

"Why don't you go get something to drink, *milenko?*" he suggested gently. "We'll be shop-talking. You will only be bored."

Wendy tucked her hair behind her ears with a frown. "I'm not thirsty," she said. "Unless you want a drink. Do you?"

"No." What he wanted, Peter realized sadly as he gazed into her moss-green eyes, was to be Wendy's partner.

He wanted her in his bed, in his arms, in his office and work and library and studio. Anywhere, everywhere. Permanently—but equally. He'd come to rely on his tigress for many things, but none of them were activities of daily living.

"Thank you." Peter lifted one corner of his mouth. "But please, get a drink to—*for* yourself."

After searching every centimeter of his face, Wendy nodded. "Okay," she said and turned away.

She'd only gone a step when she turned back to trumpet, "Shall I bring you some food—if it looks good?"

Peter closed his eyes and let his denial break—like a dam given too much dynamite.

Wendy *knew*. Somehow, either from someone's big mouth or by adding the evidence supplied by her two eyes plus two ears—it hardly mattered how now—she'd learned about his physical difficulties. And, in her clumsy, insulting way, she was trying to help him cope.

"No thanks, I'm not hungry."

After a quick hair tuck, Wendy nodded again. "I'll be right back," she said before slipping into the crowd.

He *was* a goner, Peter thought ruefully as he watched her disappear. Because his reaction to her crude attempts to protect and to aid him wasn't anger. Or embarrassment. Or raging pride. Or sorrow or disgust.

No, he found Wendy's efforts to "help" him without acknowledging why he needed it, *which he didn't*—Peter sighed fatalistically—he found them endearing rather than infuriating.

How insane was that? He'd left Katrina—hell, he'd left the continent on which Katrina lived—when she'd treated him with just such pity. But Wendy...

His response to her was completely different. Had been different from the start. Something about Wendy Marek had resonated in him from the very first moment their eyes had met.

No other woman had affected him like this. He couldn't imagine another doing so in the future. Which meant that if he let pride or anger run his mouth and drive her away, he'd have to live the rest of his life without the unique sense of connection with her that gave each day meaning.

Of course, he'd survive, but...

No buts. He didn't want to sacrifice his self-esteem just to keep Wendy as his lifelong mate, did he?

He sighed again. Apparently he wanted her even while he was upset with her.

*And now you can have her,* his internal voice pointed out. *Just let her caring nature, her inborn sympathy and kindness bind her to you for good, for life, forever.*

But, as he half listened to the latest chemistry gossip, Peter realized that he also wanted Wendy to have the life, the husband, she deserved.

And he wanted to be a choice, not a charity.

Peter rubbed the side of his face. He wasn't fool enough to force a confrontation here and now, but soon he must give Wendy her options—*love me as a man or leave me alone*—and learn his fate.

He had no idea, he realized glumly, which option she'd choose. He could only hope he was prepared for either answer.

WITH TIME RUNNING OUT and to ready himself for whatever Wendy decided, Peter completed the bulk of his remaining work on the solution to Gandel's Anomaly over the next nine days.

Then, unable to live with uncertainty a moment longer, he brought home a baked chicken, tossed a salad—and rolled the metaphorical dice.

He tried to act as normally as possible, which probably wasn't very, through dinner. Then, while Wendy went to wash the dishes, he began to pack. And pray.

When she emerged from the kitchen, a pile of neatly folded shirts and another of slacks met her at the sofa.

"W-what are you doing?"

"Packing."

The tigress muttered under her breath. Something colorful, no doubt, but Peter decided not to ask for enlightenment. His stomach already resembled macramé.

"Why are you packing?"

He managed to lift and drop a shoulder. "I'm leaving St. Louis soon, so I thought I'd begin my preparations."

*Hovno.* Her eyes widened and paled, like grass blades withering in a drought.

"L-leaving?" she whispered from behind the fingers raised to cover her mouth. The black opal of her wedding band winked at him. "Just…just like that?"

Peter's hand crept to the side of his face as he hesitated. Was he making a terrible mistake? Maybe he should wait. Why force an outcome he might intensely dislike? He sighed; his hand fell away.

He had to know how Wendy saw him: as a man she could love or as a charitable project. And he'd been a scientist too long. In the end, it was more important to know the truth than to like what he knew.

"You have forgotten? I have a commitment," he said, folding another shirt with suddenly shaking hands, "to work with Wilkersen. I must be in Los Angeles next week."

Wendy tucked her hair with a vengeance. "A-are you coming back after you…after L.A.?" She asked the question with her chin lifted.

*Now bait the hook. And see if she bites.*

Taking a deep breath, Peter let it out slowly. The knot in his stomach didn't dissolve. "No. After consulting with Wilkersen, I'm expected in Guadalajara."

"Mexico?" Wendy smacked her forehead. "You're going to Mexico? But—they speak Spanish there! Do you even know any?"

Ah, she'd nibbled the bait. With another brief prayer, Peter offered the hook. "No…"

"No? Are you nuts?" Well, she was agitated. But about what, precisely? "How are you going to get around? How will you order dinner or hail a taxi or handle the simplest things?"

"I don't know," he admitted, hoping he sounded worried. Offhandedly, of course. "I'll just…hope I make no mistakes when I shop for fruit and so forth."

The look on Wendy's face told him she remembered the melon incident—and her important role in its outcome.

"What if you do make a mistake?" Wendy demanded,

cramming her hair behind her ears. "Do you have any idea how difficult Mexico's going to be for you, Peter?"

She'd played perfectly into his hands.

"You're probably right. I will need help in such a strange place," he said, trying to keep his voice steady, his words uninflected, to keep the test fair. "So why don't you come to Guadalajara with me? We're good together, *milenko,* and we're already married. Perhaps we should...stay that way."

Wendy stood frozen. Feeling as if she'd suddenly left her body.

Strange. She'd never known that a person's whole world could fall into place—and then fall apart without making a single sound.

That a heart could break in complete silence.

"I..." God help her, she *wanted* to say yes. Yes, she'd go to Guadalajara, to Los Angeles, to that Altai place, to anywhere in the damned universe just to take care of him.

But she couldn't.

Taking care of Peter was his job.

The Czech Chest had just handed her the ultimate reality check. When push came to shove, the choice became clear, familiar: my needs or yours.

Silence filled the apartment as Wendy fought tears. Dammit, she would *not* cry!

The bottom line was so simple, so irrefutable: she couldn't give up her dreams for his comfort. Look at how much pain—for everyone—had resulted when her mother had done that. And she wanted kids...*Peter's kids.* She couldn't risk hurting them the way her mother had hurt her.

So Wendy held off the eye liquid—and the overwhelming sense of loss—using a time-honored method: she lashed out.

"Oh, why don't you knock off the pity-pot routine?" she...well, shouted. "Buy yourself some language tapes."

"Excuse? Pity-pot?"

His sexy, adorable purr only made her ache. And angrier. "You heard me—knock it off! Everybody's got problems. Some people can't read, others have asthma or debt up to their eyeballs or colicky babies. That doesn't give any of 'em the right to go around asking other people to sacrifice *their* lives for 'em. That poor-me stuff's totally bogus, Havel!

"Okay, you've got a slight problem with your balance," she ranted—er, continued, "and you've lost some hearing in that ear you're always rubbing—so what?"

Peter stuck up a hand like a traffic cop. "For the sake of complete accuracy," he said, "I also have some difficulty seeing with my left eye."

"Fine, you've got some vision trouble, too," Wendy agreed, clinging to exasperation because she was still furious and still heartbroken. "Big damned deal. You're functional—so drop the sympathy ploy."

Clasping her hands high against her chest, she adopted a falsetto tone to say, "'Ooh, I'm so helpless. Give up your life and your dreams to baby-sit me.'"

"That is supposed to be me?" Peter's purr was husky; his eyes darkened to navy, his lips curving into that geedee freaking irresistible smile. "My voice is not so soprano, *milenko.*"

Wendy could feel herself weakening as she watched his mouth and remembered how it felt against hers.

"Don't try to distract me!" she warned them both. "And I don't hear you denying that you're asking me to abandon my plans for your convenience."

"Not abandon. Merely postpone," the Czech Chest corrected. "We'll go to Paris later, I promise. *Milenko,* what we have together does not come around daily. Can you give up such rapport, such fantastic lovemaking just—" he snapped his fingers "—like that?"

No. But she had to. Oh, she was tempted, but…the lesson she'd learned from her childhood pain was still valid.

Love that could last wouldn't ask her to put his wants before her needs.

Wendy knew she had to stop this farce right now. Before her heart urged her to make a mistake she and her kids would pay for the rest of her life.

"Dinwiddie's released my portion of the trust fund," she announced. Not as firmly as she'd have liked, but she got the words out. "So I've turned in my notice to the university. I'll be leaving for Paris in a few days to enroll in the Design Institute and to find a place to live."

She hadn't planned to leave quite so soon, but...she couldn't stay here. Not now.

Shock blared from Peter's features, then quickly disappeared behind a stone mask. "But what about...us?" he asked tonelessly. "What about our marriage?"

Wendy told herself not to weaken, not to waste what she'd learned from her mother and that long-ago note that had hurt so much, in so many ways, for so long.

A new explanation of Mom's departure and a couple of amazing months with a wonderful man couldn't erase years of pain and longing. Even if they had, she still hungered to express herself. And she still remembered her vow to protect herself from the helpless dependency of her past.

"What about it?" Her gaze met Peter's; she was proud that hers held steady, too. "If you want to stay married..." Foolish to even suggest an alternative. She knew what his answer would be. *What the answer always was.* Still...the part of her that wanted to love him, heart and soul, insisted she try.

"If you want to stay married," she repeated, "come to Paris."

Peter held his hands out, palms up. *"Milenko..."* he pleaded. "Be reasonable. I have already signed the contracts."

He put his eyes to work gazing soulfully. "These obligations will only require a few months to fulfill. Can't you delay your enrollment—?"

"No!" White-hot anguish seared her soul. He knew what Paris meant to her. If he lo— Wendy realized they'd never said that four-letter word to each other, not out loud anyway. But she'd thought that what they'd shared had been more than just great sex.

She'd thought wrong, hadn't she?

"No, I can't." Wendy's smile, aimed at the wall behind him, looked brittle. "But no worries, Worthington called today, too. Said he's expediting your permanent resident-alien permit under the specialists' category. Something he apparently could have done anytime he wanted to," she added, with what sounded like bemusement.

*Hovno,* she was more interested in immigration antics than in their relationship? Had he been so mistaken about what they had together?

"Your 'green card'—which, by the way, is actually a light peach color—has been issued," she went on, still not looking at him. "So, as we agreed at the beginning of this…this… Well, as agreed, you can file for divorce as soon as it arrives."

*Then* she directed her gaze at him and he was drowning in the tigress's green eyes, reading a bone-chilling message there that was confirmed by her next declaration. "I sure as hell won't contest it."

While Peter searched frantically through his brain for words, more words, English words, the *right* words, Wendy gathered her keys and a sweater.

*Don't leave!* he wanted to beg. But he remembered Katrina saying the same thing to him and it hadn't changed a thing.

"W-where are you going?" he finally asked. Wendy was angry but she was fair. They could work out a compromise. If they kept trying.

With her hand on the knob of the front door, Wendy said, "I'm going to Patrick's to borrow some luggage. Goodbye, Peter."

As she jerked open the door, he heard her mutter, "I

can't give up my dreams for yours. I can't stay married just because I think I love you."

At least, that's what Peter *thought* he heard. It was, certainly, what he hoped she'd said. Combined with her refusal to pity him for his trifling handicaps, it was something a fortunate person could base a lifetime on.

But it wasn't something a prudent person risked misinterpreting.

She'd left the door open behind her, he noticed, and decided to classify it as a symbolic gesture rather than a simple error. He still had possibilities that way.

No more packing tonight, Peter thought as he gently but firmly closed the door, then retraced his steps as far as the TV remote. He'd watch television. Relax. Prepare. Think. Wait.

When she returned, he'd ask Wendy to repeat what she'd said just now. And he'd explain himself again. In exhausting detail. He'd spell out all his feelings, if necessary.

Yes.

They'd straighten everything out. As soon as she returned....

WENDY STARED at the big-headed, tiny-bodied figures cavorting on the screen, their potty mouths delivering allegedly droll remarks.

Well, what did you expect at two o'clock in the morning? she thought morosely.

She was horizontal on Robin's sofa, glaring at some raunchy cable cartoon show in its seventh replay of the day. The last two of which had passed before her eyes, though she hadn't *seen* either of them.

"Aw, jeez. Are you still up?" Hmm, her friend—whose spikes were mashed to her head—appeared to be somewhat crankola. "Go to bed, Wenders. It'll all look different in the morning. You can fix it then."

With another grumble, Robin shuffled back to bed.

"I wish, girlfriend," Wendy whispered after her. But she couldn't see any way the relationship could survive. Dammit, what good was great sex and meeting-of-the-minds conversation, or even love, if the two partners didn't understand—and care about—each other's needs?

It wasn't as if they'd have to be in Paris forever....

*Or in Guadalajara, either.*

Wendy groaned. "Blending two lives of equal value shouldn't be so hard," she told the doglike character doing gross things with meat patties and a fan.

When two already-full lives tried to mesh, conflict was inevitable. What she needed to know was—when it occurred, whose needs came first?

She needed to be sure she wouldn't repeat her mother's sad story.

For hours she'd been lying here, racking her brain, seeking some workable compromise, any plan that held even a slim-to-slimmer chance of resolving this fundamental dilemma. "Lots of people pull it off, don't they?"

All she wanted was a long, happy marriage and two fulfilling careers. That's all.

But she wouldn't—she couldn't settle for less.

And dammit, she shouldn't have to.

# *10*

STILL A FEW RUNGS below full consciousness, Peter swallowed…. His mouth was dry as the Sahel.

*Unnh.* Something hard was jabbing his cheek. He tried to shift away from whatever was grinding into i—

"But wait! That's not all! If you call within the next seventeen min—"

Peter leapt to his feet, swearing in Czech. After a couple of wobbles, he scooped up the remote and shut the TV pitchman off in midoffer.

Sunlight streamed through the windows. Morning, then.

So he'd fallen asleep atop the remote and when he'd moved just now, he'd pressed the Power On button.

His gaze rested on the stack of slacks he'd apparently kicked to the floor sometime during the night and the wadded pile of shirts he must have crumpled beneath him.

After Wendy left to borrow her brother's luggage. He must not have heard her return. Unless…

"Where did you go? To Robin's?" Peter wondered a minute later as he stared at the undisturbed bed, an even worse possibility occurring to him. "Or—" No, he couldn't say it.

Slowly, like a yoga master on tranquilizers, he made a quick survey of the closet and dresser, then broad-jumped into the bathroom.

What he saw sent him sinking to the cold tile floor despite that internal voice reminding him, *It's better to know the truth than to hold on to a dying dream.* He sat with his knees bent, his forearms braced on them, one hand clasping the other wrist and his forehead resting on his arms—while he listened to a silence so loud it obliterated the low surf sound that had been his companion for the past two years.

Leaping to his feet, Peter staggered through the apartment again.

That's when the last hope died. Her art supplies were gone, too.

*Hovno.* Sometime between infomercial sign-on and the sitcoms that heralded dawn, Wendy *had* returned to the apartment. To pack, turn off the TV and leave. Not to work out a compromise.

Peter swore. That's how the best relationship he'd ever been part of ended? No long speeches, no shouted recriminations, no final tally of his shortcomings or her sacrifices—nothing?

*Not even goodbye.*

''Why?'' he asked the empty silence surrounding him. ''Why couldn't we work something out?''

Bah. Why couldn't two intelligent people find a solution to something that was, essentially, only an itinerary issue?

*Because it's more than that,* advised his inner voice. *To Wendy, it's about putting her dreams first. To you, it's choosing between your professional reputation and a woman.*

He didn't want to make such a choice. He shouldn't have to.

Silence beat at him like the powerful wings of a large bird. He wasn't asking her to give up fashion design forever, just t̶ ̶l̶ay her training until he'd lectured in Guadalajara. T̶ ̶ ̶ ̶ vasn't so much to ask. A couple of months at most.

Finally, muttering in Czech, he dredged up the energy to head for the kitchen. He'd eat something, then start looking for Wendy. Try to talk sense into her. She had to be somewhere in St. Louis.

He had his palm flat to the kitchen door when the telephone rang.

He set an unofficial long-jump-over-used-furniture record. Snatching up the receiver, he put it to his bad ear, lost his balance, knocked a lamp over as he fell and finally got the damned phone aligned to his right ear.

"Darling! I was so worried—"

"Nice of you, Havel, but no need," Leippert's booming voice assured him.

Peter smacked his forehead. Of course. She was at work.

The dean charged on. "Is Wendy there? Robin said something about splitsville, which I think means she's not coming in today, but I've got a speech to give at noon and I need some figures to plug in."

"I'm sorry," Peter said slowly, his heart contracting. "She…she's not here."

As Leippert launched into a verbose, rambling response that boiled down to, "Huh, that's odd," Peter recovered the lamp and set it upright.

"I don't know where she is," he said when the man paused for breath. Hoping he didn't. Hoping she wasn't truly gone.

After disconnecting, Peter trudged back to the kitchen. He ought to come up with a plan to find her and make her see they had something too special to throw away for a city in France.

Pulling open the refrigerator door, he froze. Draped around the top of the milk jug were Wendy's keys. Propped against it, a note.

"Feel free to use the car. Leave it with Dad when you're done."

*Hovno*… Paris wasn't a city; it was Wendy's dream. One of the things he'd admired about the tigress from the beginning was her ability to make decisions and act on them.

Now, her decisiveness seemed less admirable than… devastating.

AFTER TALKING to the answering machines—that didn't— of Robin, Stefan and Patrick—and getting declarations of ignorance from two experts at it: Worthington and Din-widdie—Peter showered, dressed, scooped the keys from the fridge and took himself to the university.

Where, after one startled look, Boroni launched a discussion of the last unsolved part of the Anomaly, prodding him to participate by firing questions at a rate equivalent to a machine pistol on full automatic.

"Thank you, Emil," Peter said some five hours later.

Boroni's refusal to let him concentrate on anything but the mathematical issues raised by Gandel had given him breathing room. Restored sanity, logic and judgment to his mind.

He'd never forget Wendy, but he could live with a broken heart, as he lived with damaged sight and hearing. But he could not survive without his professional reputation—and that was built on performance and reliability.

*Which begins with showing up as promised.*

"No, Dr. Havel," the elderly professor insisted, "it is I who must thank you. With your fresh viewpoint and energy, we have extended the boundaries of human knowledge a little further."

Wrinkles wreathed Boroni's smile as he added, "I'm sure my wife wishes to thank you, too."

At Peter's questioning look, he chuckled. "Because now I am satisfied," the old mathematician explained. "For years, my wife has nagged me to spend time with our family, but I have devoted my life to learning and teaching. Once we publish our work, I will retire and Marie and I can visit our children and grandchildren.

Dr. Boroni leaned toward Peter. "Just in time," he confided. "Neither of us is getting any younger. Perhaps I should have listened to my wife. My children are strangers...."

"I'm sure they know you love them," Peter murmured. But did they?

Only if they took it on faith. And what about those children like Wendy, whose faith had been shattered? How did they know they were loved?

"Hopefully, there is still time to show them," Emil said.

Standing on tiptoe, Boroni gave Peter a hug. "Thank you, my boy," he whispered. "You've helped me leave my mark on mathematics—with time to spare."

Peter patted the old man's back thoughtfully. Is that all one's family deserved—one's spare time?

"Winning mathematics' top prize, the Fields Medal, has always been my dream," the old professor mused. "Solving the Anomaly is the opportunity I've waited for to fulfill my dream."

Didn't everyone deserve a chance to do the same?

A simple question. With a simple answer.

Peter's dream had been to be treated as an equal, not with condescension. He'd needed to know he could contribute to a relationship.

He hadn't planned on falling in love.

Wendy wanted to study fashion design in Paris. She needed to feel safe by feeling self-reliant.

Even if it should, love couldn't nullify that need.

Peter stopped to say his farewells to the chemistry professors and Dean Leippert. After fending off Robin's puzzled looks and even more puzzling questions, he went back to the apartment. To pack—not for provocation, this time, but for flying to Los Angeles.

To work with Wilkersen.

And to see if he could be happy living without Wendy.

Which meant, he realized before the captain turned off the seat belt sign, living without his heart, without his soul…hell, without a reason to get up in the morning.

Wendy had become his reason and, fool that he was, he hadn't even known how much she meant to him until she'd left for Paris.

*Sakra*, he hoped she was enjoying it.

"OUF! UNG!" Taking an elbow in the ribs, Wendy passed it along to the joker shoving her into the slightly built man in front of her, who apparently hadn't bathed this millennium and ate onions. Lots of them.

*Welcome to glamorous, sophisticated, romantic Paris.*

Yes, here she was, riding L'Metro with eight billion irritable French citizens and an equal number of surly guest workers. All crammed into this tiny car with her.

She'd have introduced "Metro rage" to them by now, except that two days after landing at Orly, she still felt like a zombie who'd been teleported to another galaxy. The jets are still lagging, she thought—and started to cry.

*And she didn't care.*

She didn't care if the other commuters compressed her to the thickness of paper. She didn't care if she never got over her jetlag or her culture shock, either. Because nothing would change the elemental, permanently mood-altering fact that Peter hadn't cared for her enough to put her needs first. Just this once.

Wendy wrenched her hand free to wipe away her tears.

Ever since their last night, she'd been telling herself she'd been smart to stick to her original plan.

Six beefy women suddenly squashed her against the onion eater on their way through the car.

Yep, here she was in Paris, living her dream. Classes at the Design Institute would be starting soon; she'd already begun auditing lectures about fabrics and findings, style history, pattern-drafting, mass-production methods, blah, blah, blah.

So why was she so miserable?

*Because it's not my whole dream any longer,* she acknowledged as the packed humanity pitched and lurched in unison with the train's halt at a station to exchange hordes. She wanted more than Paris—and the—yawn—exciting profession of fashion design. She wanted her Czech mate.

And a couple of little mateys, too.

But she'd made her choice—and even if it now looked somewhat less than totally fulfilling, she wouldn't bail on it at the first clash of priorities.

*"Pardonez moi."* Growling a perfunctory apology, a man in a rumpled suit banged her knee with his attaché case as he pushed past to claim a nonexistent space further down the car.

Wendy vowed to design a line of fashionable business accessories—without sharp corners.

And not to fall in love ever again.

"Not that there's much chance of that," she muttered— which earned her an extra centimeter of space from the onion lover.

As she understood the process, a heart was required to fall in love.

And now that it was too late, she recognized that she'd given hers to Peter. Utterly and completely—and forever.

AFTER WALKING OUT of the jetway at LAX, Peter scanned the crowd until he located a young man holding a card displaying his name—and a video camera.

"I'm Havel," he told the cardholder. "Are you Wilkersen's assistant?"

The young man shook his head. "Leroy Cooper. Film student. I'm making a documentary about Dr. Wilkersen to put on the institute's Web-site." He grinned at Peter, who managed only to grimace in return. "It's not every day I get to pick up an Olympic gold medallist who's also one of the sharpest mathematicians in the world."

"Thanks to the hockey game that won that medal, the sensory organs on the left side of my face are permanently damaged," Peter replied. Funny how little his flaws—and others' knowledge or opinions of them—mattered now. Since Wendy had accepted and dismissed them.

*And me.*

"Bummer." The Californian dealt with his revelation as

casually as he dressed—rumpled shorts, Hawaiian shirt and sandals.

After helping Peter retrieve his luggage, Cooper led the way to his car. "Handicaps like yours," he said thoughtfully, "y'know, invisible to the naked eye—must be tough to adjust to. 'Cuz, like, other people can't see what's been hurt or lost or whatever."

Peter nodded. The film student was correct. The emotional damage done when Wendy's mother abandoned her was no more obvious than his physical losses, but it was just as real. Just as life-altering.

His internal nag snorted. *Except you wouldn't.*

Dammit, he couldn't.

Or could he? A possibility crackled through Peter's brain like lightning.

"What would be required to transmit live, interactive broadcasts via the Web?" he asked.

As they joined the thousands of cars creeping along a Los Angeles freeway, Cooper launched happily into a fact-filled and very enlightening dissertation on streaming video.

WELL, WENDY THOUGHT as she followed the priest into L'Metro, she'd survived Day Twelve. Almost.

She still had to fight her way off the train and out of the station. Then walk eight boring—er, picturesque—blocks through the peculiarly Parisian dusk to her lonely little garret—er, quaint studio apartment.

Maybe she wouldn't notice the view tonight. Or maybe this time, the Eiffel Tower's twinkling lights wouldn't remind her of Peter's twinkling blue eyes. Damn the evenings in Paris.

The days were manageable—her classes were challenging and the studio work engrossing. But fashion design no longer consumed her.

She wanted what life with Peter offered. What she'd

really wanted her whole life but had been afraid to reach for.

Wendy stumbled on a cobblestone as she crossed the street. What the hell had she been thinking to make location and work more important than who you shared the location and your life with? She could design clothes anywhere. Even in sunny Mexico.

Still pondering the idiocy of ranking career-training above love and a family, Wendy turned the last corner before her current temporary home. A sound made her stop dead. An oddly familiar sound—except that she shouldn't—*couldn't* be hearing it. Not in Paris.

Her eyes widened as she stared through the Parisian dusk.

*What the hell?* Wendy's heart began racing but her feet were paralyzed, her brain frozen.

Halfway down the block, a shopkeeper stood waving his arms, shouting. A gendarme had a tall, broad-shouldered, golden-maned man in custody.

"Peter?" she whispered. Questions flooded her.

*Like monsoons inundate Bangladesh.*

She was still trying to make her feet move when the policeman pulled Peter to the edge of the sidewalk. He teetered on the uneven curb.

Then Wendy was running, flying down the street, pushing between the men, grabbing Peter with one hand to stabilize his balance, grabbing the cop with the other while yelling—er, telling him to hold it, buster.

In stumbling French she said, "Please, *m'sieur!* Be careful." Turning to the shopkeeper, she asked, "What is the problem?"

"He claims my wine is sewage!" the man cried.

"I only asked directions." Peter's bewildered purr caressed her ears.

For a moment all Wendy could do was close her eyes. Just hearing his voice, feeling the heat of his body...

All the pain and unhappiness of the past two weeks melted away.

*This* was where she was supposed to be. With the man she loved—whether that was in Paris, St. Louis or Istanbul.

"Well?" shouted the shopkeeper. "Does he think he can slander my livelihood without retribution?"

Stumbling between French and English, Wendy began to explain, apologize, and generally grovel.

When the shopkeeper uncrossed his arms, she disengaged Peter from the policeman, anxious to remove him to safety. Okay, she was wild to touch him. And it felt as electric, as wonderful as always.

They'd taken three steps when Peter turned and addressed the men in rapid fluent French.

The Parisians grinned. *"De rien, m'sieur,"* they called. *"Bon chance."*

Wendy's gaze commuted between the two men and her husband. They were beaming paternally, while Peter—Peter was flashing a sheepish version of that irresistible smile.

The one she had no intention of ever resisting again.

But, come on. She couldn't be a complete pushover. She might *feel* like it, but she wasn't going to act like it.

"What was that all about?" she demanded as they strolled toward her apartment building.

"Fear," he said, twinkling his eyes at her through the dusk.

Wendy stopped and looked at the tall, athletic Czech who, despite his physical handicaps, had built an international reputation and a personal fortune and traveled the world unaided.

"Pull the other one," she suggested. "What could *you* be afraid of?"

His hands cupped her face. "The possibility that I might have lost the one thing I could not live without."

The purred words released the titanium band of tightness that had been squeezing her chest ever since she'd left St.

Louis. But she had to be sure. The legacy of her past, but there it was.

"You mean, you want your ring back?" He wouldn't get it, and what it meant, without a fight.

"No, *milenko*," he answered. "I cannot live without the woman who—" His hand left her face to capture her fingers for an inspection that darkened his eyes to navy velvet. "Ah," he purred. "Who still wears it."

Wendy wanted to skip all the talking. She wanted to throw herself into his arms. She wanted kissing and caressing and body parts joining.

"That's why you came to Paris?" she asked.

"Yes. To be with my wife, where I belong."

Arching an eyebrow, Wendy jerked her chin in the direction from which they'd come. "And that scene just now?"

Peter chuckled.

"A test. For fear's sake. I knew that if you rescued me from the Frenchmen, you would probably also rescue me from a life of loneliness. And I in turn will show you that you can count on me for a lifetime."

"What about Guadalajara?" Not that she wouldn't ditch the Paris Design Institute, now that she understood the place a career should occupy in a person's life: second. "What about your lectures?"

"I have arranged to deliver them from Paris via live video feed on the Net."

Every prayer answered, every hope fulfilled. Wendy reached for him, but Peter stepped back. Out of kissing range.

"I'll never let logistics come between us again," he promised—while Wendy ground her teeth in frustration, "as long as I know you love me as much as I love you."

"And how much is that?" she asked. Wondering which cliché he'd mangle in the description process. And why they couldn't just spend the next fifty years demonstrating.

"The largest number known is a googol," Peter replied,

as if lecturing a class. "This is one followed by a hundred zeros. A googolplex is the number one followed by a googol of zeros. To quantify my love in mathematical terms, I love you a googolplex, *milenko*."

"And I love you double that," Wendy assured him.

Then she grabbed her Czech mate and they got down to some serious and well, naturally, French-kissing.

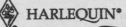

# A visit to Cooper's Corner offers the chance for a new beginning...

COOPER'S CORNER

## Coming in December 2002
## DANCING IN THE DARK
## by Sandra Marton

**Check-in:** When Wendy Monroe left Cooper's Corner, she was an Olympic hopeful in skiing...and madly in love with Seth Castleman. But an accident on the slopes shattered her dreams, and rather than tell Seth the painful secret behind her injuries, Wendy leaves him.

**Checkout:** A renowned surgeon staying at Twin Oaks can mend Wendy's leg. But only facing Seth again—and the truth—can mend her broken heart.

**HARLEQUIN®**
*Makes any time special®*

Visit us at www.cooperscorner.com

CC-CNM5

If you enjoyed what you just read,
then we've got an offer you can't resist!

# Take 2 bestselling love stories FREE!

# Plus get a FREE surprise gift!

# $ **Saving Money Has Never Been This Easy!** $

Just fill out and send in this form from any October, November and December 2002 books and we will send you a coupon booklet worth a total savings of **$20.00** off future purchases of Harlequin and Silhouette books in 2003.

## Yes! It's that easy!

**I accept your incredible offer!**
**Please send me a coupon booklet:**

Name (PLEASE PRINT)

Address                                                                Apt. #

City                         State/Prov.                    Zip/Postal Code

**In a typical month, how many**
**Harlequin and Silhouette novels do you read?**

❏ **0-2**                                    ❏ **3+**

097KJKDNC7                                              097KJKDNDP

**Please send this form to:**
   In the U.S.: Harlequin Books, P.O. Box 9071, Buffalo, NY 14269-9071
   In Canada: Harlequin Books, P.O. Box 609, Fort Erie, Ontario  L2A 5X3

Allow 4-6 weeks for delivery. Limit one coupon booklet per household. Must be postmarked no later than January 15, 2003.

**HARLEQUIN®**
*Makes any time special* ®

*Silhouette®*
*Where love comes alive™*

PHQ402